THE ASSASSINATION
OF JESSE JAMES
BY THE COWARD
ROBERT FORD

THE ASSASSINATION OF JESSE JAMES BY THE COWARD ROBERT FORD

———

Ron Hansen

———

ALFRED A. KNOPF   NEW YORK   1983

THIS IS A BORZOI BOOK
PUBLISHED BY ALFRED A. KNOPF, INC.

Copyright © 1983 by Ron Hansen

Library of Congress Cataloging in Publication Data

Hansen, Ron. [date]
The assassination of Jesse James by the coward Robert Ford.

1. James, Jesse, 1847–1882—Fiction. 2. Ford,
Robert, 1862–1892—Fiction. I. Title.
PS3558.A5133A9 1983 813'.54 83-47851
ISBN 0-394-51647-8

Manufactured in the United States of America

FIRST EDITION

To John Irving, John L'Heureux, John Gardner

Part One

———

LOOT

———

1

SEPTEMBER 7th, 1881

*His manner was pleasant, though noticeably quiet and reserved. He
listened attentively to every word that Scott Moore or I uttered but he
himself said little. Occasionally he would ask some question about the
country and the opportunities for stock-raising. But all the time I was
conscious that he was alertly aware of everything that was said and done
in the room. He never made the slightest reference to himself, nor did he
show the least trace of self-importance or braggadocio. Had I not known
who he was I should have taken him for an ordinary businessman
receiving a social visit from two of his friends. But his demeanor was so
pleasant and gentlemanly withal that I found myself on the whole liking
him immensely.*

MIGUEL ANTONIO OTERO
My Life on the Frontier

H E WAS GROWING into middle age and was living then in a bungalow on Woodland Avenue. Green weeds split the porch steps, a
wasp nest clung to an attic gable, a rope swing looped down from a
dying elm tree and the ground below it was scuffed soft as flour. Jesse
installed himself in a rocking chair and smoked a cigar down in the
evening as his wife wiped her pink hands on a cotton apron and
reported happily on their two children. Whenever he walked about the
house, he carried several newspapers—the Sedalia *Daily Democrat,*
the St. Joseph *Gazette,* and the Kansas City *Times*—with a foot-long
.44 caliber pistol tucked into a fold. He stuffed flat pencils into his
pockets. He played by flipping peanuts to squirrels. He braided yellow
dandelions into his wife's yellow hair. He practiced out-of-the-body
travel, precognition, sorcery. He sucked raw egg yolks out of their
shells and ate grass when sick, like a dog. He would flop open the limp
Holy Bible that had belonged to his father, the late Reverend Robert S.
James, and would contemplate whichever verses he chanced upon,
getting privileged messages from each. The pages were scribbled over
with penciled comments and interpretations; the cover was cool to his

cheek as a shovel. He scoured for nightcrawlers after earth-battering rains and flipped them into manure pails until he could chop them into writhing sections and sprinkle them over his garden patch. He recorded sales and trends at the stock exchange but squandered much of his capital on madcap speculation. He conjectured about foreign relations, justified himself with indignant letters, derided Eastern financiers, seeded tobacco shops and saloons with preposterous gossip about the kitchens of Persia, the Queen of England, the marriage rites of the Latter Day Saints. He was a faulty judge of character, a prevaricator, a child at heart. He went everywhere unrecognized and lunched with Kansas City shopkeepers and merchants, calling himself a cattleman or commodities investor, someone rich and leisured who had the common touch.

He was born Jesse Woodson James on September 5th, 1847, and was named after his mother's brother, a man who committed suicide. He stood five feet eight inches tall, weighed one hundred fifty-five pounds, and was vain about his physique. Each afternoon he exercised with weighted yellow pins in his barn, his back bare, his suspenders down, two holsters crossed and slung low. He bent horseshoes, he lifted a surrey twenty times from a squat, he chopped wood until it pulverized, he drank vegetable juices and potions. He scraped his sweat off with a butter knife, he dunked his head, at morning, in a horse water bucket, he waded barefoot through the lank backyard grass with his six-year-old son hunched on his shoulders and with his trousers rolled up to his knees, snagging garter snakes with his toes and gently letting them go.

He smoked, but did not inhale, cigars; he rarely drank anything stronger than beer. He never philandered nor strayed from his wife nor had second thoughts about his marriage. He never swore in the presence of ladies nor raised his voice with children. His hair was fine and chestnut brown and recurrently barbered but it had receded so badly since his twenties that he feared eventual baldness and therefore rubbed his temples with onions and myrtleberry oil in order to stimulate growth. He scissored his two-inch sun-lightened beard according to a fashion then associated with physicians. His eyes were blue except for iris pyramids of green, as on the back of a dollar bill, and his eyebrows shaded them so deeply he scarcely ever squinted or shied his eyes from a glare. His nose was unlike his mother's or brother's, not long and preponderant, no proboscis, but upturned a little and puttied, a puckish, low-born nose, the ruin, he thought, of his otherwise gallantly handsome countenance.

Four of his molars were crowned with gold and they gleamed, sometimes, when he smiled. He had two incompletely healed bullet holes in his chest and another in his thigh. He was missing the nub of his left middle finger and was cautious lest that mutilation be seen. He'd had a boil excised from his groin and it left a white star of skin. A getaway horse had jerked from him and fractured his ankle in the saddle stirrup so that his foot mended a little crooked and registered barometric changes. He also had a condition that was referred to as granulated eyelids and it caused him to blink more than usual, as if he found creation slightly more than he could accept.

He was a Democrat. He was left-handed. He had a high, thin, sinew of a voice, a contralto that could twang annoyingly like a catgut guitar whenever he was excited. He owned five suits, which was rare then, and colorful, brocaded vests and cravats. He wore a thirty-two-inch belt and a fourteen-and-a-half-inch collar. He favored red wool socks. He rubbed his teeth with his finger after meals. He was persistently vexed by insomnia and therefore experimented with a vast number of soporifics which did little besides increasing his fascination with pharmacological remedies.

He could neither multiply nor divide without error and much of his science was superstition. He could list the many begotten of Abraham and the sixty-six books of the King James Bible; he could recite psalms and poems in a stentorian voice with suitable histrionics; he could sing religious hymns so convincingly that he worked for a month as a choirmaster; he was marvelously informed about current events. And yet he thought incense was made from the bones of saints, that leather continued to grow if not dyed, that if he concentrated hard enough his body's electrical currents could stun lake frogs as he bathed.

He could intimidate like King Henry the Eighth; he could be reckless or serene, rational or lunatic, from one minute to the next. If he made an entrance, heads turned in his direction; if he strode down an aisle store clerks backed away; if he neared animals they retreated. Rooms seemed hotter when he was in them, rains fell straighter, clocks slowed, sounds were amplified: his enemies would not have been much surprised if he produced horned owls from beer bottles or made candles out of his fingers.

He considered himself a Southern loyalist and guerrilla in a Civil War that never ended. He regretted neither his robberies nor the seventeen murders that he laid claim to, but he would brood about his slanders and slights, his callow need for attention, his overweening

5

vaingloriousness, and he was excessively genteel and polite in order to disguise what he thought was vulgar, primitive, and depraved in his origins.

Sicknesses made him smell blood each morning, he visited rooms at night, he sometimes heard children in the fruit cellar, he waded into prairie wheat and stared at the horizon.

He had seen another summer under in Kansas City, Missouri, and on September 5th, in the year 1881, he was thirty-four years old.

HE HAD INVITED Alexander Franklin James over from their mother's farm in Kearney for the occasion, and dined on jackrabbit, boiled potatoes and onions, and hickorynut cake, then everyone, excepting Frank, autographed the night air with magnesium sparklers that were a gift from Jesse Edwards James, a six-year-old who thought his name was Tim. Frank presented his younger brother with a pair of pink coral cufflinks, and the two played cribbage as Zee tucked in the children, and after she retired for the evening, they rode a mule-powered street-car downtown, Frank cleaning his nails on one side of the aisle as on the other Jesse slumped down in a frock coat and talked compulsively about stopping the Chicago and Alton Railroad at Blue Cut.

On the following morning, Frank rode east and Jesse frittered that Tuesday and part of the next day through. He picked coffee beans from a canning jar and ground them fine as coal dust. He soaped his saddle and tack and glossed the rings and curb with pork lard; he carried water and cord wood; he tied onto his saddle horn a burlap sack that bore the red trademark of grain merchandisers in St. Louis. His two-year-old daughter swept his light brown beard with a doll brush, he dressed in a white linen shirt and gray wool Sunday clothes, tied a blue bandana around his neck, and climbed into a soiled Confederate offi-cer's coat that was rich with the odors of manual labor and was heavy enough to snap the pegs off a closet rack. He lunched on okra soup and kissed Zee goodbye, then rode eastward on back streets and cow-paths, his coat pockets clinking with flat pieces of slate that he skimmed into racketing trees and winged sidearm at coarse, scolding dogs.

He urged his horse in the direction of Independence and into woods that were giving up their greens to autumn gold and brown. He ducked under aggravating limbs and criss-crossed through random alleys of scrub oak and scraggle where yellow leaves detached themselves at his least provocation. He could see the Missouri River in pickets and frames to his left, wide as a village and brown as a road, gradual in its procession. He came upon a hidden one-room barkwood shack with a puncheon floor and goats on the porch and blue smoke unraveling from the chimney. A man booted with tawny mud produced a shotgun from behind a door. A woman shaded by a broad sunhat teetered with buckets in a hog pen, evaluating his carriage and disposition and horse.

Jackson County east of the Kansas City limits at that time enclosed a region called the Cracker Neck that contained ramshackle farms and some erstwhile Confederate Army guerrillas who routinely sided with the James gang, and provided seclusion to the outlaws following robberies. Within the region was Glendale, where two years earlier the gang had rifled a Chicago and Alton Railroad express car, and close to Glendale was Independence and a cooperage where Frank James squatted among the stave piles in back, eating a cucumber sandwich under the afternoon sun.

Jesse rode into the ring of shade beneath a huckleberry tree and canted his hat to conceal his face from the neighborhood; his brother tucked a sandwich corner into his cheek, regained his height, and wiped his broad mustache with his palm.

Frank was thirty-eight years old but looked a homely fifty. He was five feet ten inches tall at a time when such height was above average and weighed about one hundred fifty pounds. He had ears nearly the size of his hands and a very large, significant nose that seemed to hook and clamp his light brown mustache. His chin jutted, his jaw muscles bulged, his mouth was as straight and grim as a hatchet mark, and he'd ground down his teeth in his sleep until they all were as square as molars. He was a stern and very constrained man; he could have been a magistrate, an evangelist, a banker who farmed on weekends; rectitude and resolution influenced his face and comportment; scorn and even malevolence could be read in his green eyes.

Frank put a black cardigan sweater over his blue cavalry shirt and a gray coat over that, his scowl on two girls who lingered their dappled white ponies in the street and on a man with his hands in his pockets fifty yards removed.

Jesse yelled, "Me and him, we're circuit riders is why you never seen us beforehand."

The man continued to gawk. Frank untethered his mount and swung up and, as the two brothers ambled onto the eastward road, the man crossed to a hardware store to report his conclusions about the hard cases he'd observed.

Jesse said, "You stop for a meal in these burgs and you don't have to wait but five minutes for some fool to spend an opinion about the ugly strangers in town and what their appetites are like.''

Frank said, ''I'm gonna regret those cucumbers. They're gonna argue with me through evening.''

Jesse glanced at his brother with concern. ''What you need to do is tap some alum onto a dime, cook it with a matchstick, and lick it clean before you partake of your meals. That's the remedy for dyspepsia. You'll be cured inside of four days.''

''You and your cures.'' Frank crossed in front of his brother, jamming his horse, and they turned left on a twin-rutted road and a median strip of grease-smeared, axle-flogged weeds. A great many animals had ganged on the road for a half-mile, then shambled into cannon-high straw grass that meandered into green bluffs. The James brothers pursued eccentric routes in that general direction, Jesse weaving right or left in his boredom, bending extravagantly from his saddle as he steered, shouting questions and assessments across the open to Frank. They meshed inside the woods, Frank ducking under an overhead bough that whapped dust from his coat shoulder, Jesse yanking his horse right and into a coulee where it noisily thrashed fallen leaves.

Ahead was brown shale and green ferns and humus where the sun was forbidden, and then two naked trees connected by twenty feet of hemp rope, to which had been reined a considerable number of horses. Here thirteen men squatted with coffee and idled or cradled shotguns: croppers and clerks and hired hands, aged in their late teens and twenties, wearing patched coveralls and wrinkled wool trousers and foul-looking suit coats that exposed their wrists, or overcoats the color of nickel, of soot, that assorted weeds had attached themselves to. They were hooligans, mainly, boys with vulgar features and sullen eyes and barn-red faces capped white above the eyebrows. They were malnourished and uneducated; their mouths were wrecks of rotting teeth. Consumption was a familiar disease, they carried infirmities like handkerchiefs; several were missing fingers, one was sick with parasites, another two had lice, eyes were crossed or clouded, harelip went undoctored.

Robert Woodson Hite and his simple younger brother, Clarence, were cousins from Adairville, Kentucky; Dick Liddil, Jim Cummins, Ed Miller, and Charley Ford had been in the James gang on previous occasions, the rest had been recruited to check the horses and divide the posses and parade with Henry rifles outside the passenger cars, firing on the recalcitrant and defiant. They bunched around the James brothers when they arrived that afternoon, several exhorting and goading Frank and Jesse in an exercise of kinship or special influence, the others wary and timid, slinking over or sniggering or investigating whatever was under their eyes.

The Jameses descended from their saddles and a lackey pulled the horses to wild feed and Jesse hunkered with coffee brewed from his own fine-ground beans and chatted with Ed Miller and Wood Hite as some gangling boys eavesdropped. Jesse inquired if the Chicago and Alton managers had stationed guards in the depot or mail cars. He inquired about the nearest telegraph machine. He inquired about the time of sundown.

Meanwhile Frank quit the main group to reconnoiter the woods and the railroad and the meager farm and inhospitable cabin belonging to a man named Snead. He stood in green darkness and weeds, smoking a cigarette he'd made, perusing the sickle curve in the rails and a grade that was hard work for a locomotive. The southern cliff on which he tarried rose about thirty feet above the cinder roadbed, the northern ridge had been a lower elevation on a hill the railroad had excavated and was about ten feet above the cut. Three miles east was Glendale station. Mosquitoes and gnats hived in the air and inspected his ears but he did not slap at them because he was using his hearing to position some fool crashing through weed tangles and creepers to the left and rear of him. The noise stopped and Frank opened his gray coat to slide his right hand across to his left pistol.

"Excuse me," a boy shouted, "but I see I've sort of traipsed in and interrupted you."

The voice was genial, golden, unrecognizable; Frank trudged up the hill some until he perceived a young man in a gray stovepipe hat and overlarge black coat that was reduced and cinched by a low-slung holster. His thighs were clenched by green bushes. His hands were overhead, as if a gun were on him, and the cuffs had dropped deep on his forearms. He had ginger brown hair and very small ears and a sunburned face that could have prettied a girl except for lips that seemed slightly pursed and swollen. He looked to Frank like a simp and a snickerer, the sort to tantalize leashed dogs.

Frank queried, "Which one are you?"

"Bob Ford."

"Ah, Charley's brother."

Bob received that as an invitation to lower his hands. His face creased with a wide smile that hung on as Frank stubbed his cigarette cold on a cottonwood trunk and returned to his inspection of the geography, disregarding Bob Ford.

The boy hunkered next to Frank and swatted his stovepipe hat around, dividing screens of mosquitoes and gnats that blew awry and rejoined and touched lighter than breath on his neck. He said, "I was lying when I said I just happened on down here. I've been on the scout, looking for you. I feel lousy that I didn't say so at the outset."

Frank dug in his pockets and extracted cigarette makings. He was not inclined to converse.

Bob scratched his hat-matted hair. "Folks sometimes take me for a nincompoop on account of the shabby first impression I make, whereas I've always thought of myself as being just a rung down from the James brothers. And, well, I was hoping if I ran into you aside from those peckerwoods, I could show you how special I am. I honestly believe I'm destined for great things, Mr. James. I've got qualities that don't come shining through right at the outset, but give me a chance and I'll get the job done—I can guarantee you that."

Frank slimed the cigarette he'd made and struck a match off his boot sole. "You're not so special, Mr. Ford." He inhaled tobacco smoke and let it crawl from his mouth before he blew it. "You're just like any other tyro who's prinked himself up for an escapade. You're hoping to be a gunslinger like those nickel books are about, but you may as well quench your mind of it. You don't have the ingredients."

"I'm sorry to hear you feel that way," said Bob, "since I put such stock in your opinions." He slapped a mosquito and looked at his blood-freckled palm and stood, rehatting his short, baby-fine hair. "As for me being a gunslinger, I've just got this one granddaddy Patterson Colt and a borrowed belt to stick it in. But I've also got an appetite for greater things. I hoped joining up with you would put me that much closer to getting them. And that's the plain and simple truth of the matter."

"So what do you want me to say?"

"You'll let me be your sidekick tonight."

"Sidekick?" said Frank. He'd heard the term applied solely to matched horses in a team-span.

"So you can see my grit and intelligence."

Frank examined his cigarette, sucked it once more, and flipped it onto a roadbed tie where the butt was later shredded under a railroad detective's laced shoe. He said, "I don't know what it is about you, but the more you talk, the more you give me the willies. I don't believe I even want you as close as earshot this evening."

"I'm sorry—"

"Why don't you *go?*" Frank said and the boy tramped up the hill, slapping weeds aside.

THE LATE CLELL MILLER's kid brother Ed had imposed a large iron pot in the hoop of his saddle lariat, and he and Dick Liddil scrounged for wild onions and scarecrowed vegetables as Jesse gardened his rant into a second hour. He cut and rooted and cultivated until he'd worked on Shelby in the Civil War and the might of iron submarines and Mrs. Mary Todd Lincoln's hysterics. Often he was facetious, but no one adventured a smile until Jesse did. His audience varied according to jobs they were expected to perform—steeds needed tending, roads needed watching, rookies were bossed into cooking chores—and each vacated seat was bullied over as Jesse continued what he liked to call wabash.

His cousin Robert Woodson Hite remained on his left, sulking and mooning the afternoon through over some imagined slight. Next to Wood was his nineteen-year-old brother, Clarence, who was stooped and consumptive and slack-jawed and as void of calculation as a sponge. Persevering too was Charley Ford, who snorkled mucus and spit it, who chuckled and hee-hawed soon after the others did, continuing on with his bray seconds after the others had ceased, and who covered his left boot with a corrupted coat in order to conceal a clubfoot that practiced walking had made practically imperceptible. He had abetted the ransacking of the express car on the Chicago, Rock Island, and Pacific Railway, which the James gang had boarded on July 15th, and gave accommodations to the outlaws afterward at his sister's place near Richmond. So he was in good favor. His brother William had married the sister of Jim Cummins, which was how Charley was initially noticed, and he hunted pigeons and turtledoves with Ed Miller, who had recruited him into the James gang by introducing him to Jesse on a gambling night in 1879—he had impressed Jesse as a savvy, sporting man then; just how Charley never could fathom.

Charles Wilson Ford was a rail-thin, rough, and likeably ignorant country boy who apologized for his failings before they could be found out: there was something of a good-natured dog about him, something hungry and grateful and vulnerable that made up for his general vulgarity. His lackluster brown eyes were sunk in his skull and his right eye was slanted enough to look akilter and borrowed and slapdash. Mismatched also were his ears (the right appeared to have taken wing), and his teeth (his overbite made it seem as if he were incessantly sucking his lower lip). He had heavy black eyebrows and a black mustache no coarser than body hair, that never seemed more than a random smear of newsprint under his nose. His complexion was pestered with acne, his fingers often looked shoe-grimed, he spoke with a paltry lisp that somehow made him seem younger than twenty-four.

Jesse was on the subject of the first electric power plant, which Thomas A. Edison was constructing on Pearl Street in New York City. He explained, incorrectly, how the incandescent lamp worked, and Charley stabbed at the dirt with a stick or pinched scarlet eruptions on his shoulder and neck or measured the others with sidelong glances. Then a boy in a gray stovepipe hat emerged from the snaggles and claws of the woods and reached into the blue smoke of the fire and praised the miscellaneous stew and principally slouched about doing fraudulent chores in order to eavesdrop on Jesse. At last Clarence Hite relinquished his seat and the boy pushed John Bugler aside and capered over boots and legs and wormed down next to Charley Ford with the incivility and intrusion that bespoke brotherhood. The boy had been introduced to Jesse more than once but the outlaw saw no reason then to store the kid's name, and now, as he culled a list that Frank had read aloud Monday night, he kept returning to the name Bunny. The boy nodded like a horse whenever Jesse's words seemed to want affirmation; whenever Jesse leavened his chat with humor the younger Ford boy laughed overloudly and infectiously with whoops and idiotic rises, like a knuckle-run on a piano. His were the light-checkered blue eyes that never strayed, the ears that picked up each nuance and joke, the amen looks that suggested he understood Jesse as no one else could.

Frank returned from his reconnaissance and scowled at the loiterers even as he drank black coffee with a carefree Jim Cummins. Dick Liddil rattled a wooden kitchen tool around inside the iron pot and sang "Chowtime!" and the gang filed by the fire with invented spoons and bowls. The Ford boy was the last to get up, finding his legs only when Jesse stood and closing on him like a valet.

"Am I too late to wish you Happy Birthday?"

Jesse grinned. "How'd you know?"

Bob Ford ticked his head. "You'd be surprised at what I've got stored away. I'm an authority on the James boys."

Jesse asked, "Your name isn't Bunny Ford, is it?"

The boy was so avid to second whatever Jesse said that he nearly admitted it was, but checked himself and corrected, "Why no. It's Robert Ford."

"Of course it is."

"Bob."

Jesse simpered a little and walked to the fire; Bob sidled and hopped to keep in stride with him. Jesse said, "I don't recollect: you've never been with the gang before, have you?"

"Oh no sirree. I'm a virgin." Bob thumbed back his stovepipe hat and grinned just as Jesse might. "At least in that one respect, if you get my meaning."

"Yes?"

"I've been fretting and fidgeting like I had ants down my pants the entire afternoon. Your brother and I had a real nice visit over toward the railroad, chatting about this and that, enjoying each other's company, but otherwise I've been organizing my mind and working at calming my innards."

"Cook alum," Jesse said, and took a heaped bowl and spoon from a man in a gunnysack apron. Jesse lowered onto a stump in his vast gray coat and Bob sat on the earth at his feet with his holster removed and his own coat opened for rather overdue ventilation. Jesse chewed and wiped his mouth on his hand. "Do you know what this stew needs?"

"Dumplings?"

"Noodles. You eat yourself some noodle stew and your clock will tick all night. You ever see that woman over in Fayette could suck noodles up her nose?"

"Don't believe I have," said Bob.

"You've got canals in your head you never dreamed of."

Bob was scraping his stew out of a blue envelope. Juice broke from a corner and spoiled his trouser fly in a manner that suggested incontinence. He would not notice this until later. He flapped the envelope into the fire and licked his spoon with a hound's care before submerging it in his pocket. He said, "Your brother Frank and I had just a real nice visit this afternoon. Must've been a hundred subjects entertained, having to do with the Chicago and Alton Railroad and the U.S. Express Company and assignments on board the cars."

Jesse had closed his eyes but kept the spoon in his mouth. He exercised a crick in his neck.

Bob went on. "Well, the upshot of our visit together was we sort of mutually agreed that the best thing for all parties concerned would be if I could use my *huge* abilities as your helper and, you know, apprentice. So we could be confederates together and come out of this unscathed. That was the upshot."

13

"Well, Buck does the figuring." Jesse looked at his bowl of stew. "Do you want the rest of this?"

"I'm sorta off my feed."

"Hate to waste it."

"My innards are riled as it is."

Jesse arose and dumped his leftovers into the iron pot and gave over his bowl and spoon to a boy for washing. He said to Bob, "If you order a beefsteak in a restaurant and they don't broil it long enough? Don't ever send it back, because if you do the cook spits all over your food; tinctures it something putrid."

Bob was dumbfounded. He said, "I don't like to harp on a subject but—"

"I don't care who comes with me," Jesse said. "Never have. I'm what they call gregarious."

Bob smiled in his never-quit way. Frank was drinking coffee and scowling again as he walked over from the far side of the fire. Jesse raised his voice. "I hear tell you and young Stovepipe here had a real nice visit."

Frank looked askance at Robert Ford and flung on the ground the remains of his coffee. He dried the tin cup with his elbow. "Your boys have about an acre of rock to haul, Dingus. You'd better goose them down yonder."

THEY SKIDDED a rain-surrendered cottonwood tree down the bank and horsed it over the polished steel rails, ripping bark away from the bone-colored wood. They carried limestone and sandstone and earth-sprinkling rocks that were the sizes of infants and milk cans and sleeping cats, and these they hilled and forted about the tree as shovels sang and picks splintered and inveigling footpaths caved in along the vertical Blue Cut excavations. Jesse supervised the rock-piling, recommending land to be mined for stone, dedicating his men to various jobs once the locomotive was shut down, chewing a green cigar black. Shadows grew into giants and died as the sun burned orange and sank. Mosquitoes flitted from hand to cheek until a night wind channeled east on the tracks and carried the insects away, even tore the ash of cigarettes and battened light coats over backs on the higher exposures. Clouds bricked overhead and were brindled pink, then crimson and violet; leaves sailed like paper darts and the air carried the tang of cattle and hogs and chimney smoke.

Frank was a solemn sentinel on the southern ridge, big as a park bronze of the honored dead, two inches taller than most of his men and majestic with confidence and dignity and legend. Bob Ford heaved rock and yanked the horses to creek water and stirred the camp fire out, and each time he passed Frank James he said "Hello" or "How do you do?" until Dick Liddil indicated that robbers crossed paths with each other many times in the course of an evening to-do and Frank considered it silly to even once exchange pleasantries.

Jesse, on the other hand, was the soul of friendliness and commerce, acknowledging each of Bob's remarks, letting the boy ingratiate himself, rewarding him with trivial tasks that Bob executed with zeal. Then he asked Bob to strike a match as he read the dial of a pocket watch in a gold hunting case, stolen from a judge near Mammoth Cave. The clock instructed him and he retreated into the dark and after some minutes returned with a kerosene lantern and with a burlap grain sack over his arm like a waiter's towel. "You can stick with me but don't heel. I don't want to bust into you every time I have the notion to change direction."

Bob muttered, "I'm not a moron, for Heaven's sake," but his irritation was quiet and his head down—one might have thought his boots had ears.

Jesse wasn't listening anyway. He scrubbed his teeth with his linen shirt collar and bulged his lips and cheeks with his cleansing tongue. He curtained his coat halves over his unmatched, pearl-handled pistols (a .44 caliber Smith and Wesson and a Colt .45 in crossed holsters), but he kept his gray suit jacket buttoned at the lapels in accordance with fashion. He told the boy, "They're supposed to have a hundred thousand dollars in that express car; at least that's what the gossip is."

Bob smiled, but there was something incorrect and tortured about it. He said, "My fingers are already starting to itch."

Jesse squatted and struck a match and turned up the flame on the lantern, then wadded a red flannel sleeve around the glass chimney under the curled wire protectors. The yellow light rubied.

"That's ideal," Frank called. He was on the south ridge above Jesse and the railroad tracks, up where the grade increased and horseshoed to the right, about twenty yards east of the rock accumulation on the rails. Dick Liddil, Wood Hite, Jim Cummins, Ed Miller, and Charley Ford were near Frank, murmuring and smoking and sitting or squatting with rifles erect on their thighs, their fingers inside the trigger housings. The Cracker Neck boys, the sickly sharecroppers and havenots, had congregated with Jesse and been instructed to range along

Blue Cut's northern ridge, which they did in a lackadaisical fashion: they rambled far down the tracks, grew lonesome, rejoined, huddled, bummed cigarettes, strewed out again and perilously crossed paths with each other in the night of the woods. Frank commented, "They're going to trip and shoot each other into females."

Dick Liddil said, "I bet I can find them husbands if they do," and that jollied even Frank.

Jesse held the lantern over his pocket watch. Both hands were near the IX. He said, "About two years ago we robbed the same railroad, only it was right in Glendale we boarded her."

"I know that," said Bob, a little peeved and superior. "You may not realize it yet but I'm a storehouse of information about the James gang. I mean, I've followed your *careers*." Bob had snipped two eyeholes from a white handkerchief and this he stuffed under his stovepipe hat so that it concealed all but his mouth and chin. However, he had cut one hole slightly low and inside of where it should have been, resulting in a mask that gave the impression he was cock-eyed and pitiable, which was not at all what he had in mind.

Jesse looked at him curiously but recommended no alterations. His concerns were apparently historical. "Do you know what happened five years ago to the day? To the *day*? What happened on September seventh in eighteen seventy-six?"

"You made an attempt on a Northfield, Minnesota, bank." Bob rummaged in his memory and asked, "Was it owned by General Ben Butler? The Scourge of New Orleans?"

"That's right," said Jesse.

"Knew it."

Jesse said, "Bill Chadwell, Clell Miller, Charlie Pitts—they were killed outright. The Youngers have been in prison ever since. It's painful to recall."

Bob added unnecessarily, "And you never got a plug nickel from that bank."

Jesse failed to register a facial reaction; he merely replied, "So you can see how this date would have an aroma for me."

Then Jesse seemed to pick up a sound as a receptive animal might, twisting sharply to the east, specifying and assessing and then grasping his lantern to walk off the cliff, hopping down ten feet in three plunging, dirt-sloshing steps. He stamped his boots (a pain shooting up his injured ankle) and shook out his trouser cuffs, then knelt to hear locomotive noise translate through the rails. The steel was warm and burnished with wear and smooth as a spoon to his ear. The hum was like insects in a jar. He called to his older brother, "She's right on schedule, Buck."

Frank was smoking another cigarette and beguiling Dick Liddil and Charley Ford with long passages from *The Life of King Henry the Fifth,* ending with, " ' But if it be a sin to covet honor, I am the most offending soul alive.' "

Dick Liddil asked, "How much of that you got memorized?"

"Over a thousand lines."

"You're a man of learning."

"Yes, I am." Frank rubbed his cigarette out against the rough bark of a tree. "You'd better go down to Jesse."

Jesse raised his blue bandana over his nose as soon as he could make out the boiler cadence, and he placed his right boot on the rail as Dick Liddil slid down the southern cliff, ouching and cussing and clutching weed brakes. Dick then tied a red bandana over his nose and ambled over, shaking dust from a beige shirt and from brown pants that were so long for his legs and were so creased with constant use that they looked like concertinas.

The locomotive's chuffing was growing loud. Jesse's right foot tickled with rail vibrations. He looked around and saw Liddil to his right with his Navy Colt hung in his hand, the Hites and Ed Miller to the east, preparing to strongarm the passengers, many other boys ranged along the cut with Henry rifles slung over their wrists, Bob Ford on the cliff behind him, looking like a gunfighter.

Jesse could hear the locomotive decelerate on the grade, hear the creaks and complaints as the carriages listed north on the curve. The brass headlamp's aisle of white light filled the passage called Blue Cut and streaked across scrub brush and into the forest, causing Charley Ford to blind his eyes, and then the light bent and flooded toward Jesse. The cowcatcher hunted the tracks and the black smoke billowed into hillocks and mountains over the smokestack and train, and Jesse swung his flannel-red lantern over the rails in a yardmaster's signal to stop.

The engineer was Chappy Foote. He had his elbow and goggled head out the cab window and his left fingers on the handle for the steam brake valve. On seeing the lantern, he leaned his body out and concluded that a freight train had stalled on the grade until he saw the man's bandana and ten yards behind him the high rubble on the rails. He turned to his fireman as he yanked the valve handle and yelled, "Looks like we're going to be robbed!"

The young stoker, John Steading, cupped his ear because of the boiler roar but picked up enough of the sentence to swing out for a look and say, "Mercy."

Jesse avoided the cowcatcher and saw the toggle-joint between the brake blocks rise, compelling them against the steel tires with a scream that made him clamp his ears. Hot steam broke over him and couplings banged and sparks sliced off the rails. The running speed had been twenty-five miles per hour; it was fifteen a few seconds later; then five. Steamer trunks slid; the mail agent was thrown enough to punch through a slot of the walnut route sorter, bruising his thumbnail and knuckle; a fat man in the sleeper careered half its length and clobbered the door like a rolling piano; in the caboose a mechanic used his handkerchief to dab macaroni soup off his clothes. The engineer braked in time to creep the locomotive into the rubble, the cowcatcher just kissing the rock with the *chunk* of a closed ice-box door.

They could hear a quartet of Englishmen in the Pullman car singing pleasantly, "Come out, 'tis now September, the hunter's moon's begun, and through the wheat and stubble is heard the distant gun. The leaves are paling yellow and trembling into red, and the free and happy barley is hanging down its head."

Then the gang was running and bounding and skidding down the embankments. Jesse watched as Bob Ford slid down like a debutante in petticoats, his left hand snatching at weeds and roots as his right unveiled his eyes enough to peek around at the commotion. Men were rushing alongside the train and levering their rifles and slouching about in a manner they fancied was ghoulish and frightening. Frank James was on the south side of the train with a rifle slack in his arms, his cardigan sweater closed with a fist, instructing everybody. Steam trickled from the locomotive trucks and spirited in the breeze, and the engine huffed "church" and once again "church" and then sighed with embering fire as Jesse hiked onto a cab step and brandished his cocked revolver.

The engineer cringed down under his hands, shouting, "Don't shoot! Ain't no call for that!"

And Jesse said, "You two best come down from your machine and bring a coal pick along."

Chappy Foote replied, "You've got the gun," and obediently removed his goggles and hooked them over the brake handle. His stoker was scared sick and worked at getting his gumption back by resting on the fold-down bench, his sweat crawling over the filth of his face. He looked about sixteen. The engineer dropped a coal pick onto the cinder bed and lingered on each step as he climbed down. The stoker followed, neglecting the last two rungs. Then Jesse shook the hands of both workers, introducing himself as Jesse James, the man they'd read so much about.

AFTER THE LOCOMOTIVE slammed to a halt on the grade known as Independence Hill, a porter named Charles Williams bent down from the platform of the ladies' coach (where tobacco smoke was forbidden) and made out three or four men near the engine and Chappy Foote disembarking onto the cinder bed. Williams was a small, brook-no-guff child of ex-slaves, dressed in a brass-buttoned, navy blue uniform and a blue hat that was cocked on his head. He retrieved his lantern, intending to learn the nature of the predicament, but no sooner did he scurry around the cars than a man near the caboose shouted, "Get back inside, you black bastard!" and four bisecting gunshots sent him back onto the platform. He opened the door to the ladies' coach and saw the women inside lowering the thirty-four curtains and concealing valuables, hiking their skirts to tuck folding money under their corsets, poking jewels into their brassieres, shoving purses and necklaces under seat cushions. (One woman who had secreted over a thousand dollars and a delicate watch in her stockings would compliantly offer her embroidered handbag to Frank James and have it courteously refused.) Men rushed in from the smoker chucking dollars into their derby hats and then sloped down in their seats with their children huddled next to them or under lamp tables or between the tasseled chairs and the walls.

Williams scurried down the coach and ducked out the rear door at the end of the passageway. (The vestibules that connected coaches and kept out the weather had not yet been invented; the only protection was a platform railing and roof.) He snuck down the stairs and saw three masked men beneath the lamplit second compartment of the sleeper, one man smoking a cigarette, another kicking soot clods from the carriage. It had been several minutes since they'd stopped the train, they wanted activities and hobbies; soon they'd be looking for bottles to break.

The man with the cigarette glanced over and inched his shotgun at the porter. He said, "Better get back inside, you black devil, or you'll have your head blowed off."

That would have been Ed Miller, who was only a few months away from having his own skull shot in.

19

THE CONDUCTOR was named Joel Hazelbaker. He was a severe man who had for ten years worked on freight trains and broke most of the bones in his fists boxing hobos. When the locomotive braked he swung down to the roadbed to determine what the cause was and witnessed the gang swooping down into the cut. He told the crowd in the second-class coach about the robbery in progress and then had the presence of mind to trot around the bend toward the caboose to solicit a flag man. They'd overtaken a freight earlier and he was afraid it would crash into them (a common accident then) unless warned: the back cars would accordion, the freight's boiler would explode. Near the first-class palace cars, Hazelbaker encountered a raincoated man with two revolvers who was crouched like a nickel book gunfighter and who ordered him to halt but listened when Hazelbaker explained that he had to stop the freight train. A brakeman named Frank Burton tottered over the smoker roof and climbed down with a red lantern, and the two hurried back to the caboose but were shot at with so many rounds that Hazelbaker was momentarily convinced the outlaws commanded an R. J. Gatling cluster gun. He saw Frank Burton's coat flapping with near-misses as the boy ran on and then the shooting sputtered as Frank James walked the roadbed irritably waving his arms overhead, calling in a big voice, "Cease firing!" over and over again. Frank James simmered, searched out an oaf to hit, found his cousin Clarence Hite, and cuffed him on the ear. He then gave the conductor permission to proceed.

Hazelbaker would later recall for newspaper reporters that he and Burton needed to run less than ten rods beyond the caboose before the freight locomotive announced itself with many long whistles, the engineer having guessed at a problem ahead because of occasional boiler sparks he'd seen swirling through the crowns of trees. The brakeman motioned the lantern across the rails, as Jesse had, and when the locomotive's brakes screeched into lock on the tires, the conductor returned to the rear of the sleeper, unhooking his nickel-plated watch and chain from his vest and unsnapping a leather wallet that was big as a summons envelope and attached to his suspenders with a shoelace. He separated his seventy-five dollars from that evening's railroad collections and released his cash and time-piece into an iron water tank that was lashed next to the Pullman door. The watch made a gone-forever noise in the water and Hazelbaker's stomach queered.

ON THAT TRAIN the express and baggage and mail cars had been combined into one green, windowless coach with government property divided from the rest by means of a wooden partition and screen. The mail agent was O. P. Melloe. After the locomotive stopped, he opened the door on the north and sagged on the doorframe to observe the gang's business with the engineer. He also saw that in the rear section of the car the baggagemaster and express messenger had tilted their heads out the open door at radically different heights. The baggagemaster said, "Opie? We're going to bolt this door from the inside."

"I'd say that's a good idea," said Melloe.

Their door slammed and through the chicken wire above the partition the mail agent heard the two young men shuffle bags and boxes. He ascended canvas bags of mail until he could see the two stacking chicken coops, thereby forbidding detection underneath of the Adams Express Company safe that was also en route to Kansas City. Melloe said, "If they push you to the brink, do what you must to save your skin."

Henry Fox, the messenger, banged down a crate of plumbing fixtures and glanced around for other valuables to camouflage. Fox answered, "Thanks for the reminder, Opie."

Melloe descended from the crushed mail sacks and leaned against the doorframe with his door opened just enough to see out. A man in a Confederate officer's coat and blue bandana mask had limped down to the express section with the young fireman in tow by his shirt collar, and a wiry boy in a stovepipe hat and overlarge coat was menacing Foote in the direction of the express car.

Upon arrival at the express section, Chappy Foote ineffectually tried the doorknob and then invited recommendations about what he should do since the express company's door gave every indication that it was locked and could not be forced. Jesse recocked his revolver hammer (the clicks like a barber cracking his knuckles) and recommended, "Why don't you smash it in." He then maneuvered over to Bob Ford as Foote grunted the coal pick into an underhand swing and rounded it overhead into the door near the latch, loudly splintering the wood and embedding the spike so that he had to waggle the handle to extricate it. Jesse confided to Bob, "The locked doors and the smashing them down, that's a little skit we run through each time—sort of like grace before dinner."

The engineer oofed and drove the coal pick again and the wood submitted to the blow, screaming and folding inward near the edge. The messenger saw they'd get in anyway, so he pulled the bottom and overhead bolts free inside, saying, "All right! You can come in now!" and Jesse moved forward to sock the kickboard so that the door gave in, quivering into darkness. Henry Fox retreated with his hands high as the baggagemaster snuffed the lights. Jesse ordered the engineer to roost in the weeds with his stoker and ordered Bob Ford to guard them. Bob poked his revolver into Foote's side and the two railroadmen walked rather routinely off the cinder bed and sat down. Jesse heaved his chest onto the threshold of the express car and kneed himself into the room. Dick Liddil and the come-lately Charley Ford imitated Jesse and lighted a lantern as Jesse lifted packages and shook them and guessed at their contents. "That's a woman's satchel," he said. "All fancy beadwork and paper flowers."

"Could be," said the baggageman. His smile didn't know whether to hold on or vanish.

Jesse smashed another box on a nail and snagged it open, finding inside a photograph of a child in an oval frame, the cheek torn by the nail. Jesse flung it against the ceiling, adjusted his blue bandana over his nose, and glared at the express manager. "I want you to open that safe."

Fox looked to the baggagemaster for counsel. The man's head was down. Fox looked back at the robber with a nervous smile, his fright making him seem complaisant and insolent. Charley Ford stepped over and struck Henry Fox over the skull with his pistol, the concussion like gloved hands clapping loudly once, like a red apple pitched at a tree. The blow chopped the messenger down to his knees with blood shoelacing his face and the baggagemaster backed to the green wall with horror as Liddil said, "You didn't have to bop him, Charley."

"Yes, he did," said Jesse. "They need the convincing. They got their company rules and I got my mean streak and that's how we get things done." Charley grinned with accomplishment and Jesse cleared some registers off the only safe he could see, one no larger than the kneehole in a lady's dresser. "Come over here and attend to this now."

Melloe was at the partition. He exclaimed, "You all right over there?"

Dick Liddil heard a wild and scrambled fusillade and leaned outside to see the Crackers firing at a conductor and brakeman who were crouching with a red lantern. Frank James was hollering for them to cease, and after twenty rounds they did. Bob Ford was squatting in the weeds, his gun cocked up next to his cheek. "Scare ya?" Dick called, and Bob stood with no little chagrin. "I couldn't tell what on earth was going on!"

Fox gathered himself and dialed numbers on the U.S. Express Company vault and after two failures had the combination correct enough to jerk the door open. Then the baggagemaster helped him over the chicken coops, on which he sat down heavily, cracking two frames. The baggagemaster carefully backed onto the coop that covered the Adams Express Company safe, where the greater amount of money was.

It was Charley Ford who emptied the U.S. Express Company safe, with such concentration and sedulousness that he stole receipts, waybills, non-negotiable notes, and a calendar schedule of express deliveries, in addition to more than six thousand dollars in mixed currencies. Jesse then tested the weight of the grain sack and slunk over to the lantern, puzzling over the contents. "Isn't no hundred thousand dollars here, Dick."

Dick looked into the grain sack himself and said, "I'm *real* disappointed."

Bob Ford was standing over the engineer and stoker when Jesse jumped down to the cinder bed from the express car and encouraged the messenger and baggagemaster outside with his gun. Blood had trickled into Henry Fox's right eye, so he looked at Bob with his left as he staggered over the weeds and crashed down.

Bob gaped at the injury with some panic; Fox admitted to the railroad crewmen that he had a gruesome headache; Jesse was walking with Charley and Dick as he called that they were going to go through the cars. "If any of them so much as twitch, give their coconuts a sockdolager: that's language they understand."

BY THAT TIME Frank James had ascended the stairs at the rear of the ladies' coach, catching himself with the brass door pull as an ache branched over his chest. Ed Miller and Clarence Hite climbed after him and Ed Miller entered the coach first, his boot slamming the door aside, an eyeholed flour sack over his head, his sawed-down twelve-gauge straight ahead of his right pocket. He was reported to have said, "Throw up your hands, you sons-a-bitches!" and then, for emphasis, slapped a man in the mouth.

Then Frank James strolled inside in his gray coat and yellow bandana mask, looking colossal and mean and sick. He saw about thirty men either cowering or flinching or accusing him with censorious eyes, while the wives scrunched down behind their husbands' shoulders. He hypothesized at least twenty handguns among the travelers,

23

so he strode down the aisle, imperious as Victoria's consort, his boot-heels barking on the oakwood flooring, and he scowled and lingered over those investors and vacationers who seemed recalcitrant, ticking a button or collar with his Remington .44 Frontier revolver, which he would surrender to Governor Crittenden in little more than a year.

Frank shouted, "Are any of you preachers?"

No one raised a hand.

He shouted, "Are any of you widows?"

Some frowned with curiosity.

He said, "We never rob preachers or widows."

Four hands shot up.

"No; no, you're too late."

Having satisfied himself that he had conquered any thoughts of rebellion, Frank nodded to the rear of the coach and an emaciated Clarence Hite scuttled in, a Colt Navy .36 caliber six-gun dominating his right hand. He had a skulking hunchbacked look and his hazel eyes kept double-checking his actions with his cousin. He punched his revolver into the green, knee-length coat of a man and said, "I'm Jesse James, ya damned yellow dog! Gimme your money!"

The man fiddled his hand inside his coat and presented Clarence with a worn envelope containing seventy-five dollars and with an English gold watch that would fastidiously chime the hour no matter what skullduggery Clarence was up to at the moment. Clarence shoved the gray-haired man back and joyfully dangled the watch and envelope in Frank's direction. Frank came back down the aisle and chucked the goods inside the belly of his shirt, and Ed Miller, Clarence Hite, and the infamous Frank James sallied down the coach, stealing coins, dollars, watches, bracelets, rings, stickpins, pendants.

From the express car that was just behind the locomotive and tender came Jesse, Charley, and Dick. They clanged up the stairs at the head of the smoker, saw it was vacant, and rushed down the lighted car, sliding a little on the narrow Persian runner, ringing a brass spittoon against an oaken Doric pedestal. Upon reaching the platform, Jesse rapped on the coach's doorglass with his gun; Frank swiveled and waved him in; Dick and Charley jostled ahead into the coach as Frank shouted, "Just work your way toward the middle."

So a number of feuding, keening voices mixed as the gang visited each adult and ordered him or her to shell out. If too meager a sum was exchanged, a cocked revolver was pressed to the person's forehead and he was told to delve a little further. A bearded man with spectacles lost seven hundred dollars to Ed Miller but Jesse had a hunch about him and after a bickering investigation turned up one hundred dollars more. According to Williams, a Dutchman had managed to remain asleep ever since he dined in Columbia and when Charley socked him awake he at once assumed he was being asked for a fare he'd already paid. Charley pushed his revolver into the Dutchman's cheek and stole the three hundred dollars with which the man intended to purchase a farm in Joplin. Mr. C. R. Camp was host of a tour of New York land buyers and later tallied their losses at $4,021. Clarence Hite squatted to remove the white shoes from an infant so he could poke his finger inside and rescue God knows what. John O'Brien had stuffed inside his pants a bundle of several hundred dollars clenched by a rubber band, and on the demand of Frank James delivered one thousand dollars that had been for business expenses. The bundle of his own money slithered to the floor and rolled as Frank walked on and O'Brien's small daughter redeemed it, saying, "Here's some more money, Papa!" Frank turned and snatched it from her hand. Dick Liddil dictated that Mrs. C. A. Dunakin raise her hands overhead and whirl four times as he inspected her. He said, "Next time we pull off a job like this we'll have a lady along to search you female passengers." She retorted, "You might have a woman with you or a man dressed as one, but you'll never have a lady." An immigrant had his wallet tossed in a sack and soon beseeched Jesse to recover it so he could withdraw his insurance papers. His plea was denied as too time-consuming. Children wailed in corners, several women became hysterical and remained so throughout the night; men sat in chairs with blank faces, their hands lumped in their laps, having lost fortunes: their crabbed savings, the cost of a cottage, the auction sale of six Holstein cows, a laggard Silver Anniversary watch.

Jesse squeezed past the porter, Williams, who had already been frisked, and pushed into the sleeping car, flinging green velvet drapes aside as he passed each berth. He shocked a yellow old woman whose hair was braided, whose frail hands were in prayer; otherwise the sleeper seemed empty until he parted the exit drapes and saw in the foyer two women in nightgowns and a piano of a fat man all huddled around the conductor. Something in the group's timidity dispirited Jesse and he exited onto the platform, where he saw that Frank and some of the others were on the cinder bed shedding loot into a flour sack. Near the caboose were workers on the freight train who'd slunk forward to innocuously watch and whisper about the activities. Horses had been fetched and they nickered and fussed in the attic of weeds and timber over the cut. Wood Hite and Ed Miller had entered the sleeper with fire axes that they used to rip bedding off and snag mattresses from their boxes. The gang's visitation on the Chicago and Alton had now lasted nearly forty-five minutes and was beginning to deteriorate into carousal. Jesse went back inside the sleeping car and shouted, "Okay! Let's vamoose!" Then he twisted the neck of his grain sack and limped forward outside the sleeper and ladies' coach, exaggerating the heft of the valuables as the victims peeked under the curtains. He saw Frank Burton sitting on a platform, looking bankrupt, and asked how much was stolen from him. The young brakeman answered that he'd given up fifty cents and that was all he had.

It was later recorded that Jesse dug into the grain sack and gave Burton a dollar and fifty cents, saying, "This is principal and interest on your money."

Jesse delivered the loot to Jim Cummins, who'd reappeared after one of his typical evaporations, and he uttered a kindness to Henry Fox, who was looking scalped and catatonic, his ears sirening. (He resigned from his job within the month and sued the express company for damages, without luck.) Having been relieved of his assignment, Bob Ford scrabbled up the bank to the woods and scuttled through bracken, nettles, and thorns to the gathered horses, where he removed the white mask with the cut-out eyes. Charley Ford sidled over to his kid brother and said, "I was in top form tonight."

"That messenger, he's going to have trouble recalling his *name!*"

Charley leered. "Surely gave him a goose-egg, didn't I?"

"Goodness!"

Charley asked, "Did you see me roast that one gent for standing on his cash?"

"No," Bob said, "I missed that. I was outside, y'see."

"He kind of skidded when he walked was how I knew. Must've had his shoe atop fifty dollars. And his wife, she was in a state, her beady little eyes all squinched up."

"Really took the cake, did she?"

"Oh my, yes," said Charley. "Jesse's gonna be satisfied with me."

Jesse James was then walking the engineer to a locomotive that was slowly susurrating, his right arm slung over Foote's shoulders, his manner affectionate and delighted, his mood invigorating. At the cab Jesse athletically shook the man's hand, leaving a silver coin in the engineer's palm like a sidewalk magician. Chappy Foote later claimed he said, "You are a valiant man and I am a little stuck on you. Here's a dollar so you can drink to the health of Jesse James tomorrow morning.''

''Obliged'' was all that Foote could think to mutter.

''Now, what about that roadblock? Shall I have the gang remove those stones? I could hitch a team to that cottonwood and tow it right off the rails.''

''No, don't bother. To tell you the truth, about the best thing you could do for me is take yourself and your party far away from here.''

Jesse said, ''All right, partner. Good night,'' and clambered up the bank in his billowing gray coat, reducing into darkness.

THE JAMES GANG walked their horses south through scrub brush and over fire ash that was no warmer than a morning bed. They loped onto a road and into a gully and threshed through a cornfield with tassels high as the saddle cantles. There Frank moved among the veterans, distributing each man's allotment of cash and luxuries, auctioning off the gold watches and Mexican jewels, burning the securities and non-negotiable papers. Clarence Hite would later confess that each share was one hundred forty dollars but he was wretched at sums and unlikely to suspect chicanery, so it is probable that he was cheated, as were Andy Ryan, John Bugler, John Land, and Matt and Creed Chapman. Jesse had already piloted them over to a cowpath by a creek and, according to John Land, explained, ''Boys, we just haven't got time to divide the loot now—they're too hot for us—and we didn't get the money we expected to anyhow, but we'll all meet on the right fork of the Blue River a week from tonight and you'll get your cut there.''

He never really intended to meet them again; the country boys were only meant to provide security during the robbery and easy prey for the sheriff afterward. On the night of the 7th, they rode off in five directions, feeling rather pleased with themselves, but by the evening of September 10th, Andy Ryan and John Land had been arrested in shacks near Glendale, Matt Chapman and John Bugler had been jailed, and Creed Chapman was only weeks away from a six-month imprisonment in which he lost forty-two pounds.

The James gang segregated into three groups before riding out of the cornfield. Jim Cummins and Ed Miller navigated eastward for Miller's house in Saline County; Dick Liddil and Wood Hite crossed the river near Blue Mills in order to rusticate on the rented farm of Martha Bolton, the widowed sister of the Fords, whom they were both

27

trying to romance; the James brothers, the Ford brothers, and Clarence Hite rode west into Kansas City under a cold rain that moved over them from the north and knuckled their hats and sank their horses inches deep in the mire of wide, empty streets.

Zee James was asleep on the sofa when her husband creaked the kitchen door and surprised her awake with a kiss, and she boiled water in a saucepan as Jesse chaired himself in his soaked coat and lied unnecessarily about a cattle auction in Independence where he'd purchased twenty steers at below market price and right away sold them by an exchange of telegrams with a livestock buyer in Omaha.

Zee didn't raise her eyes from the saucepan. "So you've got money again?"

"Come out of it real satisfactory." He was jubilant and still energized by adrenaline, an excitement he had come to crave like caffeine. He jumped up from his chair and gandered out at the red barn. He said, "Guess who I ran into."

She gave Jesse a wifely look and got a jar down from a pantry shelf.

He said, "Buck, for one. Then Clarence Hite and two coves of his. They're with the animals right now."

"They do satisfactory at the auction too?"

He grinned. "About the most they ask is that they come out of a swap with all their toes and fingers." He then adjusted a dry hat on his head and without justifying his exit went out to the stables.

Red coal-oil lanterns gladdened the interior of the barn but Frank James was glooming about and glaring at the younger men's slipshod management of their horses. He saw Jesse at the Dutch door and sat on a long bench, his legs wide and his forearms on them, his rough hands joined around a yellow cigarette. The James brothers were not exceptionally close as boys and as they grew older were scarcely a pair—more than occasionally they were not even on speaking terms— so it was not particularly surprising that Jesse preferred not to seek out Frank's company but stood just inside the sloshing eave and peered at his melancholy and peaked cousin Clarence and then at Charley Ford, who gave up wiping the waxy coat of his mare to attempt juggling the weighted pins that Jesse had dropped in the stall. Then Jesse abruptly perceived that the stripling Bob Ford had approached from his right. "You must've creeped up on cat's paws."

Bob smiled. "I'll wager that's the first and last time you'll ever be caught off-guard." He no longer wore the overlarge coat or stovepipe hat, only green trousers with light green stripes and a collarless, yellowed shirt that plainly itched. He looked European, principally French, in spite of his blue eyes, and was not as scrawny as he initially appeared to be, but was muscular in a nuggety way, each sinew strapped to its bone as clearly as shoelaces on a shoe. Jesse could smell Mrs. S. A. Allen's Zylo Balsamum Hair Dressing (which he too favored) on the boy's ginger brown hair. They were exactly the same height.

"How old are you, kid?"

"Twenty," he said, and then corrected himself. "Except I won't really be twenty until January." He scratched his sleeve apologetically and answered again, "I'm nineteen."

"You *feel* older than that though, don't you?"

Bob acknowledged that he did. A pigeon stirred on a rafter and cocked its head at a man flinging wooden objects into the air.

"You enjoy yourself this evening?" Jesse asked.

"I was strung too high for much pleasure."

Jesse seemed to think that was an appropriate remark and something in the boy's manner of speaking inspired Jesse to ask, "Do you like tea?" And when Bob said he did (though he didn't), Jesse invited him up to the bungalow without saying goodbye to the others. They were then gathering around a clove cake on which orange gumdrops spelled Grampa, part of the loot that Clarence Hite had pilfered on the coach. The younger men sat on the ground around Frank, and Clarence recapitulated some of the robbery's disputes and amusements, emphasizing his valor, fabricating badly, boring both Charley and Frank in such a thoroughgoing way that they beguiled themselves by eating the gumdrops and cake, Frank ripping out large segments that he carefully squeezed into his palm until they were roundly packed, only then popping them into his mouth.

Charley listened to Hite with impatience, almost petulance, a smile tucked like licorice in his mouth, his eyes glazed. When his ear at last learned of a stillness, he awoke and lurched into long and wearying stories about the Fords. He talked about their childhood in Fairfax County, Virginia, in rented rooms in George Washington's Mount Vernon estate. He talked about sailing paper boats on the Potomac River, clambakes on the Atlantic coast, or playing doctor with the late president's great-granddaughters while guests from foreign countries walked the grounds. He talked about the Moore School near Excelsior Springs and about Seybold's Tavern and its sleeping rooms, in which the roughneck and frightening Younger gang retired on more than one occasion while the owner and his nephews, Bob and Charley Ford, looked on with reverence.

He said Bob once shot a milk cow because it kicked him in the shin during chores, that as kids they chased cats with meat cleavers and chopped off their ears and tails, that ten children once swarmed over Bob and almost choked him to death with a grapevine because he so often bullied them, that he and Bob were horse thieves in high school, rustling colts and fillies for Dutch Henry Born, who was arrested in Trinidad, Colorado, by none other than Sheriff Bat Masterson.

Frank James paid attention to the stories but didn't pretend much fascination. Charley said, "It sounds like maybe it's made up, but it's history, top to bottom."

Clarence said, "Funny things happen in Colorado. I once saw a cat eat a pickle."

Frank and Charley regarded him dully and then Frank got together two horse blankets and haggardly walked to an empty stall. "If you two are going to stay up all night, I guess I don't have to stand guard."

Clarence asked, "Do you think the sheriff's out already?"

"Generally is."

Charley worried that he might have thoughtlessly wronged Frank James or done his own cause some damage, so he slunk over to the stall and gawked as the grim man hung his coat and scraped straw into the shape of a pallet. He said, "I wasn't just flapping my lips when I spun out those yarns about my kid brother and me. What I figured was if you and Jesse could gauge our courage and daring, why, you just might make us your regular sidekicks."

Frank jerked a look of umbrage toward Charley and then spread out a wool blanket with his stockinged foot. "You're beginning to sound like Bob."

"I'll be square with you: it was Bob who put me up to it. He's sharper than I am; he's smart as a whip. And he's got plans for the James boys that I can't even get the hang of, they're that complicated."

As he settled achingly into repose, Frank wrapped a horse blanket over his cardigan sweater and supported his head with his right forearm. He said, "You might as well forget everything about that because there'll be no more monkey business after tonight. You can jot it down in your diary: September seventh, eighteen eighty-one; the James gang robbed one last train at Blue Cut and gave up their nightriding for good."

Charley hung his biceps over the topmost stall board, disappointed and skeptical. "How will you make your living?"

Frank was smoking a cigarette with his eyes shut. "Maybe I'll sell shoes."

JESSE AND BOB were by then at the round dining room table, letting Zee read the green tea leaves in their mugs. A big candle was the only light and the men's rapt faces were vaguely orange in the glow as Zee made the prescribed suggestions. They each up-ended their mugs and clocked them around three times as Zee, with a slight giggle, recited, "Tell me faithful, tell me well, the secrets that the leaves foretell." She then requested that Bob give her his mug and gazed at the green dregs still clinging to the murky bottom. "It looks like a snake."

Bob got up from his chair and gaped with puzzlement as she obligingly tilted the mug. "You mean that squiggle there?"

"They call it a snake. It's a sign of antagonism."

Jesse grinned and slid his own mug across to his wife. "She gets all the fancy talk straight out of *Lorna Doone*."

Zee peered at her husband's cup and said, "Yours is no happier, Dave."

Bob looked interrogatively at a man who was massaging his gums with a finger. "Dave?"

He said, "You know your Good Book? David is the begotten of Jesse." He winked for reasons that Bob couldn't intuit. "You might call it my alias. Give me my sorry prophecy, sweetheart."

Zee gave back the mug. "It looks like an M. It means someone has evil intentions toward you."

Jesse squinted inside and tipped the candle, pattering wax on the oakwood. "That's not exactly today's news, is it."

Zee sighed. "They're lacking in gaiety tonight, aren't they. Maybe I steeped the tea too long." She then arose from the dining room table with fatigue and announced that she'd be knitting in the bedroom if she could keep her eyes uncrossed. Jesse walked to the pantry and picked two Havana cigars from a corked soapstone jar and bade his guest follow him with the candle to the front porch, where they could rock and smoke and raise their voices.

The weather had modified into a mild shower, the night sky grumbled in the east, runnels glittered in the street, somewhere a rooster crowed. Jesse lowered into a hickory rocker and Bob Ford took the mating chair. Bob saw his trousers drip rainwater as he bent forward over the candle and resettled, blowing cigar smoke in a gush. Jesse had nibbled off the end of his cigar but let the chew lump under his lower lip to induce drowsiness. It was almost one o'clock and he assumed correctly that a posse from Kansas City would have reached Glendale and begun an investigation.

Bob said, "I can't believe I woke up this morning wondering if my daddy would loan me his overcoat, and here it is just past midnight and I've already robbed a railroad and scared the socks off some Easterners and I'm sitting in a rocking chair chatting with none other than Jesse James."

"It's a wonderful world," said Jesse.

Bob's cheeks collapsed when he sucked on the cigar and the button of gray ash absorbed him. "Have you ever heard outlaws call dollar bills 'Williams'? I read that in *Morrison's Sensational Series*. You see, Bill is a nickname for William."

"I see."

"You haven't heard anybody say it though?"

"Can't say so."

"You know what I've got right next to my bed? *The Trainrobbers, or A Story of the James Boys*, by R. W. Stevens. Many's the night I've stayed up with my mouth open and my eyes jumping out, reading about your escapades in the *Wide Awake Library*."

"They're all lies, you know."

"'Course they are."

Jesse carved cigar ash off with his thumbnail. "Charley claims you boys once lived in Mount Vernon."

"Yep. Played in Martha Washington's summerhouse, even made a toy of the iron key to that jail, the Bastille? Lafayette gave it to General George Washington and neither one of them ever guessed that Bob Ford would use the dang thing to lock his sisters up in the attic."

Jesse eyed Bob and said, "You don't have to keep smoking that if it's making you bungey."

Bob was relieved. He reached over the bannister and dropped the cigar into a puddle. It wobbled and canoed in the rain. "I was seven when we moved to Excelsior Springs. Everybody was talking about the sixty thousand dollars in greenbacks the James-Younger gang stole in Liberty. My Uncle Will lived close to you, over by Kearney—Bill Ford? Married Artella Cummins?"

"I know him."

"How we did love to go over there for Sunday dinner and spend the afternoon getting the latest about the Jameses."

Jesse searched his pockets and brought forth a cake of camphor that he rubbed over his throat. "You know what he also said? Charley said you once had a shoebox practically filled with James boys mementoes.''

Bob submerged his resentment and acrimony behind a misleadingly shy smile. ''That must've been a couple of years ago.''

''Or maybe it was Bunny who did that.''

''You're making sport of me, aren't you.''

Jesse caught Bob's wrist and put a finger to his lips in order to shush the boy, and then inclined out over the porch rail to inspect the composition of the night. He resettled and patiently rocked the chair on its complaining runners and then Bob saw a stooped man with a lunch pail tramping through the rainmuck of the street. He was Charles Dyerr, assistant foreman at the Western Newspaper Union and next-door neighbor to a man known only as J. T. Jackson. Dyerr would much later claim he rarely saw Jackson engage in gainful employment and guessed he was a gambler, just exactly the sort of man that Dyerr held in deepest contempt.

Jesse called out, ''Evening, Chas!''

Dyerr glanced to the porch and changed the grip on his lunch pail. ''J.T.''

''They've got you working late again.''

''James gang robbed another train.''

''You don't mean it!''

Dyerr apparently felt he'd already spoken at compromising length, for he crossed up into his yard without another word.

Jesse called in his shrill voice, ''If they put a posse together get me into it, will ya?''

They heard a woman speak as Dyerr opened the screen door and the man responded, ''Just that so-and-so next door.''

Bob said, ''You really are the cool customer they make you out to be. I'm impressed as all get-out.''

Jesse's cigar had gone out. He reached to ignite a match off the candle flame on the porch floor. He seemed suddenly glum, almost angry.

''I've got something I want to say.''

Jesse glared at him.

''It's pretty funny actually. You see, when Charley said I could come along, I was all agitated about if I could tell which was Jesse James and which was Frank. So what I did was snip out this passage that depicted you both and I carried it along in my pocket.''

''Which passage would that be?''

"Do you want to hear it? I'll read it if you want."

Jesse unbuttoned his linen shirt and rubbed the camphor over his chest. Bob assumed that meant he should read it. He pulled a limp yellowed clipping out of his right pocket and announced, "This comes from the writings of Major John Newman Edwards." He dipped to pick the candle up and placed it on the rocking chair's armrest. "I've got to find the right paragraph."

"I'm just sitting here with nothing better to do."

"Here: 'Jesse James, the youngest, has a face as smooth and innocent as the face of a school girl. The blue eyes, very clear and penetrating, are never at rest. His form is tall, graceful, and capable of great endurance and great effort. There is always a smile on his lips, and a graceful word or compliment for all with whom he comes in contact. Looking at his small white hands, with their long, tapering fingers, one would not imagine that with a revolver they were among the quickest and deadliest hands in all the west.' "

Bob raised his eyes. "And then he goes on about Frank."

Jesse sucked on his cigar.

Bob tilted toward the candle. " 'Frank is older and taller. Jesse's face is a perfect oval—Frank's is long, wide about the forehead, square and massive about the jaws and chin, and set always in a look of fixed repose. Jesse is light-hearted, reckless, devil-may-care—' " Bob smirked at him but read no reaction. " 'Frank sober, sedate, a dangerous man always in ambush in the midst of society. Jesse knows there is a price upon his head and discusses the whys and wherefores of it—Frank knows it too, but it chafes him sorely and arouses all the tiger that is in his heart. Neither will be taken alive.' "

Bob flipped the clipping over and continued. " 'Killed—that may be. Having long ago shaken hands with life, when death does come it will come to those who, neither surprised nor disappointed, will greet him with the exclamation: "How now, old fellow." ' "

Jesse creaked his rocker, scraped the fire from his cigar with his yellowed finger, and made the ash disintegrate and sprinkle off his lap when he stood. He said, "I'm a no good, Bob. I ain't Jesus." And he walked into his rented bungalow, leaving behind the young man who had played at capturing Jesse James even as a child.

2

1865–1881

We have been charged with robbing the Gallatin bank and killing the cashier; with robbing the gate at the Fair Grounds in Kansas City, with robbing a bank at St. Genevieve; with robbing a train in Iowa, and killing an engineer, with robbing two or three banks in Kentucky and killing two or three men there, but for every charge we are willing to be tried if Governor Woodson will promise us protection until we can prove before any fair jury in the State that we have been accused falsely and unjustly. If we do not prove this then let the law do its worst.

We are willing to abide the verdict. I do not see how we could well offer anything fairer.

JESSE W. JAMES
in the Liberty Tribune, *January 9, 1874*

HIS WIFE WAS Zerelda Amanda Mimms, a first cousin to the James brothers, her mother being their father's sister, their mother, Zerelda, being the source of her Christian name. She'd nursed Jesse through pneumonia and a grievous chest wound at her father's boardinghouse in Harlem, which is now northern Kansas City, and Jesse would later claim with great earnestness that he never looked at another woman after that. He lost thirty pounds, he coughed blood into his fist, he sank into fevers that made his teeth chatter, she told him, like five-cent wind-ups. He fainted sometimes while throned in plumped pillows, while Zee spooned him gravied vegetables and noodles; he hacked into a tin spittoon and cleaned his mouth with a bedsheet and apologized to his cousin for his sickness, said he normally had an iron constitution and the endurance of an Apache.

Jesse was eighteen and glamorous then; Zee was twenty and in love. She'd grown up to be a pretty woman of considerable refinement and patience. She was conventional in her attitudes and pious in her religion, a diligent, quiet, self-sacrificing good daughter who was prepared for a life quite apart from the one that Jesse would give her. She was small and insubstantial then, with a broad skirt and corseted

35

waist and breasts like coffee cups. Her blond hair when unpinned could apron her shoulder blades but she wore it braided or helixed (each morning a new experiment) and she combed wisps from her forehead with jade barrettes. Her features were fragile but frequently stitched with thought, so that even when she was most serene she seemed melancholy or, when older, censorious; Jesse could be as shy and restrained as a schoolboy around her, and she would often consider him one of her children after they were married.

But in 1865 she'd heat towels with tea kettle water and carefully drape them over her cousin's face; she'd wash his fingers as if they were silverware and close her eyes as she bathed his limbs and blow his wet hair as she combed it. She hunched on a Shaker chair beside his bed as he slept and stitched JWJ on his four handkerchiefs and on the region of his long underwear where she presumed his heart was seated.

They'd been playmates in childhood. Frank was two years older than she was and too rough and refractory to be good company for a girl, but Jesse was a good-natured, adoring boy two years younger than she was and he was willing to do whatever she suggested so long as they didn't amalgamate with his grudging big brother. When her mother died Zee moved from Liberty to Kansas City, where she grew up in the family of her older sister and Charles McBride, and they kept up a haphazard correspondence until the Civil War. Long, illegible letters would come to the girl from Jesse, the first offering his sympathy for "your mama's being called back," but many of them telling how much he missed his papa (who'd died of cholera on a mission to California) and how unhappy he was with his own overbearing mother and his stepfather, Dr. Reuben Samuels. He wished he could have gone to Kansas City with Zee, or he wished that it had been he who'd died in infancy rather than Robert, the second-born son. On one occasion he ran away from Kearney to be with her at Hallowe'en, but they most often saw each other on holiday visits when Jesse would ask if there were any boys he could fight for her or would beg her not to think that his kissing a girl named Laura meant he was no longer obligated to Zee.

The Civil War interrupted their romance. Desperate, inept, and undisciplined Union Army troops were meddling with and imprisoning much of Missouri's civil population, often plundering their crops and supplies or pillaging their shops, so that their Southern sympathies were magnified. Indignant young men who couldn't sign on with General Shelby and the Confederate Army were joining with the irregular guerrilla bands, such as that of William Clarke Quantrill, which Frank was riding with by 1862, and in reprisal, the pro-Union state militia punished the families. They went to the Kearney farm and roped Dr. Reuben Samuels as he tried to escape into a root cellar, but he wouldn't give them any intelligence about the guerrillas' plans or movements so they flipped the rope over the limb of a sideyard coffee bean tree and snugged a noose around his neck, jerking him off the ground four times, nearly strangling the man, and causing slight brain damage that would increase as he grew older. They then pressured Mrs. Zerelda Samuels for information, manhandling her even though she was pregnant (with Fannie Quantrill Samuels), and, giving up on her, went after the sixteen-year-old boy who was working the bottomlands. Jesse would write, days later, that he was wrangling with a walking plow when he glanced to his right and saw the militia galloping toward him, their guns raised, their coats flying. They ran him until his legs were rubber and one man scourged him with a bullwhip as Jesse dodged from one cornrow to the next, striping his skin with so many cuts and welts his back looked like geography. Only weeks afterward, they arrested Mrs. Samuels and his sisters Sallie and Susan (aged four and thirteen) on charges of collaboration, locking the mother and two daughters in a jailhouse in St. Joseph. Quantrill's lieutenants, among them Bloody Bill Anderson and Cole Younger, organized for a raid on Lawrence, Kansas, where they slaughtered one hundred fifty defenseless males in less than two hours, looting and burning the town's buildings, and then getting drunk in the pillaged saloons to glorify their victory. Frank James was there. General Thomas Ewing issued General Order Number 11 in reaction to the massacre, evicting more than twenty thousand residents from counties in Missouri that were congenial to the guerrillas. Dr. Samuels gathered their belongings and moved his family to Rulo, Nebraska, just over the border, and soon after that communications and Sunday visits from Jesse ceased and Zee learned, in 1864, that her wild and willful cousin was riding with Bloody Bill Anderson.

He was called Bloody Bill because of gossip that he'd chopped off enemy heads with his pirate's sword and rode under the Black Flag with seven scalps joggling against his saddle. Jesse James was his preferred recruit; of the boy, Anderson would say, "Not to have any beard, he is the keenest and cleanest fighter in the command." And Jesse responded to the praise with worship and imitation.

Jesse snuggled inside two coats in his sleeping room as he storied with Zee about days and nights of looting, robbing, and setting fires. He said he'd been with Arch Clement when he executed twenty-five

Union soldiers on furlough whom they'd come across on a train from St. Charles, and he'd charged Major A. V. E. Johnson's company at Centralia with Frank and two hundred guerrillas, annihilating over one hundred men in less than twenty minutes and killing Major Johnson himself. (Frank still wore the Union Army cartridge belt that he stole from a victim there.)

He said he'd drawn the short straw and been selected to reconnoiter a Union bivouac: he'd slithered into their midst at night with a tanner's knife and had come out slimed with blood, having slit each of the six men's throats from ear to ear. He told her how a Yankee bullet smashed his left middle finger at the nail and ruined his rifle stock. His brother made him so intoxicated on whiskey that Jesse couldn't end his sentences, and then Frank snipped at the bone and skin with barber scissors until he'd neatened the finger to his satisfaction. At Flat Rock Ford two months later, a Minie ball punctured his right lung and he was assumed dead at seventeen, but he was walking again within four weeks and was exacting his vengeance in six.

And then, he told Zee, in August of 1865, five months after Robert E. Lee surrendered his sword at Appomattox, Jesse had returned from exile in Texas and had ridden with a detachment of Southern partisans into Lexington to receive a parole that was promised them. But members of the Second Wisconsin Cavalry overlooked their white flag of truce and fired broadside on the Confederates. Jesse was slammed in the chest not an inch from the earlier scar and he was nearly crushed beneath his stricken horse; but he extricated himself and staggered into the woods where two cavalrymen hunted him in seizing thickets until he shot a snared and rearing horse and the soldiers lost stomach for the chase. Jesse said he slept that night through in a creek in order to cool his fever and watched his blood curl into the water and unweave. He maintained it was his delirium and pure orneriness that enabled him to tow himself with roots and weeds into a field of timothy grass where a plowman discovered him and doctored him with liniments and cooked chitterlings before delivering Jesse to Major J. B. Rogers, the Union commander at Lexington. A surgeon delved into the gunwound with some ambivalence, then let the bullet remain and ruled that Jesse was all but deceased, and the government paid his railroad fare to Rulo, Nebraska, where his mother and kin still were. After eight weeks Jesse's health was so little restored that his mother boated with him down the Missouri River to Harlem so that he would not die in a Northern state. "And you were here," Jesse said with no little melodrama, "and you anointed me with ointments like the sisters of Lazarus, and I have come forth from the tomb."

As Jesse talked the sun down, the hours late, Zerelda smiled and dreamed of him as he had been and was and would be. It seemed everything about him was dynamic and masculine and romantic; he was more vital even in his illness than any man she'd ever known. And he wooed her after a fashion. He was fascinated by attitudes and accomplishments her sisters would have considered common, he was attentive to her silky voice, her sweet disposition, he commended her spelling and her penmanship, which he thought was perfect as that of Platt Rogers Spencer (it was not). She would do kitchen chores with her sisters and feel constantly criticized; she would dine at the long boardinghouse table with sour renters and feel juvenile and undiscovered; she would shop in Kansas City and feel indistinguishable from every other woman she saw, so that she couldn't wait to get back and gain in stature with the stairs to his room.

When Jesse complimented her she said, "No, I'm not pretty; but it's all right for you to say so." And when he first kissed his cousin with passion, Zee said, "If you told me three years ago that this was going to happen, I would've laughed, and then I would've dreamt about it all night."

She awoke before sunrise to collect bowls of colorful autumn leaves for his bedside and to furbelow her ordinary dresses and cook him batches of sugared delicacies that he could eat, possibly, the corners of. She thought of her mountainous meals for Jesse as communications of her enormous love and of her condition, without him, of famine. She wished to know all he knew, to feel what he did, to touch him and inhabit him and let him learn her secrets and desires. She wished to observe him as he chewed and shaved and read the testaments and asked for the vase and urinated (even that, she was loath to admit; that in particular). She made believe Jesse was her husband; she mourned that she wasn't more beautiful, more sophisticated, that she was most likely the lowliest female her cousin had ever encountered. She worried that Jesse would someday leave the Mimms boardinghouse without discerning her affection; she hoped—and then chastened herself for it—that Jesse would never get well but would forever need her and demand her attentions so that she could surrender her father's prissy name, renounce her unimpassioned life, and marry into the grueling pursuit of caring for and worshipping this Jesse Woodson James.

On Thanksgiving Jesse decided he could venture downstairs and did, leaning on her and smiling with mortification as the diners toasted and cheered. He asked to make a benediction over the food and recited from Luke, "When thou makest a feast, call the poor, the maimed, the lame, the blind: And thou shalt be blessed; for they cannot recompense thee." He had become reverent and grateful in his recuperation and intimated his vocation would be to follow his deceased father into Georgetown College in Kentucky and vest himself as a minister of God. He interlocked his fingers with those of his nurse and said he was so indebted to her it brought him to the brink of tears. "I don't know how to thank you," he said.

Zee answered softly, "I can think of a way," and on Christmas he proposed marriage.

THE ENGAGEMENT LASTED nine years. He returned to the farm of his mother and stepfather, three miles northeast of Kearney, Missouri, about twenty miles from Kansas City. He was reinstated in the New Hope Baptist Church and went to the river on christening day in order to cleanse the Civil War from his soul, but received no instructions in religion beyond those he could glean from revival tents and what were then called protracted meetings. His mother scoffed at his inspiration of joining the clerical life and he could find no other work so he divided his time between agriculture and Sundays with Zee at the Samuels table.

The farm had remained much as it was when his mother inherited it from Reverend Robert Sallee James's estate: about three hundred acres of corn and oats and meadows, thirty sheep, some cattle, a stable of horses, a yoke of oxen, a barn, a four-room house with seven-foot ceilings and a portico lifted by white posts, and two freed black servants left over from a chattel of seven slaves. The house contained two brick kitchen fireplaces that were wide as a jail, secondhand furniture hauled up from Kentucky and polished with linseed oil, and a library that dealt with mathematics, theology, astronomy, horticulture, oratory, Latin, and Shakespeare. Jesse would escort his cousin into the sitting room and break the binding of a book to read aloud whatever passage caught his fancy and then he'd grin at Zee as if he'd done something beguiling and quaint.

He'd visit his fiancée in Harlem and they'd stroll in the cold, embracing their fleece coats, or trade sips of cherry squeeze and soda water near the furnace at the apothecary. They'd chat about neighbors and relatives, give each other nicknames, or recline on their backs and oversee the fire's slow extinction behind the sitting room grate. His health was still so precarious that he needed to stop on each step he climbed and his stomach couldn't always completely capture his food, so their activities were constrained, their nights early, their social engagements were often fraught with illness and regrets.

She introduced Jesse to her girlfriends at parties but it seemed all he could do not to nod off over his tea; sometimes she lost him entirely to other rooms and attics where he could browse like an auction bidder. Whereas his own chums delighted him; he sent coded letters to aliases at tavern addresses and was jubilant when a note came back; even after his friends had taken leave he would savor their conversations, retell stories to Zee that were still vile and indelible in her mind, indicate the characteristics he found most attractive in the rowdies.

Jesse introduced Cole and Jim and Bob Younger to her in Kearney and she sat through a meal and several foul cigars with the four before she excused herself to walk on the lawn in her sweater so she could hear silence and take in the dark like a sedative and become somehow less alive. Jim and Bob were fine—cordial and slender and irresistible—but Cole was a red-haired beef of a man with sideburns and a horseshoe mustache, even more boisterous and extroverted than Jesse, a twin to him in his facial features, and the two in combination were so electric and incandescent Zee felt slow and shut-in and scorched.

And Cole was cruel; he fetched the viciousness in Jesse; he boasted with sayings like "I cooked his hash," and frightened Zee with a Civil War tale about fifteen Jayhawkers he'd tied belly to back in a row in order to test an Enfield rifle at close range. Cole's first shot bore into three men instead of the ten he intended and he had commanded, "Cut the dead men loose; the new Enfield shoots like a pop-gun!" He needed seven shots to slaughter all fifteen and said he reverted to the Army Springfield .45 from then on. Jesse listened with cold-blooded admiration, as if he'd had a rather intricate mathematics problem broken down on a blackboard; Zee brooded on how harrowed and deserted the last man killed must have been, hearing the rifle detonations and the moans of the Kansas soldiers, sustaining the lurch and added strain of cadavers on the ropes as execution moved toward him a body at a time.

And she would remember later that Cole mentioned the robberies of the banks in St. Albans, Vermont, where Confederate soldiers in civilian clothes showed their grit by getting the money in broad daylight and walking right out into the street. She would remember that because of a St. Valentine's Day newspaper account about two men in soldiers' overcoats who'd robbed the Clay County Savings Bank in Liberty,

Missouri, and ridden off with twelve accomplices into a screening snowstorm.

Jesse came to the boardinghouse with divinity fudge and a red paper heart on which he'd doggereled about ardor, and as Jesse nudged a lizard's fringe of flame from some embering logs, they talked about the crime, Jesse saying that it was really only just deserts for all Easterner-owned corporations like that. He asked, "How much loot does it say they got?"

She read that the thieves filled a wheat sack with sixty thousand dollars in currencies, negotiable papers, bonds, and gold. She also noted that a boy who happened by was killed by one of the men and that he was a student at William Jewell College, where Jesse's father had once been on the board of trustees. "George Wymore?" she said.

Jesse was still a moment and then said, "I know his folks."

She asked, "You don't think it was the Youngers, do you?"

He flicked the oiled paper back from the divinity fudge and broke off a sliver before sitting down on the floor next to her. He said, "I only know Cole's been poor and Frank's been with him." He glared at the fire for a minute, his good lung not yet strong enough for him to breathe without gasps, his skeleton so evident that he seemed a young man dying. He said, "I'll bet it was accidental," and then he changed the subject.

Alexander Mitchell and Company, a banking house in Lexington, had two thousand dollars stolen from a cash drawer in October 1866. Five months later six bandits walked inside a firm in Savannah and demanded that Judge John McLain hand over the keys to his vault. He wouldn't and an incensed man shot him in the arm (which in result was amputated), but the outlaws exited without McLain's cash. And in May 1867, a rustler told his jail inmates in Richmond that the local bank would be robbed that afternoon. The rumor carried and the town square was monitored, deputies were readied, and the teller locked the two wide doors of the Hughes and Wasson Bank. Then twenty yipping, howling outlaws in slouch hats and linen dusters galloped onto the main street and fired at second-storey windows. A robber broke the clasp lock with a bullet and six men marched inside and the bank lost four thousand dollars. But citizens constructed a roadblock and resistance. Mayor John B. Shaw was killed while rushing the thieves, his revolver kicking with each wild shot. Several men in the gang had ridden over to the jail in order to release Felix Bradley, the rustler in confinement there, but a boy named Frank Griffin raised a cavalry rifle in the courthouse yard and fired on them. Someone aimed an answering shot at him and his forehead was staved in. His father was Berry Griffin, the jailor, who went insane when his son was killed and raced across the dirt street and tackled a robber's boot and stirrup. The horse skittered and screamed. The robber looked at Griffin as if he were an inconvenience, and he lowered his revolver to the man's head and fired, burning hair with the gunpowder spray. The man sank under the horse with a section of his skull blown off and the robber fired a second time to make sure the jailor would remain dead. And then the gang rode out of Richmond without any casualties of their own, although Felix Bradley was soon lynched by an angry mob.

Zee Mimms read that account as she'd read the accounts of the other robberies, and then she knelt with her arms crossed on the windowsill, her chin on her wrist, looking out beyond the pink blossoms of the yard's cherry trees to the cinder alley that Jesse would trot along on another man's horse. He would arrive with something expensive and inappropriate—a brass candelabrum, a garlic press, a wire dressmaker's dummy—and if she broached the issue of the Richmond murders, he'd maintain he hadn't yet heard the news and then look sick with sorrow and pity as she told him about the Hughes and Wasson Bank and Mayor Shaw and the Griffins; or he'd maintain the marauders were most likely driven to the crime by an unforgiving enemy that would never give ex-guerrillas a chance at more regular jobs. He would ignore her questions or laugh about them and he'd grow forbidding if she insisted he tell her where he'd been over the week, and yet when Jesse came—with a walnut metronome—Zee decided to find out what her fiancé did with his hours: Did he weed and water? Did he drink? Did he whore? Did he mumble-the-peg, fling sticks to dogs, whittle turtles from oakwood? Did he ride into peaceful towns and train his pistols on shopkeepers and college boys as outlaws ransacked the bank? She jested her inquiries so that she would not offend, but lies and evasions were what she received in answer, or Jesse cartooned his endeavors, saying, "I've just been sitting around the house practicing the alphabet."

She said, "You haven't been doing anything bad, have you?"

"'Course not."

"You haven't been gallivanting around with the Youngers?"

He glowered at her and said, "I guess that's my own business, isn't it."

Zee looked pained but practical. "I'm going to be your *wife*."

His eyes seemed hysterical and what strength he had seemed governed only with great difficulty. He struggled with a thought and then shrugged back into his riding coat. "I can't remember when I worked the farm last. I'm always changing horses and I'm gone for days at a time. I've got shotguns and six-guns in every room, I've got gifts to bring you and I've got greenbacks in my pocket and if you look in my closet you'll see more fancy clothes than you will in all of Clay County. So you tell *me* what I do for a living. You figure something out and then you tell me if we oughta forget about getting married."

And Jesse was outside and climbing onto a stolen horse as Zee angrily shut the curtains. She folded up the newspaper and slid it under a cobbler's door down the hall, she put a picture of Jesse at seventeen inside the top drawer of a jewelry box, she pushed the metronome's pendulum and as it ticked in three-quarter time she gradually crouched by it with her crying eyes in her palms.

THE JAMES AND YOUNGER BROTHERS larked into Kentucky in March 1868, and at the same time a man calling himself a cattle dealer visited the Nimrod Long and Company Bank in Russellville, Kentucky, chatted about escrow accounts, and departed. Soon thereafter the cattle dealer returned with four other men who drew revolvers from under their coats and received over twelve thousand dollars, which was thrown into the same wheat sack that had been noted in the Missouri robberies. Shopkeepers located revolvers and fired on the robbers in their ride out but ten sentries who were stationed on the avenue covered their getaway.

A Louisville detective named Yankee Bligh took on the Russellville case for a consortium of financiers and he identified Cole Younger and his confederates as the probable bank robbers. He was also concerned that two men named Frank and Jesse James had bloodied the bedsheets of a hotel in Chaplin, more than a hundred miles from the incident. A sallow man under a greatcoat had clutched his side as he slunk away from the open hotel room door and his grave older brother had informed the maid that the man's Civil War injuries were still uncured. His wince when he moved, however, persuaded her that the wound was reopened in a scrap. And Jesse sealed the detective's suspicions about the James brothers' involvement when he mailed his fiancée a card that said a physician had instructed him to go to California or else lose his vitality.

He went to the Paso Robles Hot Sulphur Springs resort owned by his uncle, Drury Woodson James. There he mended his lung and recovered from an ear infection by consuming lemons and oranges and castoreum in addition to a pound of fish every day. A photograph of him at the time showed a cadaverous man with sunken cheeks and eyes darkened with hollow, his left hand clutching a cane; he would never again be as sick as he was then: Jesse would later say it was a condition that was brought on by being away from Missouri and Zee.

It took him four months to convalesce and then he vacationed in San Francisco on stolen cash that he doubled with casino roulette and monte. He lounged in steam baths, he stood at the prow of a ferry, he ate six-course meals in French restaurants, he sinned in fandango saloons where the ''pretty waiter girls'' wore ostrich-feather bonnets and red silk jackets but nothing whatever below that except shoes, and for a dollar would let Jesse contemplate what he had never spied outside of art museums. It all made him feel guilty and unmoored, and it wasn't long before he was climbing aboard a train that would carry him back to Missouri and make him himself again.

Zee was visiting her Aunt Zerelda at the Kearney farmhouse when Jesse arrived. His mother made an opera of his coming home and cooked a supper of pork and pies, complaining all the while of the illnesses and sleepless nights her boy's going had brought her, and reporting on the many deputies and Pinkerton detectives who were skulking around the place. ''Seems like I'm spending every minute making up alibis for you.'' She proclaimed, as they were eating, that she'd attempted to get cash for some negotiable papers ''the boys'' had swiped from the Clay County Savings Bank but that a manager had snootily refused her. She asked if Jesse knew that it was Mr. Nimrod Long of Russellville who paid half the tuition for Jesse's father to go to Georgetown College. She asked if Jesse wasn't ashamed of himself. Through it all, Jesse miserably eyed Zee but saw that she was simpering at Zerelda as if she were speaking the lightest of gossip. And as the couple strolled down to Clear Creek to flip pebbles into the water and chat, Jesse saw that the woman he was pledged to had changed. Zee called herself a milkweed, a nuisance, a scold; she regretted her prying into his affairs, regretted giving him arguments when she knew that he needed allegiance and love. She wanted to accommodate him, to be a good wife to him, and nothing else really mattered to her. And that seemed to be true, for thenceforth Zee avoided all rumors and newspaper stories about the James-Younger gang, she shied from conversations about criminal acts and politics, she refused invitations into society, she never inquired again about the robberies or murders attributed to Jesse; instead, she'd accepted a simple, stay-at-home life for herself and was no more conscious of the James brothers' crimes than she was of the Suez Canal or the mole on her back or the dust kittens under the sofa.

And yet Jesse made some efforts at conventional work: he was a millwright, a machinist, a coal salesman; he plowed in the sun with three pistols hooked onto his belt; he swapped cattle at the livestock shows. He would start a job with good will and industry, but then he would walk away from it because he was belittled or maltreated or weary and bored. Each occupation became a day- or week-long deception, for he was twenty-one years old and had already settled into the one career that suited him.

During the five years between 1869 and 1874, the James-Younger gang robbed the Daviess County Savings Bank in Gallatin; stole six thousand dollars from the Ocobock Brothers' Bank in Corydon, Iowa; six hundred dollars from the Deposit Bank in Columbia, Kentucky; four thousand dollars from a bank in Ste. Genevieve, Missouri; two thousand dollars from the Chicago, Rock Island, and Pacific Railway near Council Bluffs, Iowa; twenty-two thousand dollars from the Iron Mountain Railroad at Gads Hill, Missouri; three thousand dollars from the Hot Springs stagecoach near Malvern, Arkansas. And so on. Jesse shot John Sheets in the head and heart and the banker drained off the chair; his clerk scurried into the street and the bandits fired twice, catching him fat in the arm. A cashier named R. A. C. Martin was told to open a safe and answered, "Never. I'll die first." "Then die it is," said Cole and raised his dragoon revolver to Martin's ear and fired. An iron rail was winched off its tie as a passenger train slowed on a blind curve and the locomotive tilted into the roadbed and then crashed to its side in weeds, crushing John Rafferty, the engineer, and scalding Dennis Foley, the stoker, so badly that he died within weeks. The six thieves were dressed in the white hoods and raiment of the Ku Klux Klan—for what reason, no one knows—and collected three thousand dollars in compensation for putting an end to two lives.

Stopping the increasingly common robberies became so paramount that the United States Secret Service and private detectives from Chicago and St. Louis joined the Pinkerton Detective Agency in stalking the James-Younger gang. Allan Pinkerton's son William established headquarters in Kansas City and split his operatives between pursuit of the Youngers and the Jameses in the counties of Jackson and Clay; and yet, though many could recognize the gunslingers and their regular sanctuaries were known, investigators only came to misfortune when they got close to the gang.

John W. Whicher was assigned Dr. Samuels's farm and, upon receiving a spy's report that the James boys were present, walked there with a carpet bag and in poor man's clothes on a cold night in March. He'd just crossed the wooden bridge over Clear Creek when he caught a slight noise, and then Jesse jerked the man's chin back with his wrist and asked, "You looking for something?"

Arthur McCoy and Jim Anderson (Bloody Bill's brother) scrabbled up from under the bridge with guns out and Whicher said, "I'm only looking for work. I was hoping to find a place on a farm. You happen to know of any?"

"Yep," said Jesse. "I know just the right place for you. And Satan's got it all prepared."

Whicher was seen again at 3 a.m. near Owen's Ferry, his mouth gagged and his legs tied astride a gray horse; and on March 11th his body was discovered in a cistern, still gagged and riddled with bullets. A note was pinned to his lapel that read: "This is the way we treat Chicago detectives; if you've got any more send them along."

Only days later Captain Louis Lull and two associates were overtaken in the rain-soaked woods of St. Clair County by John and Jim Younger. They cocked shotguns and ordered the operatives to drop their pistols. They complied. But then Lull's right hand glided down to a derringer and he shot it at John Younger, cutting into the jugular vein so that it surged red sleeves of blood out even as the dying boy got off a shot and killed Lull. One of the scouting party sprinted away through the woods but Jim Younger only gazed at his kid brother, who was tangled under his frightened horse. He then gazed at Edwin Daniels, the man who brought the operatives there, and calmly triggered his shotgun, catching the guide in the neck.

At Gallatin an overexcited black racehorse had torn from the rail before Jesse had mounted. He was dragged forty feet on a frozen dirt street, his greatcoat lumping up near his neck like a plow collar, before he could disentangle his boot and broken ankle from the stirrup. He hopped one-footed and climbed Frank's arm and the two brothers galloped off on one horse as the filly sulked on a church lawn, her saddle rocked over to her flank, the left stirrup clinking on the flagstones when she browsed.

The filly was incontrovertible evidence linking the James brothers to the Missouri robberies, and yet they were again supported by Major John Newman Edwards, the grandiloquent author of *Shelby and His Men* and *Noted Guerrillas, or The Warfare of the Border*, in which Frank and Jesse James were gloriously mentioned. Edwards helped

Jesse inscribe a letter to Governor McClurg denying involvement in the
Gallatin crimes, claiming he had not murdered John Sheets, had not
even been near Daviess County, that he had sold the filly a week
beforehand and could furnish a receipt; however, he could not give up
just yet and risk a vigilance committee that might lynch him.

> Governor, when I can get a fair trial, I will surrender
> myself to the civil authorities of Missouri. But I will never
> surrender to be mobbed by a set of blood-thirsty poltroons.
> It is true that during the war I was a Confederate soldier and
> fought under the Black Flag, but since then I have lived a
> respectable citizen and obeyed the laws of the United States
> to the best of my knowledge.

Frank James smiled uncharacteristically when he read that and
commented that he thought he was guilty of all those crimes but now
he was having an argument in his mind about it.

If the James-Younger gang was beginning to be looked upon by
the common people as champions of the poor, it was principally due to
Jesse, who was the originator of their many public relations contriv-
ances: the claims that Southerners and clerics were never robbed, the
occasional donations to charity, the farewell hurrahs in honor of the
Confederate dead. The James-Younger gang stole the treasures from
each ticket holder in the Hot Springs Stagecoach except George Crump,
of Memphis, who revealed he had been a soldier under the Stainless
Banner. When they robbed the Iron Mountain Railroad at Gads Hill,
they searched the passengers' hands for calluses because they had
purportedly forsworn harming workingmen or ladies in order to
concentrate on "the money and valuables of the plug-hat gentlemen."
After ransacking the express car there, Jesse inserted an envelope into
the conductor's coat pocket and said in practiced words, "This contains
an exact account of the robbery. We prefer this to be published in the
newspapers rather than the grossly exaggerated accounts that usually
appear after one of our jobs."

The press release declared: "The most daring on record—the
southbound train on the Iron Mountain Railroad was robbed here this
evening by several heavily armed men and robbed of _____ dollars."
It rehashed their methods and indicated the direction of their flight and
the colors of their horses, concluding, "There is a hell of an excitement
in this part of the country."

They rode west across Missouri, staying on farms overnight, one account saying they "conducted themselves as gentlemen, paying for everything they got," and that fact alone seemed by then enough to certify that the criminals were the James-Younger gang; and yet when the St. Louis *Dispatch* printed its story implicating them in the robbery, Major Edwards sent a Western Union telegram to the city editor, saying: "Put nothing more in about Gads Hill. The report of yesterday was remarkable for two things—utter stupidity and total untruth."

At the 1872 Kansas City Fair, Jesse and Frank and Cole brushed ahead of an idled line to the entrance gate, fastening red neckerchiefs over their noses. Cole and Frank extracted revolvers from beneath linen dusters and Jesse snatched the ticket seller's tin cash box. He knelt in the dirt and pilfered over nine hundred dollars in greenbacks and coins as Cole and Frank rotated with irons and menacing looks. A thousand gawkers milled around, amazed by the convincingness of the actors and the skit as a ticket seller ran from his booth and wrestled Jesse for the cash box, beckoning for assistance. Cole knocked a woman aside and shot at the seller and missed but ruined the leg of a small girl. And then the three outlaws shoved through the crowd, unhitched their horses, and cantered off.

Days later Jesse showed himself at the Harlem boardinghouse, shaved and hair slicked and redolent of witch hazel. He was jovial and jittery and couldn't sit still. He chewed mints. He was solicitous of his cousin, asked about Zee's health, her moods, her pastimes. They snacked on sliced bananas and milk. And when she washed the dishes, he eased behind her, girdling her small waist with his hands, then massaging her back and shoulders. He moved her blond hair aside with his nose and kissed her neck. "Oh, that gives me goosebumps," she said, and clacked a bowl in a bowl. His hands widened their transit over her ribs until his fingers grazed the sides of her breasts and withdrew and then insisted on more sensation of Zee with the next advance. Zee dried her hands and revolved and kissed Jesse on the mouth and they moaned in embrace for a minute. Jesse said, "If someone's ear was to the door just now they'd think we were moving furniture."

She smiled. "Oh, I cherish you so."

He caressed her and asked, "Do you mind if I get liberal with you?" and she answered, "Yes," at the word liberal, and "Yes," at the end of the sentence.

"You *do* mind."

"I'm unmarried," she said, and then it registered that she was stopping a man who robbed and shot at people from fondling parts of her that she would otherwise pay scant attention to. Zee decided to relent when next he asked, but Jesse didn't ask, he simply scratched his chestnut brown hair and smiled and looked for whatever exit that offered itself. He reached under his coat to the back of his trousers and hauled out a folded Kansas City *Times* that he flattened on the kitchen table. "If you don't read another thing in your life, this is what you should last feast your eyes on." He rapped his knuckles on a newspaper column and Zee bent over the table to see it, drawing a swing of hair away from her cheek.

It regarded the robbery at the Kansas City fairgrounds as "a deed so high-handed, so diabolically daring and so utterly in contempt of fear that we are bound to admire it and revere its perpetrators."

Jesse straddled a chair. He blinked and darted and exercised his eyes. He followed a finger to the side of his head and back, and then to his nose, his chin.

The heels of Zee's hands had numbed from her lean and hair had again fallen across her brow. She stopped reading and simply said, "The boarders will be coming down for supper in an hour and I've got to cook it by myself."

"Can't that man write though? He's got more ee-magination than Georgia's got cotton."

Zee unsacked hard biscuits onto a plate. She cut tomatoes over a saucepan and juice ran down her wrists. Lard melted and slowly twirled in a skillet over a fire. Jesse grew morose as she ignored him. She saw him glaring at her once and then she saw him reading another newspaper that must have appeared from another pocket.

He read: " 'The Chivalry of Crime. There are men in Jackson, Cass, and Clay—a few there are left—who learned to dare when there was no such word as quarter in the dictionary of the Border. Men who have carried their lives in their hands so long that they do not know how to commit them over into the keeping of the laws and regulations that exist now, and these men sometimes rob. But it is always in the glare of day and in the teeth of the multitude. With them booty is but the second thought; the wild drama of the adventure first.' "

She pulled down a jar from the pantry and kept her back to Jesse as she dipped into the jar with a spoon. He continued: " 'These men are bad citizens but they are bad because they live out of their time. The nineteenth century with its Sybaritic civilization is not the social soil for men who might have sat with *Arthur* at the Round Table, ridden at tourney with *Sir Launcelot* or won the colors of *Guinevere*; men who might have shattered the casque of *Brian de Boise Guilbert*, shivered a lance with *Ivanhoe* or won the smile of the Hebrew maiden; and men who could have met *Turpin* and *Duval* and robbed them of their ill-gotten booty on Hounslow Heath.' "

Zee reached for but overturned a canister of black seasonings that spilled across the counter. Her creased dress as she tidied and the rucked wool stockings at her ankles were all that Jesse could see. He rocked forward in his chair as if his boots were stirruped. He said, "Just let me read on a little bit," and he moved his finger along as he did: " 'It was as though three bandits had come to us from the storied Odenwald, with the halo of medieval chivalry upon their garments and shown us how the things were done that poets sing of. No where else in the United States or in the civilized world, probably, could this thing have been done. It was done here, not because the protectors of person and property were less efficient but because the bandits were more dashing and skillful; not because honest Missourians have less nerve but because freebooting Missourians have more.' "

She said in mute tones, "I don't care what John Newman Edwards says."

"How's that?"

She wheeled with storm and sorrow in her face, her hands locked on her ears. "I don't want to know!" she cried. She even stamped a shoe. And then she hustled out, her skirt inch-raised, and the swinging door clapped her departure.

Jesse limped over to the stove and clamped a potholder around the handle to move a skillet that was beginning to smoke.

A general mopiness and depression began to plague Jesse, and Frank sought to dispel it with a trip to the Hite property near Adairville, Kentucky. However, it was there Jesse learned his sister, Susan Lavenia James, was planning to marry Allen H. Parmer, a man whom Jesse despised. The very idea of Susie's being private with Parmer so plunged Jesse into despair that he chewed sixteen grains of morphine in a suicide attempt.

By the time a physician came, Jesse was sleepwalking and there seemed to be no hope that he'd recuperate; but Frank persuaded his younger brother to keep moving by whispering that the Yankees were coming or that Pappy was being strangled in the coffee bean tree. He gave Jesse two empty .44s so he could rage around the room, crying and carrying on until he collapsed with the morphine overdose and all they could do was pray for the repose of his soul. Just about sunrise Jesse abruptly woke up with a powerful appetite, as if he'd experienced only a peaceful sleep, and that evening he journeyed back to Kansas City where he prevailed upon Zee to marry him by convincing her of his complete repentance.

ON APRIL 24TH, 1874, Reverend William James, an uncle to both parties, joined Zee Mimms to Jesse James at the Kearney home of the bride's married sister, who also served as the bridesmaid. Zee wore her mother's white wedding gown though its train and veil had been browned by an attic trunk. They were shivareed in a one-room log cabin near Noel, and then journeyed to Galveston, Texas, accompanied by Frank, who would marry Annie Ralston two months later.

After a week in Galveston the couple was supposed to steam south to Vera Cruz, but Jesse had boated the Gulf of Mexico with his brother one afternoon and the blue water terrified him. The waves were big as the roofs of houses. He allowed a lead fishing weight to sink and it had gone so deep it stripped all the reel line from his spool. Who could prove it ever bottomed? Maybe it banged up against a China Sea junk at the other end of the world.

So they leisured at a coastal hotel and Zee peeled and sliced apples for her husband under a broad pink umbrella as a correspondent for the St. Louis *Dispatch* interviewed the famous Jesse James. The newsman was amiable and cautious and needed little more than social notes but it was nevertheless a catechism and the first of her husband's characterizations she'd witnessed. His manners were decorous, his charm, while charlatan, was fetching, his sentences were dexterous, his thoughts glanced away from ensnarements like minnows. Zee pared a careful, red-skinned spiral from the fruit and listened with amazement as he braided and invented, and she wondered if she'd underestimated Jesse and scaled him too small, if she was so accustomed to him she hadn't realized he was still as romantic and remarkable as the near-dead eighteen-year-old she'd nursed. She was ready, that season, to revise all her opinions of him. She had shrunk into a maiden who was deferential and daughterish, and it pleased Zee beyond good sense when Jesse placed his excellent hand atop hers.

She saw that the correspondent had apparently asked the groom for a sentiment about his bride, because Jesse looked at her with amorous concentration and said, "We had been engaged for nine years, and through good and evil report, and notwithstanding the lies that have been told about me and the crimes laid at my door, her devotion to me has never wavered for a moment. You can say that both of us married for love, and that there cannot be any sort of doubt about our marriage being a happy one.''

It wasn't at all happy for the first year. At summer's end the couple returned to Missouri and concealed themselves in the sewing rooms and harness sheds of relatives until Jesse could get around to renting and cultivating a farm. Meanwhile she was rooting out a scandal that claimed it was the James-Younger gang that stopped two omnibuses on each side of the Missouri River one Sunday afternoon in August. Even though he was one of the victims, Professor J. L. Allen went so far as to blather, ''I am exceedingly glad, as it looks I have to be robbed, that it is being done by first-class artists, by men of national reputation.''

And on December 8th, five men caused the Kansas Pacific Railroad to brake at the Muncie, Kansas, depot by stacking ties on the tracks. They uncoupled the Pullman coaches and towed the express and baggage cars ahead some two hundred yards before ransacking them of thirty thousand dollars. The express company immediately tendered a reward of one thousand dollars for each outlaw, dead or alive.

In early January Jesse shook Zee awake and read the verses in the Gospel of Matthew pertaining to the Holy Family's flight from Herod into Egypt, saying he'd been getting premonitions and thought they ought to fly from Missouri. He was somehow so persuasive that Zee yielded to his proposition and by the next week they were renting a house in Nashville, Tennessee, where they would soon be joined by Frank and his new wife, Annie. (Annie Ralston had told her parents that she wanted to visit relatives in Kansas City and left home with a valise and trunk. Frank met her train and eloped with Annie to Omaha, whence she sent the note: ''Dear Mother: I am married and going West.'' Her parents had no idea who her husband was, or even that she'd been courted, and her father was understandably shocked when detectives surrounded his house and ordered the occupants out with their hands up.)

So the James boys were not in residence on the night that Allan Pinkerton's detectives sloshed through snow to the Kearney farmhouse they called ''Castle James.'' In order to smoke the criminals outside, the Pinkerton operatives soaked a cotton wad in turpentine, tied it around a rock, and pitched it through windowglass into the kitchen, spritzing flames across the plank flooring. Dr. Samuels got up from his sleep and, when they called for the James boys to give themselves up, yelled out that his stepsons had disappeared, then poked the cotton wad into the fireplace as Zerelda spanked out the fire with a dishtowel. No sooner had the couple done that, however, than a soot-blackened railroad potflare smashed through another windowpane, and when Reuben Samuels swatted it onto the coals with a broom, the cauldron accidentally exploded.

Shrapnel tore through the stomach of Archie Peyton Samuels, the James's nine-year-old stepbrother, and the boy died within hours. A maidservant who slept by the pantry had a slice taken from her cheek and swooned for loss of blood. And Mrs. Zerelda Samuels suffered such a mangling of her right hand that surgeons had to saw it off above the wrist.

The James brothers' only public reaction to Archie's death and the maiming of their mother came in an impassioned, misspelled letter from Jesse that appeared in the Nashville *Banner* in August. He listed once more the misrepresentations about his activities and then centered his fury on Allan Pinkerton, writing:

> Providence saved the house from being burnt altho it was saturated with Turpentine & fiered with combustible materials and the shell did not do fatal work and they fled away to the special train that was waiting to carry them beyon the reach of outraged justice. This is the work of Pinkerton, the man that sed in his card that he just wished to set himself right in the eyes of the world. He may vindicate himself with some, but will never dare show his Scottish face again in Western Mo. and let me know he is here or he will meet the fate of his comrades, Capt. Lull & Whicher met & I would advise him to stay in New York but let him go where he may, his sins will find him out. He can cross the Atlantic but every wave and white cap he sees at sea will remind him of the innocent boy murdered and the one-armed mother robbed of her son (and Idol). Justice is slow but sure and there is a just God that will bring all to Justice. Pinkerton, I hope and pray our Heavenly Father may deliver you into my hands & I believe he will for his merciful and protecting arm has always been with me and Shielded me, and during all my persecution he has watched over me and

protected me from workers of blood money who are trying
to seek my life, and I have hope and faith in Him & believe
he will ever protect me as long as I serve Him.

Jesse and Zee were then renting a cottage at 606 Boscobel Street
under the aliases of J. D. and Josie Howard; Frank leased the Big
Bottom farm as B. J. Woodson, and Annie added the first letter of his
Christian name to become Fannie.

Zee gave birth to a son on New Year's Eve, 1875, and they
christened him Jesse Edwards, for his father and the newspaper editor,
but discretion caused them to call him Tim, and he was seven years
old before he learned his actual name. Jesse would saunter downtown
with his son hipped like a paunchy cat or bundled inside his overcoat
so that the infant's bewildered head poked between the lapels. He sat
the baby in his homburg hat, he dangled him over rivers to give Zee a
fright, he snuck him looks at his pinochle cards, hung a blue derringer
over his crib, screwed a unlit cigar in the child's mouth and practiced
ventriloquism in taverns.

Zee choired at church, she conversed happily with her sister-in-
law as they stewed and pickled vegetables or grated cucumbers and
onions for catsup, she cooed to her child as he suckled; but alone
outside her home she felt shadowed and stalked—footsteps stopped
when she did, curtains dropped when she turned her head—and she
became so leery and aloof that shopkeepers and neighbors assumed
she was snobbish or persnickety or perhaps a little simple.

Her lone male friend was Dr. John Vertrees, whom Jesse hired to
live with Zee and her son during the weeks of absence he attributed to
his work as a wheat speculator. (The doctor assumed that was a lie
manufactured to cover a secret addiction to cards and horse races, for
Mr. Howard dressed like a boulevardier and wore a derringer in a
hideaway shoulder harness and once presented to his wife an envelope
of diamonds.)

Little is known about the James brothers' activities on the road
while they resided in Tennessee, except for the summer and autumn of
1876 in which the James-Younger gang committed two robberies, the
second of them being the fiasco at Northfield, Minnesota, in September.

LESS THAN TWO MONTHS earlier they had robbed the Missouri Pacific
Railroad of over fifteen thousand dollars near Otterville, Missouri. As
the badmen looted the Adams and U.S. express companies, a minister

conducted the timorous through canticles and evangelized for the repentance of sins, and a newspaper account later complimented the robbers who "were well versed in their business" and "remarkably cool and courageous throughout the whole affair."

But then the St. Louis chief of police arrested a man who'd been bragging about the loot he'd gotten from the robbery, and after rough interrogation, Hobbs Kerry confessed that he was one member of a gang that was governed by Jesse James and included Frank James, Cole Younger, Bob Younger, Clell Miller, Charlie Pitts, and Bill Chadwell.

Jesse sent a letter (which was probably rewritten by Edwards) to the Kansas City *Times*, contending that "this so-called confession is a well-built pack of falsehoods from beginning to end. I never heard of Hobbs Kerry, Charles Pitts and Wm. Chadwell until Kerry's arrest. I can prove my innocence by eight good and well-known men of Jackson County, and show conclusively that I was not at the train robbery." He closed with another plea for a fair hearing and signed it "Respectfully, J. W. James."

By the time the letter was published, on August 18th, Jesse and his brother and Cole, Jim, and Bob Younger were sitting on a railway coach headed four hundred miles north to an area in which the citizens would not be so cautious or on the lookout for thieves. Clell Miller, Charlie Pitts, and Bill Chadwell knitted into the group at depots in Missouri and the eight toured St. Paul's gambling houses and sat through a Red Caps and Clippers baseball game before they bought thorough-bred horses and tack and rode the Minnesota River to scout Mankato and then Northfield.

Cole Younger coveted retirement in a foreign country before September stripped away but thought he needed more of a subsidy than a Swedish mill town could muster. Meanwhile Bill Chadwell, who'd lived in the state, boasted about the ease of larceny in placid Minnesota and indicated secluded routes and short cuts that could spirit the outlaws to Iowa like a whirlwind in the Book of Kings. And good authorities had told him that General Benjamin Butler of Massachusetts, the man called "The Scourge of New Orleans," was an investor in the First National Bank of Northfield: they could revenge his confiscations and slaughter of Confederate soldiers. And that argument worked. Cole Younger later confessed that once they heard about Butler's involve-ment in the institution, they "felt little compunction, under the circum-stances, about raiding him or his."

Northfield it was then. On September 7th, Jesse James and Bob Younger and Charlie Pitts dressed in cattlemen's linen dusters and rode across the iron bridge over the Cannon River into Mill Square, where they hitched their splendid horses. Jesse's was the grayish brown color that is called dun, the other two were bays; and each had such thoroughbred conformation that men sidetracked to scrutinize and assess them and wondered who the visitors were as the outlaws strolled over to the Scriver Block, which contained the H. Scriver and Lee and Hitchcock merchandise firms and, around the corner, the First National Bank, on Division Street.

At J. G. Jeft's restaurant each man ordered eggs and bacon and apple pie and dawdled over two pots of coffee as they consulted about varieties of rifles with the same tedious overattention that other customers were giving sorghum and Holstein cows.

Bob Younger was a debonair man with a blond mustache and short brown hair and expressive eyebrows that seemed to crave a monocle. Charlie Pitts was an alias for Samuel Wells, a sometime cowhand with a handsome sunburned head that was square as a chimney, whose skin was so unclean dirt laced it like rainwater stains on tan wallpaper. Jesse had just turned twenty-nine but he seemed to uncle them both, and he took care of the check when Frank slouched by the plate glass window, cuing his younger brother about the tranquility of the town.

So Jesse, Bob, and Charlie returned to the Scriver Block, sitting atop dry goods boxes outside the Lee and Hitchcock store, cutting slivers of wood from the boxes and loafing in the sunlight until two o'clock, when Cole Younger and Clell Miller rode into Division Street from the south. Cole stopped his racehorse and pretended some annoyance with the cinch, winking over the animal's withers at Jesse, who then stood and walked around the corner to the First National Bank, swiveling into the narrow, windowed doors and slamming both into jolts against brass hindrances on the baseboards. He snicked back the hammer on his .44 and hurtled onto the walnut counter at the unrailed teller opening as Bob Younger yelled out, "Throw up your hands!"

Clell Miller followed the three to the bank, shutting the two doors behind them and standing on the sidewalk with his right hand inside his long linen duster, glancing everywhere. Mr. J. S. Allen crossed the street to see if anything peculiar was happening but Miller prevented the man's approach. Allen stepped back and then rushed around the corner into an alley, screaming, "Get your guns, boys! They're robbing the bank!"

A University of Michigan medical student named Henry M. Wheeler was frittering away the afternoon under the green awning of his father's drugstore, just across Mill Square from the bank. He saw the man in the ankle-length coat impede J. S. Allen and heard the merchant screaming his news; he cried out, "Robbery! Robbery!" to the customers in the drugstore and ran into the Dampier House to retrieve a Spencer carbine he'd seen in the hotel's luggage room, then scrambled up to the second-floor window that looked onto the street, with three waxed paper cartridges in his hand.

Cole Younger and Clell Miller jumped onto their racehorses and caterwauled and hooted and shot Colts overhead and about, at shingles and signboards and brick corbels, wherever chance swerved their muzzles, and three horsemen clanked in race over the iron bridge and racketed onto Division Street, so that five wild men careered around in an area eighty feet wide, clattering over the planks in the crosswalks and banging away in the air with their guns, cocking their horses after whosoever had not as of then scuttled into commercial buildings.

Jesse James by then walked off the counter in a four-foot drop to the floor and scowled at the two clerks, Alonzo Bunker and Frank Wilcox, who shrank from Jesse as from a furnace, retreating to the bookkeeping alcove. The cashier was attending the 1876 Centennial Exposition in Philadelphia; the acting cashier was Joseph Lee Heywood. Bob Younger was saying, "We're going to rob this bank. Don't any of you holler. We've got forty men outside."

Jesse sauntered over to Heywood and asked, "Are you the cashier?"

Heywood said he wasn't.

Jesse looked with puzzlement at Bunker and Wilcox and put the same question to them. They crouched away from his left-handed gun and shook their heads in the negative.

Jesse returned to Heywood with ire in his blue eyes and said, "You're the cashier. Open that safe quick or I'll blow your lying head off."

Charlie Pitts saw Clell Miller in argument with J. S. Allen and guessed rightly that they'd already lingered too long. He lurched over the counter grill and clumsied down and Heywood bolted to close a vault that was the size of a walk-in closet. Pitts snagged Heywood's sleeve and retarded him and the two scuffled, Heywood shouting, "Murder! Murder!" until Jesse jabbed a revolver into Heywood's cheek and said, "Open that safe inside there now or you've got one more minute to live."

And to convince the acting cashier of that, Pitts snuck behind him with a pocket knife and slit the skin of his throat. Joseph L. Heywood was stunned. He was a slender man in his thirties with a dark beard and a scholar's look—he could have been an algebra teacher, someone conservative and cultured, and he was, in fact, a trustee at Carleton College. Cut, he looked at Jesse with rebuke in his face as his neck unsealed and blood rolled down his collar like a red shade being drawn.

Jesse ordered him again to unlock the safe and Heywood held a handkerchief to his neck and croaked, "It has a time lock. It *can't* be opened."

Jesse struck him cruelly on the skull with his revolver and the cashier caved in. He sat down on the floor and his eyes rose in his skull with faint and he laid himself down with caution for his rickety condition. Jesse then ordered the clerks to unlock the safe, but they said they couldn't, and had Jesse only made the attempt himself he would have found out that the stove-sized safe at the rear of the walk-in vault had already been unlocked at nine that morning.

Gunfire was now regular outside and Jesse caught a glimpse of Frank and Cole reeling their horses around, one of them cantering up onto the sidewalk, loudly clobbering the wood. Bob Younger had climbed over the counter and insisted that the two clerks kneel as he rifled the till drawers. The cash had been removed from the wooden trays, as it happened, and all he could find were rolls of pennies and nickels in the midst of deposit and withdrawal receipts. Had he looked to a second drawer below he could have gained three thousand dollars.

The clerk named Bunker, who was also a teacher at Carleton College, saw that Jesse was looking on with peculiar fascination as the cashier gave blood to the floor, and that Younger was preoccupied in seeking the currencies. So he rocked back on his shoes and then dashed for the director's room and the alley door. Charlie Pitts aimed at him and burst slivers from the doorjamb with a shot and the clerk ducked outside. Pitts fired a second time and Bunker floundered down the alley, a rift in his right shoulder next to the collar bone.

Chaos ruled outside. The gang had expected the Northfield residents to cower beneath their onslaught, but the citizens had instead rushed into whatever rooms were close by to search out weapons and ammunition. Elias Stacy claimed a shotgun from a hardware store and tore open a box of shells and chambered one without noticing that it was bird shot. Some businessmen retrieved desk pistols and derringers, common laborers crossed the town from their work with rakes and straw forks and sickles, and boys dodged into the street to pitch rocks and bottles at the skittish, prancing horses. The steam whistle at the river mill was screaming over and over again, girls were yanking steeple ropes so that the church bells were clanging, and men were grunting wagons into the streets in order to restrict the available exits.

A Scandinavian immigrant named Oscar Seeborn mistook the pandemonium on Division Street for a celebration of some sort or as the general brand of American violence that he'd been warned about on his passage west. So he barged ahead with innocence and neutrality evinced in his smile even as an outlaw instructed him to go back in an English he couldn't yet understand. When Seeborn stepped away from the man's pistol he was murdered.

At about the same time, Clell Miller saw Elias Stacy walk into the street with a shotgun and raise it in his direction, and then Clell was clouted off his mount with a load of bird shot in his cheek and forehead like a black tattoo of a constellation. Though blood ran down his face in bars, Miller ascended onto his saddle again and raked his horse toward the man who'd shot him so that when Clell returned the exchange it would be from inches. But Henry Wheeler had his carbine trained on Miller from overhead in the Dampier House and a lead ball the size of a blouse button slammed into the outlaw's clavicle with such force it towed him off his horse and flat on his back in the street.

Cole Younger fired at Stacy and missed, then at the Dampier House window, but Henry Wheeler crouched back into the room. Cole descended from his horse and asked Miller, "How bad is it, Clell? Do you think you can ride?"

"I don't know." His subclavian artery was severed. All his blood was in his chest. He raised on his elbow and looked around as if he'd awoke in an unfamiliar bedroom. Then he died and bowled over onto his nose in the dirt. Cole unbuckled Miller's ammunition belt and leaped back onto his horse.

Anselm Manning owned the hardware store across the alley from the First National Bank and he sidled down that alley with a rifle that could only be loaded with one cartridge at a time. It made him concentrate. He walked out into the street and judged his chances of getting the moving outlaws and when he saw two just beyond the racehorses tied in front of the bank, he trained his sights on them. But they dodged him by sinking low, so he adjusted slightly lower and killed the closest horse. He then levered the rifle in the alley but realized the ignited cartridge was lodged in it, so was obliged to go back to his hardware store for a ramrod. He was back at the alley entrance within a minute and looking around the corner when he spied Cole Younger. His shot strayed wild but caught a signpost in such a way that it glanced right and tore into Cole Younger's side, making him groan and grit his teeth as his horse jerked around in fright.

Manning retreated again and grinned at a man in the alley. "Got lucky,'' he said and then walked out, loading a third shell in the breech and cocking the rifle as he maneuvered to get his sights on Bill Chadwell, who was sitting on his horse eighty yards away, acting as a sentry. Manning was a thoroughly unguessing man and he gave his body as a target as he calculated and engineered, causing men in the alley to anxiously call him back. But he stayed out there just long enough to get off a shot that went through Bill Chadwell's heart, killing him at once, so that Chadwell slowly declined from his saddle in the graceless swoon and slide of happenstance and gravitation, until his fingers lightly swished the dirt with each ungainly horse motion.

Cole Younger, who could calculate the odds against success better than the more unyielding James brothers, got his horse close enough to the windowglass to yell in to Jesse, ''The game's up! They're killing all our men!''

Jesse had already guessed that. He'd heard the gunfire and seen blue gunsmoke roil and churn against the glass. He reconsidered the First National Bank's untampered-with safe for a second but sleeplessness or panic had snailed his brain and all he could do was blink. He said, ''You two go,'' but as Charlie Pitts and Bob Younger scurried out, Jesse walked back to Joseph Heywood, who was blacked out on the floor. Then he reached his revolver down and blew the man's skull into fractions.

Outside, a man named Bates crossfired from the second floor of Hanover's Clothing Store, and Elias Stacy ran up the outside stairs to a corner office on the Scriver Block from which he continued to fire bird shot down on the thieves. Henry Wheeler had loaded another cartridge and crept up to the Dampier House window. He saw Stacy's bird shot smack Cole Younger's hat off and in the next instant triggered his second cartridge, which tore off a segment of the man's shoulder.

Jim Younger was shot in the mouth, obliterating his front teeth, and he spilt blood like coffee as his horse racked in front of the drugstore.

Bob Younger's bay horse was the one killed by Manning, so he slunk over to some crates and boxes for cover. But Manning jogged around the Scriver Block to get to the other side of the outlaw and his gunshot made Bob Younger's right sleeve sail as the ball crashed into the man's elbow. Younger switched his revolver into his left hand and crouched around to get even with Manning, but Henry Wheeler looked down and with his third cartridge wrecked Bob Younger above the right knee.

Frank James reared his horse to twist it toward the Dampier House, but then felt a hurt in his thigh as if someone had driven an iron stake into the bone. He could feel his blood run down his shin into his boot, and he saw Jesse come out of the bank like a sleepwalker, easily climbing onto his grayish brown horse and cantering west on Division Street without giving anyone more than a few shots. And so Frank shouted, "They've got us beat!" and five shellacked horsemen raced toward the Cannon River bridge until Cole looked for his brother Bob and saw him scarecrowed in the street, broomsticked on his good left leg. Bob cried, "Don't leave me! I'm shot!" and Cole pivoted around as many guns shot at him, reaching to Bob with pain as he said, "Get on behind me," and gripping Bob by the cartridge belt to bring him up onto the croup of his horse. And then they sprinted out over the iron bridge, jouncing with agony in the gallop, their blood coasting back from their wounds.

TELEGRAMS THAT WARNED of the outlaws' flight were by then being sent to each Minnesota sheriff's office, but the James-Younger gang enjoyed the good luck of riding through Dundas, three miles west, as the telegraph operator was eating lunch. Shoppers and street people looked on in surprise as the spent and collapsed party in cattlemen's dusters loped by on expensive racehorses that were dripping blood.

They stole a Morgan draft horse from a man's wagon team and then got a saddle on loan from a farmer by saying they were deputies in pursuit of some horse thieves. They then strapped Bob Younger to the Morgan horse but within a mile the cinch snapped and Bob flopped off to the road. Jesse looked upon him like something peculiar in the road and pranced his racehorse impatiently as Cole picked up his unconscious brother and put Bob's feet in his own saddle stirrups, riding with his arms around him as Bob rolled sloppily in their run.

When they ascertained that they were not being followed, the six washed and drank in the Cannon River and sat with exhaustion in the haven of shade trees. Charlie Pitts was unscathed so he watered and soothed the horses. Jim Younger sliced his linen coat into strips and tied the bandages over his mouth. Frank James numbed his injury with a tourniquet that he released a little with each minute. Cole Younger fabricated a sling for Bob's arm and a binding for his leg, then wadded a bandana inside the shoulder of his coat and beanied his near-bald head with soaked leaves. They weren't penitent over what they'd attempted; their sorrow reached to the limits of their bodies and no further, all their anguish was in their skin. Jesse came back from his reconnaissance and slid down the river bank, threshing weeds aside.

Their predicament made him pitiless and when he looked at Bob Younger's sleep, he spat. He said, "I don't have a clue about where we are. Could be Delaware for all I know."

"Could be Sherwood Forest," said Frank, who in normal circumstances was never droll. And then he said, "Maybe we ought to go."

Cole threw a stick. He and Jesse hadn't been on good terms for more than two years—they were always vying for management of the gang and Cole regarded Jesse as too headlong in attitude—so he generally ignored what Jesse said, giving his ear only to Frank. Cole said, "Bob's too sick."

"Then let's leave him," said Jesse.

Cole glared up at the man and said, "I've still got my gun, Jess."

And Frank angrily said to his brother, "Go gather the animals."

Jesse ascended through the green weeds and grass, yelling back, "Give up that one man and you just might save five!"

By that time, the bodies of Clell Miller and Bill Chadwell were seated on a parlor bench in Northfield where their shirts were removed and their wrists crossed on their laps and photographs were taken. Their cameos later centered a souvenir card: the catch of death made them look bewildered and frazzled. Soon thereafter the cadavers of McClellan Miller and William Chadwell were sent to the University of Michigan medical school for classroom dissection, and for more than fifty years the skeleton of Clell Miller stood forlornly in Dr. Henry A. Wheeler's consultation room.

The James-Younger gang meandered the woodlands of Rice, Waseca, and Blue Earth counties for a week, sometimes recrossing the same ravine four times in their windings, or clocking a village so that stores and hovels shied from at noon were confronted a second time at two. With Bill Chadwell gone, they were gloomily lost in green woods or limited by foreign creeks and rivers that were too deep to ford. Even as late as four nights after they'd run out of Northfield, the bedraggled gang was spied by boys who lived no more than fifteen miles away. At a small hotel near Shieldsville a posse of ten from Faribault was eating supper when the gang rode up to water their horses and became perplexed by the great variety of shotguns and rifles angled against the hotel's porch railing. Jesse crept up to the porch and pressed against the screen, peering in. The posse men stopped talking or chewing or lifting their spoons and looked at Jesse with apprehension or stupidity, perceiving at once who he was; and they sheepishly permitted him to jump down and sprint away with his gang before they got up from their suppers.

The rains came and the gang was in swamplands with nearly one thousand manhunters looking for them. They gave up their horses and walked on foot at night, sleeping during the day under tents made from sopping blankets and shrubs. They couldn't hunt wild game so they chewed grass and wild mushrooms, growing weaker as the nights grew increasingly cold. Jesse's stamina was extraordinary, however, and he couldn't stand the recurring pauses and delays. He complained that they were procrastinating and that it was like trying to make a getaway while pulling a hospital along. He considered the Youngers, and especially Bob, as impediments to ever getting back to Missouri, and once, in mean temper, put a gun against Bob Younger's skull and was going to pull the trigger when Cole lunged at him, and only Frank and Charlie Pitts together were able to wrestle him off.

It was then that the James brothers split from the Youngers and Charlie Pitts. Days after they parted company, Jesse's predictions came true, for Sheriff Glispin and his posse surrounded the four in the Younger gang. They were slogging through the mires of the Watonwan River near Madelia, and a gunfight ensued. Charlie Pitts was instantly killed with a Minie ball that crashed through his chest at the collar. Bob Younger was shot in the right lung but survived, as did his brothers, although Cole was stricken with eleven gunshot injuries and a blackened eye that gloved the entire right side of his face, and Jim fell with five wounds that included a cartridge ball that crannied beneath his brain and another that so shattered his jaw he could never again chew food.

The Youngers were medicated at the Flanders House in Madelia and were viewed in the Faribault jail by Pinkerton detectives and newsmen and crowds of the inquisitive, for whom Cole sorrowed about his sins and cited scripture and broadcast his love for mankind and the Baptist church, even cunningly leaked a tear or two so that resentments might be lessened. At the Younger brothers' trial each man acknowledged his crimes and his guilty remorse so that instead of execution the judge sentenced them to the state penitentiary at Stillwater, Minnesota, there to remain for life.

The James brothers' tracks were lost outside of Sioux Falls in the Dakota Territory, where it seems they rustled two blind horses from a farmer and, having long since become peeved with each other, gladly separated. The next information about either man was in a letter sent by some chagrined Pinkerton operatives who had relaxed from their hunt for the Jameses in order to dine at the Whaley House in Fulton, Missouri, and had invited to their table a man who had charmed them with wicked stories and then left a note under their hotel room door, educating them about the fact that he was Jesse James. It was the sort of bravura performance that had become typical of Jesse James in society: he would later palaver with detective Yankee Bligh in Louisville and make the same admission about his identity via a postcard that read: "You have seen Jesse James. Now you can go ahead and die."

MRS. ZEE JAMES conceived a second time in 1877, within a few weeks of Annie, and the two women exhausted entire mornings reporting their sensations and cravings, but the James brothers rarely saw each other and if they met didn't speak. Frank thought Jesse had overtaxed his mind and saw good evidence for that judgment, for Jesse had silenced himself around Zee, he ate alone on the back porch, he followed his shoes as he walked; he ignored his wife's condition until the last months, then made her hide from public view.

He was one to read auguries in the snarled intestines of chickens, or the blow of cat hair released to the wind, and the omens since he arrived in Nashville had forecast three years of bad luck that moated and dungeoned him. And he saw verification of his forebodings in all he tried to do. He had invested in commodities and lost so much he'd been forced into weekend work hauling rubble and trash. He had sold corn and seen the proceeds thieved by a rich landowner named Johnson who had no inkling who J. D. Howard was and paid insufficient attention to his menacing letters. He had traveled to Chicago in order to assassinate Allan Pinkerton but never found an occasion that did not seem devious and dishonorable. (He wanted a duel at sunrise with flintlock pistols. But instead he was offered potshots as Pinkerton exited from buildings or cabs, or nasty incidents in restaurants while he dined with operatives and their ladies—blood would spray the waiter's coat, Pinkerton would tow the tablecloth as he sank, screams would shatter the glassware.) So Jesse went dejectedly home while sleuths and local constabularies continued the hunt for the Jameses in four states.

He had headaches that were fierce as icepicks behind his eyes. The cottage was wreathed by high bushes and lowering trees so it was as gloomy as twilight through the afternoon, and Jesse would sit alone in that eerie calm like broken furniture surrendered to a black lagoon. He'd purchased a contraption for peeling apples that he would dismantle and oil and reassemble, but his rifles dulled with smut, his horses ganted in their barn stalls, he wore the same clothes for weeks. He was like a man in a wheelchair, a man enfeebled with a stroke; his words were slurred, he noticed events seconds after they occurred, his neck seemed too frail for his head and his eyes sank to consider his brittle fingernails. Then he would awake and he would be transformed, his movements were raced and his mind was electric and his comments were snide and sarcastic, so that whenever he left for his livestock auctions and farm sales and derbies or wherever it was he went, Zee was relieved to see him go and welcomed Dr. Vertrees as one would a rescuer.

Twin sons were born to Zee in February 1878, and she named them Gould and Montgomery after the two doctors who'd delivered and cared for them until they succumbed to the crib deaths that were common among infants in that era. About then Annie gave birth to a boy who was christened Robert Franklin James and Zee had the minor consolation of nursing him when Annie's milk was insufficient. But Jesse's grief was huge. He thought of himself as the cause of their miseries and Zee would awake at night to see him sitting on the edge of the mattress, his blue nightshirt rucked and screwed about him, a white buttock windowed by the gather at his waist, his papa's pencil-marked Holy Bible open in his hands.

He began to call himself Dave, a nickname from childhood that Zee never really got accustomed to, and he began gathering in the cottage some rough guests from Missouri: Tucker Bassham, a man called Whiskeyhead Ryan, a good-looking horse thief named Dick Liddil, an ex-Confederate soldier named Jim Cummins, and Clell Miller's brother Ed. Zee regarded them all unfavorably but gave Jesse no instructions about them for they seemed to gratify him in a way she could not, and she was pregnant again and wanted nothing more than an unchallenging life in Nashville, Tennessee.

She knew Frank James was getting along: his pedigreed hogs were awarded first prize for Poland Chinas at a county fair; when the crops were in he made cedar buckets for the Prewitt-Spurr Lumber Company; he was registered to vote and among his friends were the sheriff of Davidson County and a judge from the Eighth Circuit Court. But Jesse only raced horses—Roan Charger, Jim Malone, and one that especially pleased him, Skyrocket—and when she brought up the notion of a farm, Jesse agreed with her but thought it ought to be in the New Mexico Territory, and in July 1879 journeyed west to Santa Fe and the Las Vegas hot springs, staying there with a boyhood friend named Scott Moore so that Zee gave birth to their daughter, Mary, in a room at Frank and Annie's house, and the child was a month old before her father ever saw her.

Annie partially convinced Zee that Jesse was a preposterous, irresponsible man, but America seemed spellbound by him. Correspondents sought to locate him, mysteries about the James brothers were considered in editorials, reports of their robberies seemed to be such a national addiction that nickel books were being published in order to offer more imaginative adventures. Insofar as it wasn't them that the James gang robbed, the public seemed to wish Jesse a prolonged life and great prosperity. He was their champion and their example, the apple of their eyes; at times it even seemed to Zee that she wasn't Jesse's only wife, that America had married him too. And it seemed a joy to many of them when a reinvigorated James gang—without the man's more prudential older brother—robbed the Chicago and Alton Railroad at Glendale, Missouri, in October 1879.

Some men with six-guns pushed the checker players at Joe Molt's corner store fifty yards to the Glendale depot, where the station attendant ate the barrel of Jesse's revolver until he agreed to whatever the outlaw commanded. Jesse then wrecked the telegraph apparatus with a crowbar (Tucker Bassham thought it was only a sewing machine) and the red flag was raised next to the railroad tracks in order to notify the engineer that passengers wanted on. After Dick Liddil climbed aboard the locomotive, Ed Miller sledged in the express car door, and currencies, bonds, and securities were swept into a meal sack and divvied six miles out of town, each in the company receiving $1,025, more than most of them could make in a year. The engineer told newspaper correspondents that the captain of the group had come up to him prior to riding off and had said, "I didn't get your name, but mine is Jesse James."

His pretext was that setting up a farm required a great deal of money, and he made an effort to persuade Frank to join him when again the James gang was plundering, but Frank was settled and intransigent and in the course of one of their increasingly common arguments Frank smashed a beer bottle against the Colt that Jesse had pulled in exasperation.

So Frank was again not with the James gang when, in November, they moved against the Empire City Bank. It appeared, however, that someone had spoken of their intentions, for the gang was forestalled by a preliminary reconnaissance that showed more than a dozen townsmen inside, each with more pistols and shotguns than he could possibly use. The gang therefore fragmented, with most of them returning to their chores as if they'd merely been on a club excursion, but Jesse and Whiskeyhead Ryan met again in September 1880 to rob the Mammoth Cave sightseers' stage in Kentucky. Five men and Judge Rutherford Rountree and his daughter, Lizzie, were ordered out of the stagecoach at gunpoint and gave up $803 and jewelry, including a diamond ring that Jesse would later slip on his wife's finger, and a gold watch that was a gift to the judge from the governor of Kentucky and was found two years later among the belongings of Mr. Thomas Howard of St. Joseph, Missouri. Ryan sipped from a pint bottle of whiskey during the presentation, and, as Jesse jumped onto his horse, complimented the passengers for their graciousness, drinking to their continued well-being. Judge Rountree would later recognize T. J. Hunt as one of the culprits and the poor man would be imprisoned for eighteen months before the judge's mistake was repaired.

Jesse displayed the ring, the gold watch, and the money to Frank James, and then made a practice of sashaying by his older brother's workplace in his gentleman's clothes. The temptation of an easier income at last became too persuasive and Frank joined Jesse and Whiskeyhead Ryan when they stopped a government paymaster on the road to Muscle Shoals, Alabama, in March 1881, splitting a five-thousand-dollar payroll three ways.

It was Frank's ill luck then that he was immediately suspected of participation in the Muscle Shoals holdup, the only robbery he'd committed since Northfield in 1876, and it was only the compelling polemics of his lawyer, Raymond B. Sloan, that kept him out of jail. Then, on March 26th, Whiskeyhead Ryan gripped a mahogany bar in a grocery store saloon and swallowed a shot glass of sour mash after each of twelve cove oysters. He got surly and then he got arrested and in his buckskin vest was found more gold than a man of his capabilities ought to have owned. Descriptions of him were telegraphed to police departments around the country and Kansas City responded with a wire petitioning the state of Tennessee to extradite William Ryan to the state of Missouri.

Overnight the B. J. Woodson and J. D. Howard families vanished from Nashville, and by the summer of 1881, Zee was again in Kansas City and mothering a six-year-old son and a two-year-old daughter in a bungalow on Woodland Avenue. Jesse was calling himself J. T. Jackson in remembrance of Thomas Jonathan "Stonewall" Jackson, the Confederate general, and Zee was again feeling dwarfed by her husband, subsidiary to him. It seemed they moved and lived and concealed themselves according to his will, and she dwindled under him like a noon shadow, she was no more than an unnoticed corner of the rooms he filled. She could imagine a life without Jesse but knew it would be without consequence or surprise, nothing would be in jeopardy, and she would die a completely ordinary woman, one as insipid and colorless as the girl who stitched initials into handkerchiefs and read Robert Browning by candlelight. Much later Frank Triplett would write that Jesse "married a woman, who while amiable, good, and true to him in every sense of the word, yet possesed no will of her own, and whose mind, weak, plastic, and yielding, took form from, rather than shaped that of her husband. To such a mind as this, no matter how good, no strong effort is a possibility, and it will sooner drift into the channels of excuse and justification than to make a bold, strong stand against wrong."

Zee could only agree.

ON THE NIGHT of July 14th, Sheriff Pat Garrett stole into a sleeping room on Pete Maxwell's ranch in the New Mexico Territory and there shot and killed the twenty-one-year-old outlaw who was known as Billy the Kid.

And on July 15th, two days before Mary James's second birthday, two wary men of unequal heights and qualities bought tickets for a Chicago, Rock Island, and Pacific sleeper to Des Moines, Iowa. They would not stay on the train long enough to conclude the journey. They were overdressed, as was common then, even in a sultry July: each wore a gentleman's vest and suit cut in the English style, a black slouch hat, calf-high Wellington boots, and an open white linen duster of the sort that cattlemen used to keep cow grime off their pants legs and to protect against railroad soot and sparks. It was not immediately evident that they were carrying heavy Navy Colt revolvers or that the jaunty sport of the two had shoe-dyed his spruced hair and beard.

They lodged themselves magisterially in an opulent, chandeliered drawing room that was called a palace car. Shades were still strapped down to the sills to keep out the pernicious late afternoon sun and Jesse pushed them aside to peer out at the porters and railway policemen. And when they jolted into motion, Jesse moseyed from one coach to the next, stooping to look at the countryside, tipping his hat to the more antique women, pivoting only slightly away if ever a railroad employee approached.

He interrupted his partner's nap at six to suggest they visit the dining car, where some passengers would later recall their speaking about the robbery of the Davis and Sexton Bank at Riverton, Iowa, four days earlier, a holdup then accredited to the James gang, but which the two men were positive was actually accomplished by Poke Wells and his gang.

The man eating across from Jesse was Ed Miller, the ruggea, unintelligent younger brother of the late Clell Miller, and a good friend of Charley Ford, whom he'd introduced to Jesse at a poker game in 1879 and whom he'd arranged to make part of the James gang of late. Ed Miller looked much like Clell—brown eyes and waxy brown hair the color of coffee beans, and a smug, vulgar, open-jawed face that seemed rigid enough to barge through wooden doors. He sank into the dining car chair as if he were delighting in a too-occasional, good hot soak and Jesse guided a match beneath his cigar until a duplicate flame licked up from the tobacco. They talked about the new governor, Thomas T. Crittenden, a Democrat and a onetime Union colonel who'd been financed by the railway companies in his 1880 campaign. His inaugural address in January pledged the government to the job of ridding Missouri of the James gang, and Jesse said he was going to take measures to guarantee his men's allegiance. He whispered, "You won't none of you get away with bargaining or making exchanges. I've got a wife and two children I've gotta look out for."

"You can trust me," said Miller.

Jesse rocked back in his dining car chair, his fingers lacing his hair like a shoe, his green cigar angled up, and he gave himself over to a long thought before saying, "I know I can, Ed."

Then a middle-aged conductor in a blue suit and cap tapped the dining car table with a finger as he politely carped that cigars could only be enjoyed in the smoking car. Jesse reacted genially, saying that was exactly where they were going.

Soon after 9 p.m. on the milk-stop train, they were in Cameron, thirty-five miles east of St. Joseph, and stepping up into the smoking car were two glum, sweating men in long wool coats who—though they'd been chatting together on the depot platform—diverged once they were in the smoker, the younger sitting forward, the larger man sitting just ahead of Jesse James and Ed Miller. The man sitting forward was Robert Woodson Hite, the Kentucky cousin of the Jameses, and the man closer to Jesse was his brother, Frank, his sandy sideburns shoe-dyed black and lifts in his riding boots giving him two inches in height. He looked just once at Jesse, tilting up his exaggerated nose, and then he lighted a cigarette and looked out at the Cameron buildings that were slowly gliding away.

They were going eleven miles north to Winston. A good many yards beyond that was a stone trestle that bridged Little Dog Creek and there Dick Liddil, Charley Ford, and Wood's brother, Clarence Hite, were tying seven horses in a copse of trees. They then trudged back along the roadbed with Dick assigning jobs to his more agitated partners. They could hear crickets and frogs in the weeds and as they gained the Winston depot they could hear singing in the Presbyterian church.

Already on the depot platform were Mr. A. McMillan, a masonry contractor, and a crew of four that included his two sons. They were going home to Iowa that Friday night and were joshing and goosing each other; the James gang avoided giving the crew their faces when they achieved the platform, and the three were straggled along it when the locomotive's headlight yellowed their skin. McMillan and the four got on, but the brooding gang lingered. Conductor Westfall slanted out from the smoking car, his left arm hooked in the grab rail, and hollered, "All aboard!"

Dick Liddil called out that they were only waiting for somebody, and when the conductor swung back inside they plunged through engine boiler steam to jump up onto the front and rear porches of the U.S. Express Company car, just behind the coal tender.

Conductor Westfall moved down the smoking car, gripping seats to steady himself when the rolling stock jerked forward, spraddling his legs out like a man on a horse when he stopped to punch a spade design into a passenger's ticket. He didn't see the guns in Frank's hands, didn't see Ed Miller's glare.

They'd gone only forty yards and Westfall was checking a sleeping man's ticket when Frank pushed a blue mask over his nose and pulled himself up, yelling, "Stay in your seats! Don't move!" And when a man laughed at the joke of that James boys act, Frank fired his guns every whichway, into the floor, the gas lamps, the ceiling, making ears ring and making the forty passengers sink down beneath their crossed arms. Westfall straightened at the gun noise and edged just enough into it that he caught a shot between two ribs. His right hand went to the injury and he groaned and then staggered out of the smoking car as Ed Miller and Wood Hite joined in the gunfire; but Jesse James gave Westfall only the chance to get out the car door before his unaccidental gunshot killed the man and Westfall teetered off his legs, banging down the iron stairs and sliding off the train onto the roadbed.

Frank McMillan and John Penn were standing outside the smoking car in the July night when the gun noise began. They crouched down and a lead ball crashed through an overhead window, spiderwebbing the glass, and John Penn jacked himself up to peek inside and drop down again. McMillan asked, "Who is it?" and Penn said, "I can't tell," and Frank McMillan was craning his neck to look inside for himself when a lead ball punched into his forehead above his right eye, stopping his life instantly. His body collapsed just as the air brakes screeched and McMillan too slipped off the slackening train.

Jesse, Wood Hite, and Ed Miller were by then running forward through gunsmoke to get into the express company car, and Dick Liddil and Clarence Hite were scuttling over a coal pile to the locomotive in order to guarantee that it wouldn't go further than their horses. But a crewman had switched on the automatic air brakes, which meant Dick had to command the engineer to bring the train gradually along until it was over Little Dog Creek.

Charley Ford was standing by the baggage agent's passageway with a disguise on, a gun cocked near his ear, but he gave way to Jesse, who rammed against the wooden door as if his bones were made out of timber, slamming the door into a packing case. He slapped aside the agent, Frank Stamper, and then rammed against an interior door as Charles Murray, the express messenger, was jarring an outside door shut. Ed Miller pushed Stamper into a wall and pressed a revolver into the agent's cheek, saying, "You get out of here!" Stamper stepped outside and looked at the long gray beard hooked over Charley Ford's ears, and Frank James, who was by then walking along on the ground, gripped the baggage agent by the leg and jerked him into a pratfall. "Keep your seat," Frank said.

Jesse scared Murray into yielding the key to the express company safe by saying one man was already killed so they had nothing to lose by killing him too. The only light in the express section was a coal-oil lantern that was hanging from a finger hook and though Jesse was thorough in gathering over three thousand dollars into a grain sack, he missed a good deal more in gold bullion and grieved about it for a week.

He then said to Murray, "Get down on your knees."

The messenger glowered. "Why?"

"You oughta pray; I'm going to kill you."

"Hey?" Miller called.

"Get down!" Jesse said.

Murray withdrew a little and replied, "You'll have to make me."

"All right," Jesse said, and surprised him by socking his pistol into the man's skull so that Murray dropped like emptied clothes. Jesse looked abjectly at the man he'd so easily rendered unconscious and then he cocked his pistol to put it against Murray's head.

Ed Miller cried, "Don't shoot him!"

And Jesse grinned and uncocked his pistol and then picked up the grain sack. He said, "Don't you tell me what I can and can't do," and then jumped down from the express car.

And then the robbery was over. The James gang sprang down to the ground and down through the weeds and ran into the night, cutting their reins instead of untying them and then riding south through the woods.

CHICAGO NEWSPAPER PUBLISHERS —who were still smarting over the loss of immigrants to St. Louis and Kansas City—made a great deal of the Winston train robbery, alleging that "in no State but Missouri would the James brothers be tolerated for twelve years." Missouri was being called "The Robber State" and "The Outlaw's Paradise," and yet the governor had the authority to offer only three hundred dollars for capturing the outlaw. Governor Crittenden would later write: "Concluding that the James gang pursued its lawless course for the money in it, oftentimes acquiring large sums, I determined to offer a reward of $50,000; so much for each capture and conviction, which in my opinion would be a temptation to some one or more of the gang to 'peach' or divulge on their associates in crime. As money was their object in the first place in their lawless pursuit, I believed an offer of a large sum as a reward would eventually reach those who had become tired of the life, and more tired of being led on in blood and crime by a desperate leader."

He arranged a meeting with the general managers of the railroads and express companies operating in Missouri and persuaded them to contribute to a common fund from which the governor could offer rewards of five thousand dollars for the arrest and conviction of each person participating in the robberies at Glendale and Winston, with a further five thousand going to anyone who could bring in Frank or Jesse James.

Jesse organized the September 7th robbery of the Chicago and Alton Railroad at Blue Cut to "spit in the governor's eye," and again the James gang got away with it, and Jesse brought Frank and Clarence Hite and two Ray County boys named Ford to the bungalow in Kansas

City. And it seemed to Zee it could go on and on like that, with Jesse going off for days and weeks and then coming back with the jolly good cheer of a man given money and youth. It upset her but she didn't complain; instead she looked for messages in the green tea leaves and made herself giggle when that seemed the right thing and then she stayed with her knitting like an indulgent mother until Jesse limped into the room and whispered, "You go to sleep."

Then she was awake again and the tattercrossed quilt was under her chin and the grandfather clock had chimed three. She closed a robe around herself and huddled a little at the bedroom door and saw Jesse in a ladder chair next to the side window. He sucked on a lump of chewing tobacco and seemed to contemplate the moon. Raindrops tracked reeds on the misted glass and wind disarranged the trees. His night thoughts seemed to walk the room. His eyes were on the street. A cocked revolver was across his knee but he lent it no more notice than a smoker would a cigarette.

Zee watched Jesse sit there for several minutes and didn't say a word, and then she felt someone watching her and saw in a corner of the room the boy who called himself Bob Ford. He looked at her spitefully, and then he receded into darkness and she heard the screen door latch shut.

Part Two

—

NIGHTHAWKS

—

3

SEPTEMBER–DECEMBER

1881

*They were not the ordinary rough-shod highwaymen typical in the
Western country, but were more of the nature of modern Robin Hoods,
who robbed the rich and gave to the poor; who took human life only
when they deemed it necessary for the protection of their own and their
liberty; who were addicted to none of the ordinary vices of the bad men;
who used liquor, tobacco or bad language sparingly, and who, in many
particulars and traits, would have been model men had their vocations
been honest and their lives unmarred by bloodshed and robbery.*

EDGAR JAMES
*The Lives and Adventures, Daring Hold-ups, Train and Bank Robberies
of the World's Most Desperate Bandits and Highwaymen—The
Notorious James Brothers*

ANNIE RALSTON JAMES invented an alibi for Frank by visiting Sonora,
California, with their three-year-old son, Rob (who was being
dressed as a girl then, and was being called Mary), and by writing
letters to her parents that depicted the sights she and Frank were viewing out West. But following the Blue Cut robbery, she journeyed back
to Kansas City and signed the registration book in the St. James Hotel,
and on September 14th she and their "daughter" were in a phaeton
carriage as Frank said goodbye to Zee in the kitchen of the bungalow.
Jesse sat in a backyard rocking chair, ignoring their flight to the East,
but Zee was getting mailing addresses in Chattanooga and Baltimore
and young Ford was giving the glum man whatever intelligence about
the coastal cities he could recall from his reading. He said Salem,
North Carolina, was overrun with diphtheria owing to the sewers not
being up to snuff. And Raleigh was a dead town with no sizable
manufacturing establishment in it. And he'd heard tell that Richmond,
Virginia, was all yellow-flagged because of an epidemic of small-pox.

Frank simply circled his hat in his lump-knuckled hands and said, "I guess I'll know who to come to the next time I plan a trip."

Bob poured another cup of coffee and in a pout replied, "I was only trying to be helpful."

Zee went outside to hug Annie and to grasp Rob to her bosom and then Frank received her kiss like medicine, glaring once to the backyard to see that his younger brother was angrily looking away. He said, "I'd better get to the depot," and soon after that the Frank James family was gone.

Bob peered out from the kitchen window to see the phaeton pull away, then dropped his coffee cup in dishwater and moseyed toward the clothesline pole where Jesse was sitting in a rocker that was submerged to its seat in straw grass and weeds. Bob thought he could say something about getting a goat to chew the yard down a little, but before he could get the sentence together, Jesse said, "My brother and me, we're not on speaking terms these days. I can remember years at a time when we were scarcely civil to each other. I'll get lonely though and invite him back and old Buck'll be in the neighborhood before the week is out. You might say we've got an arrangement." He glanced up at Bob and rubbed about in his chair. "That's why I didn't say goodbye."

"I wasn't going to mention it."

Jesse reached under the rocker and into a tin cake closet from which he hauled up two writhing garden snakes. "You scared?" he asked.

"Just surprised a little."

The snakes flicked their forked tongues out and the heads roamed the air from side to side as if searching for relatives in a crowd. Jesse said, "These aren't as succulent as I like and they're the devil to clean but if a man skins and fries them in garlic and oil—*mercy*, it's good eating."

"I've never been that hungry."

Jesse allowed the snakes to crawl his sleeves and nose his vest and slide down to the bunched wool of his trousers. He unfolded a four-inch knife and lifted the head of the browner snake on the blade, but it glided onto his thigh. "Must have at least twelve of these critters in the yard. Sometimes of an evening I'll sneak out here barefoot and listen to them slither over to where they don't think I can catch them. Then I snag them with my toes just to prove there's no getting away from Jesse." He crooked a snake head around with his knife and read its cruel face before it ducked under the steel and veered to his elbow. "I give them names."

"Such as?"

"Such as enemies. I give them the names of enemies." He then carefully laid the snakes on the wooden arm of the rocking chair and sawed off their heads with his knife. The bodies curled and thrashed over his wrist. He flicked their heads into the straw grass. "Go tell Clarence and Charley to get their gatherings together."

"Me too?" Bob asked.

Jesse glanced at him sharply but then changed and said, "You can stay."

The suggestion to leave struck Clarence Hite hard and he bickered with Bob about it when Bob nudged him from his nap. "I'm his cousin!" he said. "My momma was his daddy's—?"

"Sister," said Bob.

"That's right! So how come it's me has to rattle his hocks outta town?"

Charley sacked turnips and acorn squash he'd grubbed from the vegetable garden. "If I know Jess, what it is is there's some real nasty sad-Suzie work that's got to be done around here and Bob's the ninny that has to do it."

"I'm willing," said Bob. "Don't know why exactly. I guess that's the noble and benevolent sort of person I am."

Clarence commenced coughing until he'd expelled something into a handkerchief. He peeked at it and then wiped his mouth.

Bob said, "He probably would've picked Clarence except he was a little jumpy about finding goobers in his soup."

"Well," said Clarence, putting the foul handkerchief in his pocket. "He certainly didn't want you around for your charity toward others." He climbed into his horse's doghouse stirrups and rode out of the barn as Charley chaperoned his mare from her stall.

Jesse was at the compost crib, drooling the snake bodies onto the corn shucks and vines. He called, "Clarence? You tell your daddy I'll be in Kentucky in October and maybe we can hunt some birds together."

Clarence complained, "But how come it's Bob who gets to stay?"

"Bob's going to move my gear to a house down the street."

Charley winked at his kid brother. "See?"

"I don't mind," said Bob, though of course he did. "Sounds like an adventure." He tore up a foxtail weed and stripped it between his teeth.

Charley jumped onto his mare and said, "If you ever need me to swing the wide loop or, you know, make smoke someplace again, a body can usually find me at my sister's—Mrs. Martha Bolton?—over to the Harbison homestead."

Jesse tipped his head and smiled. "I'll keep it in mind."

Clarence said, "You know where I'll be."

Jesse limped over to the bungalow, saying, "It's been pleasant," and at the porch door gave Bob an exacting look that implied he was already beginning to suspect his own judgment. "You've got some packing to do, kid," said Jesse, and Bob traipsed after him.

THEY MOVED to 1017 Troost Avenue at night so that the neighborhood couldn't get a good look at them or their belongings, with Bob carrying single-handedly most of what Jesse called gear. And then he thought Jesse would give him eight hours' sleep and a daydreaming goodbye; but Jesse forgot to say anything about it that night or the next morning and with a second day in the J. T. Jackson house, Bob thought he might never go but might be brought in as a good-natured cousin to the boy and a gentleman helper to Zee. Bob followed Jesse wherever he went, hawked him in his city rounds, watched him from a barn stall. He curried the horse next to the horse Jesse curried. He smoked a cigar that matched the cigar Jesse smoked. They rocked in chairs on the front porch and made trips to the Topeka Exchange saloon, where Jesse could spend nearly sixty minutes sipping one glass of beer and still complain about feeling tipsy. Bob would rarely vouchsafe his opinions as they talked. If spoken to, he would fidget and grin; if Jesse palavered with another person, Bob secretaried their dialogue, getting each inflection, reading every gesture and tick, as if he wanted to compose a biography of the outlaw, or as if he were preparing an impersonation.

One night Jesse and Bob and the boy, Tim, walked down a towpath with bamboo poles and dropped shot-weighted lines into the Missouri in order to snag some catfish. Jesse walked down from the cliff and waded the shallows with tobacco in his cheek and his trousers rolled, cold bottom mud surging between his toes and clouding brown over his white calves. Bob nannied Tim on the steep, damp bank, snatching insects with his shrewd left hand, his swift right. Tim asked the name of the yellow country across the green churn of the river and Bob told him Kansas. Tim pointed northwest. Nebraska. And then Bob crouched so close to the boy his ear might have been a fragrant flower. "Here's what we'll do: rifle your arm out like so, keep that finger unbent, and let me turn you clockwise. There's Iowa above us. Still Iowa. Still Iowa. Illinois. You ever heard of Chicago?''

"Yes."

"Chicago's in Illinois somewheres."

"I mean: no, I haven't."

"You haven't heard of Chicago?"

Tim shrugged.

"Isn't no such place as Chicago," Bob said. "I was just making that up." The boy looked at him strangely but Bob continued. "You're on a raft on the Mississippi now and that's as east as the state of Missouri goes. South. South. Quincy. Alton. St. Louis. Cape Girardeau. The Ohio River marries into the Mississippi and ol' Miss fattens up and then it's Kentucky for the blink of an eye, maybe forty miles or so, and Tennessee for another forty, and then you've got a skirt along the bottom and it's called Arkansas, Arkansas, Arkansas. And then lookout, child, you better cover that scalp! It's Indian Territory! Choctaw, Chickasaw, Cherokee, Creek, and Seminole, maybe a thousand of them yelping and slinging their arrows at you!"

Jesse had sloshed over the bank and scrambled up to the cliff, ripping a maple branch into a stick. He overheard the geography lesson and smiled at Bob with brown tobacco blotting out some teeth. The sun was gone and only an orange glow along Kansas recalled it. Jesse gazed down at the fishing lines and asked if there'd been any nibbles.

"Can't say I've felt even a twitch, Jess."

Jesse cautioned, "Little rabbits have big ears, Bob."

"Dave," Bob corrected. "Could be it's not night enough yet, Dave."

Jesse unfolded his pocket knife and whittled with the stick so close his eyes crossed. Blond shavings boated on the water eight or nine feet below them. When the stick was arrowed, he gave it to Tim. "You want to go play?"

The boy slid down the weeds without saying, going down to the water his father had walked in and then flinging the arrow into it. Jesse sighed as he watched the stick navigate the currents out and then he unlidded a mason jar that was not there when last Bob looked. The odor was that of lager beer. Jesse drank and sleeved his mouth and mustache. "You want some?"

Bob swallowed some but tilted the mason jar too much, spilling beer on his chin.

"Good?" Jesse asked.

Bob grinned. "Good as baby Jesus in velvet pants."

81

Jesse scowled at the blasphemy but then sat back on an elbow, clicking stones in his palm. "Your people God-fearing, Bob?"

"Oh heavenly days, yes. My daddy's a part-time preacher."

"Rich or poor?"

Bob thought about it. "Prosperous, I guess. He could give me plenty of money but he's got this philosophy that his boys ought to feel some hardships or else they'll all spoil."

"A man of principles," Jesse said.

"People say that about themselves when really they only want to make you unhappy."

Tim swatted the river with a washed-up board but when Jesse called, "What're you doing down there?" the boy said he was letting minnows tickle his fingers. Jesse called, "Don't get yourself all soaked now, you little honyock." And on second thought, in a voice meant only for Bob, Jesse asked, "You ever meet Zerelda? Mrs. Samuels?"

"Haven't had the pleasure."

"The Good Lord really accomplished something. Giant woman; eight feet tall. If she'd been a man she'd be governor now." Jesse looked for his red socks and rolled them onto his feet without brushing the silt off his ankles and soles. He then lunged his stockinged feet into his high boots and stuffed his gray trouser legs inside. He said, "You ever hear any gossip about my father and Frank's being two different men?"

"Yes."

"They say that was the reason my papa went West in the gold rush: he couldn't support the shame of it. What do you think of a story like that?"

Bob said, "I'm personally more interested in what *you* think about it."

Jesse glared at him and in a growl of a voice said, "I think it's a goddamned lie."

"I'm with you then; and I won't hear another word of it if the subject ever comes up." Bob removed his stovepipe hat and scratched at the circled indentation of his ginger brown hair. "Since we're telling stories, have you ever heard the one about the James gang robbing this one railroad?"

"You're not giving me enough clues."

"It's a funny story."

Jesse shook his head in the negative and then raised the mason jar, swallowing a long sentence of the lager beer.

Bob continued, "You see, the James gang is robbing this railroad train like you do, and going through the passenger cars and on board is this Quaker minister or something, some old coot with a long beard and, you know, a mean disposition? You can tell he's no joy to be around, but he's got this pinched-up wife with him and she's shivering with fright and clutching the preacher's sleeve and so on. You're sure you haven't heard this?''

"I would've stopped you by now."

"How's it go? I've gotta get this right. Oh! I guess it's you. You stand in this railroad coach and everybody's cowering, of course, and you holler, 'I'm Jesse James! And here's what I'm gonna do! I'm gonna grab all your money. I'm gonna grab all your watches and jewelry! I'm gonna grab everything you own!' The preacher's wife is cringing now and the old coot's guarding her and you say, 'And then I'm gonna go down the aisle and rape all you women!' "

Jesse said, "I don't like the way this story's headed."

"Well, everyone knows it's not true, Jess; it's just sort of comical. You see, after you say what you do about raping the women, the Quaker ups and says, 'Surely you wouldn't rape a preacher's wife!' And this is the funny part; his wife gets mad and gives her husband an elbow and says, 'Shut up, Homer! It's Jesse's train. Let him rob it the way he wants to.' " Bob's eyes slanted to Jesse and he saw the man wasn't laughing. "You don't think it's funny?"

"Well, hell, how could I if it isn't true?"

"Jokes don't need to be, Jesse."

"You're gonna have to explain why I oughta laugh then."

Bob said with great impatience, "Why don't we just forget it," and instantly felt in jeopardy, for his impudence was plain and Jesse's countenance was stern and it seemed just possible a boy might find Bob chambered in the river some morning. His hair would float in the water, his body would yeast until his clothes' buttons popped, an elm blowdown would bash out his eye, and then the river would abandon him on a levee where snails would feel his skin with cold horns and red crawdads would cling to his ankles. He said, "I didn't mean to sound sharp just then."

Jesse simply adjusted his jacket sleeves on his arms and said, "I've got a good story for you that's true as a razor. This'll give you an example of Frank and me putting a man in his place, and it don't depend upon any prevaricating. Once me and Frank were riding in the countryside and got hungry, so we went up to this farmhouse and asked would this widow lady make us some supper."

"Oh, that one," said Bob.

"You've heard it?"

"Only about twenty times."

Jesse was as still as a shut-down machine.

Bob said, "I'd love the chance to hear you tell it, though. I imagine you'll make it more interesting."

Jesse resumed, " 'I'll gladly pay you,' I say, and she said that was all right, we looked like genuine Christians and she'd do us the good turn. Kid, I want to tell you, that was one scrumptious supper. She went all out. But Frank saw she was crying and when he asked why, she said the mortgage was coming due and that the loan manager or whatever was going to be there any minute to repossess the place. And her a poor widow! Can you imagine? Well now, Frank and me, we insist on paying her something; and you know what we gave her?"

"Enough to pay off the mortgage," Bob said.

"You *have* heard this one."

"But no one ever said the supper was scrumptious. This is fascinating."

"So we gave her what she needed and we go, and on the highway who's coming our way but the loan manager. He greets us but doesn't give Frank and me a second thought, he's that greedy to get hold of that farm. Much to his surprise, of course, she paid him off and in no time he was plodding along the road with his wallet bulging his coat out and his grin a little tighter. And that's when Frank and me come out of the woods with masks on and steal all our money back." Jesse laughed uproariously, like a plowboy. He even slapped his thigh.

"And you're saying that's a true story."

"Is!"

"Jesse!"

"You calling me a liar?"

Tim crawled back up from the river, pretending to be something that he was not, and when he approached the two he said matter-of-factly, "I saw your pole dip, Cousin Bob." And Jesse slipped out of anger into eager regard for their fishing, winding the line around his right hand as he pulled it up to check on Bob's hook. The smelly mystery compound he'd gobbed on the hook was gone and he charged himself with the responsibility of baiting the snare again, adding to it a smear of tobacco that he wiped from inside his cheek. With that accomplished, Jesse swigged some more lager beer and put his boy in his lap, snuggling his chin beard into the boy's neck and munching his lips along Tim's ears in order to make him giggle. He said, "Do you know how to make a fire, Timmy?"

"Yes."

"Bob'll say you're lying if he don't see it."

The boy angled forward to glance at Bob. He said, "I can."

"You go ahead and make one for us. Show Cousin Bob you're a six-year-old." Tim got matches from his father and then went into the woods again to gather kindling and rotted logs. Jesse sipped some beer and then covered the mason jar with oiled paper and screwed on the lid. "You remember John Newman Edwards?"

"Newspaper man," Bob said.

"He'd misbehave himself for two or three weeks at a time; drink himself nearly cross-eyed; and then he'd come back to Kansas City and say, 'I've been to the Indian Territories.' Always tickled me to hear that."

"I've been to the Indian Territories," Bob said to get it right.

There was a pause and then Jesse said, "Garfield is dying real gallantly," and he went on to speak of the published newspaper interviews with Charles J. Guiteau.

On July 2nd President James A. Garfield had strolled into the Baltimore and Potomac Railroad station with Secretary of State James G. Blaine in order to meet a morning train that would take the president to Long Branch, New Jersey, where his wife, Lucretia, was convalescing. They'd crossed a ladies' waiting room without noticing a deranged evangelist and general miscreant named Charles J. Guiteau who'd spent the preceding three months in pestering them for the Paris consulship, and since June had been preparing to "remove" the Republican president. He crept up behind Garfield, straightened a .44 caliber British Bulldog revolver, and shot the president once in the right of his back, and as the man struggled around and cried out, "My God! What is this?" shot him again in the arm. Guiteau then slipped out of the station but was caught by a policeman, to whom he said, "Keep quiet, my friend, keep quiet. I wish to go right to jail."

Jesse knew a great deal about Charles J. Guiteau: that he was five feet five inches tall and thirty-nine years old and once claimed his employer was Jesus Christ and Company. He was a swindler, insurance salesman, debt collector, a member of the Illinois bar; he skipped out on hotel bills, published a book on religion called simply *The Truth,* and had assigned his collected papers and .44 caliber pistol to the State Department library.

Jesse James, Jr., would grow up to be a good-looking man but he was a grouchy, ill-favored boy with ash blond hair that spiked up from his scalp and a mouth that was always pouting. But he put together fire sticks with some proficiency and was squatting by his woodstack, guiding a match along some kindling in a grandfatherly way, as his father continued to speak about the July assassination and Bob attended to what he was saying like a paid companion.

Tim plopped down in his father's lap and asked Bob, "Do you see the fire?"

"It's really burning, isn't it?"

The boy said, "I made it myself."

"Hup?" Jesse said. "I just felt something. Might've had a nibble."

Bob gingerly cupped his fingers around the bamboo pole and gazed down into the night-blackened water. The moon was out and the evening was cooling. Tim threw a rock and the river glunked and Jesse said, "Don't do that, son. You'll scare all the fishes away."

"Daddy, I'm boring."

Jesse laughed and said, "You mean, you're bored."

"Yes."

Jesse hugged the boy to him with his right arm. "Maybe a fish will come and you can get all excited."

"I don't like fishing."

"Sure you do. *I* do. You must."

The boy shrugged and sank into the man's wool jacket. Bob unscrewed the mason jar and swallowed the lukewarm bottom inch of beer. The river was the only noise.

Jesse said, "You know what we are, Tim? We're nighthawks. We're the ones who go out at night and guard everything so people can sleep in peace. We've got our eyes peeled; no one's going to slip anything past us."

"I've got something!" Bob said.

"You sure?"

"It's heavy!" Bob had whipped up the bamboo pole at the first twitch and then jumped to his feet, bending the tip so low it made a parabola.

Jesse sidled next to him and clearly struggled with the temptation to grab the pole from Bob's grip. "Don't horse it, kid. Bring it up easy."

There was no reel on the pole, so Bob stepped on the bamboo and tugged the fishing line up with his right hand, looking over the cliff into the river but getting no sight of his catch. He could hear it thrash out of the water and he began hauling the weight up with both hands and with great strain heaved onto the river bank a gruesome fish that seemed overdue for extinction. It was orange in the firelight and round as a dog and over its eyes were crimson feelers that moved like thumbs on its skull. Tim backed into his father's leg but Jesse crouched close to examine the catch. "God damn it, but that's an ugly thing."

The fish seemed unperturbed even though cruelly hooked in the mouth. Its teeth meshed and unmeshed with a click, its red tail and gill wings undulated, and its frosted blue eye stared with calm accusation at the fishermen until Jesse grew disgusted and said, "Kill him, kid." And Bob did as he was told, taking a burning stick from the fire and stabbing it into the fish over and over again until Jesse said, "That's enough!" and then looked at Bob as if he'd been given a sign and would now act accordingly.

BOB WAS SENT AWAY cordially the next day, just as he knew he would be, with a goodbye from Jesse but nothing from Zee beyond what good manners demanded. It was forty miles to Martha Bolton's farm from Kansas City and it was already noon by the time he attained Liberty, where he watered his common horse at a trough and sank a dipper in a water pail outside a dry goods store. But as he lifted the dipper he viewed himself in the store window and was discouraged by the picture of a scroungy boy in a ridiculous stovepipe hat that was dented and smudged, in an overlarge black coat that was soiled and stained and plowed with wrinkles and cinched at his waist by a low-slung holster. He thought he looked goofy and juvenile, so he went inside the store and cruised the aisles.

A gentleman's clothes then were generally English: Prince Albert suits, greatcoats with caped shoulders, knee-length frock coats and knee-high Wellington boots into which pin-striped pants legs were stuffed. Men wore bowlers, derbies, fedoras, slouch hats, and short-crowned, wide-brimmed felt hats that were cooked stiff as boaters and were worn tilted back on the head so that a pompadour showed. Robert Ford was not yet extraordinary in his clothes and at the dry goods store selected a fine white shirt and a starched white collar that could be attached with a stud, white underwear with wooden buttons that ran down its middle, and a heather green suit with lapels that were abbreviated so they could be fastened nearer the throat than has been the fashion since. And he crowned his head with a black bowler hat that was ribboned with black silk, a hat that suited a boulevardier but did not particularly suit Robert Ford.

The store owner stacked the bundles and scratched their prices on a newspaper and totaled them after licking his pencil. "You come into some money, is that it?"

"You might say that."

"Do you mind if I ask how you got it, being's you're so young?"

"I can't see that it's any of your business."

The store owner tore off a long sheet of brown paper and folded it around the bundles with a great deal of noise. "I'd just like to know out of curiosity. Maybe I could get into your line of work and buy myself a year's clothes in one afternoon."

"Only thing necessary is a great aunt who loves her nephew to pieces."

"Inheritance. I see."

Bob put his finger on the twine intersection so that the store owner could make a knot. "You were probably thinking I got the cash like the James gang would. Am I right or wrong?"

The store owner leaned his arms over the counter and winked. "Don't think I don't appreciate the business." He looked out the window as Bob rode off and then he crossed to a livery stable, where he talked to Sheriff James Timberlake.

MRS. MARTHA BOLTON rented the Harbison farm in 1879, just after becoming a widow, and she made a good income by giving rooms and meals to her brothers, Charley, Wilbur, and Bob, in exchange for chores and fifteen dollars per month. The wood frame house was two storeys high, the roof was buckled, an elm tree raked the shingles in storms. White paint blistered and scaled from the boards, oiled paper was tacked over the broken windows, the road door was nailed shut and a calico skirt insulated the cracks of the sill and sides. Martha raised chickens that nested under the porch and cows that watered at a wooden tank near a windmill. Elias Capline Ford ran a grocery store in Richmond, but mowed and maintained the agriculture on weekends. Wilbur, a brother two years older than Bob, was the enormous and morose hired hand and he lived a secret life in a room that clutched the earth brown barn.

When Bob arrived a black surrey sat in the weeds, a barn cat licking its paw on the surrey's seat, and a number of horses drowsed in a rickety limb corral in which straw scattered on the wind. Dick Liddil was at the yard swing with Bob's niece, Ida, twisting the slat seat until the raveled ropes squashed down on her hips. He released the seat and she twirled, squealing, her auburn hair flying out, and Dick fell backward and admired the girl. Wood Hite stood on the roofless kitchen porch, his fists on his hips, stern as John the Baptist. He called, "You're gonna make her sick! She's gonna upchuck, you don't watch out!"

Dick ignored Wood and rose to cuff the girl's dress so that it bloomed and revealed her thighs. She wailed unconvincingly, "You're not supposed to peek, Dick!"

"But you're so pretty! I can't help myself!"

Bob hollered hello to Dick but the man was inattentive. Wood slammed the kitchen door behind him. Bob rode into a barn stable and had removed most of his tack before he saw his brother Elias on his back under a borrowed McCormick reaper that was clotted with weeds.

"Howdy do!"

Elias smeared grease from his brow, a screwdriver in his left hand. "Here to work, Bob?"

"Well, I've been on the road and—"

"Didn't think so," his brother said, and continued with the machine.

Bob clomped into the farmhouse, saw Wood on the sofa frowning at no one in particular, and heaved the clothes bundle onto Martha's bed downstairs. She and Clarence Hite and Charley sat in the kitchen at a round oak table that was wide as a pond. Clarence slouched in a chair with his socked feet on an upended basket and sawed at warts on his hands with a paring knife. Blood trickled down to rags that were tied around his wrists. Charley slumped over the table with his chin on his thumbs, his sunken eyes closed, his boots hooked around the rear legs of the chair as he listened to Martha read about him from an astrological almanac.

Bob said, "Howdy!" but there was no response.

Martha read: "July ninth. 'Diligence, tact, a keen sense of responsibility, and a capacity for detail are your dominant traits. Your sense of duty is strong. You have poise and meet every situation calmly and resourcefully. Home means much to you in your daily existence.' "

Bob said, "Howdy!" a second time, but it appeared that snubbing the last-born was a custom his siblings still kept. Bob snuck over behind Martha as she distributed her long reddish hair away from her cheeks, and he idiotically pulled her apron bow through the slats of the chair. Martha fetched the ties with a nuisanced look at her kid brother, and with a smile as wide as a kazoo, Bob said, "I'm finally home!"

Martha riffled the almanac and said, "I'm real glad, Bob."

Clarence said, "Read the birthday sayings for Jesse James."

And Bob asked, "Do you want to know where I've been?"

Clarence said, "Read Jesse's birthday."

Bob uncinched his cartridge belt and holster and clattered them onto a counter. He smiled. "I've been to the Indian Territories."

Martha asked, "What day was Jesse born on, Bob?"

"September fifth, eighteen forty-seven." He swiveled a chair around and sat on it and scowled at Clarence Hite's slashed fingers and the blood that cross-hatched his hands. "What are you *doing,* Clarence?"

"Skinning off warts."

Martha read, "September fifth. 'You are a person of quick and rash judgment, violent moods, and vast enthusiasm. Temper your emotions with poise and self-control. You are lively, always active, and fond of pleasure and the society of friends.' "

Clarence said, "That isn't Jesse."

Charley said, "Why, I was about to say the opposite! That's him like he was sitting in that chair and sipping Doctor Harter's Iron Tonic."

Bob said, "Read mine."

The girl, Ida, had come in from swinging and she moved over to the round oak table with an apple in her hand, the red peel corkscrewing from the pulp. She looked down with consternation and said, "Clarence! What—"

He interrupted to say he was skinning warts off, and Charley said, "He's about twelve shy of a dozen in the smarts department, Ida. He's about a half-bubble off level."

Bob said, "Read January thirty-first, eighteen sixty-two."

Martha flicked several pages without care about whether she tore the sheets. "For some reason I thought you were January twenty-ninth."

"No. That's Zerelda Samuels, Jesse's momma. Eighteen twenty-five."

The congregation in the room all looked at Bob strangely. Charley sniggered and then said, "Isn't he something?"

Bob justified himself by saying, "I don't *try* to remember those things; I just *do.*"

"January thirty-first," Martha read, and Bob rocked forward so that the chair back rubbed the oak table. " 'You are kind, generous in judgments of others, and possess a discerning, artistic temperament. You are not afraid of hard work,' " (Charley hooted) " 'yet are easily disheartened by obstacles and temporary failures. Be firm in your resolves and keep trying.' "

Bob took the almanac from Martha and said, "How come mine is the only one that's negative?"

"Generous," Martha said.

"Just that."

"Artistic," she said.

"You bet," Charley said. "Bob can't make the ends of a circle meet and he's supposed to be artistic."

Bob grinned and said, "I can't even draw flies."

Wood Hite clomped in from the sitting room. "How come you all are in the kitchen chatting, and I'm all by myself?"

Martha said, "You old stick-in-the-mud! What do you expect? Always fuss-budgeting around, telling people what they can and can't do."

Robert Woodson Hite was a man in his late twenties who was so crotchety and orthodox that he seemed almost elderly and was known among the James gang by the nickname "Grandfather Grimes." His mother had contributed many of the James genes to his physical characteristics and he looked more brother to Frank than Jesse did—the same large ears, the same anteater nose, the same scorn and malevolence in his scowls. Martha had spurned his affections, so he pursued her daughter, but Ida was too young to be more than perplexed by his attentions, thus he'd spent most of the afternoon in a pout.

But Bob Ford rocked back in his chair and experimented one more time. "Wood?" he said. "I've been to the Indian Territories, Wood."

Wood was in a mope. He dully asked, "How was it?" and frowned at Clarence's wart work.

Bob couldn't think of a sassy answer. He thumped his chair forward and said, "About like you'd expect." He stood from the table. "Guess I'll go get myself duded up. These clothes are a little rancid."

And Wood said, "I'm in that room too, Bob. Don't mess up my things."

Bob sneaked from the overcoat a cigar butt smoked on September 7th after the Blue Cut robbery and then he scurried up the stairs to a room with twin beds and a cot in it. The cot was against an east wall that was covered with the corset advertisement pages from newspapers and Wood's razor, comb, toothbrush, and toothpowder were laid out at the foot of the cot on his folded green blanket as if it were a toiletries salesman's display. The twin bed next to the mullioned north window was Charley's, the mating bed was Bob's, a slat bed with a duck feather mattress that lumped like melons as he slept. Close to the closet door was a lady's white dresser and screwed to it was an oval dresser mirror where Bob could watch himself practice moves and feints he hoped to use, veering left and fanning his thumb like a gunslinger's hammer, blowing muzzle smoke from his index finger.

Bob kicked under his bed with his foot and hooked out a shoebox. He sat on his mattress with the box in his lap, removed the lid and clamped it against his neck with his chin. He rolled the cigar butt inside the white handkerchief with the cock-eyed holes cut into it, and poked it into a corner. He squirmed his boots off and flung off his month-old clothes until all he wore was a nasty union suit, then he took on loan a towel and cake of Ivory soap and a tile brush from Ida's pink bedroom across the hall, and he crept downstairs and across the cold earth to the cattle lot and broad water tank.

Two calves stared with worry as he stripped off his underwear and they trotted six feet when he shooed them. Scum floated on the water but rocked away when he washed his hand across the surface. He lifted a snow white leg and sent it into cold water, then crashed over into the tank with such noise Martha was at the kitchen window when he stood, catching his breath. She smirked at his nakedness, so he lowered and rotated. His neck, wrists, and ankles were black in the creases and murked with road dust and wood smoke and his skin was reddened wherever he scoured with the tile brush. A breeze puckered the water and cast goose pimples over his back. He bent over to rinse soap from his hair and shook water like a hound. The calves backed a little and to terrify them more he smacked the water so that a clear sheet curved over the tank and tattered and tore apart in the air. And then he noticed an amused Dick Liddil standing as close as a tailor. He was hatless and his blond hair straggled in the wind.

"How long you been there?"

"Just now arrived. Did I miss much?"

Bob stalked the Ivory soap cake on the water. "Not unless you've never seen a man wash his dirty carcass before."

Dick said, "Hear you've been to the Indian Territories."

Bob scrubbed an elbow as if that could shift the conversation elsewhere.

But Dick continued, "It's all anyone can talk about."

Bob checked his other elbow. "Don't try to fish me because I won't hook."

"Is that what the Indian Territories do? Make you turn over a new leaf?"

Bob swished his hands underwater and reexamined his nails. "That territories business is one of Jesse's stories, is all."

"You've got a big pecker for being such a little squirrel."

"Is that what you come over here to see?"

Dick bent for the towel and some good nature slid from his face. He was perhaps five feet seven, an inch shorter than Bob, and twenty-nine years old. He grew a comma of light brown hair on his lower lip and his combed mustache was curled with wax so that he looked a Southern cavalier, and he considered himself a ladies' man in spite of a right eye that strayed toward his cheek, the result of a childhood accident with a stick. He tossed the towel at Bob's nose and nibbled his mustache as Bob rubbed his hair wild. "Your brother said Jesse kept you on in Kansas City some extra days. What was the reason?"

Bob covered his face with the towel as his mind motored a second or two. "Well, I'm not at liberty to say exactly. I will confess we had ourselves an adventure or two, the like of which *you'll* never experience, but as for details and whatnot, that would be confidential."

Bob straddled the tank and then hopped to the dirt. Drops of tank water pocked the earth where the cattle had churned it soft. Bob swatted the dust from his union suit and started to climb into it but Dick said, "Why don't you burn that instead," and Bob bunched it and surrounded himself with the towel.

Dick said, "Let me ask you this: did Jesse mention that me and Cummins were in cahoots?"

"Is that so?"

Dick smiled. "Oh dear. I've went on and said too much."

"Who else is partners with you two?"

"You'll just go and squawk about it to Jesse."

"Ed Miller?"

"He'll cut our throats if he finds out. You don't know him like I do. You do Jesse dirt, you connive behind his back, he'll come after you with a cleaver."

"He can be spiteful, can't he?"

"Ho. You're darn tootin'."

Bob cleaned between his toes with the towel and said, "Don't see why he'd give a dang since he and Frank've called it quits and scattered the James gang hither and yon."

Dick assayed Bob's countenance for clues about what he understood or withheld but saw neither cunning nor deception. "Boy, you are slow as peach mold, you know that? Tucker Bassham's already gone for ten years and Whiskeyhead Ryan's in jail; soon as one or the other feels the urge he can give the government all he knows about Jesse and then go out on the street scot-free. Jesse don't want us giving ourselves up and he don't want us getting caught and he don't want us gathering loot except if he's in charge.''

The two heard a gate creak and saw big Wilbur strew a shock of garden corn stalks into a feed trough next to the barn. He doused the stalks with salt water from a tea kettle in order to lure the milk cows, and then seemed inclined to visit his shivering younger brother. But Bob shook his head in the negative and Wilbur changed his mind and maundered across the yard to the kitchen, banging the tea kettle with his knee. It was near dusk and the weather had cooled and Bob wanted a coat, but instead he asked, ''So what're you three cahoots cooking up?''

''Don't know that I should say.''

''Much loot in it?''

''Thousands and thousands of dollars.''

''I don't want to wheedle the dang news from you, Dick.''

''How about let's leave it a mystery and then we won't neither one of us regret our little chat.''

Bob clamped the tile brush with his teeth and crossed his eyes at Dick in a measure of exasperation, then clutched the towel around himself and reached down for his holster. Dick pinned it with his boot. ''Let me carry your six-gun for you, Bob.''

Because of the brush in his mouth, Bob's ''All right'' came out ''Awri.'' And he had taken no more than two strides toward the house when he felt Dick cuddle to him with the cold revolver insisted under the towel and blunt against his scrotum. Bob let the brush drop and shrank a little from the ice of the nickel barrel. He said, ''Feeling lonely, are you, Dick?''

''You and me, we horse around and josh each other with lies and tomfoolery, but now and then we need to get down to brass tacks. Which is: you so much as mention my name to Jesse, I'll find out about it, you better believe that. And then I'll look you up, I'll knock on your door, and I will be mad as a hornet, I will be *hot*.''

''You be careful with that iron.''

Dick removed the revolver and smacked it into Bob's leather holster. He walked beside Bob. ''You know where I stand on these matters and that's all there is to it. We can be friendly as pigs from now on.''

"Could be I'll never see Jesse again."

Dick drew the screen door wide for Bob and restricted it with his shoulder as he pried his boots off on a mud-caked iron jack. He said, "Oh no. I've got a hunch about it. Jesse will come a courtin' Ed and Jim and me, and then he'll find himself in the neighborhood and call on them two Ford brothers. Jesse don't miss much. He has a sixth sense."

Inside, cooking smells maneuvered through the house: cow liver, sweet potatoes, stewed onions, cabbage—scents that were as assertive as colors. Dick moved sock-footed into the kitchen, bumped Clarence aside, tendered Martha's rump with his hand and removed it before she could skirt from him, and spoke heartily to the assembled. Bob went to his sister's bedroom, where he ripped the brown shop paper from his clothes and dressed in his new white underwear. Over Martha's chiffonier was a square mirror that he could tilt to admire himself from toe to topknot, and he'd just noted his cowlicked, straw-wild, ginger brown hair when an intuition sickened him and he rushed the stairs to the room overhead, where Wood and Charley were rooting through his mementoes. The shoebox was crushed, newspaper clippings skidded on the floor with each wind puff, everything he'd stolen or saved was sinking shadowed cups in his soft pillow: a compass and protractor encased in a box of blue velvet; a green tin of playing cards missing only the three of clubs, once used by a Mr. J. T. Jackson at Ed Miller's Thursday poker game; an item that was short as a thumb and wound in a linen handkerchief; a barkwood pocket knife with two blades and an awl, filched from Jesse's stepbrother, John; a magnifying glass; brittle licorice that no one could chew; a sardine can that clattered when Wood shook it; a bag sachet that smelled of lavender.

Bob shouted in a juvenile voice, "You two have some nerve!"

Wood looked at him with more consternation than guilt. "What *is* this junk?"

Charley said, "Thievings; isn't that right, Bob." He was at the nightstand drawer, stirring his finger among yellowed book pages and tattered newspaper columns that were knitted together with shirt pins. His brother bodied Wood aside and gleaned the articles on the bed as Charley peered at a Civil War photograph and skittered it into the drawer. "This ain't Jesse."

"You don't know that."

"Never wore no mustache; never was anywheres *near* a cannon."

"I can't even calculate what I'm lookin' at," said Wood.

"Ever since he was a child, Bob's collected whatsoever he could find about the James brothers. Got himself a little museum in this room."

Bob rammed the nightstand's drawer closed. "Next time you snoop around up here, you'd better strap on a shootin' iron."

Charley showed his buck teeth when he smirked. "You can see how scared I am."

Bob scowled at Wood and said, "You too, Wood Hite. You cross me again and I'll put a bullet through your head."

"Now is that any way to talk?" Charley asked.

But Wood simply extended his fingers to Bob's chest and disdainfully flicked a wooden button on Bob's union suit and Bob sat on the mattress as if he'd been muscled backward. Wood sneered, "You better recollect who my cousin is. You seem to've misremembered that Jesse loves me like the Good Book. Jesse's my insurance. You can play like you're a dangerous person with people at the grocery store, but don't you misremember who you'll be accounting to if I so much as have my feelings hurt. I'd be gooder than you've been to me if I was in your shoes."

Martha climbed a stair riser and called. "Do I have to yell suwee?"

Charley said, "Why don't everybody make up and be pleasant for once? Why don't we pass the evening like pleasant human beings?"

IT WAS THE EVENING of September 19th and President Garfield was on the New Jersey shore, fighting chills and nausea as surgeons talked about his degeneration and newspaper correspondents smoked cigarettes on the seaside lawn. An aneurysm that had developed over a ruptured artery apparently collapsed at about ten o'clock, for the president woke from sleep, complaining of an excruciating pain close to his heart. And at 10:35 p.m. James A. Garfield died.

Perry Jacobs stopped by the Harbison place at noon on the 20th to pass along that telegraphed news and he sipped coffee with Martha and Bob as Wood Hite and Dick Liddil packed for a trip east to Kentucky. When Dick came downstairs with his coat and bags, Martha kissed him on the lips and whispered something to his ear. He smiled and said, "Oh, goodness! Maybe I'll change my mind." But then Wood was behind Dick and bumping him toward the door and after some speedy farewells they were off.

They rode east sullenly, rarely speaking, rocking on their horses. Wood read a penny newspaper four inches from his nose under the brim shade of his hat; Dick counted crows and chewed sunflower seeds and watched the geography snail by. Brittle weeds slashed away from the horses; children clattered down cornrows with gunnysacks after school, jerking orange ears from the stalks; a young brakeman in a mackinaw sat on a freight car with a slingshot that knocked on far-off barn doors. "Cecil?" someone called out. It took them a week to reach St. Louis, where Dick caroused with someone named Lola who danced on a grand piano. Then the two ramped up onto a Mississippi River barge and worried throughout the long slide south to Cairo. The outlaws couldn't swim and their water fright contaminated the animals so that they reared and bucked and showed their teeth with each crabbed movement on the current.

Then as the two outlaws crossed southwest Kentucky from Cairo, Wood began nagging and carping at Dick for his pettiness, his chicanery, and his philandering with Martha, pushing on to an imaginary problem with the divvy at Blue Cut. It was Wood's contention that Dick stole one hundred dollars from his grain sack in the second-class coach and that he'd never turned it over to Frank when they apportioned the loot afterward. But that was all a smokescreen for his trepidation that Dick would try to romance Wood's stepmother, Sarah, who was known to be susceptible to passionate attentions.

Wood's father was Major George V. Hite, once the richest man in Logan County, Kentucky. He owned a grocery store, a mansion, and six hundred acres eleven miles south of Russellville, close to the Tennessee border, and was said to be worth one hundred thousand dollars when just one dollar represented a man's daily wage. But he'd invested in the commodities market and lost so much on tobacco and cotton that he filed for bankruptcy in 1877. His first wife, Nancy James Hite, died a year later and he was sundered. After a suitable period of mourning, however, he began to consort with and court Sarah Peck, who was referred to by a newspaper reporter as "the pertest and prettiest widow in all this whole country." And yet the community was scandalized by their eventual engagement, and the Hite clan was incensed, for Sarah was considered carnal and licentious and was even rumored to have been enjoyed by Jim Cummins in the course of an Easter visit. When Major Hite married the widow, most of his children left the mansion in anger, but the James gang would return whenever they needed seclusion and Jim Cummins made a second career of boasting that he'd tampered with Sarah in a pantry as pork chops burned in a skillet. And by the time Wood skidded the main gate aside and rode onto the Hite property, his case against Dick was so repeatedly and tempestuously made that the two were not speaking at all and only Dick's promise not to toy with her feelings kept him from being prohibited from the grounds.

Beautiful thoroughbred horses milled about on the green pasture, colts dashed along the fence and cut away for no particular reason. Two ex-slaves threshed in a golden field a quarter-mile off, a black woman pinned laundry on a clothesline, and Mrs. Sarah Hite was weeding among the withered remains of a vegetable garden, five acorn squash sacked in her apron. One rolled out and dropped to the earth when she waved.

Wood said, "She eats men alive."

Dick licked sunflower seeds from his palm and never paid attention to her; nor did he look at Sarah much at supper when she sat next to her emaciated husband, speaking wifely courtesies into his black ear trumpet. And because his shyness and silence were beginning to show, Dick leaned over his pot roast and asked, "You cook this, ma'am?"

She shook her head and said, "I've got a nigger woman."

Hite inclined toward his wife with the trumpet. "Hmmm?"

"Dick asked if I cooked this."

"Did you?"

"No."

Major Hite picked up Sarah's white hand, which was wristed with lace, and showed it to the assembled like a lovely greeting card. "You boys ever seen such dainty nubbins?" He grinned at her red-faced resentment and said, "Sarah's my plump little plum."

Dick looked at his knife and fork and Wood said, "She knew what he was like when she married him."

After dessert the Hites and Dick repaired to the broad porch, where they were seated on chairs that the butler, John Tabor, skidded across the floor. The talk was dull and void of thought, consisting almost entirely of observations that were manifestly true—the railroads make money going each way; it's no fun being sick; sometimes you don't know you've eaten too much until you get up from the table. At eight-thirty the old man stood with pain and yawned until his body shuddered and said, "Morning comes awful early." But Sarah said she wasn't sleepy and stayed with a wicker rocker and embroidered daisies on a kitchen hot pad as the men chatted—Wood and Dick and George Hite, Jr., the grocery store manager, who was grotesquely hunchbacked and lame. Wood prevailed upon Dick to sing Confederate Army ballads and Dick complied in a tenor voice that was so tragic and piercing that Sarah momentarily put down her needlework. Then a stillness came and there was only the creak of the chairs and the Hite brothers retired, and though Wood scowled at his young stepmother, she obstinately remained in her rocker with her stitching, a squat candle between her black, buttoned shoes, a silver thimble clinking whenever she drove the needle.

Sarah was buxom and broad as a stove and was considered voluptuous. Her eyes were bright blue, the sort that can seem a mosaic of silver and white, and her hair was the color that was then called nut brown, and it curtained her cheeks as she concentrated on the flower's yellow disk.

Finally, Dick said, "I guess we're the night owls, you and me."

She simpered but did not look up. "I'm glad."

"Oh?" Dick asked, as if he were Clarence. "How come?"

She made an ambiguous motion with her shoulders and smiled at her shoes. "I could listen to you sing and carry on until sunrise. You have a real pleasant disposition; and you're interesting to look at; and, I don't know, you sort of make me warm all over."

"I'm what they call a worldling."

"Well, I knew there had to be a name for it."

"You and the Hite family don't get along, if I'm to trust Wood and his version of the situation."

She let her hands and sewing sink in the navy blue lap of her dress. Orange candlelight raised and lowered on her face and she tucked her bottom lip with her teeth. "We hate each other like poison, if you want to know the truth. Most of the Hites wouldn't spit on me if I was on fire."

Dick never missed even the most concealed insinuation. He said with a wink of his skewed right eye, "They say when a woman catches fire you're supposed to roll her around on the ground and cover her with your body." And Sarah laughed so loudly she clamped her mouth, and then called him a naughty tease and said he tickled her to such an extent her cheeks were burning up. And then Wood was at the screen door in a nightshirt, his hair as sprigged as a houseplant. "Isn't it just about bedtime?" he asked, and Dick kissed Sarah's dainty nubbins as he exited for the second-floor bedroom.

Dick took off his boots and clothes and tucked himself under the bedsheet. He wacked the pillow, he rustled and stirred, he announced that he'd drunk too much coffee. He saw Wood in the bunk across from him as he arose in his longjohns and woolen socks. Wood's eyes glared at him. "I need to visit the privy something terrible," Dick said.

What he did was sneak down the first-floor hallway and touch the master bedroom door two inches inward to see Major George Hite alone in the room, puttering a snore. Dick did not allow the screen door to clap as he went outside. He walked around the rocking chair and across a cold lawn to a two-hole outhouse in back. The board walls showed interior candlelight at each severance and crack. Dick paused and looked around at the night, then slid into the outhouse and shut the door carefully behind him.

The candle was tilted in a tin cup that was nailed below a small side window and Sarah sat next to it, prim as a child, her dress hiked up and collected like laundry, her pale thighs squeezed and puckered a little with fat, her ankles thin above her shoes. He could see her blush and her downcast eyes were a maiden's, but she seemed less shocked than amused. She said, "This is embarrassing."

"You can go ahead and do your duty; I don't mind."

"Well now, I've sort of got stagefright with a strange man in the commode with me."

"You look awful pretty."

"Do I?"

"I've never seen such well-shaped limbs."

She glanced fleetingly at the bent pronouncement at his crotch and then at his chill blue eyes. "Is Wood awake?"

"Just me."

She contemplated her knees for a moment and then blew out the candle. She rose with her navy blue dress still bunched at her waist and shyly moved toward Dick. She said, "I bet you thought I was a lady."

DICK LIDDIL stole into the house at eleven o'clock, crawled up the stairs so that the footboards wouldn't creak, and saw that Wood's bunk was empty. He reclined on the mattress for a minute or two, contemplating causes and effects, then sat up and removed his revolver from its scabbard and slid it under the woolen blanket like something pleasurable. And he awoke at sunrise to the calm voice of Wood Hite in middle sentence: "—moonlight and held a conversation with myself over what I should and shouldn't do. Should I blow the sidewinder to kingdom come? Should I chop his perty face into hash? Maybe I could cut his oysters off like a steer."

He sat on the bunk across from Dick, his eyes pouched and green with sleeplessness, his nose colossal beneath the strip of daylight allowed by a window shade. Dick's pistol had somehow been fished from its place and was squashed under Wood's thigh. Wood continued, "But I took into account our months together on the wrong side of the law and what I come up with is you and me should duel; and may the best man win."

"You're making this more grievous than you oughta, Wood."

Wood smacked him with a pillow. "The honor of the entire Hite family is at stake!"

So the two accordingly stood back to back on the cold, dew-white lawn, revolvers raised like ear contraptions, Dick in his longjohns and boots. Wood created gentlemen's rules for the duel as Dick kidded and negotiated and finally counseled Hite about the jeopardy to his very being that was forthcoming. Nevertheless, Wood counted out numbers in a stately, funereal measure and the two marked each word with a stride, greening the grass with their boot tracks. But Dick was a man who left nothing to chance; not only did he angle toward a broad ash tree as he walked, but he turned at nine instead of ten and fired at Wood's left ear.

Wood ducked in reaction to the gunshot and the sizzle of a miss that veered wide of his skull, then he crouched and spun around to see the green lawn in streaks that slewed toward the ash and a flicker of yellow hair next to the gray bark. He clutched at his trigger and the revolver jumped so violently it sprained his wrist and a chunk of ash tree exploded. Dick bent out and shot at Wood a second time—his arm kicked up, there was a noise akin to a window that has crashed down in its sash, blue gunsmoke ballooned and then dwindled, and another noise like the snare of a saw cut the air near Wood's neck.

The gunpowder noise surprised Wood's relatives and servants from sleep and they rushed down the hallway to the screen door, closing robes around their nightshirts and nightgowns, as Dick discharged his last round and crackled branches in a woodrow next to the road. He snapped the hammer into three detonated cartridges, saw the Hites behind the screen door, and ran to them in the clomping, clumsy way of a cowhand unused to his legs as Wood shot at his back twice, neglecting to lead Dick each time.

Dick struck the last riser on the stairs with his toe and walloped into a slide across the porch. Major Hite flattened his nose to the screen as he hollered, "Here now! Stop this! Wood? Wood! I won't have any gunplay on my property! I've told you a thousand times."

Dick slithered toward the old man's bare feet and Wood shot another time. It shattered a chair strut and nailed a dark hole in the windowsill. Major Hite stamped down on a throw rug and yelled, "Wood! You listen to me! No more!"

Wood looked down the revolver muzzle and clicked the chamber around. "That was my last bullet anyways." He eyed the revolver at a bird feeder. "Something must be wrong with the sight on this thing."

George Hite, Jr., was bent next to his father. He said, "You'll notice I wasn't in on it, Daddy. Don't even own a shooting iron."

Major Hite looked down at the man cowering near his white calves. "What's the reason for this ruckus? Huh?"

Dick saw Sarah slink over to her husband, pink slippers on her feet and a patchwork quilt shut around her. Dick arose and said, "Me and Wood, we woke up on the wrong side of the bed this morning, is all."

Major Hite showed no signs of hearing Dick; he merely waited for the man's mouth to stop moving and then said, "You know what? You've worn out your welcome, young fellow."

DICK LEFT AT ONCE and rode north as far as Russellville, where he rented a room with a concealed stairway above a blacksmith's shop and worked infrequently for ten cents per hour and chewed tobacco on a store bench with veterans of the Mexican-American War. Afternoons he roistered with Mrs. Sarah Hite when she could visit town, or she arranged strange venues with Dick, sunrise on Mud River, or midnight near a revival tent, or noon underneath a railroad trestle, where she smeared a bedsheet flat over the weeds.

Her go-between in arranging these meetings was the ex-slave, John Tabor. He'd stand in the alley as the blacksmith rammed the ceiling overhead with a rod and Dick would skip downstairs in his socks; he'd throw twigs at Dick's window, announce a time and location when the sash was raised, and then slip off into darkness.

One Thursday at nightfall, John Tabor lightly rapped a restaurant's window near the table where Dick swabbed stew from his dish with pumpernickel bread. Dick went outside and the butler gave him a come hither look that lured him into an alley. John Tabor was reed thin, close to fifty, the brown of saddle leather, and he liked to claim a resemblance to the Great Pacificator, Senator Henry Clay. He twisted his coat collar up and blew in his fists and invented Alaska out of the nip of the air. "I won't be delivering no more notes," he said. "I won't be fetching Sarah no more for you, neither."

Dick saw that his checkered dinner napkin was still tucked under his belt. He removed it and stroked his wide mustache with a corner. "You in a snit, John?"

"Yeah. Uh huh." He looked over his shoulder into the empty street and then he bowed closer to Dick. "Wood seen me and it don't make him happy, a colored man owning a white lady's secrets, setting her onto a backdoor man which ain't her husband. He don't know much yet but he *suspects*. That's more than plenty right there. He'll cut me dead, I don't be careful."

"Naw."

"Said he would. Said he'd stick an axe betwixt my eyes."

"She does want to meet me though, doesn't she? You've come so far, you may as well tell me where she'll be and make them your last words."

Tabor gripped his coat and walked into the wind but as Dick hunched next to him the butler said, "At creekside, over near the pigsty; tomorrow evening, about nine. Now my mouth's gonna be shut, as far as you're concerned. You ain't gonna hear no more from John Tabor."

Dick Liddil saddled his bay mare at seven the next evening and rode south in a slow walk, his stomach so queasy that he submitted to one of Jesse's prescriptions and ate salts of tartar and powdered gum arabic. And as he crossed onto the Hite acres, panic overtook him; he sometimes circled his horse around to check the night woods, to decipher the crackle of autumn leaves, to cock his Navy Colt at a raccoon that truckled into the creek. Trees groaned and sighed as the wind pressed against them; grasses rolled with the soft susurration of mourners whispering in a candled parlor; and Dick was conjuring phantoms, he was as spooked as a man alone in a room who watches a closet doorknob turn and the door ever so slowly open.

He crossed a meadow and motivated his mare down the creek bank, where she sloshed in water that was as shallow as the coronets of her hooves. The pigsty was a low barn with a roof over the feedboxes and the rest a mud roll-around inside an ill-made slat fence. Dick creaked his saddle and read his pocket watch with a matchstick and looked around for Sarah. He slid off the mare and let her drag her reins over to leafmeal as he walked to the brow of the hill.

Hogs oinked and grunted and climbed over each other for corner food. Weeds lowered under the wind and apprehensions spidered his back. He wandered about and broke sticks in his fists. The hogs snorted and crowded and there was a sound like pages being torn from a book and pigs screeched around a sow that was greedily wolfing something down as she trotted away from the corner. Dick leaned on the sty's fence like a slow country boy and asked, "What the heck are you critters chewing on?"

Then Dick saw a shoe and ankle wobble as the hogs shoved and scuffled above a muddied wool coat. His skin nettled cold and water came to his eyes and he screamed at the animals as he swatted them in the hocks with his hat. They scampered and squealed and snorted the earth. A sow remained and wrenched at a cord of sinew that made the body jerk but Dick shot a bullet that punched into the mud and the sow scurried back with the others.

The wool coat was screwed around to the side and one sleeved arm was crooked beneath the man's back while the other lolled over the bottom slat on the fence. Dick could see that the skin on the man's knuckles was brown but that was the sole clue that this was John Tabor, for most of his throat and face were eaten off, there were only red sinews and laces of muscle and cartilage and the blood-slick bones of the skull.

Then there was a low moan that could not have issued from Tabor, that came from the pigsty, and Dick crouched with his Navy Colt lifted toward a collection of juts and ovals and shadows. "Wood?" he shouted. He clicked back the hammer, steadied the quavering revolver with his other hand, and shouted, "Jesse?"

The shadows broke and reconnected and he saw that the creature was closer by a foot and Dick jibbed to the side like a boy playing dodge ball, and he listened for the corduroy sound of a careful slide of iron from leather. "Can't we talk about it, Jesse? Or Wood?"

The creature moved and Dick called out, "I'll shoot! So help me, I'm scared enough to be real undependable with this Colt." There was a snuffle and a sob and he called out, "Sarah?" and he turtled around the sty, his Colt raised, his coat sleeve skating off the fence rail, until he could make out Mrs. Hite. She was feeble with shock and her eyes were cloudily bottled by tears. The acid stink of her vomit was on her dress and for one insane moment Dick was ready to murder the woman because she smelled bad.

"Did Wood kill him?"

Sarah's neck seemed restrained by a shackle and then she was able to nod, twice.

"You tell the sheriff that. You tell the sheriff that Wood Hite is a killer. You swear out a warrant for his arrest, but don't you say word one about the James gang, and don't let my name cross your lips."

And then Dick walked by her without even nicking her dress, sliding down the creek bank to his mare. Sarah was standing in the same position, motionless, staring at the remains, her hands gloved with blood and stalled at her sides as if sewn there. Dick climbed into the saddle and trotted his horse westward across the Hite meadows and never saw the woman again.

JESSE JAMES RODE INTO KENTUCKY in October as he'd promised Clarence Hite he would, but he went by way of Louisville and then south into Nelson County, where his cousin Donny Pence was a sheriff. He stayed a week, hunting pigeons and quail in the daytime with Congressman Ben Johnson and playing cards in the Pence sitting room at night. Johnson would later retell how they were reading the newspaper one evening when Donny gave J. T. Jackson a page with an article about the James gang robbing a train in Texas. The man slapped the newspaper down and walked over to a windowpane, there scratching into the glass with a diamond ring: *Jesse James* and *October 18th, 1881*. He then turned to the congressman and said, "I want you to be my witness that I was in Kentucky on this date and not in Texas." And then, having compromised himself, Jesse forgot about going south to Logan County and instead journeyed west to Missouri, stopping off in Saline County at the cabin and sixty miserable acres owned by Ed Miller.

He rattled the cabin's cloth-screened door on its hook and looked around at the yard, at a bruised mule harness, a perilous rake, and a rusted plow embedded in soil, and then Jesse looked back at the door and saw Ed Miller with a gun in his hand and fright in his eyes. Ed asked, "You come by for a visit?"

"You going to let me in or do I have to talk through the screen?"

Miller flipped up the hook and Jesse pulled the door, passing the speechless man as he walked inside.

The room was a mess: in it was a kitchen table on which smeared dishes were stacked, a green suede of mold on their caked meats and rinds; newspapers were shocked like corn against a couch, a chair was tipped over, a patched shirt was draped over a closet door, a cat was on the kitchen cutting board licking something from the sink. "You aren't much of a housekeeper, are you?"

"You didn't just *happen* by," Miller said.

"Why not?" Jesse glanced at the gun and Miller put it on the grimy table. Jesse said, "Clell kept himself so untidy you could rub his neck and make dirt worms." He sat down on a ringed rug and nodded toward a sagging couch. "Go ahead and take the load off your feet."

Miller did as instructed and looked out the window, twisting his unclean hair with his fingers. His clothes were as wrinkled as crumpled paper, his fingernails were outlined with filth, a corner of his mouth was stained brown with gravy or tobacco juice.

"You ought to get yourself a wife."

Miller glared briefly at Jesse and then shrugged. "I was going to ask Martha—Charley's sister? I was going to ask her if she could imagine it, but I guess Wood has plans of his own, and there's always Dick Liddil getting in the way. I've give it some thought." He picked something out of his hair and wiped it on a pillow. He couldn't seem to put his eyes on Jesse; his right foot rapidly tapped the floor.

"Your crops in?"

"Don't got much," Miller said. "A garden patch and pasture. I was sick at planting time."

"How you feeling now?"

He glanced fleetingly at Jesse and asked, "Why?"

"You're acting queer."

"You and me, we haven't been just real good friends lately. It's not your fault, you understand. You hear talk though."

"Talk."

Miller explained, "People tell you things."

"Give me an example."

Miller sighed. "Jim Cummins come by. Oh and Jim says—you know those boys got caught for the Blue Cut deal?—Jim says he got word—don't ask me where—that you're planning to kill them."

"Why would I do that?"

Miller shot a glance at Jesse's gun hand and then reestablished his gaze on the yard. "It's just talk probably."

"To shut 'em up?"

"Just talk."

"Cummins say anything else?"

"Nope. That was it basically."

"It don't explain why you're scared."

Miller looked at Jesse with watery eyes and spit on his mouth, light glinting off the oils on his skin. "I'm in the same position, you see? I was *petrified* when I saw you ride up!"

"I just happened by, Ed."

"Suppose you heard gossip though. Suppose you heard Jim

Cummins come by here. You might've put two and two together and thought we were planning to capture you or Frank and get that reward. Isn't true, but you might've suspected it."

Jesse got up, leaving coins from his pockets on the rug, and jiggled a pants leg over his boot. "Haven't heard a lick of gossip lately." He looked out at the road and at a sky that was pink with sunset. He grinned at Miller and said, "I'm glad I happened by."

Miller worked at a smile and said, "Me too."

"I want to put your mind at rest."

"I've got six hundred dollars stashed away; I don't need any governor's reward."

"It's the principle of the thing too."

Miller pulled himself to his feet and swept a hand over a plate to shoo away flies. They sewed in the air and resettled. "I can't offer you supper; my cupboards are empty."

"How about if we go for a ride? I could buy you something to eat in town and then be on my way."

Miller gathered his mare in the paddock and saddled it as Jesse sat on a gelding with the night all around him. Then they trotted westerly, their bodies jumping off the saddles until the horses eased into a graceful lope and then into a walk. A farmer with a hayrake recognized Ed Miller and waved and Jesse nudged his horse to the right so that he couldn't be seen. He said, "It's a great month, October." Some minutes later he said, "Your mare's cheating on her right leg. Looks like she might be wind-galled."

Miller couldn't get himself to say anything.

Jesse pretended a cinch problem, slowing his horse, and said, "You go on ahead, partner. I'll catch up."

Miller slumped in his saddle and peered ahead.

Jesse gentled his gun from the leather holster at his left thigh and thought for a second or two before jogging his horse ahead.

When he got close enough, Jesse angrily said, "You ought to get better at lying."

Miller stopped his horse but apparently couldn't persuade himself to drop a hand to his pistol until he'd spun around, and just then Jesse tripped the hammer and a cartridge ball pounded into Miller's cheek, snapping his head to the side and propelling his body off the mare so that he walloped onto the road.

Jesse stepped his gelding forward through gunsmoke and peered down at a man whose mouth and eyes were open in the rapt look of death. He got off the horse and tugged at Ed Miller's legs, swatting weeds flat beneath the man's coat, swishing leaves aside with each surge, towing the body under sumac and elm trees.

The mare was found browsing in its paddock two days later, a saddle rolled counterclockwise on its cinch until it was almost under the animal's belly, the saddle fenders and stirrups sloppily bird-winged. Ed Miller was not found for many weeks and by then the coroner could only guess that the body was male and not yet middle-aged, it was little more than a bird-pecked skeleton with yellow teeth and a hank of black hair in clothes that had squashed flat in the rains.

Jesse disappeared.

DICK LIDDIL SOLD HIS HORSE in Kentucky and took a train to Kansas City, where he spent October and November in the apartment of Mattie Collins, his common-law wife. They'd met in a courtroom following her cross-examination by a prosecuting attorney. She'd killed her brother-in-law, Jonathan Dark, as he was punching his wife and she pleaded her case so convincingly that the gunshot was ruled justifiable. Dick had just been paroled from the Missouri penitentiary in which he was serving time as a horse thief and in which he'd developed an interest in legal manipulations. Mattie Collins seemed sharp, prudential, accomplished, and when she stepped down from the stand, Dick leaned over a bannister to whisper, "I admire your spirit." Within weeks they were a couple. Their marriage was more tempestuous than happy, though, and Dick periodically separated himself from Mattie, repeatedly coming back just as he did in October, with a robbery in his past, anxiety in the present, and a promise of constancy in the future. He lied to Mattie about the previous two months; she grew petulant and burned a mincemeat pie and pitched asparagus soup at him; she coldly apprised him of his limitations and cruelty, his inability to love, the shipwreck he'd made of her life, and by midnight they were compromised.

He passed his days with sleeping and pool and penny-ante poker. Mattie took him shopping and made Dick buy her, over the course of the month, a veiled black hat, an oyster shell pillbox, eight damask naperies, and white gloves with four pearl buttons that were near her elbows when worn. Liddil kept seeing Pinkerton operatives in every floorwalker, newspaper reader, or common man poking about in a store; in the evening he would insist there were prowlers and make a simpleton of himself by going out in his nightshirt and gun. And even in the pool hall he was getting the feeling that each shot was being watched, each comment was being overheard, until the creepy sensations at last grew so strong that he spun around and saw Jesse step into the lamplight. "You want to go for a ride?" he asked, and Dick could only agree.

It was the weekend after Thanksgiving and cold weather was so regular that they gave it little attention as they rode out from Kansas City in the morning. Jesse could wake up with a speech prepared, but Dick was just the opposite, sleep kept him in its grip until he'd been up and around for an hour; so as they rode east, Dick Liddil listened and Jesse slipped in and out of topics like a man at a clothing store trying on coats. He was happily loquacious and Dick was suspicious and unnerved, but he gradually relaxed and even grew drowsy within Jesse's spindle of yarns. His was a pelican's nest of unlinked sentences, fragmentary paragraphs, scraps of extraordinary information, variations on themes, but the issue he kept nipping at and tucking into everything else was that of the Jackson County court trial of Whiskeyhead Ryan.

He said a prosecuting attorney—who'd been elected on the basis of a campaign against the James gang—had released Tucker Bassham from a ten-year sentence in the Missouri penitentiary in return for his craven testimony about the Glendale robbery in 1879. According to the newspapers, Jesse said, Bassham took the stand and testified that it was Bill Ryan and Ed Miller who recruited him into the James gang, and he furthermore claimed that he was ordered around at Glendale by none other than Jesse James, who was the man who'd looted the express car. Jesse said Cracker Neck boys had bullied some witnesses, Tucker Bassham's house was burned to the ground, and railroad men were so scared off that none of them showed up in court; and yet, Whiskeyhead Ryan was convicted and sentenced to twenty-five years at Jefferson City. "I can't have that happening," Jesse said.

"How can you stop it?"

Jesse didn't say. He looked up into cross-hatching trees and said, "The wind serenades a purified man." He leaned back on his saddle cantle, his right hand on his bedroll supporting his weight. "Did I tell you that I moved out of Kansas City?"

"Where to?"

Jesse ignored that and said, "I'll strap a chair on my back and walk out into the wilderness some nights. The prairie sounds just like a choir."

"Are we going to your place?"

Jesse hooked a finger inside his cheek and flicked out the last of his tobacco chew. He wiped his finger clean on his trousers. "I got word about you and Wood. You two ought to patch things up."

"I'd still like to know where we're going."

"You seen Ed Miller lately?"

"Nobody has."

"Must've gone off to California." He scratched his neck beard and saw Dick looking at him with perplexity. He said, "If you were going to see Jim Cummins, wouldn't you follow this road?"

"I guess so."

"God damn it, Dick; use your head."

James R. Cummins had served in the Civil War with Frank and Jesse under Brigadier General Joseph O. Shelby and in the late seventies had participated in many of the James gang's robberies, though his reputation in Jackson and Clay counties was merely that of a common horse thief. His sister, Artella, married William H. Ford, Bob and Charley's uncle, in 1862, and it was partly that connection that caused the Ford brothers to join on with the gang. And it was to Bill Ford's farm near Kearney that Cummins withdrew after Blue Cut, prior to leaving the state for the hot springs in Arkansas.

He was already gone when Jesse and Dick approached the Ford house in late November, and Bill Ford was out in the meadow, doctoring sheep. His boy, Albert, scrunched at a tall window off the sitting room and stared at the two as they climbed down from their saddles at the rail fence. Then the raised curtain dropped from the boy's shoulder and the stuck mahogany door screeched open.

Albert was fourteen and good-looking in a choirboy way—his cheeks dimpled when he smiled and there was a scampishness to his eyes. He wore black trousers with a scrim of straw and mud on the cuffs, and a green pullover sweater that was rotted at both elbows. The boy said hello but was ignored for a minute as Jesse reconnoitered the yard and then gravely ascended the steps. Dick could see past Albert to the kitchen, where Mrs. Ford and her daughter, Fanny, stirred clothes in a steaming laundry boiler. Jesse peered into other rooms.

The boy asked Dick, "Are you friends of my pa's? Because if you are, he isn't here right now but you're welcome to sit a spell and enjoy our hospitality until he gets back."

"We're friends of Jim Cummins," Jesse said, and rolled a cigar in his mouth.

"Oh?" said the boy. His Uncle Jim had schooled Albert on how to answer a sheriff's interrogations. Albert gained thirty years, became sullen. "Well, it so happens he's been gone since August and never said where he gone to."

"I'm Matt Collins," Dick said, and shook the boy's hand.

"Very happy to meet you."

Jesse strode over and clenched the boy's hand and introduced himself. "Dick Turpin."

"Pleased to make your acquaintance."

Jesse smiled around his cigar but stalled the shake and crushed Albert's hand in his until the boy winced. Albert was about to cry out when Jesse clamped his left hand over the boy's mouth and yanked him into the yard. Dick softly shut the mahogany door.

Jesse manhandled the boy toward a red barn, once slamming Albert into a cottonwood tree so that he lost his wind and water came to his eyes. Dick shambled after the two, looking apprehensive and ashamed, backing sometimes so he could check the road, blowing on his red fingers.

When he was rear of the barn, Jesse twirled and threw the boy to the earth and stepped a boot onto Albert's throat. "Don't you yell," he said. "Don't you say nothin' except how I can find Jim Cummins. Matt, aim that six-shooter."

"Come on, Jesse! He's just a kid."

Jesse glowered at Dick for letting his name slip, then returned his attention to the choking boy. "He knows where his Uncle Jim is and that's gonna make him old pretty soon."

The boy shook his head as he brawled and kicked at Jesse.

"Maybe he doesn't know," Dick said.

"He knows." Jesse fell to his knees on the boy's biceps and Albert cried "Ow!" and his mouth was clutched closed in Jesse's left hand. Four bruises later colored his cheek like blue nickels. "You need to ask and ask sometimes. Sometimes a child won't remember much at first and then it'll all come back." He twisted the boy's ear like a clock wind-up and Albert's eyes showed agony, his body racked wildly, his boots thudded against the earth. "Just tell me about your Uncle Jim, that's all! Where'd he sneak off to; where's he hidin' out?"

The boy purpled and his swats at Jesse lessened with exhaustion. Jesse screwed the left ear more and Albert's scream was snared in Jesse's palm as he bent over with the cigar in his cheek and scrutinized the injury. "My gosh, I believe it's about to tear, sweetie. Just a little more to get her started, then I can rip your ear off like a page from a book."

Dick was slumped against the barn, sick to his stomach and overwrought. He moaned, "Let the kid *go*."

"He's lying."

"Jesus; he can't even talk!"

"Where's Jim?" Jesse asked, and then chanted it: "Where's Jim? Where's Jim? Where's Jim?"

"Quit it!" Dick yelled and slapped Jesse's hat off and immediately felt juvenile.

But Jesse squatted back and reconsidered and rubbed his hands on his thighs and the boy wept but couldn't make words. He wiped his nose and eyes with his hands and shuddered with sobs as he sucked for air and when at last he spoke his voice scaled like a child's. "You bastard! I don't *know* where he is and you won't *believe* me and you never gave me a *chance* you kept my mouth squeezed shut so I couldn't breathe and my ear, my ear's burning up, how'd you like me to do that to you? I never know where Jim is or when he comes so leave me alone, get off me, you son of a bitch!" Grunting, Albert bucked under Jesse and shouted again, "Get off!" and Jesse rose.

The boy rolled over and Dick walked around the barn and to the road, his hands fisted inside the pockets of his sheepskin coat, his neck splotched crimson with fury and disgust. When Jesse came forward, Dick was already in his Texas saddle. His face was moon white, his mouth was weak, and he looked at his boot toe in order to talk. "I'm worn out, Jesse. I can't—" He sighed and abandoned the sentiment and squinted down the road a mile until it was not more than a needle. The curdled sky was the color of tin and the woods were rose and gray in the twilight. Dick said, "My mind's all tangled anyway. Little deals like that just make me feel dirty."

Dick looked over to collect Jesse's reaction to this and was astonished to see him caved forward into his bay horse, his nose flattened against its neck and mane, his mouth in the crescent of a man noiselessly crying, a grimace of affliction in his face.

"You all right, Jesse?"

He nuzzled into the gelding's winter hide and muttered words that Dick couldn't master. The boy limped toward the Ford house, tenderly cupping his left ear and crossing his nose with his sweater sleeve.

Dick said, "Maybe you better ride on to wherever it is you're living now, and maybe I'll sell this animal and skeedaddle on over to Mrs. Bolton's and, you know, apologize to the Fords; put everything in its best light and so on."

Jesse accorded his back to Dick and scrubbed at his eyes with a blue bandana. "I must be going crazy."

Mrs. Ford and Albert and Fanny were at the tall windows but when Jesse glimpsed them the curtains closed. Jesse dickered with his left boot until it thrust into the stirrup and then he swung up with an elderly sigh and rode off without a word.

CONCERNING ROBERT WOODSON HITE and what Clarence called "Wood's scrape with the Negro," it is only necessary to know that Sarah swore to a murder warrant and Wood was arrested by two deputies from Russellville, the county seat, as he fished in a creek with a bamboo pole. He'd become cold-blooded and complacent and unconcerned, and he seemed so tractable that the marshal rented an upstairs room in a city hotel rather than lock him in the crowded jail. A man sat outside the room with a shotgun but he appears to have been bribed by the Hites, because Wood was able to walk down the stairs one afternoon and exit the hotel through the chandeliered lobby, and ride out of town on a saddled and provendered horse that was hitched next to a tobacco-store Indian. Thereafter records lose Wood Hite in his torpid pursuit of Dick Liddil until finally in December the cousin who was given Jesse's middle name was seen in Missouri.

Wood rode from Saturday night to Sunday morning, rocking sleepily inside a once-white goat-hair coat and long blue muffler, with his eyes shut and his left wrist tied to the saddle horn so he'd know if he slid. His face was bricked with windburn, his mustache was beaded and jeweled with ice. Snow made boards of his trousers and sleeves, his nose was injured with cold, and sometimes sleet sailed piercingly into whichever eye was open. Wood reached Richmond before six, warmed his cheeks and ears and backside at a railroad switchman's stove, and turned toward Mrs. Bolton's farmhouse. He saw Elias Ford near the corn crib shooing cattle toward the silage he'd scattered on the snow. Elias lectured the animals but his words were lost on the wind; quills of gray smoke left his mouth and disappeared. When he saw Wood he was startled, for he assumed it was Frank James who glowered at him from the road—the resemblance was strong even without the deception of darkness. Elias threw up his arm in greeting and then invited him in from the cold, pointing first to the stables and then to the farmhouse.

Wood walked his horse inside a stall, threw a moth-eaten brown blanket over it, and shoved a tin pail of oats at its nose to entice it to alfalfa. Then he walked to the kitchen with Wilbur, who was teetering with a milk can. Wood inserted his mittened hand in the can's twin grip to make the carry less clumsy. He shouted into the arctic wind, "How come it's always you does the chores?"

"Charley and Bob pay extree to Martha so's they don't have to!"

"Still don't seem fair!"

"Well," Wilbur said, then lost whatever their justification was and pitied himself for a moment or two. Then he shouted, "You know how I could tell it was you? You was carrying but the one six-shooter and the others carry two!"

Wood pulled the storm door for the man and he banged the milk can inside. Wilbur said, "I'd take a rag to my nose if I was you; it's unsightly."

Martha dumped bread dough onto a floured board and kneaded it with both hands. Oatmeal boiled in kettle water on the stove and her daughter yawned as she stirred it with a wooden spoon. Wilbur strad-dled a chair and blew into his hands; Wood removed mittens that dangled from sleeve clips like a child's. A coal-oil lamp was on the fireplace mantel and Martha saw her shadow leap and totter against the wall as the lamp was moved to the oak table. She turned and saw Wood thawing his right ear over the lamp's glass chimney as he stuffed a handkerchief up his coat sleeve.

"Look what the cat dragged in," she said.

He rotated his head to thaw the left ear.

"You come from Kentucky?"

Wood circled the chimney bowl with his hands and looked at Martha in order to construe what she did and did not know. "You mean the news never got this far?"

Wilbur enlightened his sister. "Wood and Dick had a shooting scrape month or two ago."

Elias closed the kitchen door behind himself and stamped his boots. "I thought you was Frank James when I saw you. I thought, 'What in tarnashun is Buck doing here?' " He buffeted his ears with his mitts and, apparently captivated by his earlier stupefaction, repeated the query: "I thought, 'What in tarnashun is Buck doing here when he's supposed to been gone East?' "

Bob was awake upstairs and sore from a night on the duck feather mattress. The north window was raised and the room was so cold spirits left him with each exhalation. He attached the flame of a match to a floor candle and lay back with his hands behind his head and a socked foot dangling near the heat as Charley snored and Dick mewled. Over the breakfast noises he heard his sister Martha say, "Look what the cat dragged in." Bob stared at the brown smudges of squashed spiders on the bedroom ceiling and pondered women and money until Wood's voice penetrated the kitchen chat.

Then Bob bolted out of bed and crouched next to the inch-wide crack of the door. He missed some words from Elias and then Martha said, "Cover the kettle, Ida." Bob could hear his sister trickle coffee beans into the box grinder, could hear a chair moan as someone skidded it on the boards. His sister said, "What on earth did you and Dick get into a fracas about?"

Bob scooted over to the cot and pressed his left hand over the Navy Colt beneath the pillow before he said with insistence, "Dick!"

Liddil automatically reached under the pillow but discovered the pistol trapped and saw Bob with his ginger hair jackstrawed, his eyelids welted green with worry and sleeplessness.

"Wood Hite's downstairs."

Dick boosted onto his right elbow and Bob released his hand from the pillow and the Navy Colt beneath it. Both listened to Wood claim yet again that Dick stole one hundred dollars from his Blue Cut loot— perhaps he'd said it so often he was now convinced that that was the cause of his ire. Martha cranked the coffee grinder and Wood claimed he'd been in the wilderness since October. He made no mention of Sarah or John Tabor or his recent arrest for murder.

From above the two heard Martha say, "I-da! Don't stick your thumb in the cream when you skim it! Goodness sakes."

And Wilbur said, "Dick told me a complete other version of that affray."

Bob and Dick listened as a chair screeched on the floor and Wood said, "You mean he's here?"

"Come in late last night."

Dick cocked his revolver and nestled it under the five woolen blankets on the cot and said, "I'm going to play possum." Bob shrank back, then crawled over to the nightstand between the twin beds as Elias told Wood to simmer down and Martha said, "Don't you boys get into a fracas up there. I've almost got breakfast cooked."

Bob extricated a loaded revolver from Charley's holster and hunkered low and shivered as Wood made a racket on the stairs. Wood slammed the bedroom door with his boot so that it bashed the wall and plaster dribbled from the doorknob's concussion and Charley jolted up. Wood strode into the room in his tall black boots and hairy coat, a blued Peacemaker outreached so that it was trained on Dick's twirled and blond mustache. Wood kicked the cot and it jounced an inch. He roared, "Come on outside, you oily sack of puke!"

Bob saw Dick flutter his eyes a little and then the wool blankets lashed with the gunpowder's detonation and Dick's shot smashed a hole in the bedroom door. Wood ducked aside from the shot and then regained himself and fired once at Dick and strewed pillow feathers, and a second time as Dick rolled off the mattress, the ball striking short and swiveling a slipper.

The noise muffled Bob's hearing until afternoon and left a high wail in his ears for days, so he couldn't make out what Dick or Wood or Charley was yelling, nor could he see them much because of the gunsmoke that seeped from the accumulated blankets and moved over the room like desultory weather. He cowered next to the slat bed and clicked back the hammer on the revolver, so scared he could neither shudder nor swallow nor shut his eyes though they burned and itched with gunsmoke. He created rules and modified them—if Wood shot at Bob, Bob would kill him; if he murdered Dick, Bob would kill him; if Wood merely confronted Bob with his gun, surely Bob would need to kill him; if he looked at Bob, then kill him—until it seemed there was nothing left but to kill Wood, kill him soon.

Bob saw Dick dive across to the lady's dresser and miss another shot at Wood that ripped a calendar down. Charley got out of bed and lunged to the windowsill, where he bent to squirm under the sash. Wood shot at Charley but missed; Bob nearly shot at Wood's neck but checked himself because of scruples and Charley slipped on the eave shingles and slid off the roof and wumped into a snowbank that was twelve feet below.

It was when Wood was foolishly turned toward Charley that Dick triggered a shot meant for Wood Hite's heart that snagged Wood's right arm like an angry wife. Blood flowered under the goat hair of his sleeve and Wood cradled his arm, cherished it for a second, then dipped under the gunsmoke to see Dick slithering backward on the seat of his red union suit to the nook next to the closet door. Wood pointed the Peacemaker at the paramour's groin but his injured muscles crippled with the revolver's weight and the cartridge ball veered into Dick's thigh and blood swatted the floorboards and bedsheets and Dick rocked with agony. Yet he lifted his Navy Colt again as Wood lurched around the doorjamb into the corridor and peeked back. The Colt's hammer snapped against an empty chamber and Wood switched his pistol to his left hand and squinted the muzzle's sights in line and it was then that Bob Ford, with calm intention and without malice, shot Robert Woodson Hite.

The round went in just right of his eyebrow and made a small button of red carnage that shut Wood's motor off. Bob felt his wrist and arm muscles twitch spasmodically when the revolver jolted and he saw Wood's skull jar to the side, saw Wood collapse to his knees as his brown eyes jellied and reason vanished and a trickle of blood lowered to his blue muffler, and then Wood fell to the left with a concussion that jostled the room, his cheek wetly smacking the boards.

Bob started to rise, but couldn't. Dick looked at him with consternation, as if Bob had grown antlers or spoken in tongues. Bob released the revolver onto his mattress as he rose over it and walked around to Wood with sickness in his stomach, an apricot in his throat.

Dick asked, "Has he passed away?"

Bob cupped his ear. "What?"

"Is he dead?"

Bob moved him some with his foot and Wood's maimed right arm slipped from the heap of his coat. Wood's chest swelled and gradually relaxed and then expanded again. Blood pooled wide as a birdbath under his skull. "He's still sucking air, but I think he's a goner."

Dick collared his thigh with his hands and choked it and brushed his eyes on either shoulder to quench the tears that collected. He said, "Hitch my leg up onto the bed so it won't dispense so easy."

He gritted his teeth when Bob seized his ankle and sagged back with a moan when Bob lifted it onto the mattress. Bob snuffed the candle on the floor and walked out to the corridor and looked down at Martha and Elias on the bottom stairs. "Maybe you oughta come up and wish him well on his journey."

Blood crept away from Wood and drooled into board cracks that languidly conducted it toward the door. Bob stared at it as the stairs creaked, and on hearing the rustle of his sister's dress, said to Martha, "He's losing all his stuffing."

She bumped past Bob, removed her apron, and carefully wadded it under the exit wound. "Do you want to be moved?"

Wood said nothing. His eyes were closed. A string of saliva hung from his mouth to the floor and it bowed with each cold draft of air. Martha tugged the blue muffler off and picked the blood-tipped hair from his brow.

Elias squatted next to her and canted his head to examine the injuries, inquiring here and there with his thumb and then wiping it off on his shirt. He said, "You were a good fellow, Wood. You talked kindly and you took care of your horse and you always pulled your own weight." Elias looked around, somewhat embarrassed, and then arose with effort.

Martha said, "I hope the pain isn't frightful, Wood. I'd fetch something for you to drink but I'm afraid it would just make you choke." Martha paused and added, "Little Ida's going to miss you. So is the rest of the family."

She moved off to the side with Elias and cinched the muffler around Dick's thigh as Bob came so close his toes brushed Wood's cold fingertips. He said, "Just in case you never noticed, it was me who shot you. I don't harbor any ill feelings toward you, I was just scared and looking out for my own well-being." A finger ticked on Wood's left hand and Bob retreated an inch or two and then recovered his composure. He said, "You've done a gallant job of dying so far and have nothing whatsoever to be ashamed about."

ACCORDING TO MARTHA'S April confession, Wood Hite died "when the sun was an hour high"; at which time the men removed Wood's clothes and lifted the corpse onto Bob's twin bed and Dick Liddil onto Charley's. Dick drank from a bottle of corn whiskey as Martha bathed Wood and anointed his chapped skin with alum and oil of sassafras, then Elias cared for Dick's mutilated leg with veterinary medicines and a sewing kit that was such an affliction to Dick that he swooned.

Bob put Wood's goat-hair coat on a closet hanger and balled everything else up in a box. He dressed in the heather green suit he'd purchased in Liberty and he slicked his hair in the mirror over his sister's chiffonier. He sat down to breakfast and saw Charley sitting under a striped blanket on the stove, steam growing off his back, his sprained ankle round as a melon. Wilbur stood at a window vagrantly lettering the mist on the glass; Ida was weeping on the sofa; Martha served cold oatmeal and boiled milk and frequently rubbed her eyes with a dishtowel. Only Bob seemed without melancholy, only Bob seemed uninclined to brood. He showed Wilbur the shell of the bullet that murdered Wood Hite and loitered about the kitchen sniffing the burned gunpowder in it. He carried in a jorum that was packed with snow and made Charley step down into it in order to relieve his swollen ankle.

Neighbors visited on their return from church and Wilbur was dispatched upstairs to shut the bedroom door. The wife talked about the preacher's inspiring sermon and about the peace that always descended upon her on Sundays, and her husband, John C. Brown, followed his nose through the house, slapping his prayerbook against his thigh. "Do I smell gunsmoke?"

Bob explained, "I ought to get our flue pipes cleaned. Might be chimney swifts in them. I might could do that today."

"You ought to keep the Sabbath, Bob."

"You got your religion, I got my own. It isn't right to spoon it down our throats every Sunday."

"It's just that me and the missus, we're Spirit-fired people, and when you think you've got the answer, well, you want to share it."

"I'd just as soon you didn't," said Bob.

Then it was afternoon and the neighbors were gone and no one mentioned Wood or an undertaker, nor wrote a letter of condolence to the Hites in Adairville, Kentucky. Ida mooned in her mother's room, bread rose in towel-covered tin pans, Elias kept his scowl in a coffee cup, and Wilbur tinkered with a broken clock. Martha sat mute and motionless across from Bob, who intently perused *The Farmer's Alma-nac*. Charley hopped into the kitchen on one foot and snared a cookie in an earthenware jar. He said, "One thing's settled: can't take him into Richmond."

Wilbur looked up. "How come?"

Charley munched the cookie, sprinkling crumbs on his chest. He licked his scant mustache and said, "One: the sheriff will put Bob away in jail. And two: Jesse will find out his cousin Wood's been shot dead in our house and that'll be the end for each and every one of us."

Bob clenched his teeth so that his jaw muscles twitched, but resisted any comment. The conversation languished and Charley hopped back to Ida with the cookie jar. Martha simmered tea and served it to herself. Ice melted from the eaves and peppered the snow underneath. The sun approached the mullioned windowpanes at four o'clock and then it was colder and the sun was screened by the southwest woods and Elias made himself portly with sweaters and coats and patiently waited at the door until Wilbur could torture his feet into Wood's fine leather boots.

Bob followed Elias and his chores from the kitchen window, squeaking an eyehole in the glass with the elbow of his suit coat. The oven door clanked as Martha took out four bread loaves and Ida came inside from the root cellar with jars of vegetables clenched by their lids. Bob could see the girl in the looking-glass of the evening-darkened window. She gazed at him with misgiving and asked, "Does Uncle Bob like okra, Momma?"

"Can't you see him standing there? Why don't you find out for yourself?"

Bob smirked. "She's afraid of me, Martha." He saw Elias and Wilbur in conference next to the water tank and he then tacked on, "You all are."

He sliced a loaf on a tin plate, dipped a knife into molasses, and let the syrup braid off onto the bread. Then he climbed the stairs with it and looked into the bedroom from the corridor. The candle was on the nightstand and Dick was moving his lips as he read a yellow book about a woman of riotous appetites. Wood's mouth was open but someone had covered his eyes with spoons. Dick licked a finger and turned a page without looking over the book at Bob. "He ain't disappeared, if that's what you were hoping."

"What chapter are you on?"

Dick said, "She's seen some young swell and got herself all agitated."

"How's your leg?"

"Full of torment, Bob. Thanks for asking."

Wood's skin was sallow and smirched slightly green where veins branched at his neck. His fingers were vised together at his stomach. Bob ate over Wood but the syrup was tainted and it was a penance to chew and swallow the bread. He set the tin plate down and lowered onto Dick's bed and examined the excavation in Wood's stern and arrogant skull.

"I ought to feel sorry but I don't. I'm just glad it's Wood who's dead and not me."

Dick stared at Bob, his book closed on his index finger. "You and me, we'll have to sit down and talk a few things over. Circumstances have changed."

Then Elias was there with a moth-eaten brown blanket that smelled of animal sweat. His cheeks were clownishly red with the cold and moisture was clinging to the end of his nose like a teardrop. "Ready?" was all he said.

They lifted Wood and let him sink onto the brown horse blanket. They then towed him across the boards and skidded him down the stairs so that his skull thudded and his body fished from side to side. Charley and Wilbur solemnly rose from kitchen chairs as Wood was carried out; Ida covered her face with her palms and Martha turned to the stove.

The December cold sliced inside Bob's coat sleeves and across his ears. His knuckles ached with the cumbersome load and the brothers periodically let the body down to relieve their backs and exercise their fingers. "Nippy," Bob said once, but Elias must not have heard. After they'd achieved the second rank of the woodrows, Elias concluded it was enough of a remove that the stink wouldn't reach the cattle lots, and they rolled the naked body into a snow-filled ravine that was once a sweetwater creek. Elias slid Wood to the right with his boot, then crouched to tuck the horse blanket over him. The two cleared snow and kicked at the ravine so that its dirt banks spattered down, then they collected whatever rocks and slabs were near. Elias swarmed apple leaves and strewed them over the cadaver as Bob ripped dead branches off the trees and swooped them down onto the long mound.

Then Elias stood there lugubriously, his arms crossed over the hat at his chest, and Bob stuffed his hands in his coat pockets. Elias prayed, " 'Blessed are the poor in spirit: for theirs is the kingdom of heaven. Blessed are they that mourn: for they shall be comforted.' " He paused and then petitioned Bob with his eyes.

"Meek," Bob said.

" 'Blessed are the meek: . . .' " After a moment Elias beseeched his brother again.

And Bob recited, " 'For they shall inherit the earth.' "

4

DECEMBER 1881 –

FEBRUARY 1882

No one should know more about Jesse James than I do, for our men have chased him from one end of the country to the other. His gang killed two of our detectives, who tracked them down, and I consider Jesse James the worst man, without exception, in America. He is utterly devoid of fear, and has no more compunction about cold-blooded murder than he has about eating his breakfast.

ROBERT A. PINKERTON
in the Richmond Democrat, *November 20, 1879*

A MAN ON A CHESTNUT HORSE walked the road next to the Ford brothers' farm at least once each week after the Blue Cut robbery. He wore a blue watchcap under a gray hat and he lived for hours at a time in the woodrows, as motionless as a clocktower, staring across the cow-ruined cornfields to the busy kitchen and the barn.

He was Sheriff James R. Timberlake of Clay County, and whenever a caller rode in, the sheriff noted in a journal the animal's color and gender, the rider's physical characteristics and comportment. His stakeouts were intermittent and without system however, whatever he encountered was by chance; and Timberlake's information was so inadequate that on Monday, December 5th, he recorded the arrival of Jesse James but ascribed it to a visit from a Methodist circuit rider with whom Jesse shared a resemblance.

The man came at dusk and tied his bay horse to a Martin box, then peered through two windows and entered the house without announcement, greeting the Fords in a country way and letting the door blow wide until a girl pushed against it. The sheriff saw what he could of the man companionably roughhousing, rowdily swatting shoulders and biceps, receiving the Ford brothers' handshakes, but soon the night was too cold and black and Timberlake lost patience with the dreariness and solitude and rode west from Ray County to Clay.

Bob was in the living room when Jesse arrived. Ida embroidered next to a candle and Bob sank in a chair across from her, poking grit from a comb with a sewing needle, listening to clockworks as they counterweighted. He saw branches veer over a windowpane and tremble still, and as he thought about it he became so spooked that he swiveled and adjoined his eyes with an apparition that receded from the glass. And then Jesse was inside the kitchen, as loud and large as a beer wagon, and Bob was scuttling up the stairs.

Dick Liddil was already hopping one-leggedly toward the closet, wincing with each movement.

"Why'd he come by, Dick? Does he know about Wood, do you think?"

"I can't figure it, Bob. I only know that he don't miss very much."

"What should I say about you if he asks?"

Dick let himself slide down into a corner and consider for a moment, then said, "Just tell him I'm in K.C. with Mattie." Dick swaddled himself in yanked-down petticoats and crinolines as Bob closed the closet door.

When Bob shied into the kitchen, Jesse was at the stove in a mountain of clothes that included a reddish beaver coat that was stolen, he claimed, from a Hapsburg crown prince on a buffalo hunt in Nebraska. He turned with a coffee cup at his mouth but lowered it when he viewed Bob. "Why, it's The Kid!"

"How's everything?" Bob asked.

Jesse ignored the question and took off his hat with care and slid it onto a breadbox that was crudely ornamented with painted gladiolas. His skull was encompassed by a brimline that divided reddened skin from white and scored his oiled brown hair. He wrestled out of his massive coat and laid it over a chair, then unbuttoned a cardigan sweater that showed a burn hole at the belly. No one talked as Jesse moved—it was as if his acts were miracles of invention wondrous to behold. Martha stared at Jesse as she cooked, Ida was moonstruck as she set down another dish, Charley and Wilbur grinned gregariously whenever his eyes floated near. He said, "I never take off my gunbelt."

And Wilbur said, "Good thinking."

Jesse walked back to his coffee and Charley hitched aside. "Hurt your leg?"

Charley smiled. "I slipped off the roof and smacked down into a snowbank like a ton of stupidness. One second I'm screaming, 'Whoa, Nelly!' and the next second, poof! I'm neck-deep in snow."

"The roof! Whatever possessed you to climb on the roof in December?"

Charley lost his smile and saw the criticism in Bob's expression. "There was a kite—what am I saying? There was a *cat*. A cat was on the roof and I went after him. A tom cat. Yowling and whatall; and I slipped." Charley rubbed his slanted right eye and coughed into his fist.

Jesse winked and said, "I thought maybe your clubfoot was gaining on ya," and Wilbur guffawed as if that was funny and Charley noised the room with his hee-haw laugh and Jesse smiled at his own zaniness as Martha carried a bowl of ham hocks to the table.

Bob said, "Dick was here for a little bit and then he went on to Kansas City to be with his wife."

Jesse acted as if he hadn't heard and presumptuously sat down at the table and there tickled Ida's side and stomach, saying, "Kootchy kootch," as if she were two, until the girl was sore with giggles and the fun was over and Martha at last said, "Oh, quit it, you two."

Jesse's mood was genial and he reacted to Martha's regulation without anger, immediately diverting his attention from the daughter to her mother and tucking a napkin under his collar as he began a disquisition on the subject of Charles Guiteau. His court trial for the assassination of President Garfield had commenced just three weeks ago and was already a gaudy spectacle, one or two columns about it opened every newspaper, and Guiteau gloried in the publicity, giving outrageous speeches, interrupting the prosecuting attorneys, generally playing the wild-eyed maniac as correspondents ecstatically copied down his every pronouncement. Following prosecutor Corkhill's examination, Guiteau jumped up and said, "It is the unanimous opinion of the American people that you are a consummate jackass," and as a surgeon gave his testimony, Guiteau screamed, "Is there any limit to this diarrhea?"

Jesse went on and on about it, a one-man show, a sorcerer, so physical and passionate his audience seemed no more than weeds. For more than an hour over a meal and chocolate cake and coffee, Jesse's shrill voice contained the Fords, contained the room; he seemed to fill the house like a foot in a shoe; and it was only Bob and Martha who seemed to remember the Sunday murder, the body covered in apple leaves in the snow, Dick Liddil upstairs concealed in a closet, Cousin

Albert roughed up by this man. Ida was girlishly in love with Jesse, Wilbur chuckled and shook his head with mirth at each sentence, Charley toyed with his gossamer mustache and crossed his legs like a gentleman and rivaled Jesse now and then with his own penny yarns and paltry jokes about Charles J. Guiteau. Jesse graciously gave him audience and acknowledged the news items with "Fascinating" and then developed another description.

At seven Martha collected the dishware and Ida scraped garbage into a battered tin bucket for swill and Charley said, "Here's a cute story, Jess. Bob and me went to the Moore School as children over toward Crescent Lake? And what with it so near Kearney, conversations just naturally had to do with the exploits of the James-Younger gang. Well, Bobby was—what—eleven or twelve? And he couldn't get enough. He practically *ate* the newspaper stories up. You were by far his most admired personage. It was Jesse this, Jesse that, from sunrise to sunset."

"Fascinating," Jesse said.

"No; there's more. This is cute. We're at supper and Bob asks, 'You know what size boot Jesse wears?' "

Bob said, "Jesse doesn't care about this, Charley."

"Oh, shush now, Bob. Let me tell it. Bob says, he says, 'You know what size boot Jesse wears? Six and a half,' Bob says. He says, 'Ain't that a dinky boot for a man five feet eight inches tall?' Well, I decided to josh him a little, you know, him being my kid brother, so I said, 'He don't have toes, is why.' "

"Really stupid," Bob said.

"Shush. Then my momma pipes up and says, 'He *what?*' and I'm not letting on. I say, 'He was dangling his feet off a culvert and catfish nibbled his toes off.' Well, Bob taxed himself trying to picture it until Momma let on that I was playing him the fool. And Bob says—I want to get this right. What was it exactly you said, Bob?"

"I said, 'If they'd been catfish he'd a drilled them with his forty-four.' "

Charley clapped his hands sharply and laughed. "Yep, that's the exact words, exactly."

Jesse looked at Bob without comment.

Bob said, "It'd be a good joke if it was funny."

"You've got to picture it though. Bob saying you would've shot them catfish, then smiling in every direction, real satisfied with himself. Oh! And you know what he said next? He said, 'You *need* your toes.' "

"How'd I miss this?" Wilbur asked. "Where was I?"

Charley carved a shred of pork from between his bucked teeth and licked the meat off his nail. " 'You *need* your toes.' "

" 'Course you do," Jesse said.

"Isn't that a cute story?"

Jesse suppressed his opinion. He was no longer galvanic; he'd turned the voltage down. He seemed preoccupied, slightly pained; he regarded Bob in a way that implied the sight was disappointing. He searched under his cardigan sweater and removed a cigar that he skewered with a tine of his fork. "Give me some other conversations, Bob."

Bob was reluctant. "You know how children are."

"It'd be cheery to hear what you fancied about me," Jesse said. "It might make me laugh and help me forget my cares and woes."

"I can't recall much of any consequence."

"I got one," said Charley. He smiled at Jesse, whose eyes were crossed on a match flame below the green cigar. "This one's about as crackerjack as the one about your toes."

"Which?" Bob asked.

Charley looked over at him. "About how much you and Jesse have in common."

Jesse said, "Why don't *you* tell it, Bob; if you remember."

Bob inched forward in his chair. "Well, if you'll pardon my saying so, it *is* interesting, the many ways you and I overlap and whatnot. You begin with my daddy, J. T. Ford. J stands for *James!* And T is Thomas, meaning 'twin.' Your daddy was a pastor of the New Hope Baptist Church; my daddy was part-time pastor of a church at Excelsior Springs. You're the youngest of the three James boys; I'm the youngest of the five Ford boys. You had twins as sons, I have twins as sisters. Frank is four and a half years older than you, which incidentally is the difference between Charley and me, the two outlaws in the Ford clan. Between us is another brother, Wilbur here (with six letters in his name); between Frank and you was a brother, Robert, also with six letters. Robert died in infancy, as most everyone knows, and he was named after your father, Robert, who was remembered by your brother's first-born, another Robert. Robert, of course, is my Christian name. My uncle, Robert Austin Ford, has a son named Jesse James Ford. You have blue eyes; I have blue eyes. You're five feet eight inches tall; I'm five feet eight inches tall. We're both hot-tempered and impulsive and devil-may-care. Smith and Wesson is our preferred make of revolver. There's the same number of letters and syllables in our names;

I mean, Jesse James and Robert Ford. Oh me, I must've had a list as long as your nightshirt when I was twelve, but I lost some curiosities over the years.''

Jesse was still as a photograph; he could have been a man of cultivation at a concert. His hands were assembled at his stomach, his collar was concealed by his two-inch brown beard, smoke spiraled from his cigar in a line and then squiggled above him like sloppy handwriting; but his eyes were active, cagey, they calculated and appraised and then carefully looked at the green cigar as Jesse tapped ashes into his coffee cup.

He said, "Did I ever mention that scalawag George Shepherd to y'all?" He grinned at Bob and reached a right hand to grip Bob's forearm in apology while saying, "George was one of Quantrill's lieutenants and he gave me a story like Bob's, is why I thought of him, giving me everything we had in common and so on, just so he could join the gang. How could I know he had a grudge against me and was lying to get on my good side? I said, 'Come on aboard, George. Glad to have ya,' and so on, but I got good old Ed Miller to keep his eye peeled.'' Jesse gripped his fingers once more and then released Bob's forearm, bringing his right hand back to shave the ash from his cigar with the lip of the coffee cup. He said, "I'm talking about eighteen seventy-nine. November. I was arranging to rob a bank in Galena, Kansas, and sent George on in to look at it. Did I say he only had one eye? Used to wear one of them pirate eyepatches and flip it up or down, depending on how much he wanted to scare ya. So: he goes to Galena, but then my spy, Ed Miller, comes back and reports that Shepherd went and sent a telegram to Marshal Liggett, giving him the date of the robbery and whatall. It's ten o'clock the following morning and Shepherd comes riding into camp, bump-be-dump-be-dump, and much to the poor man's surprise about twenty guns open up on him. He's banging away and hating himself for being so goddamned stupid when I hear a ball whiz by my head and just then I make up my mind to pretend I'm a goner and flop to the ground. George hightails it with Jim Cummins giving him what-for for maybe a mile or two, and the next thing I see in the papers is George Shepherd running off at the mouth about *killing* Jesse James. Yes! Lordy; here's the end of my cares and woes, I'm thinking. Jim Cummins goes up to Clay County and says what George is been saying is true, and I get some of the boys to slaughter a cow and once it's stinking pitch it into a coffin that they wagon on through Kearney, I even get Zee to put on black and weep her way up to my momma's place. I forgot to let Momma in on all this, though, and she's the one got the sheriffs onto me again. She says, 'Don't you all have any common sense? You need *two* eyes to get Jesse.' ''

Charley and Wilbur laughed for a suitable period of time and Jesse laughed with them until coughing made him stoop with the cigar near his ear and scrub his mouth with the checkered tablecloth. He rubbed the water from his eyes as he said, "My goodness, that Zerelda. She's a caution."

Bob said, "You oughtn't think of me like you do George Shepherd."

"You just brought him to mind."

"It's not very flattering."

Martha waitressed around them and took their cups and saucers; Jesse returned the cigar to his mouth and made himself complimentary. "Good eating, Martha."

"Glad you liked it," she said.

Bob asked, "How come George had a grudge against you?"

Jesse cocked an eyebrow. "Hmm?"

"You said George Shepherd had a grudge against you and I've been wondering what it was."

"Oh. George asked me to protect this nephew of his during the war and it so happens the kid had five thousand dollars on him. The kid winds up killed, and all that money swiped from him, and when George was in prison someone whispers to him it was Jesse James slit the boy's throat."

"Just mean gossip, was it?" Charley asked.

Jesse looked at his cigar and saw it was out. He then made a comic gesture of presenting it to Bob, who glared at him icily, and dropped the cigar in a pocket, saying, "Bob's the expert; put it to him."

Bob rose with his knuckles on the table and was cautious lest he shove his chair awry on exit and appear a stamping boy in a snit. "I've got something to do," he said.

"I've made him cranky," Jesse said.

Wilbur snickered and Bob said with august gravity, "I've been through this before, is all. Once people get around to making fun of me, they just don't ever let up."

Martha said, "Someone's speaking awful fresh over there!"

Bob was forced to walk past Jesse to reach the main room and Jesse kicked his left leg out across Bob's path, clouting the floorboards with his boot. Bob glanced down at the bogus grin of a playground bully, and at the suggestion of menace that was beneath Jesse's antics. Jesse said, "I don't want you to skip off to your room and pout without knowing why I dropped by for this visit."

"I suppose you're going to tell us how sorry you are that you had to slap my cousin Albert around."

Such great heat seemed to come then from Jesse's eyes that Bob nearly glanced away as from sunlight, but in a second the man cooled and said, "I come to ask one of you two Fords to ride with me on a journey or two. I guess we've agreed it ought to be Charley; you've been acting sort of testy."

Bob was pale and silent. He stepped around Jesse's obstructing boot, calmly climbed the stairs to the upper room, and carefully shut the door. Dick shoved open the closet door with his toe and stared at Bob from among the women's things. "I'd say that was really stupid."

Bob covered his mouth and slid his back down the newspapered wall to a sit.

JESSE AND CHARLEY rode west at nine and after twenty miles in the cold chose to risk a Pinkerton investigation by staying over at the Samuelses' long, ramshackle house.

A dog slept by the fireplace in the kitchen, an alphabet sampler was on one wall, the ceilings were only seven feet high; snores came from the sleeping rooms and Mrs. Zerelda Samuels sat in a motionless rocking chair as Jesse sipped the cocoa she'd cooked. She was a huge, mannish, careworn woman with a mercurial temper and the look of a witch. A robe sleeve was limp where her right hand and wrist had been blown off, her white hair scattered wide when let down, and she sucked her lips over violet gums that contained no more than twenty teeth. She said, "You're Charley Ford."

"Yes, ma'am. You seen me once or twice with Johnny."

"But you're not my son's age."

"No; that's my brother Bob."

"You got the consumption or don't you eat right?"

Charley shrugged and grinned at Jesse with shame. "I guess what it is is that I'm just skinny."

She massaged her right forearm and said to her boy, "I got a letter from George Hite. Hasn't seen hide nor hair of him."

129

Jesse squinted at Charley. "And you say you haven't seen Wood?"

"Can't imagine where he could be."

Zerelda rose from the rocking chair and said, "I best get some shut-eye. I've gotta be up and at 'em by six."

After his mother left, Jesse settled down on a cot that was under a window the size of a man. Charley tucked his wool bedroll into a pink davenport and was out as soon as he completed his prayers. But he awoke at four and saw Jesse seated on an abused Queen Anne chair, absently scratching the sole of a foot through his sock. "You finished with your sleeping?"

Charley switched cheeks on his bedroll. "I could use one or two more hours if it's no trouble. I can't operate on less than five. I run into walls and fenceposts."

Jesse said, "I've been holding a discussion with myself over if I ought to tell you this or no. My good side won out and now, well, I'd like to make a clean breast of things."

"My mind is cobwebby yet, is the only drawback."

Jesse crossed to the davenport and sat so close his right knee encroached and Charley retracted his leg. Jesse smelled of onions and camphor. He asked, "Can you hear me when I whisper this low?"

"Just barely," Charley said.

"You knew I went into Kentucky?"

"Yes."

"I'm talking about October now. I come back through Saline County and thought to myself, 'Why not stop by and see Ed Miller?' So I do and things aren't to my satisfaction at all. Ed's got himself worked up over something and I can tell he's lying like a rug and I say to myself, 'Enough's enough!' and I say to Ed, 'Come on, Ed; let's go for a ride.' Do you understand what I'm saying?"

"Going for a ride is like giving him what-for."

"Exactly. Ed and Jesse, they argued on the road and when push come to shove, Jesse shot and killed him."

"Jesse did."

"You've got it."

"You."

Jesse condescendingly patted Charley's knee and rose up from the davenport. "So you see? Your cousin got off easy. I was only playing with Albert."

Charley said, "I've made him squeal once or twice myself. I'm just not as thorough as you are."

"You want to swap a tale with me now?"

Charley camouflaged his fright with ignorance. "I don't get your meaning."

"If you've got something to confess in exchange, it seems to me it'd only be right for you to spit it out now."

"Can't think of a single thing."

"About Wood Hite, for example."

"I've been saying over and over again I can't figure out where he's gone. I'm not going to change my story just to have something to spit."

"Why was your brother so agitated?"

"Which?"

"Bob."

"It's just his way. He's antsy."

The dog in the kitchen sighed; Jesse reseated himself in the Queen Anne chair. He said, "You can go back to sleep now."

"You got *me* agitated now: you see?"

"Just ain't no peace with Jesse around. You ought to pity my poor wife."

"Ed Miller was a good friend of mine. He introduced me to you at that one poker game. I'm a little angry with you, if you want the God's honest truth."

Jesse crossed his legs at the ankles and shut his eyes. He pushed his hands deep in his pockets. He said, "You ought to pity me too."

THEY AROSE with the colored cook but did not remain for breakfast. Instead, Jesse fished around in the chicken coop until he could show off three brown eggs crammed between the fingers of one hand. He chopped the shells open with a pen knife and drank the yolks down, slobbering his chin with the clear albumen, and proffered one to Charley.

He shook his head in the negative, saying, "I can get along without breakfast. I'll eat something on the way."

"It's a good journey."

"It isn't Kansas City?"

"I moved again. San Hose-say!"

"Don't know that—"

"Saint Joseph!"

"Oh."

It was late afternoon when they arrived and their horses were sore in their mouths from the clove bits, and yet they were spurred into a leisurely walk so Charley could see the wonders of a city of thirty-four thousand. Jesse saved for the last the marvel that was the grand, red-bricked World Hotel, where wooden chests that contained bathtubs were rolled from room to room by bellboys, where gas lamps burned all night long in the corridors, where a sanitarium for epileptics covered one entire upper floor and was run by Dr. George Richmond, the inventor of an elixir called Samaritan Nervine.

Charley was nearly overcome. "There must be something to see every dad-blamed place you look!"

"It takes getting used to; there's no argument on that score."

Shopkeepers were locking up and girls in long woolen coats were crouching out of the evening cold as Jesse and Charley roamed south on Twenty-first Street to Lafayette, where Jesse had rented a cottage in November. It was common and white and sat on a corner behind the shade of a wide porch that curved around it like the bill of a cap. Because the lot was small, they stabled their horses elsewhere and on the walk back Jesse instructed Charley about his assumed identity. He said he was listed in the city directory as Thomas Howard. His occupation was supposed to be that of a cattle buyer, so he made a point of visiting the St. Joseph stockyards once per week, but he spent much of his time there in speaking about two fillies he was racing in Kentucky so that his nonappearances wouldn't be suspect.

"I can't remember all this."

"You've got to, Charley."

"Do I get another name? I mean, I can't be plain old Charley Ford, can I?"

Jesse considered options as they walked through a crust of snow to the cottage and stomped their boots on the porch. "Johnson," he said at last. "Why don't you call yourself Johnson?"

(It was not until much later that Charley learned Johnson was the name of a man in Tennessee whom Jesse had sued for "acting under false pretenses.")

The front door sucked open and the storm door rattled in its frame. Zee was there in an orange gingham apron and Mary was riding the saddle of her broad hip, her face lowered as she cried. Zee looked sadly at Jesse and then pushed open the fogging storm door. "So. It's Charley this time," she said.

DICK LIDDIL RECOVERED from the gunshot slowly because of a maroon-colored infection that swelled from his thigh muscle like a split apple, but within a week of Jesse's visit he had mended well enough to ride and it became common for Dick and Bob to eat lunch in Richmond and clerk or play checkers at Elias Ford's grocery store. They claimed they were looking for income opportunities, but they also claimed prior commitments if work was offered. They made some vague inquiries about the James gang, the sheriff's office, Allan Pinkerton's detectives, and the manhunt for the perpetrators of the Winston and Blue Cut train robberies. And increasingly Bob noticed a man alone at a cafe table, jotting notes in a journal, leaning on a pool cue and staring at Dick over the foam on a beer, or riding on a chestnut horse on the street and swiveling in his vast gray soldier's coat to see them stamp the snow from their boots and walk into an apothecary.

At last at lunch in Christmas week, Bob carried a plate of pigeon pie over to a round rear table and cut the meat with a spoon as he measured the stern man sitting there. Compared to Bob he was enormous, as tall as Frank James but more muscular, six feet two at a minimum and wide as a gate in his shoulders and chest. He was exceptionally handsome in a foreign, somewhat villainous way. He looked like a circus lion tamer or the leering remittance man in a melodrama; his skin was as chestnut brown as his horse was, his mustache covered his mouth like a crow's wings, and his eyes evinced the black shimmer of coffee in a cup as they studied Bob with an arrogance that was close to animosity.

Bob said, "Sorry for the intrusion. I didn't mean to interrupt your meal, but I've seen your face off and on around Richmond and I can't place who you are."

"I own a livery over to Liberty; maybe that's where you seen me."

"Of course. That must be it."

The man looked around Bob to Dick. "Why don't you call your friend over here and we'll get acquainted."

Bob considered it for a second, then motioned, and Dick slid off a stool and limped over with a mug that sloshed pennies of coffee on the floorboards. The man skidded two chairs out with an unseen boot and Bob and Dick warily sat down.

"I was constable of Liberty Township for two years; that could be where you seen me too."

"No, it must've been the livery," said Bob. Dick bent over his coffee in order to conceal as much as he could of himself.

The man continued, "And I've been sheriff of Clay County since eighteen seventy-eight, so I'm in the public eye a lot."

Dick kept his face lowered but angrily kicked Bob in the shin. Bob restrained his ouch.

The man rose an inch from his seat and shook Bob's limp hand. "My name is James R. Timberlake."

"Very pleased to meet you," said Bob and then sat back on his fingers.

"You're?"

"Bob."

The sheriff looked with interest at Dick and he responded without raising his eyes from his coffee. "Charles Siderwood. I'm just on a visit and . . . Well, there isn't no *and,* I'm just visiting is all." He drank from the mug as if he were suddenly parched.

Timberlake licked a thumb with his lower lip and flipped the pages of his journal, scanning each like a librarian until he located the correct description. "Robert Newton Ford. Born January thirty-first, eighteen sixty-two. Presently living on the old Harbison farm. Single, average height and weight, brown-haired, clean-shaven. Occupation unknown. No prior arrests." He smiled very briefly and then looked at Dick and reviewed several pages before he ironed one flat with the heel of his hand. "You're Charles Siderwood?"

Dick glanced at him from under his eyebrows. Timberlake wrote down the name. Bob said, "I've always wanted to be written about in a book."

Timberlake inclined massively toward Bob, overwhelming the table. "Do you think I *care* about you two and who you are and who you aren't? It's the James brothers I want. I've been on the loop for Frank and Jesse since eighteen seventy-six and by God I'm going to get them."

Timberlake withdrew a little and considered his thoughts; a round businessman made an entrance into the cafe, making noise about the cold, whacking snow off his trouser legs and calling, "Mollie, why don't you cut me some of that good apple pie?"

Mollie said she'd sold the last of it and the businessman winked inclusively at Bob. "Well, give me some of that good chocolate cake so I don't shrink away to nothing."

Timberlake rolled a cigarette and licked it and struck a match off Dick's coffee mug. He winced when the smoke broke against his eyes. He said, "Do you know about the governor's proclamation?"

Dick gave Timberlake his rapt attention but Bob pushed away from the table and said, "This is all very interesting, but if you'll excuse me, I'm going to order some of that good chocolate cake I've heard so much about."

"Sit down." The sheriff picked a shred of tobacco off his tongue, flicked it onto the floorboards between his boots, and dried his finger on the tablecloth. Then he unbuttoned a broadcloth shirt and retrieved from inside it a parchment that was torn at the corners and folded in quarters. He slid the parchment across to Dick, and Bob reached across the aisle to slide his cold dish of pigeon pie onto another table.

Dick perused the document as he imagined an attorney might, with concentration and no little scorn and with occasional nods of concurrence. "It mentions Glendale and how certain parties confederated and banded together to steal what was on the train. It goes on about the Winston shebang last summer and how 'in perpetration of the robbery last aforesaid, the parties engaged therein did kill and murder one William Westfall,' and so on. Ta-da-ta-da-ta-*da*, 'I, Thomas T. Crittenden, Governor of the State of Missouri, do hereby offer a reward of five thousand dollars—' " He looked for a reaction from Bob and then from Sheriff Timberlake, who canted into the windowsill and placidly smoked without comment. " 'And for the arrest and delivery of said Frank James or Jesse W. James, and each or either of them, to the sheriff of said Daviess County, I hereby offer a reward of five thousand dollars, and for the conviction of either of the parties last aforesaid of participation in either of the murders or robberies above mentioned, I hereby offer a *further* reward of five thousand dollars, in testimony whereof, I have hereunto set my hand,' and ta-da-ta-dum."

Timberlake took Dick's coffee mug for his cigarette ashes. "You know why I gave that to you, don't you, Mr. Siderwood."

Dick scratched at a circle of starchiness in his trousers, where his wound had festered into the cloth. The pain seemed to reach into marrow and muscle like the roots of a sturdy weed. Dick said, "I meet a friend of mine, a friend who'd made some mistakes and maybe got himself into a mean scrape or two. You think I could tell him the government will erase whatever's on the slate just for helping your people?"

"You go talk to Henry Craig in Kansas City if you want to make arrangements." Sheriff Timberlake drew on a cigarette stub that was now so short it must have charred his mustache. He released it into an inch of coffee, where it hissed succinctly and floated. He said, "You

135

tell your friend the governor's got a regular toothache over the James gang. My guess is he'd agree to do just about anything if it'd make the pain go away."

SOMETIME IN CHRISTMAS WEEK, Thomas Howard and his cousin, Charley Johnson, ascended Lafayette Street on foot, in slush, with a city councilman named Aylesbury who wanted to rent out a seven-room house owned by Mrs. August Saltzman. The rise was steep as a playground slide and on several occasions Aylesbury needed to rest in order to catch his wind.

Jesse smiled and said, "At least if you get weary of climbing this hill you can always lean against it."

Aylesbury shook his head and respirated, his gloved hands on his hips. "I don't know if I want stairs or a block and tackle."

Charley reached the crest at 1318 Lafayette Street and there slouched around a one-storey, green-shuttered white cottage that was called the House on the Hill. He counted two scantily furnished bedrooms, a sitting room and a dining room, and a recently attached kitchen with a shaded rear porch that looked eastward over a ravine into wilderness. He could see fifty miles of countryside to the north, east, and west, and if he walked onto a neighbor's corner lot, Charley could see Kansas, the brown Missouri River, an iron bridge that was the color of rust, the shuttle and steam and collision of boxcars at the railroad yard, and brick stores and downtown businesses with their streets of mud and brown snow and with a roof of coal smoke overhead.

Charley saw Aylesbury skid a shoe in the snow to reveal the loess soil underneath and he slunk after the two men as they clambered through snowdrifts to a smokehouse, to a stable that was cut into the earth, to a shed for "garden tools and what-have-yous," and a warm outhouse that could seat two.

"You can see into next week from here," Charley said. "You won't never be surprised by company again."

Jesse did not acknowledge the remark.

The city councilman walked from room to room in the cottage, his arms wide, his voice dwindling in closets. He shut doors, he raised and lowered windows, he sat on mattresses and sofa cushions, he informed Mr. Howard that across the street was Thomas Turner and his wife, along with a niece named Metta, who was three.

Jesse seemed lost in reveries. "So my little girl will have a playmate."

"And it's romantically situated, isn't it? Here on this lofty eminence?"

Charley said, "I like the address most. Lafayette Street. When I was a kid I used to tinker with a French music box that the Marquis de Lafayette gave the father of our country."

This was such a startling bit of information from such an improbable source that Aylesbury only looked over his nose to evaluate Charley for a moment, and then returned to the man he knew as a cattle buyer named Thomas Howard. "The rent is fourteen dollars a month."

Jesse squinted at the councilman and slowly walked to the kitchen.

Aylesbury said, "I've priced about twenty places in town and that's what a cottage goes for these days. I may even be a little low." Jesse leaned on a kitchen window sash in a black mood, looking out. His coat shadowed the room like shutters. Aylesbury called, "How much is comfort and contentment worth?"

THE THOMAS HOWARD CLAN moved into The House on the Hill on December 24th, and in the late afternoon Jesse and Charley strolled downtown St. Joseph with a list Zee had written out: candies and chocolates and peppermint canes, a cloth hand puppet with a porcelain head, ivory barrettes carved to represent angels, and *Five Little Peppers and How They Grew,* a children's book by Margaret Sidney. Jesse bought what he could with the little cash he had, then Charley saw a notice that said the Second Presbyterian Church was holding its annual Christmas party that evening, and the two walked over to Twelfth Street, slipped into the unlocked basement, and stole a game of feathered darts, a green metal hoop and stick, a rubber ball and six jacks, a sack of popcorn balls that were covered with molasses, a reed whistle, and a red Santa Claus suit and a white whisker set that was constructed from baling wire and painted binder twine.

At nightfall Charley cleaned the snow off his boots and softly knocked on the cottage door. Zee opened it in her apron, a streak of flour on her cheek. She asked where Jesse was and Charley answered that the Turners had invited their new neighbor over for an eggnog. Then he sat with Tim and Mary on the twin bed in the sitting room. He said, "Don't you wish Santa would come now instead of midnight when you're asleep?"

Tim looked at Charley with mistrust. "Yes."

"Let's squinch our eyes shut and wish that Santa would come right now."

Charley and Tim squinched their eyes and Mary sucked her thumb and then the kitchen door was slugged in and sleigh bells jingled and Santa Claus jollied into the sitting room, his red coat made fat with straw. He shouted, "Ho ho ho," in a voice that was low as a kettledrum and he seated himself on a wicker chair and bestowed sweets and toys to the children as Zee reminded them of their manners and smiled.

Tim collected his gifts within the metal hoop and then pestered Santa for more, investigating pockets, sticking his hands into straw, lifting the sides of the red coat until he contacted a Smith and Wesson revolver. The boy snatched his hand back as if it were burnt and scowled at the man in the red suit. "You're not Santa Claus; you're Daddy."

Charley called across the room, "He's one of Santa's helpers!"

Jesse sat low in the chair with his boots kicked out, drew off the soft red cap by its cotton ball, then reached out and snuggled Tim close to his chest. He said, "Let me tell you a secret, son: there's always a mean old wolf in Grandma's bed, and a worm inside the apple. There's always a daddy inside the Santa suit. It's a world of trickery."

THE FAMILY ATTENDED a Christmas service at the Second Presbyterian Church, at which time the Santa suit was returned before it could be missed. Afterward Jesse showed Tim how to roll his hoop on the cottage floor, Charley played jacks with Mary, Zee served an extravagant breakfast in a gift dress of black satin that was slightly too small and was unbuttoned beneath her apron. Then Jesse and Charley rode a noon train forty miles southeast to Kearney and visited the Samuels farm, an occurrence that was so inconceivable to Sheriff Timberlake and his deputies that no men were stationed on the road.

Mrs. Samuels cooked a goose and presented it with browned whole onions and candied yams and biscuits and turnips and cucumber pickles. A green rag carpet covered the floor, a wood heating stove was connected to the screened fireplace, a glassed case of yellow waxed flowers was on the cherrywood mantel; a scriptural engraving, a picture of "The Death of Stonewall Jackson," and a sampler stitched by Zerelda Cole as a girl at St. Catherine's Academy were nailed up on the plastered walls. Dr. Reuben Samuels sat dopily at the long table's head, admiring his huge congregation: his eldest daughter, Sallie, her husband, William Nicholson, and child, Jesse James Nicholson; his eighteen-year-old daughter, Fannie, and her husband, Joseph Hall; his son, Johnny, who was twenty years old and the only child who still lived with them; Jesse's younger sister, Susie, and her husband, Allan Parmer; Charley Ford, who shocked corn for him once; and none other than Jesse Woodson James. According to custom, a chair was left empty in memorial to Archie, the son accidentally slain by the Pinkerton Agency in 1875; and at the foot of the table, ruling it like Queen Zenobia, was the doctor's overbearing and refractory wife.

A girl brought in a gravy boat that she'd allowed to cool so long the gravy curdled and Zerelda flew into a rage, clubbing the girl with her mangled right arm and yelling that she was an ignoramus. Jesse appealed to Dr. Samuels, "Pappy?" and the man grinned benignly at his stepson. Jesse said, "She's acting up."

Reuben looked to his wife and called, "Mother? She's got to bring the goose in yet."

"You shut up, Pappy," Zerelda said. "She's been snappish and peppery with me all day."

Reuben simply commenced to ask for the Good Lord's blessing on all the good food that had been prepared and brung over and Zerelda gave an amen to the prayer, permitting the girl to go back to the kitchen. Then Zerelda began talking about a Christmas letter she'd received from Frank that she was sure had been steamed open in Kansas City and only then sent on to Kearney. Annie and Rob were fine, the letter said; Baltimore was gloomy and crowded; Buck had seen Shakespeare performed in an opera house and nearly wept with joy. Zerelda talked about the nightwatchers, the town criers, the gossips, and many black-suited men, each thin as a coffin nail, who lurked in alleys and atop shop roofs in order to spy on her. She said she consistently claimed she hadn't seen Frank for seven years and was scared he'd died of consumption. And as for Jesse, she'd initiated the misleading rumor that her third-born had passed away from this vale of tears too and was now planted under the gladiolas. Zerelda then ceased in midsentence and Charley turned from his victuals to see her mouth tremble and her white head gravely lower.

Reuben suggested, "Don't get started again, Mother."

But Zerelda flamboyantly covered her eyes with her coarse left palm and cried, "Doomed! Hunted down and shot at like coons in a tree! Soon every one of my boys will be killed and, oh, how will I endure it? My heart will crack in two!"

Charley chewed deliberately and swallowed; Jesse studied his plate; his half-sister Fannie said with annoyance, "Momma! You've embarrassed every single person at this table. You quit your ranting and raving. It's Christmas."

Mrs. Samuels reached out the stub of her right wrist to touch Jesse's cuff and she looked at her son with red eyes and unflinching melodrama as she asked, "How can I continue without you? How can I bear to let you go?"

Jesse was so abashed and perplexed by his mother's mawkishness that as the supper continued he refrained from anything other than a jocose comment or two over the butter dish, and after the four o'clock exchange of Christmas presents—receiving a cruet of elegantly scented hair oil and a red cravat made of silk—Jesse convinced the Samuels family that the Fords had an evening celebration prepared, and he'd promised Charley that they'd attend.

Charley took up the invention and inquired, "You think you can eat another goose?"

Jesse ticked his head and said, "Don't know. My pants are getting sort of personal with me already."

Everyone yelled goodbyes back and forth outside for several minutes, then Jesse and Charley climbed into a two-horse phaeton and steered it east at a trot. Jesse sighed, "Mercy!" and then was mute for a mile. He said at last, "She wonders why Frank's in Baltimore and I wonder why I'm not."

Charley complimented Jesse on all the pretty things in the house and Jesse said, "You can have a palace of carpets and gold and expensive paintings but they aren't worth the mud off your feet if it isn't full of God's peace."

"I suppose," Charley said, and then he found silence practical, and he practiced it for most of the trip to Richmond. But as they neared Martha's rented farm, he remembered Wood Hite mouldering in the creek bed and imagined a yellow cadaver, its withered skin retracted from inch-long teeth, its mouth in a scream, cavities in its skull where the eyes once were, and sitting, for some reason, on the sofa, like a circuit rider at Saturday tea. They rattled onto the road to the barn, slewing aside in the snow, and Jesse clucked the two horses toward the stables.

Charley moved off the seat, letting a lap blanket slide to his boots, and Jesse slowed the team. "What's made you so jittery?"

"I better go ahead in case my sister's in the altogether."

Jesse smiled. "That'd be jim dandy!"

"And there's Ida to think about. You know how young girls are with gentlemen; how they're so modest and everything." And before Jesse could contradict him, Charley jumped off the carriage and fell to his knees in the snow, then violently brushed himself and galumphed to the kitchen door.

Bob was in a chair, wan and shyly startled, his arms beneath the oak table like a schoolboy sticking gum.

Charley asked, "Is Dick still here?"

"Kansas City."

"Anything you should hide?"

"Jesse?"

Charley nodded and removed his coat. "Don't let him see us so much as wink at each other. He's suspicious as a danged coyote, and he don't trust you one iota."

Bob lifted a cocked revolver from under the table and carefully let the hammer click forward. "I guess that makes us even."

Then Jesse came inside in his reddish brown beaver coat, frost on his dark brown mustache and beard, moisture in his eyes from the cold, and communicated amicably with Bob, joshing as he jigged at the stove fire, creating Christmas cheer. Then as Charley vagrantly talked about the weather, Jesse played truant and roamed the second floor of the house, nosing into closets and cabinets seeking evidence. His footfalls overhead were faint: Bob presumed that Jesse gently pushed the shut doors so that they swung ever so gracefully into the night of the rooms.

Bob touched his own lips to stop Charley from speaking and the two brothers listened as Jesse knocked a chair akilter and carefully righted it. Bob said, "Dick might be making arrangements with Henry H. Craig."

"Oh? And who would that be?"

Martha came into the kitchen fastening a yellow robe around herself. Her auburn hair was wrecked with sleep and her complexion was very pale. She murmured, "Are you telling him?"

"Maybe you better," said Bob. "I'll stand at the door."

Charley said in a constrained voice, "This is mysterious."

Martha poured water into a tumbler and turned with it near her mouth. "It's just a guess on my part." She sipped water and put the tumbler down. "Mr. Craig is an attorney and a Kansas City police commissioner; has an office in the Times Building. Dick said he was going to give Mattie a Christmas gift, but my guess is he's actually going to see Mr. Craig and give him you two for the reward."

Bob bent into the sitting room and craned to see the stairs. Jesse was apparently motionless somewhere above them, letting his fancies run like red-eyed ferrets, letting the experienced air educate his senses.

Bob could just make out his sister's words as she informed Charley about the governor's reward, about plea bargaining and immunity, about exoneration. She sipped water and told him Craig could only negotiate for Jackson County, so she and Bob were considering a visit with Governor Crittenden to see if he couldn't guarantee the Ford brothers wouldn't be prosecuted—in exchange for that they'd promise the governor to help him capture Jesse James.

Bob leaned his back against the kitchen doorframe and saw Charley contemplating his toes, his face temporarily sixty years old. "Charley?" Bob whispered.

His brother raised his brown eyes.

"You can forget about Wood Hite and about Jesse getting back at us. You won't go to jail for your train robberies. And you'll be a rich man come spring."

"You're both talking too fast for me. I can't get it straight in my mind."

Martha said, "Just let us take care of it then."

They listened to the crump of Jesse's slow descent on the staircase and Bob started to move out of the kitchen.

Charley said, "He'll kill us if he catches wind of it. He'll cut our throats in our sleep. He's already put away Ed Miller. Said so like it was something piddly he'd done."

Bob sauntered into the sitting room and saw Jesse crouched on the stairs, scratching his thumbnail on a riser. Jesse considered the nail and then sniffed it. "Is this blood?"

Bob sat nonchalantly in the rocker. "Could be. Clarence Hite was here for a week and never could get the best of that miserable cough; could be he was spitting blood and had himself an accident."

Jesse rubbed his thumb on the seat of his trousers. "You don't suppose it's consumption, do you?"

"Oh, Lord; I hope not. I never gave it a *thought*."

"In England they eat lemons. Twelve per day isn't too few." Jesse removed his broad hat and attended to the almost inaudible conference near the kitchen stove. "And they sip boiled water at bedtime." He turned to Bob. "They talking about me?"

Bob rocked and smiled. "Probably. You're the topic of conversation in every part of the country."

Jesse extricated himself from his heavy coat and laid it on the sofa with his hat. "Did I ever tell you about meeting Mark Twain?"

"No."

"He was in this country store and I recognized him, of course, and went over to shake the man's hand and congratulate him on his good writing. I said, 'You're Mark Twain, ain't you?' and he nodded yes he was, and I said, 'Guess you and I are about the greatest in our line.' He couldn't very well agree since he didn't know who I was, so he asks and I say, 'Jesse James,' and scoot on out of there. Hear tell he still talks about that. They say you go over to Europe and the only Americans they all know for certain are Mark Twain and yours truly.''

"I'm not surprised."

Jesse seemed to peer at Bob through a jeweler's bifocals. "You've got a bullet hole in your bedroom door."

"Oh?"

"Could've been put there when old man Harbison ran the place."

"You never can tell. If you look you'll find holes in the kitchen too. Gun-cleaning accidents, maybe."

Jesse batted the Christmas ornaments on a measly spruce that was wired into a tin bucket, and Wilbur came in from the privy, rigorously abrading his sleeves. Jesse asked, "Dick Liddil come by yet?"

"Nope."

"You know why he hasn't?"

"Maybe Mattie's got him on a short leash these days."

"I've got my own theory. I say it's on account of him and Wood having a run-in like they did in Kentucky. It's my theory he killed my cousin and he's scared he'll meet me here."

Bob gripped the rocking chair arms and tried to appear simply inquisitive.

Jesse said, "I'd appreciate it if you'd spread the word that I'm offering a reward for Dick. One thousand dollars, dead or alive. And let people know I'd prefer him dead."

"You're saying that in the heat of passion."

Big Wilbur came in with a jar of honey and a finger in his mouth. "Merry Christmas, Jess!"

"One thousand dollars," Jesse said.

Bob indicated the sheet that skirted the Christmas tree and asked, "Did you notice there was a present under there for you?"

Jesse beamed. "You're teasing." He stooped under a cincture of popcorn blossoms sewn with a thread and retrieved a cardboard box that was the size of a brick and wrapped in blue tissue paper. He shook the box and the contents clobbered inside. "Heavy!"

"I can't wait to see your eyes twinkle."

Wilbur grinned at his brother. "It's a gun, ain't it, Bob."

"You'll see soon enough."

Jesse ripped off the paper and the box flap and with childish astonishment withdrew a black, ironworked model of a salacious naked woman, her arms crossed beneath her head, her legs lewdly cloven and lifted.

"It's a bawdy bootjack," Bob said.

"I've wished I owned one a thousand times."

"Well. Now you do."

Jesse stroked the woman's round breasts with his thumb and blushed as he smiled. "I love Christmas."

"I can see that."

He imitated shame. "But I don't have anything for you! I never dreamed—"

"Your friendship is plenty."

Charley slunk in from the kitchen and then warily approached Jesse to examine the articulation of the ironwork. He asked his brother, "What is it?"

"It's a bawdy bootjack," he said.

"It's something I'll cherish always," said Jesse.

"Then we both have something to cherish," said Bob.

JESSE REMAINED on the farm that Christmas night and Bob remained awake. The moon was in the window and a window of moonlight was on the floor so that Jesse was unkenneled, released from the room's darkness and there on the cot like a man on a coffin, a man collected and in arrangement. Bob sat in his bed in his gray underwear, his wrists crossed, his ankles clasped, incapable of movement. He could see that there was a gun on the nightstand to his left and could imagine its cold nickel inside his grip, its two-pound weight reached out and aimed, but he couldn't even maneuver toward it, it was like a name he couldn't remember. He was a boy again, a rube, there were connections he was missing; and there across the room was Jesse, placid and sovereign, certain of both Heaven and Earth. His color in the night was the blue in veins of marble and the handsome head that rested on the pillow was appetitive and proud and pleased with itself.

And even then, with the man asleep, with his acute senses unattended, his keen reflexes numbed and slowed, the exact location of his firearms possibly forgotten, Bob could not screw up the courage to act. It was as if some spell or sorcery had rendered him meek, infirm, confounded. He could contrive many ways of snaring Jesse; he could invent a thousand deaths; but Bob feared it would always come to this, he would see a chance and then he'd interpret it and speculate on its consequences, he would ponder each option and particular and soon the opportunity would pass away, or qualms would overmaster him, conscience make him impotent.

Bob consoled himself with the thought that next time he would not stall so long—later, when Jesse was sickened or sorely distracted or the right situation presented itself, when Bob had mustered his courage and was not so susceptible to uncertainties. Bob was not yet twenty, after all, while Jesse was thirty-four and in physical decline; each calendar week subtracted from Jesse the powers that Bob accrued. So Bob could afford to wait if Jesse would only let him. And that, of course, he did.

With that, Bob slid under the covers and closed his eyes in imitation of Jesse and he woke next at sunrise to noises in the kitchen. Charley still snored to his left, but the cot across from Bob was vacated and downstairs a tea kettle piped once before it was removed from the stove. Bob skulked down the staircase and across the sitting room, tomfoolishly tiptoeing to the kitchen entrance and peeking around the doorjamb.

Jesse had amassed his suit clothes next to the butter churn and skidded a laundry boiler into the pantry, where he stood naked in two inches of steaming water, wringing a soaped washcloth over his skull, spitting the water that trickled into his mouth. He didn't notice Bob in the room. He scrubbed his elbow and knuckles with a tile brush and rinsed his arm and coughed twice and then again until he was racked like a chain-smoker for more than a minute and Bob smiled as he thought, *You are old, Jess. You are dying even now.*

His skin was white as sheep's wool and the scars on his chest were red as slaughter. He was muscular in the back and shoulders and sinews crossed his pectorals like laces and his biceps bunched when he lifted his wrist to tenderly examine it, but his ankle was knurled where he'd broken it, varices mapped his calves and thighs, his buttocks were flat as books, there were wrinkles of skin at his kidneys and neck, his ribs could be easily numbered, his shoulder clicked when he circled it, he bent with apparent pain. The many injuries of a reckless career had made him prematurely decrepit, as ancient as the Noah that Ham spied on in the tent.

Jesse coughed into his fist once more and swished his hand in the water at his feet, then lifted an ocean shell ashtray and sacredly doused the crown of his head. It was then that he saw Bob Ford and said, "Go away."

"It never crossed your mind that I was here and it's been nigh on to three minutes at least."

"You sure of that?" Jesse stepped from the laundry tub onto a red flannel shirt on the floor. He covered his face with a dishtowel and then rankled his dark brown hair with it as he smiled insincerely at Bob. "Maybe I was fooling you. Maybe we're playing cat and mouse."

"I've never seen you without your guns neither."

Jesse towed a bath towel off a chair and revealed, almost incidentally, a twelve-inch Remington revolver on the seat. "Don't happen more than once a year."

But Bob simpered with self-satisfaction. "Isn't no one can sneak up on Jesse James, is the way it used to be."

Jesse shawled himself in the white bath towel and sat down on the chair to soothe his feet in the laundry tub. "And now you think you know otherwise; maybe that's just what I wanted."

"I'm making fun is all, you understand. I wouldn't dream of mocking you or causing you any ill feelings."

Jesse rounded forward under the towel and cozied his feet in the bath water. It was as if no one else were around and Jesse was once again alone and at ease with his meditations. He said, "I can't figure it out: do you want to be *like* me, or do you want to *be* me?"

ON NEW YEAR'S EVE, Bob and Wilbur attended a party at Greenville. Since it was too cold to use the milk barn, George Rhodus, the host, had moved and stacked his Colonial furniture and rolled the blue carpet against the north wall and installed a string quartet in the dining room so the guests could waltz to Viennese music or converse around a galvanized bucket that was filled with hot cider and spiced apple slices. Bob and Wilbur lurked in a corner and exchanged pleasantries with whoever chanced by but mostly restricted themselves to occasional greetings and nods and otherwise sipped from glass cups and looked sly.

Then Jesse's stepbrother, Johnny Samuels, came in, uninvited, with two churlish companions who smutted the atmosphere. John was the comeliest of Zerelda's children; records mention a graceful young man with luxurious golden brown hair, liquid blue eyes, a soft, combed mustache and beard, and the complexion of a girlchild—one writer even compared his beauty to that seen in Flemish paintings of "the calm, benignant face of Him who died on Calvary nearly two thousand years ago."

He slunk over to Bob and Wilbur and asked, "You two seen Dave?"

Bob said, "He came on Christmas but went off with Charley the very next day."

Johnny seemed to want no more than that. He scooped up apple cider with a tin can that once contained apricots and then joined a man with a scar through one eye socket who spiked Johnny's cider with clear grain alcohol. Mr. Rhodus sent the hooligans a not-in-my-house-you-don't look but it didn't curtail what a guest would later call "their boozing," and by midnight George Rhodus and two enormous sons were steering Johnny Samuels outside into the cold. He squirmed and tried to jerk free as Rhodus said, "I've had about enough of you, young fella. I've had a belly full! I don't care who your brothers are!"

Bob heard Johnny scream, "Come back here, Rhodus! Rhodus! You coward! Come back out here and settle this!" Wilbur moved a window curtain aside and Bob saw Johnny spit on the shoveled brick sidewalk as his two friends punched their hands into woolen mittens and tramped across the yard to a wide string of brown horses. John Samuels was not about to give in so easily, however. He made a snowball and threw it but it sifted like sugar on the winds. He shouted oaths at Rhodus and kicked at short clumps of peony bushes. There was a bird feeder with icicles on it like the cushion tassels then in fashion and these Johnny collected with a sweep of his hand and pitched them with violence at the front door, so that a cluster of knocks startled the ladies inside.

Wilbur said, "Johnny's lost his sense of humor, ain't he."

Bob continued to stare without emotion as Johnny blasted snow with his tall black boots and tantrumed like a caricature of his wild and hot-tempered stepbrother. The front door whined open and cold rushed into the room and Bob heard Rhodus bellow, "Now that's enough of that carrying on, John! You're all liquored up and angry about nothing! You three boys go on home now and sleep it off and let's let bygones be bygones!"

Johnny moved onto the road, where he stood with his boots wide, clutching his wool coat closed. He shouted, "I ain't *on* your goll-danged land, George! I'm standing on public property!" And he skipped and clogged in the snow for the jeering show of it.

Rhodus became overexcited with that and went to a closet for a gun. He shouldered past men who tried to muscle him back inside and then was on the sidewalk with a Confederate pistol raised at Johnny's flat-brimmed black hat. He shot once and a woman shrieked and the three boys on the road squatted.

"Go!" Rhodus cried out, but John Samuels rose with a brick that he'd somehow unearthed from the sidewalk and he trotted forward and heaved the brick at Rhodus with great strain. The brick crashed through a tall window, bursting glass like ocean spray, swatting a curtain into the room, savagely denting the cherrywood floor on its strike, and in the next moment the revolver went off again, blue smoke billowing gray in the cold, the noise so loud it seemed two shots or three. And this ball socked into the right side of John Samuels's coat, swiveling him on his boot. He staggered as if he'd been thrown something cumbersome and then clutched at his upper ribs and looked toward the lit Rhodus house with disappointment and tribulation and abrupt sobriety, then he tilted backward and fell and his skull knocked the road like wood block against wood.

Great consternation followed, of course. John Samuels was carried into the Rhodus house by six men and laid next to the fire embers, where his clothes were removed with exceeding delicacy and his naked skin cooked to the warmth of a Sunday roast. An osteopath was in the neighborhood and was soon kneeling over John, manipulating the injury, resting his ear against the right lung. And while hypotheses and rumors and wild speculations about why John was shot were communicated and contradicted, George Rhodus invited some male partygoers to a conference in his upstairs bedroom, where they were evidently sworn to secrecy about what they each termed "a mishap."

It was then that the Ford brothers discreetly left in order to avoid any appearance of collusion, and for all of the next week Bob rode to Richmond so he could scour the newspapers for information about the shooting and its aftermath. "Young Samuels," the Kansas City *Journal* stated, "is reported as being quiet and orderly when sober, but is decidedly wild when under the influence of liquor, and it is in that condition he attended the dance, where he became engaged in a quarrel and was put out of the house, and in retaliation threw a brick through a window." The shooting was recounted and the medical circumstances were conveyed along with the prognosis that "death has been daily expected since." Concerning George Rhodus, however, there was little news—a sentence or two regarding a sheriff's investigation or a notation about a forthcoming grand jury inquest into the misadventure—with the result that Bob would ride back to the farm each afternoon with a feeling of astonishment. He kept expecting an obituary for George Rhodus, a news item about a Greenville dairy farmer who'd succumbed to a grisly execution: skewered, perhaps, by his Confederate Army sword while contritely praying at a chapel kneeler, or murdered as he napped on a parlor sofa, carbolic acid having been poured into his ear through a funnel.

But nothing happened, nothing at all. Johnny Samuels was dying and yet Jesse James was not going to avenge him. Soon the court reporters forgot about the Greenville incident except for a brief note that said the grand jury "failed to find a true bill" against the man who shot Jesse's stepbrother, and Bob Ford came to a new appreciation of just how much was possible.

ON JANUARY 4TH, Dick Liddil boarded an afternoon train to Richmond and hiked out to Mrs. Bolton's farm in smarting cold. He could smell snow but it only started to lick into him when he crossed onto the rented property at nine. By then Martha was asleep, so he went to the untidy room off the barn where Elias, Wilbur, and Bob were gambling pennies at cards. Dick sat close to the hayburner stove and acquainted them with a highly selective history of his days in Kansas City, and though Bob asked in every way imaginable if he'd made an arrangement with Police Commissioner Craig or Sheriff Timberlake or Governor Crittenden, Dick never strayed in his denying.

Elias and Wilbur would be at their livestock chores before sunrise, so they turned in at eleven, and Bob and Dick sat alone at the oakwood kitchen table, chatting in voices so low they would not buckle a candle flame that was two inches from their mouths.

Bob seemed more mature to Dick, more intuitive and shrewd; it was almost as if he'd taken a wife. Gone were the giddiness and ingratiation, though his good manners still seemed artificial and the air of performance and duplicity was still very strong. He listened attentively as Dick presented his plan to get involved with racehorses and eventually own a string, but he pulled away from any further exposure of his intentions when it seemed that beneath Bob's occasional comments there were sharp questions that would never be asked, inferences that Dick had inadvertently encouraged, implications that Bob was making of his omissions. Bob finally pushed the dialogue closer to his own prescriptions by asking if Dick remembered the July newspaper reports about Sheriff Pat Garrett and the killing of Billy the Kid.

Dick made no reply.

Bob asked, "Do you know what the Kansas City *Journal*'s comment was? They said a sheriff like Pat Garrett was just what Missouri needs:

a man who'll 'follow the James boys and their companions in crime to
their den, and shoot them down without mercy.' "

"You say this was in a newspaper?"

"Yes! And I'll quote you something else too. They said the man
who gunned down the James boys would be 'crowned with honors by
the good people of this commonwealth, and be richly rewarded in
money, besides.' "

Staining the oakwood was a dark ring that Dick rubbed with his
thumb. He said, "Maybe I *did* read that after all."

"You recollect it?"

Dick glanced away from Bob to the sitting room. The yellow eyes
of a cat were looking at him and then the cat curled down to lick at its
chest. Dick said, "You're not as hungry when you get to be my age,
Bob. You get to be twenty-nine years old and you look back and see
you've never done anything good that you can brag about and you sort
of forget all your pipe dreams. I gave up all my ideas of grandeur."

Bob slid his chair back and moved the coal-oil lamp from the
kitchen to the sitting room. He said, "Oftentimes things seem impossible up until they're attempted." Then he lidded the chimney glass
with his palm and suffocated the light.

CLAIMING A MORNING APPOINTMENT with a dentist in Richmond and
some chores to accomplish afterward, Bob left the house at dawn on
January 5th and surreptitiously journeyed to Kansas City by railroad
car. He dunked cinnamon doughnuts in coffee at a Kansas City cafe
and scanned three Missouri newspapers for more information about
John Samuels but saw not a word about him, only about Charles Guiteau:
a jailkeeper had allowed more than three hundred visitors "to inflame
and gratify the assassin's vanity and indulge their own morbid curiosity
by an admission to Guiteau's cell." The correspondent went on to say,
"It is an admonition to persons about to commit murder: 'Choose a big
man for your victim. Shoot a President; club a Cabinet Minister; creep
up behind a Senator and kill him with a slingshot; but don't kill any
private citizen, for if you do the Court will deal harshly with you.' "

Bob brushed cinnamon off his mouth and tie, tipped the counter-
man a nickel, and browsed through a clothing store's city directory for
the address of Police Commissioner Henry H. Craig. He noted the
cross streets on his shirt cuff and walked outside.

The streets were mud and slush and rutted manure, coal smoke
cindered the sidewalks and made the air blue, telegraph, telephone,

and electric wires criss-crossed overhead and chattered when a wind rose. He was slightly lost but could tell this was the commercial district: male accountants, secretaries, clerks, and commodities brokers stood under lowered awnings conferring about the universe, all in creased and corrugated suit coats that were black or navy blue in color so that they need never be cleaned. Bob cut between two surreys to cross a street and saw a boy with unsold copies of the Kansas City *Times* rolled under his left arm. He followed the boy down West Fifth to Main and then into the Times Building, where Henry H. Craig leased a law office in room number 6.

He blew his nose and knuckled the sleep from his eyes. He removed his bowler hat and slicked his fine brown hair with his palm. He rapped twice on a window of frosted glass and saw a faint blur become a man's black form and then he was being appraised by an apprentice attorney-at-law who seemed scarcely seventeen. Bob said, "I'm looking for Commissioner Craig. I've got some information about the James gang."

The apprentice glanced down to see if Bob carried a gun, then invited him in and shut the door. He asked for Bob's name but Bob wouldn't give it. He said Mr. Craig had a client with him at the moment and Bob said he expected the information would keep. The apprentice disappeared for a minute and then invited Bob into a room that contained green chintz furniture, tall bookcases of Kansas and Missouri statutes and judicial opinions, and a cherrywood box with a crank and black ear trumpet, which Bob took to be a telephone.

He heard the room's door creak and click shut and turned to see a stern man in his late forties with his suit coat off and circular bifocals on. His left eyebrow was cocked in a manner that made him look quizzical; his wide brown mustache was streaked with gray and covered his mouth and chin with shadow, so that he seemed even more severe than he was. "My assistant mentioned something about you and the James gang."

"Yes sir. I want to bring them to justice."

"The James gang," Craig said.

"Well, not each and every one all at once. Maybe I'd start out with the lowlier culprits and that would give me the opportunities I need to capture Jesse and Frank."

Craig squinted at Bob. "Who sent you here?"

"Sheriff James Timberlake of Clay County. Sort of indirectly. By that I mean he mentioned you but didn't know I was coming."

Craig hooked a finger inside his cheek and flicked a smidgen of chewing tobacco into a brass cuspidor. He moved his tongue around inside his mouth, then bent over and spit. He asked, "How do you know the James brothers?"

Bob foresaw the snarls of cross-examination and answered, "Did I say that I did?"

"Do you spy on them?"

"You'll excuse me for saying so, but isn't what matters the fact that I can round these culprits up?"

"I get told that once a week, and they're still uncaught. You can see how I'd be skeptical."

Bob lowered into a magisterial chair and rested his bowler hat in his lap. He let his palms appreciate the sculpted mahogany armrests. "Just lately?" he asked.

"Just lately what?"

"Anybody come to you lately saying he could bring in one or two of the James gang?"

Craig cleaned his eyeglasses with a white handkerchief. "Why do you want to know?"

"I just sort of thought they might've."

"It was a woman."

"She give her name as Mattie?"

Craig moved a chair over and sat across from Bob, shrugged forward like a rowing coach, his elbows on his knees. "You tell me. Her name was Mattie. Mattie what? Who was she acting for? Who were they going to bring in? You in Dutch with Jesse? Or is it only the reward money? You've got to give me something. I don't even know your name."

"It's Bob."

"Just Bob?"

"Right now, yes; for the time being."

Craig flickered a smile and combed the broad wings of his mustache with his thumb. "What's the first name on your list, Bob?"

Bob rose from the green chintz chair and walked over to the telephone. He could see that copper wires were attached to brass screws at the rear but couldn't fathom what they were for. He flicked one with his index finger and a stab of electricity twitched into his wrist.

"Did it nip you?" Craig asked.

Bob shook his hand and smiled with embarrassment. "I never knew these contraptions had teeth before." Bob looked down at it. "How's it work?"

Craig sinuated his right hand. "Your voice moves on undulating electrical currents. You scream into that mouthpiece to talk and then stick your ear next to it to listen. Most times you feel like a damned fool.''

"What was the joke I read in the newspaper? Oh yes: 'The telephone has developed an entirely new school of *hello*-cution.' Do you get it? *Hello*-cution? Like elocution?''

The commissioner stared at Bob without a word. A streetcar outside rattled and clanked. Girls screamed with laughter in the corridor. Bob said, "He's a friend. I don't look on it like I'm betraying him though. Jesse means to kill him, even offered a thousand-dollar reward for his carcass. I look on it like I'm saving him from injury.''

Craig remained as he was.

"Dick Liddil," said Bob.

Craig was unmoved. "Do you know where we can find him?''

"The reason is, Dick's a conniver and I can't figure out what his plans are, I just know he's got some fancy tricks up his sleeve and he won't pity me.''

Craig walked to a chest-high accountant's desk and flipped open an inkstand to scratch Bob's information into a journal ledger.

Bob said, "He can't know it was me.''

Craig attended to his notes. "You give me an exact time and location where we can catch him, and I'll guarantee your name will never get out. You'll be cited as an anonymous spy; not even Timberlake will know. If there's a reward, you'll get it, but beyond that I can't offer you any legal or physical protections." Craig looked over his shoulder and saw that Bob's brow was stitched, his mind in a careen. "Do you get the gist of what I'm saying?''

"Absolutely.''

"Do you know where Jesse's living?''

"He *was* in Kansas City.''

Craig registered incredulity and said, "You're pulling my leg.''

"Over on Woodland Avenue; and then Troost. He's moved again though. My brother knows where but he's been and gone before I could ask.''

Craig inscribed something in the journal and Bob walked over to study the entry. "Does the name Bob Ford mean anything to you?''

Craig dipped his quill in the ink bottle and scripted cursively on a brown blotter. "Is that your actual name or your alias?''

"Actual," said Bob, and he grinned with delight when he saw the name recorded in Craig's elegant calligraphy. "Pretty soon all of America will know who Bob Ford is.''

BOB TOLD THE COMMISSIONER that Dick Liddil was sleeping over at their rented farmhouse while his maimed leg mended and then created a crude map of the Harbison property, leaving out the creek where Wood Hite's remains now mouldered but including Richmond and country roads and nearby railroad tracks.

That afternoon Commissioner Craig activated a special unit of the Kansas City Police, a company of twelve that included himself and Sheriff Timberlake, a Sergeant Ditsch, two detectives, a constable, and six city policemen. They were called to the central station at nine that same evening, received instructions and coffee, were issued revolvers and rifles and cold weather gear, and after midnight on January 6th, climbed aboard a chartered train that consisted of a locomotive and two blackened smoking cars. The locomotive accelerated to a speed approaching fifty miles per hour until Lexington Junction, where it was switched to tracks that carried the men beyond Richmond to a cross-roads a short walk away from the Harbison farm. They came without horses and that would matter later—Craig wanted no noise.

The January thaw lasted only two days; by late afternoon on the 5th the sun was cast over by a latticework of clouds, by evening it had started to rain, and by the time the twelve moved into the woodrows the rain had turned to sleet that made tree branches clatter and iced the snow so that it was like saltines. The company circumnavigated a white, ramshackle house with oil-paper windows and a buckled roof and an elm tree that scratched at the shingles, and for a time some men tilted along a ravine that might have introduced them to the orange and petrified cadaver of Robert Woodson Hite, but the moment never came; instead of continuing on that route, the men circled close to the cattle lots and made a reconnaissance of the brown, leaning barn, then scuttled back to the fruit trees where Sheriff Timberlake and Commissioner Craig were in anxious consultation.

It was about 3 a.m. and every vista was blue or black and the sleet scored their cheeks like a cat scratch. No one could tell if any were awake inside, if rifles rested on the windowsills, if the communication with Ford were merely a preposterous bluff made to lure them into a skirmish and counterattack from the James gang. And it was the if of Jesse's being there, the maybe, the perchance, that persuaded Commissioner Craig and Sheriff Timberlake to practice care and prudence and to wait in the cold until sunrise.

So they remained in the woodrows and neither talked nor smoked nor stamped their boots to the earth. Cold watered their eyes and cemented their mittens to their rifle stocks and turned their feet into flatirons. Craig looked at his vest watch and clicked it shut and minutes later checked the vest watch again. Then the night lessened, the clouds ashened slightly, and the men became starkly black and brown against the gray of the snow. Craig walked out to scan the east and saw pink in the mile-off woods and he turned connotatively to Sheriff Timberlake.

The sheriff whistled succinctly and motioned forward for the deputies to move on the farmhouse and the twelve crept forward. Craig sucked on his index finger to thaw it, then nestled it next to the rifle's trigger. Timberlake waved the company in a circle around the house and saw a boy wipe an upstairs windowpane with his fist, peer out sleepily, and withdraw into the room.

That was Bob. He woke without really knowing why and listened for a clue, which came as a clink and then as the crunch of boots in rain-iced snow. He scurried from bed in his nightshirt with one name only on his mind and with a cavity inside his chest, and at the window he made out six armed men and maybe more, as rounded-over as hedgehogs, coming out of the woods as if they were created there. "Dick!" he insisted, and swatted the sleeping man's foot.

Dick inclined on an elbow, rubbing his eyes, then slanted over just enough to see a man in a city coat slugging his legs through a knee-deep snowdrift, a rifle crossed at his chest. Dick shot from bed, collapsed a little on his wounded leg, and hopped on the good one to the clothes he'd thrown over a chair. "Who is it?"

Bob climbed into cold woolen trousers and hooked suspenders over his nightshirt. "I saw a tin star on someone's pocket; that's all the information I need."

Dick said, "God damn Mattie anyhow," and buckled on his gunbelt.

Bob looked down into the sidelot. A young deputy genuflected into the snow and steadied his arm and rifle with a raised knee. If he fired, glass would crash across Martha's four-poster bed. A big voice in the yard called, "Jesse!"

Dick was in his knee boots and corduroy trousers, one suspender twisted on his shoulder. He bundled his coat and gloves at his stomach and asked, "How do I find the attic?"

"We know you're in there!" Timberlake cried out. "Come on outside with your hands up!"

Sheriff Timberlake was near the iron well-pump in the dooryard. His eyes watered in the wind, his iced mustache was like an ivory comb, and though he may have been mortally afraid at that moment, he looked austere and authoritative. He bracketed his mouth with his mittens and shouted, "You boys are cornered! If you know what's good for you, well, you'll come out peaceably and no one will get shot up!"

Timberlake saw the kitchen door suck inward and he crouched down. The storm door misted with the inside warmth and then it was pushed open and Bob Ford leaned outside. "Don't shoot!"

Timberlake turned to Craig. "You know who that is, don't you?"

Craig claimed he hadn't an inkling.

"Bob Ford. He lives here with his sister." The sheriff called, "Come on out and show yourself!"

Bob took a probationary step out onto the porch and then rooted there with his hands squeezed under his arms. He rubbed a stockinged foot on his calf. "If *this* isn't a surprise!" he said.

"That's how we intended it," the sheriff said, and slogged forward with Commissioner Craig and two Kansas City policemen as Bob Ford courteously butlered at the door.

Martha was at the oaken table, a frayed blue bathrobe clutched at her throat, her feet in scruffy white stockings. Craig withdrew circular eyeglasses and hooded them over his ears but resisted looking at Bob. He tilted his head to listen for footfalls overhead.

The sheriff asked if Jesse James, Jim Cummins, or Ed Miller was in the house and Bob said no, they weren't. Craig asked if Dick Liddil was perchance there and Bob responded in like manner. "Your friend, Charles Siderwood," the sheriff said. "Is that actually Dick Liddil?"

"No; that's Charles Siderwood."

"Is he here?"

Bob said, "You can look around if you want, but you won't find whoever it is you're after. It's just me and my kin here."

Craig instructed the sheriff to stay with the boy and took Sergeant Ditsch and two policemen with him to the second floor. Timberlake stood Bob in a corner and then poked charred stovewood with a fork, seeking red ash or embers.

Martha consented to start a fire and Timberlake invited the rest of the company inside out of the cold, which, as it turned out, was a compassionate but careless action to take. The sheriff moved around in the sitting room and kitchen and occasionally pulled out a counter drawer. Ida sleepily walked in with a wool coat over her nightgown and stared at the many policemen with big-eyed bewilderment. Martha set a coffee kettle on the stove and a coal-oil lamp on the sideboard. Smoke fluttered two feet above it. She kept trying to interpret Bob but couldn't tell if he was pretending innocence or if he'd caused the posse to come. She remembered how Bob used to lick sugar from his palm; he used to throw apples on the roof when she had girlfriends over; she'd once chased him into the creek because he dumped mustard powder into her cake pan.

Bob could hear the party moving through rooms on the second floor, yanking and overturning drawers, rummaging through clothes. "Come *on*," he muttered and the sheriff scowled at him. Martha carried empty coffee cups to the men. The kitchen was still so cold that their breaths steamed before them when they chatted. Martha came around with a coffee kettle and filled the cups and though Timberlake meant to smile at the widow, he sneered and then returned his glower to Bob Ford. He was six inches taller than Bob and sixty pounds his better, and Bob didn't risk a sip of his sister's coffee for fear the sheriff would punch the cup into his mouth.

Sergeant Ditsch came down to summon Bob to the second floor and Timberlake followed them upstairs. Bob said, "You're not going to find anything. My momma and daddy brought us Ford children up right. I sleep in the presence of angels."

The sergeant frowned at Bob and at Timberlake as he unclosed the bedroom door. Timberlake shoved past Bob into the room, saying, "Don't mind what the boy says. Butter wouldn't melt in his mouth."

Commissioner Craig was sitting on a mattress with Bob's shoebox in his lap. He said, "You're quite the packrat."

And Ditsch said, "Show us how to get to the attic."

"You mean you haven't been there already?"

Craig looked over his round eyeglasses and squinted sourly at Bob. "I don't think we're going to find much in the attic. I think our spy sent us on a wild goose chase."

Bob said, "You need to move the boxes on the closet shelf. They left off the stairs to the attic and cut out a cubbyhole in that closet."

Timberlake slid the boxes off the shelf and threw them, casting black dresses and crinolines across the floorboards where Wood Hite left the world. Bob sat down on the cot and rested his skull against the newspaper corset advertisements on the wall. He didn't care if Dick shot at the men when they entered the attic; he didn't care if Dick surrendered and confessed all and he himself was convicted for murder. He was shivering and sick to his stomach and wished only to lie down. The lady's white dresser that was next to the closet now lacked its three drawers; coats and trousers rugged the floor; books had been tossed like cow chips.

As Craig and Ditsch looked on, Timberlake climbed on a chair and whammed at the ceiling cover with his elbow until it skipped up off its wooden frame and the sheriff could slide it aside. He then drew his revolver and raised it and called, "You there! Give yourself up!" He looked to his knees as he waited for some sort of answer, then received a lit candle from Sergeant Ditsch and rested it inside the attic.

Craig scowled at Bob and Bob confidentially nodded and Craig said, "Go on in, Jim."

So the sheriff boosted himself over the frame and they could see his legs swivel as he looked around the attic but there were no shots, no sounds at all. "Sparrows," he said once, then, after a movement, "You've got a window open, you know that?"

Craig said, "Come on down, Jim," and took his eyeglasses off to clean them. "Looks like our spy was playing games."

Martha was in the corridor in a blue gingham dress and white sweater. She saw the chaos in the room and with sarcasm said, "I thought a man's home was his castle."

Craig smiled inauthentically and made some notes in the journal and closed it. "Why don't you show us the stable and barn, Mr. Ford?"

Bob buttoned on a coat and circled a wool scarf around his neck and Timberlake accompanied him across the snow as if they were two chums out on a skate. The sheriff said, "They're going to love a pretty boy like you in the penitentiary. You won't never be lonely again."

It was then about twenty minutes after sunrise. Wilbur came forth from his shack accoutered for chores and the sheriff and two detectives searched the lofts and crannies of the barn.

Bob remained outside in the cold with his fists in his coat and squinted at the attic's north window. He could see it had been jimmied open. A strip of white cloth blew from the sliver that snagged it; a sparrow was on the sill; shingles showed in the snow rut that Dick had cleared away as he silently skittered down off the roof. His boots made buckets in the snow. The left veered a little, like a comet's tail, as if he'd hurt his ankle on the considerable drop to the earth.

The two detectives had by then discovered the snow destruction of a mounted horse running north into the orchard, but since they were on foot they couldn't chase after Dick, so they merely cussed their luck.

Bob listened to them and closed his eyes. The stable door creaked and Bob smelled chewing tobacco and looked to see Commissioner Craig there next to him, considering everything. Craig said, with some irritation, "God takes care of fools and children."

And Bob said, "Not all the time He doesn't. I think this is an exception."

A PHYSICIAN INFORMED Clarence Hite in October that his coughing was due to consumption, and so he went back to Kentucky to recuperate, though life wasn't especially pleasant there. Mrs. Sarah Hite ran away following the killing of John Tabor; Wood Hite was jailed, then escaped, then disappeared; and word came that Ed Miller was found decomposing in the woods. And then, Clarence would later confess, "about a week before Johnny Samuels was shot, Jesse wrote me a letter. It was postmarked Kearney, Missouri, but I think was written in Kansas City. He said in substance that I had better leave home; Dick was in with the detectives and they would soon take me away."

How Jesse could have known that remains a mystery: it could be he was guessing; it could be that clairvoyance was one of his gifts, just as he always claimed. In any case, Jesse was a month premature, for it was on January 24th, 1882, that James Andrew Liddil gave himself up to Sheriff Timberlake in Liberty, Missouri. Henry Craig had kept his promise and permitted no one else to know that it was Bob who put Dick Liddil in jeopardy, and Dick perceived Bob as such a friend that he pleaded with him to act as an intermediary between himself and the government.

Dick was sent to Kansas City with Sheriff Timberlake and two deputies and was met at the depot by Commissioner Craig and Police Chief Thomas Speers, who scuttled him into the Second Street jail before reporters could learn his identity. Sitting on a slat bed in his jail cell was the Jackson County prosecuting attorney, William H. Wallace, and on a chair was a skinny amanuensis who wore half-moon spectacles. It was night by then and the jail was so cold that mists came from their mouths, and yet Wallace interviewed Liddil for more than three hours. A physician visited the cell and scolded Liddil about his injured leg as he milked pus from the wound and sprinkled it with powdered rosin before wrapping it in cloth.

Clarence Hite was by then doctoring himself with a weed called candlewick that he steeped like tea, and he was brewing a pot of it in February when he responded to a voice like Bob Ford's calling him into the yard. Clarence went to the windowed door in his long underwear and a woman's bathrobe, a red handkerchief flowered at his mouth. It was night and he couldn't see anything outside a hanging lantern's yellow circle of light. He squeezed out between the door and doorframe and saw Bob Ford shying away from reproach and Dick Liddil in a rocking chair, blowing clouds into his manacled fists. Then a man who would later introduce himself as Henry Craig came forward and asked Liddil, "Do you know this man to be Clarence Browler Hite?"

Liddil nodded with sorrow; Clarence merely examined a stain of blood on his palm and wiped it on his seat.

Craig shouted to Bob, "Mr. Ford?" Bob raised his stare. "Do you identify this man as one of those who committed robbery on the Chicago, Rock Island, and Pacific Railway at Winston, Missouri?"

Bob said, "You don't look any too sassy, Clarence."

Clarence acknowledged the remark with a cough. He seemed to have shrunk two inches in every direction. "I've been sort of wolfish about the head and shoulders for nigh onto four months now."

Craig nudged an arrest warrant into Hite's ribs and recounted its contents as Clarence puzzled out the great seal and the signatures of the governor and the secretary of state. Sheriff Timberlake connected handcuffs to his wrists and Clarence called to Bob, "You know them warts I cut off? They come back, every last one."

Clarence Browler Hite was remanded to Daviess County on February 13th and there two indictments were made, one for the murder of William Westfall and a subsidiary one for participation in the Winston train robbery in July. He was arraigned within weeks and, to the dismay of his defense attorney, pleaded guilty to the charge of robbery just so he would not be cross-examined and perhaps spill something important that the government could use. He was sentenced to twenty-five years in the penitentiary in Jefferson City, and in 1883, when his private information had long since ceased to matter, he would make a confession of his crimes and then he'd promptly die of consumption, as he'd predicted he would.

SNOWSTORMS MOVED over Missouri on Sunday, February 19th, and shut down commerce for more than two days. The snow removed roads and made hammocks of telegraph wires and submerged cattle high as their shanks. It cut off every railroad line east of Kansas City to St. Louis, it stopped the mail somewhere south of Omaha, its run-off would make the Mississippi sixty miles wide around Helena, Arkansas, and yet it couldn't prevent Bob Ford from presenting himself to Governor Crittenden at the Craig Rifles Ball on Wednesday. He rented two rough brown horses and a wooden sleigh with steel runners that initially marked the snow with rust and he guided the team with reins that were so cold they branched out from Bob's mittens like ribbons of tin. The horses clouted through snowdrifts for two or three miles, sometimes sinking so deep that they lunged and swam with fright, but then Bob reached a main road and steered into twin gullies made by another sleigh and the horses clopped along at a trot. The sunshine was radiant on the snow. The woods were rose and brown against white. The sky was blue and with only gray wisps of clouds overhead, like scriptures of chalk erased from a slate. Bob crouched out of the cold and clenched into himself, his ears scarfed in a girlish way, listening to the whisper of the sleigh runners in the ruts.

He arrived in Kansas City late that afternoon. Coal smoke gloomily darkened it and the streets were stacked high with muddied snow and Catholics walked the sidewalks with a priest's cross of soot on their foreheads. February 22nd signaled the joint celebration of George Washington's birthday and Ash Wednesday, the beginning of Lent, and as Bob slipped along toward the St. James Hotel, he could hear church bells as well as artillery salutes. He liveried the two workhorses and strolled the purple carpet of the hotel lobby, thawing his fingers at his mouth, until he figured out where to ask for Henry Craig's room number and took the steps three at a time.

The commissioner shouted for Bob to come in at his rap, and Bob sidled inside like a cat. Craig was naked in a wood and tin bathtub that was narrow as a coffin, scrubbing a foot with a pumice stone. "Didn't expect you to make it."

Bob seated himself in a Queen Anne chair and slid his bowler hat beneath it. "I couldn't pass up meeting the governor. Me and him've got some important matters to take up."

Craig cast an intolerant glance at Bob and then nodded toward a squat glass and a green bottle of whiskey. "How about some roockus juice?"

Bob shook his head in the negative and smiled. "Doesn't take more than a sip to make me want to bite off my own nose."

Craig sloshed messily out of the tub and swallowed what remained in the glass. Soap suds eased down his back. "Well, this is my day!" He tottered just a little and refilled the glass with whiskey before raising it. "Here's to the Craig Rifles and to the great man who leads them so magnificently."

Bob asked, "Can I climb into that bath water? I caught a chill on my sleigh ride and that water might be accommodating."

"Go ahead," Craig said and rigorously toweled himself as Bob stripped and sank into the tub with a groan. Craig said, "There's something real seldom about you, Bob."

At about that time, Thomas Speers, the chief of the Kansas City Police Department, came up to the commissioner's room with Dick Liddil. Craig invited Speers to gladden himself with the whiskey and Bob scuttled into a coal black closet, where he fumbled into underwear that was not his own, that was laundry-marked H.C. He came out just as two waiters trollied in a meal cart of covered silver dishes, and he slicked his wet hair with his sister's ivory comb as he sat down to carrots and rare steak. Bob cut into the meat and then considered the other men's plates. "Is your cow still moving?"

Dick rose in his chair to see the color. "Just singed it a little, did they?"

"I've seen critters worse off than this get well."

Craig said, "You're not going to be complaining all evening, are you?"

"Me? I'm happy, Henry! It's the Craig Rifles Ball! It's your night!"

"Don't give the governor your smart aleck talk," said Craig, sniffing a wine cork and then pouring a burgundy for Speers and himself.

Plates were cleaned, opinions swapped, and then two policemen were sent up to sit with Dick and Bob as Commissioner Henry Craig and Police Chief Thomas Speers made their grand entrance at the party in the second-floor ballroom. The policemen opened a pack of cards, Dick put his ear to the carpet in order to listen to opera adaptations, Bob flipped through pages of the newspapers on the bed.

On January 30th, a jury decided that Charles J. Guiteau was governed not by God or insanity but by his own wickedness, and they returned a verdict of guilty as charged for his killing of President Garfield. Judge Cox sentenced him to public execution and Guiteau screamed, "I am here as God's man! God Almighty will curse every man who has had anything to do with this case!" Soon after that, correspondents stopped filing stories about the condemned man, but on February 22nd, there was an item that Bob read aloud: " 'Guiteau is said to believe that he would be a great success in the lecture field. There is no doubt that his next appearance on the platform, June thirtieth, eighteen eighty-two, will be hailed with great satisfaction by the American people.' "

Dick snickered a little. "Anything else interesting?"

Bob looked. The newspaper reminded its readers that it was Ash

Wednesday, and that the following forty days were "a time for penitential retirement from the world and abstinence from the festivities of ordinary life in order to afford an opportunity for reflection, undistracted by secular pursuits, on sins committed and preparations to do battle in the future against temptations and fleshly lusts."

Bob skipped to another column and then slapped the newspaper pages together and jumped up from the bed. He called to the policemen, "Do I have to stay cooped up here? It's only Dick who's under arrest."

The policeman in charge made Bob leave his gun and overcoat and then let him out to saunter from floor to floor and linger by the St. James Hotel's grand ballroom. The orchestra was in recess and a boy of twelve was on a stepladder above a respectful crowd, reciting a poem about George Washington. "Hail! Natal day of Freedom's son, his country's boast and pride—our own beloved Washington, who Tyranny defied."

Gentlemen in tails were stamping snow from their shoes in the corridor and ladies in ankle-long cloaks and satin gowns and perfumes of mimosa were greeting each other and patting wrists and laughing as they sashayed in. Bob followed them and slunk over to a corner and tarried there as he listened to the boy continue: "We share the glories that he won and, should the need arise, could still produce a Washington to lead, protect, advise; the hero's progeny survives, engaged in useful, peaceful lives."

The crowd applauded with greater sympathy than appreciation and the boy crept down from the ladder to be superseded by Commissioner Henry Craig. He hooked an arm around a stepladder strut to stop his slightly drunken sway and then joked and kidded and made the silly remarks of a master of ceremonies. The crowd's laughter was contrived and overly hearty and Bob muttered aloud, "You're not so great," at which a woman glared. His look was too nighted, his blue eyes skittered, he knew he seemed callow and uncouth, and yet he moved closer as Craig exclaimed about the vigilant governor of Missouri whom it was his incomparable honor to serve. And without further ado, Craig flung out his left arm toward a round table at which sat the lions of industry and property and their sumptuously ornamented wives. The reassembled orchestra played music Bob couldn't recognize and wine glasses were chimed with spoons until the governor rose up and produced silence among them by dispensing his palms.

Governor Thomas Theodore Crittenden was a stout man of fifty with perfectly combed white hair, penetrating brown eyes, and a white mustache that was clipped so close it was little more than a chalky bristle. He loved the grandeur and pomp of high office and he paused sublimely, gathering everyone's attention, before he greeted his audience and graciously bowed to Craig. He said, "I deem it a great privilege on this glorious occasion to recognize publicly the intelligent and efficient assistance that Captain Henry Craig has thus far provided the State of Missouri and myself in our joint quest to extirpate the James band from Jackson County. The aid rendered by this gentleman is invaluable to me, and without it, the duty devolving upon me would be much more difficult, if not altogether impossible to accomplish. The task Henry Craig has assumed requires fearless courage, extraordinary vigilance, and an unerring selection of instrumentalities. He is always ready to undergo any labor, danger, or exposure in pursuit of the outlaws, and in every action Henry Craig has committed himself to the highest standards of the Craig Rifles and the Kansas City Police Department, and to that I unhesitatingly bear official testimony." The governor glanced to his right and smiled with good humor at the audience. "My wife has just signaled that I should leave well enough alone, so I'll leave you all with the wish for an enjoyable evening and with the hope that I may have the pleasure of meeting you each before this celebration is ended."

By then Bob was only five ranks away from the round table and yearning for acknowledgment. He jostled closer, rustling belled, chiffon skirts, pushing a goateed man aside, and lifted an arm in a joyous and juvenile wave that Governor Crittenden squinted at. And Bob was insinuating himself close enough to give his name when his collar was snatched and both biceps were painfully grasped by two of Craig's policemen. He was going to shout but his mouth was clasped shut, and he was going to kick free when he was socked in the groin and collapsed in agony. Some people looked at him reproachfully and then the orchestra was playing a waltz and they simply passed around him as the policemen picked him up.

Craig was at the ticket table next to the door prizes of japanned dishware and a Singer sewing machine. The policemen shoved Bob into the corridor and Bob sagged against an ornate mahogany pillar. Craig said, "You're more trouble than you're worth."

"I was just going to say hello."

"That isn't why you're here. Get upstairs now and see if you can't keep your identity secret."

Dick Liddil was in a soft chair next to a coal-oil lamp, reading the newspapers; the two policemen were smoking cigarettes with their coats opened, their eyes on the snow in the streets. Dick was telling them, "Representative Thomas Allen is dying of cancer, it says. Richest man in Congress too; worth fifteen million dollars."

A policeman said, "The grim reaper don't care who you are."

Bob flopped down into a chair and put his stockinged feet up on an ottoman. He said, "You can read about your captains of industry in *Frank Leslie's Popular Monthly.*"

Dick looked over the top of the newspaper and asked, "How was the party?"

Bob said, "You take Alexander Stewart. He stocked his dry goods store in New York with only five thousand dollars to his name. He was nineteen years old at the time. And when he kicked the bucket he was worth somewheres close to fifty million. Commodore Vanderbilt is another case. He started out on the ferry boat from Staten Island to New York City and he's got a fortune of about one hundred million dollars now. Look at Jay Gould. He's as crooked as a coat hanger and doesn't care fiddlesticks about public opinion, but you know what? He's forty-five years old now and he *owns* the Missouri Pacific Railroad. Probably worth fifty million. And guess what else. Jay Gould wasn't but a surveyor when he was twenty."

Dick said, "You'll catch him in no time, Bob."

"Don't laugh. I'm going to have a good start on it pretty dang soon."

IT WASN'T UNTIL MIDNIGHT that Commissioner Craig returned to the room. Dick was asleep and Bob was shaving with Craig's toiletries and bleeding from two nicks. Craig waggled Dick's foot until he awoke and then frowned into the dresser mirror at Bob.

Bob said, "What're you looking at now?"

"My God, have you no respect for private property?"

Bob patted his face dry and lamely said, "*I'm* the one who's cut."

Craig walked to the corridor, saying in a peremptory way, "The governor's in his suite."

The corridor was carpeted in purple and ceilinged in white fleur-de-lis. Gas lamps whispered as they passed. Dick yawned loudly, like a dog, and Bob inquired about salutary topics of conversation. Craig ignored him. Craig was no longer intoxicated and the aftereffects were making him grouchy.

The governor met them in a red silk robe that was sealed like an envelope around his starched white shirt and tuxedo trousers. On his feet were calfskin slippers and on his cheeks he wore cologne. Craig made cursory introductions and Crittenden neglected to shake their available hands as he settled into a Chippendale settee and specified green wingback chairs for his guests. He said, "My wife is asleep in the next room, so let's speak as quietly as we can."

A gold tea service was on the oiled table at his shins; gold candelabra were stationed near the settee arms and the smoke from the candle flames rose straight up. A glint of light was on the governor's nose and his brown eyes glittered as he regarded the two strangers. "You're Dick Little."

"Liddil."

"I beg your pardon?"

"I spell it with two d's."

The governor accepted the correction and Craig said, "He's given us a confession but so far the newspapers haven't caught onto it. You've guaranteed him a conditional pardon and amnesty for his robberies."

Crittenden arranged two pillows beneath his left elbow so that he could lean confidentially toward Bob. "You're Robert Ford."

Bob grinned but could think of nothing to say.

"How old are you, Bob?"

"Twenty."

"Did you surrender to Sheriff Timberlake as well?"

Craig said, "It was his brother Charley who was in the James gang. We couldn't find anything on Bob. He's acting in the capacity of a private detective. He helped us make the pact with Liddil, and he was one of the party that captured Clarence Hite in Kentucky."

"I see." The governor poured green tea from the elegant gold kettle and said, "Jesse James sent me a telegram last month. It said he'd kill me if he had to wreck a train to do so and that once I was in his hands he would cut my heart into strips and eat it like bacon." Crittenden sipped the tea and touched his mouth with a napkin. "I'm going to wreck his train first."

Bob scoffed and the governor sent him a scalding look. Bob said, "I'm sorry, Your Excellency. I was laughing at something else."

Crittenden lounged with a china saucer aslant on his stomach. His complexion was pale as his shirt. He said, "Jesse James is nothing more than a public outlaw who's made his reputation by stealing whatever he could and by killing whoever got in his way. You'll hear some fools say he's getting back at Republicans and Union men for wrongs his family suffered during the war, but his victims have scarcely ever been selected with reference to their political views.'' The governor set the teacup in its saucer with a click and slid both onto the gold tea tray. "A petty thief is generally despised and easily convicted; but one who steals millions becomes a sort of hero in the estimation of many. A man who commits one sneaking murder is regarded as the meanest of criminals and fit only for a speedy halter; but there is an illogical class of persons who cannot restrain a sort of admiration for one who has murdered many and shown no mercy, who has hesitated at no deed of darkness and inhumanity. Do you see what I'm saying?''

Bob made no acknowledgment.

The governor's wife moaned in the other room. The governor tempered his voice. "I'm saying his sins will soon find him out. His cup of iniquity is full. I'm saying Jesse James is a desperate case and may require a desperate remedy.''

Dick expected a reply from Bob but realized that his companion was overpowered by assumptions and suppositions. He looked sleepy, pessimistic, depressed, and incapable of speech, so Dick responded for Bob by telling Governor Crittenden, "You've got the right man for the job.''

5

MARCH–APRIL 1882

The pitcher goes often to the fountain, but it is broken at last. The longest lane comes to an abrupt and unexpected turning. The wild career of the James Brothers had gone on unchecked so long, that there is no wonder that many regarded them as invincible if not invulnerable. They seemed to bear a charmed life. And though they were scarred and wounded, and bullet-laden, they lived on defiantly as if they dared fate to the uttermost. But fortune is a fickle jade. She turns her mystic wheel with a capricious hand. She smiles to-day with little cause for smiling and the next day frowns without any cause at all. The fabled Nemesis waits long and patiently by the wayside, but at last vengeance wakes, and doom comes swift as lightning and awful as death.

ANONYMOUS
Lives, Adventures and Exploits of Frank and Jesse James

ACCORDING TO LATER courtroom confessions, Charley Ford stayed with Jesse James from December 6th to April 3rd, either in St. Joseph or on the road in Missouri, Kansas, and Nebraska, assessing farmland and small-town banks. The Boder Brothers' Bank in Troy, Kansas, was considered but when Jesse asked that a hundred-dollar bill be broken down into smaller denominations, as was his custom in bank robberies, Louis Boder got an inkling that something was amiss and lied that their currencies were already locked in the vault for the night. And Charley later recalled that Jesse "liked the way the bank in Forrest City was situated, and said he wanted to take that bank, but I told him I did not want to go into that, as I was sick then." Robberies were conceived, but never carried out, in Humboldt, Nebraska, Maryville and Oregon, Missouri, Sebitha and Hiawatha, Kansas. And of course Jesse would later contemplate an April 4th assault on the Wells Banking Company in Platte City, but that too would never come to pass.

It was February when Jesse lumbered through snow that was high as hip waders in order to inspect a corn crib and silo near Pawnee City. Charley sat on a mare and smoked a cigarette. The Nebraska cold cut his feet off at the ankles and the wind on his cheek was like thistles, but Jesse was ecstatic. He sat down in the chair of a snowbank and shouted, "I could purchase maybe a dozen long yearlings and breed the heifers at twenty months or fatten them until they're all twos and threes. I could put the calves to grass as soon as they learnt to chew it. You can wean them on skimmed milk. I'd feed the young ones shelled corn and oats, and I'd give hay to the dry cows; no grain. I'd sorta like to try beets and parsnips in cold weather. Your German scientists swear by it."

Charley let his mare garden the brown weeds that stemmed above the snowcrust. "Somehow I never seen you as the proud owner of a cattle lot. This is going to take some adjusting on my part."

Jesse scooped up snow and ate it and swatted his mittens as he arose, rejoicing over his prospects. But when they visited another property the next afternoon, Jesse was so wary he wore three revolvers under his Confederate officer's long wool coat and knotted a blue scarf over his nose and mouth in order to remain incognito. Charley made conversation with the owner as they walked from room to room and saw the grange and barn and stables, but the man seemed either too inquisitive or too comprehending and Jesse trudged to his horse through the snow, leaving Charley to say goodbye and make apologies.

However, by March 2nd agriculture was on his mind and Jesse wrote, in his gnarled and negligent scrawl, this letter of inquiry to J. D. Calhoun of Lincoln, Nebraska:

Dear Sir:

I have noticed that you have 160 acres for sale in Franklin County, Neb. Please write me at once and let me know the lowest cash price that will buy your land. Give me a full description of the land, etc.

I want to purchase a farm of that size, provided I can find one to suit. I will not buy a farm unless the soil is No. 1.

I will start a trip in about 8 days to northern Kan & south Nebrask, and if the description of your land suits me I will buy it. From the advertisement in the Lincol Journal I suppose your land can be made a good farm for stock and grain.

Please answer at once.
Respectful

Tho Howard.

Then the spell apparently wore off because Calhoun received no acknowledgment of his reply.

Charley and Jesse visited Kansas City once at about this time and there Jesse called on Mattie Collins as Charley supported his weight on a pool cue in a smoky Twelfth Street saloon.

Much later, Mattie admitted to a "great fondness" for Jesse and said they "were in constant communication," which prompted many rumors about a love affair between them, but it is just as likely Jesse visited her in hope of private intelligence, rewarding Mattie with presents for whatever she volunteered. Years afterward, when it no longer mattered, Mattie would claim she couldn't love another man, that she was married body and soul to Dick Liddil, and she'd further claim that she'd never told even one of Dick's secrets, so it could be Jesse never received what he really wanted, which may have accounted for his tart gloominess and the sting of his words when he collected Charley at the saloon that night.

He was increasingly irritable and suspicious, and a cantankerous mood could fly over him as quickly as the shadow of a bird. But Jesse was neither close-mouthed nor sulky for long, and over the weeks that he and Charley were on the road, he unscrolled yarns and anecdotes that excited interest in Charley only insofar as they permitted him a corresponding reminiscence.

Jesse revealed that for two months one summer, using the alias of John Franklin, he conducted a singing school for the Unity Baptist Church in Calloway County. He said he once intended to steal a Lutheran minister's cigar box of coins but learned the German's salary was a mere two hundred dollars per year and Jesse returned the box, avowing, "I'm not as bad as some people think."

He chronicled a visit to a chum named Scott Moore at the Las Vegas hot springs in the New Mexico Territory. Moore and his wife, Minnie, ran the Old Adobe Hotel there and served gigantic eight-course Sunday dinners that could beguile the gold right out of your teeth. It was there, in July 1879, that Jesse was introduced to none other than Billy the Kid. Billy was slack-jawed and broad in the sitdown and the corners of his mouth collected white saliva when he talked, but he was otherwise an agreeable, generous boy who gloried in the coincidence that the two scariest men in America both wore left-handed guns. They buried him in leg-irons, Jesse said. His English was lazy, his Spanish exact, and Billy's last words had been "Quién es?"—Who is it? "He was more sinned against than sinning," said Jesse.

"Like you," said Charley Ford.

He told Charley about the uncle for whom he was named, and how Jesse Cole had become overwrought by various illnesses and had therefore resolved to permanently end them. His uncle had walked out to a summer lawn, removed his coat and vest and rested a silver watch on them, and then grandiosely lay down, unbuttoned his shirt, and shot himself in the heart.

Jesse swiveled a little in his saddle to see Charley plodding his mare along to the right. "You ever consider suicide?"

"Can't say I have. There was always something else I wanted to do. Or my predicaments changed or I saw hardships from a different slant; you know all what can happen. It never seemed respectable."

"I'll tell you one thing that's certain: you won't fight dying once you've peeked over to the other side; you'll no more want to go back to your body than you'd want to spoon up your own puke."

It was March then and the weather was nasty and the road was ice and muck and scrambled wagon ruts. Their saddles creaked with every movement and their two horses were morose: their nostrils were frosted and their manes were braided with icicles and if they rested the animals their coats would steam in the cold. Charley's motor worked in the considerable silence between the two men and then he said, "Since we're looking to robbing banks, I was wondering if I could go so far as to recommend we add another feller to the gang and sort of see if we couldn't come out of our next job alive."

Jesse seemed transfixed by his saddle's left fender and stirrup, and would not raise his stare.

Charley went on, "Bob wanted to know at Christmas could he ride with us next time we took on a savings bank or a railroad."

Jesse sneezed and then sneezed again and he scoured his nose with his yellow glove, examining the dark streak on the leather.

Charley said, "Bob isn't much more than a boy to most appearances, but there's about two tons of sand in him and he'll stand with his shooter when that's what's called for. And he's smart too—he's about as intricate as they come."

"You're forgetting that I've already met the kid."

"He surely thinks highly of you."

"All America thinks highly of me."

"Still. It's not like you've got two million names you can snatch out of a sock whenever you need a third man. I mean, who else is there that isn't already in jail?"

Jesse sighed and said, "You're going to try and wear me down on this, aren't you."

Charley smiled. "That was my main intention," he said, and went on to cite his brother's constancy and his acquaintance with the Jameses, his many attainments and capabilities, his unqualified allegiance and courage, and eventually Jesse said Bob could come along as soon as they'd settled on a situation and a gratifying corporation to rob.

And with that he lost his audience. Charley looked to his left and saw that Jesse had peeled off and was maneuvering through clusters of hickories and hackberries, so that pickets of him appeared vividly against the snow, then vanished into gray air and deep brown trees where branches snapped sharply and shrieked off his coat. Charley wasn't sure if it was Jesse he was pursuing or if he himself were not being pursued. Then he caught a fuller glimpse and nudged his horse to catch up and after some time he reached Jesse at a creek that was arrested in amber ice and partially covered by snow.

Jesse leaned in his saddle, his arms crossed on the pommel, and considered the small, three-dashed tracks that arrowed across the snow. He winked and said, "I see our supper."

"Rabbits," said Charley Ford.

A NOTE WAS MAILED to Bob Ford with the news that Charley and Jesse would come to Ray County within the next few weeks. Martha collected the letter at the post office and sent word of it to Commissioner Craig in Kansas City because, as a precaution against any slip-up or vendetta, Craig had moved Bob to a room over the National Bank on the corner of Fifth and Delaware streets, and had moved Dick Liddil to Sheriff Timberlake's house in Liberty, Missouri.

Bob Ford would later be cross-examined repeatedly about Craig's instructions to him and he never swerved in his recollection: that the commissioner enjoined him to return to Elias's small cottage in Richmond to await the arrival of the two, that Bob was told to communicate their whereabouts to Sheriff Timberlake via William Ford, Bob's uncle, or his brother Elias (who was a secretly sworn deputy then, on the lookout for Jim Cummins or Frank James), and furthermore if Craig did not receive word from Bob within ten days after Martha reported him gone, the government would consider the Ford brothers already slain and would move against Jesse without regard for their safety.

Craig said all that in a stoic, lawyerly, teacherly way, as if making simple calculations or performing a regular task that was then no more than routine. Bob accepted the counsel as an ignorant boy would, nodding general agreement at every phrase, veering his eyes toward a noise in the street, anticipating the conclusion to each sentence without fully appreciating the contents. Then he left Kansas City and spent two or three weeks with Elias in Richmond, where he showed uncommon industry by clerking in the grocery store.

Sheriff Timberlake prowled the store once, priced a tin of tooth-powder, and then slipped into the storeroom and made a cigarette, smoking patiently until Bob could join him.

When he could get away from the grocery buyers, Bob said, "Haven't seen any sign of him."

"Do you know where he's living?"

"No."

The sheriff sighed and gazed at a box containing Baker's Breakfast Cocoa. "I can't guess how he does it, but he's always knowledgeable about what's going on. He'll know you've been with me. You ought to take that for granted. And he'll kill you if he gets the chance."

Bob scratched at his neck and slid his eyes away.

The sheriff asked, "You willing to risk that?"

Bob jiggled his head in agreement and then said, "Yes, I am." He fastened his eyes on Timberlake and it was as if a shade had been drawn over the boy's face: gone were Bob's ingratiation and ingenuousness; all the sheriff could see was longing and misery. Bob said, "I've been a nobody all my life. I was the baby; I was the one people picked on, the one they made promises to that they never kept. And ever since I can recall it, Jesse James has been big as a tree. I'm prepared for this, Jim. And I'm going to accomplish it. I know I won't get but this one opportunity and you can bet your life I'm not going to spoil it."

Sheriff Timberlake winced from cigarette smoke and edged away. "Capture him if you can when he first comes to meet you. If you can't do it, wait for your chance. Don't allow yourself to be found alone with him if you can avoid it. And don't let him get behind you." The sheriff then ground out his cigarette and exited through the loading door.

Bob remained standing there and then kicked a cardboard box many times and fell down to his knees.

Meanwhile Jesse and Charley meandered, riding eighty miles per day for weeks at a time. On March 8th a newspaper reported that Jesse James was "shot full of holes" in a skirmish at a log cabin in Kansas. The man with him was said to be Ed Miller. Seven deputies were killed, the writer claimed, "in the enterprise of capturing the desperado." The notice was recanted within the day, but not before one-eyed

George Shepherd took exception to it. He immediately wrote a letter to the newspaper in which he jeered at every official pronouncement about the gang and every incompetent posse that went out after them, concluding, "I am of the opinion that there are hundreds of officers and detectives today hunting for the James boys and praying to God not to find them."

A man who was retired from the Hannibal and St. Joseph Railroad maintained that he saw Jesse and another man in Lincoln, Nebraska, around this time, but a millworker claimed they bought flour from him in Memphis, and there were occasional other reports of Jesse's being sighted in Texas, Colorado, and the South; but he was actually spending the greater portion of his time in St. Joseph: Zee was pregnant once again and he sought to spare her the drudge work of keeping the cottage.

On March 17th, Jesse curried a stallion named Stonewall, braided green ribbons into its mane and tail, and rode magisterially in the St. Patrick's Day parade with St. Joseph's many cattlemen. He raised a broad white hat to the ladies, he cast rock candies to the children, he carried on like an army general or someone running for election, and yet no sheriff or Pinkerton operative recognized the outlaw, which may have been a disappointment to him.

It was also in March that Jesse and Charley visited Maryville and ordered steamed beer in Mike Hilgert's saloon. A big, cruel, irascible man named Omaha Charlie—who would later be hanged with great enthusiasm from a railroad trestle for murder—moved about the saloon, noisily inviting various customers to play pool. He finally approached the newcomers, Jesse accepted the invitation, and Omaha Charlie immediately commenced insulting him for the swank of his clothes, his gentleman's bearing, his high voice, the scrupulous method with which Jesse chalked his warped cue.

Jesse ignored the man and bent to the pool game with good humor, sinking five stripes in two turns, which caused Omaha Charlie to squinch up his eyes and call Jesse a cheat (according to plan) and tilt toward the stranger with his pool cue raised.

Eyewitnesses later recalled that the gentleman remained calm, almost pacific, but concentrated his cold blue eyes on Omaha Charlie and said with grave intention, "Stop where you are. You are threatening the wrong man."

Omaha Charlie stalled for a minute and apprehensively reconsidered, then clapped the cue down on the pool table, slouched back to a corner chair, and occupied himself with his boot socks. Jesse James and Charley Ford merely lingered over their steamed beers, voted against inspecting the Maryville bank, and walked out.

Mike Hilgert then winked and called to the corner, "What made you so sociable all of a sudden?"

Omaha Charlie angrily removed himself from the saloon but reportedly said later, "I could see Hell in that man's eyes."

In Graham, Missouri, Jesse asked a blacksmith to renail a shoe, thawed his knuckles at a fire, and only then noticed that the man in the leather apron was Uriah Bond, whose son John was in grammar school with the James brothers in the late 1850's, then joined the Northern Army and was murdered by Jesse in the Civil War.

Uriah Bond snuck looks under his eyebrows at the two as he worked on the hoof with his nippers and clawhammer. Jesse walked over with a rasp so the blacksmith could smooth the nails after he'd clinched them. He said, "You know who I am, don't you."

Bond remained bent over and silent. He swiveled the hammer and broke a nail end off with a jerk of the claw. Then he just hunched there and a broad hand covered his eyes as he shook with rage and grief and hopeless fright.

Jesse said, "You won't tell anyone, will you," and Uriah Bond mentioned the afternoon visit to no one until he saw the photograph of Jesse with his eyes shut, his arms crossed at his wrists, his body roped to a cooling board and tilted so that he seemed to stand.

On a night in Kansas when the rain came down like cold coins, the two outlaws retreated into a small white hotel with a coven of rooms and rented one on the second floor. Two orange gas lamps sissed on the walls, the wide bed was tautly made, the closet and armoire were empty. But an eighteenth-century highboy in the corner contained a locked middle drawer that Jesse scratched at with a six-penny nail as Charley squirmed out of his clothes. The lock clicked open and Jesse said, "Presto chango!" and slid the drawer out. Inside were a night-black silk cravat that was striped in red, a starched white shirt that was still wrapped in blue laundry paper, and a crisp celluloid collar that was exactly his size (14½). According to an interview with Charley in the Richmond *Conservator,* those were the clothes that Jesse wore on the morning of April 3rd.

THEN IT WAS the third week of March. Cold spells and winds were only occasional, the pasturelands were greening, there were rucks and islands of snow only in the shade, city streets were sloppy with mud that agglutinated on buggy wheels and slowly baked in the noontime sun and then peeled off like tree bark. Jesse mentioned robberies, but only as one might mention a sparrow's nest in the eave or an annoyance in a mail-order shoe. His wife was pretty sick until noontimes, so he merrily took over some of the cooking and cleaning work, even walked into an apothecary and ordered Lydia Pinkham's Vegetable Compound. (Advertisements called it: "A positive cure for all those painful complaints and weaknesses so common to our best female population.")

He made macaroons with an apron on, he invited some girls over to visit Zee and kissed their gloved hands in greeting; he seemed to have subtracted from his make-up whatever was cruel or criminal and substituted for those qualities congeniality and inertia. He accorded to everyone, he spoiled his children, he offered Charley a substantial allowance as if Charley were his profligate but much-preferred son. He seemed resigned, placid, grandfatherly; he seemed to have given up.

So it was a surprise when Jesse threw a chinchilla coat at Charley's sleeping face and said, "Get your gatherings together. You and I are riding south."

South, of course, meant Richmond, which they achieved on March 23rd. They looked for Bob in Elias's unlocked house, then found him in the grocery store with a clerk's apron on, a feather duster jutting from a rear trouser pocket, climbing onto a wooden stool to stack jars of Heinz tomato ketchup on an overhead shelf. Only two customers were in the store: a woman was examining various lengths of penny shoelaces that were draped over a jacket peg and an elderly man was sliding a flour sack along an aisle that was coated with sawdust. Bob leaned to swish the feather duster over a row of applesauce lids and Jesse startled the boy by announcing, "You've been chosen."

Bob swiveled around and nearly slipped off the stool, his arm nearly flew up to cover his eyes. The color was leached from his face but he managed to squirm a smile onto it. He asked, "What do you mean?"

"Your brother said you wanted to join us. But maybe you like this grocery store more than you said you did."

Bob looked for a clue from Charley but his brother was fixed on the store's entrance, smoking a cigarette and coughing. Bob counterfeited bravura and arrogance, saying, "I'll walk out of this crackerbox without so much as a fare-thee-well. This piddly work is beneath me." He tore off the apron by way of illustration and dropped the feather duster handle-down in a water glass, and as he printed out a note to

Elias that read, "Gone fishing," he talked about what a sight for sore eyes the two of them were.

Jesse smiled. "So you missed me?"

"I've been crying myself to sleep every night."

Jesse rang open the cash register and praised the morning's receipts. He stuffed cigars in his vest pocket. He took carrots out to his horse. By then it was noon and the three horses were nipping ears and politicking about seniority and Charley was already in the saddle, murmuring about what he'd packed for his brother and how they'd stolen a horse for Bob. They ceased talking when Jesse came out, correcting the crease in his black fedora. He slipped his left boot in the stirrup and asked, "Do you see him?"

"Who?"

"A man in the cottonwoods with a spyglass. He followed us from your sister's."

Bob turned. He could barely see beyond the schoolyard; the cottonwoods were no more than a caterpillar of green against the light blue of the sky. "Do you think it's the sheriff or a railroad detective?"

Jesse climbed into his saddle and hooked his horse around to the left. "Hell, you'd have to lift their tails to tell the difference."

It was, as it happened, their brother Elias. He took the road to Kearney with them for two miles and postulated that they would stop at the Samuels farm that evening, but for reasons of his own, timidity probably being foremost, Elias forgot to report that information to Sheriff Timberlake and only communicated that the three men rode off into the west.

JOHNNY SAMUELS SANK against the stained pillows and feebly greeted the legendary stepbrother who'd come, he thought, to oversee his laggardly dying. He napped feverishly most of the day, arising only to urinate in a tin pail that Charley gripped for him. He did not recognize the Fords nor did he speak to them; he seemed *non compos mentis*. Reuben too was increasingly mentally ill and spent much of the late afternoon sitting with an arm on the windowsill, an apple peeler in his lap, swarmed in a moth-eaten shawl and four or five coats and mittens. Zerelda cooked with her good left hand and caressed Jesse's cheek with the stump of her right wrist and mothered her son and cried over him and asked the ceiling how she could continue to live without him, asked if she wouldn't have been better off never to have married at all, asked if Jesse ever once considered his poor momma when he chose the lot of a criminal. Her ravings were so crowded with recriminations and insults and petitions, with weeping and caterwauling and wild expressions of love, that it seemed bewildering to Bob and Charley that Jesse remained there for minutes, let alone hours; yet he did. She was four inches taller than Jesse, a giant of a woman, but she made him seem even smaller, made him seem stooped and spiritless. She made him kiss her on the mouth like a lover and rub her neck and temples with myrtleberry oil as he avowed his affection for her and confessed his frailties and shortcomings.

And then, at the six o'clock meal, she concentrated on the Fords, requiring opinions of them and explanations of why they wished to accompany Jesse and what they hoped to gain. To the last query Bob responded that they were afraid to stay at home what with the rewards being offered and every scoundrel in the county gunning for the James gang.

Zerelda gazed at Bob and mushed vegetables with zig-zag motions of her gums, her lips protruding like the clasp of a purse. She looked to Jesse and said, "I don't know what it is about him, but that boy can aggravate me more by just sitting still than most boys can by pitching rocks."

Jesse stared across the table at Bob, a teaspoon in his mouth.

The virago covered Bob's right hand with her big-knuckled left and said, "I want you to swear to God that you're still Jesse's friend."

Bob swore, "Just as I hope for mercy in the hereafter, I'd sooner die than see your son harmed in any way."

"Read Galatians," she said. "Chapter six. 'Be not deceived; God is not mocked: for whatsoever a man soweth, that shall he also reap.' "

Charley and Jesse played checkers after supper while Johnny looked on with the languor and apathy of the dying. At nine Dr. Samuels pulled himself to his feet with the arms of his chair and recited, as if he'd just created it, "Early to bed and early to rise makes a man healthy, wealthy, and wise."

Zerelda said she believed she'd follow Reuben's good advice and shoved her knitting into a sewing basket. She extinguished two coal-oil lamps, banked the fire with a charred board, and kissed Johnny on each eyelid.

Her third-born son stacked checkers in a glass and then, as Charley collected his things for a night ride, Bob saw Jesse slide into his mother's room in order to wish her goodnight.

Bob caught a glimpse of Mrs. Samuels as Jesse pushed open the door. A black net covered her hair and the doctor eased his sore neck with a red hot-water bottle, his eyes shut so tightly his face frowned. Zerelda asked if Jesse was liverish and if that was why he was so moody, and Bob heard him answer, "I guess I'm not feeling well tonight. I'm a little low-spirited." And then there was a silence in which Jesse's expression or stance must have changed and he continued melodramatically, "Maybe I'll never see you again."

It seemed more a calculated statement than a candid one, it was as if it were meant to arouse her operatic emotions, or as if it were meant to be overheard. Zerelda exclaimed, "No! No! No!" and cried without restraint and noisily called for the intercession of angels and saints, and Bob scuttled over to the corner where Charley was plucking the straw flowers in a porcelain vase.

Bob murmured, "He knows."

Charley didn't turn. "Knows what?"

"I've talked with the governor about him."

Charley scowled over his right shoulder at his kid brother, no nettled conscience in his look, only a toothache of concern and skepticism.

"He needs to be stopped," said Bob.

Charley reconsidered the vase without comment and Bob walked back to a chair, where he sat as a model student sits when the teacher is out of the room. Jesse came to them with a bottle of sherry smuggled inside his long coat and asked the Ford brothers, "Ready?" and the three rode in a cold rain until they reached a Lutheran church twenty-eight miles from St. Joseph.

It was wooden and painted white and the cross atop the steeple had a lightning rod attached. The minister was a cook in a restaurant that was known for its clam chowder. The double doors were unlocked, as was the custom then, and inside the church was clean and dark and smelled of floorwax and candles. Jesse threw his greatcoat on a pew and lit an altar candle that he carried into the sanctuary. Bob kicked his bedroll flat on the floor as Charley climbed on a rear pew to light an unornamented chandelier.

Bob said, "If we're ever alone for more than a minute, I'd like a chance to speak with you further."

Charley carried a flame from one candle to the next and pretended not to have heard.

Jesse came back from the sanctuary with a crockery jug cradled in the crook of one arm, a ribboned Bible in the other. He smiled at the two and said, "Grape juice and sherry," but only remained with them a short while before he cloaked his shoulders with his coat and riffled the Bible, seeming to read whichever page his thumbnail settled on.

Bob slept twenty minutes on the punishing floor and then awoke with the sensation that he'd been unconscious for much longer and might have missed something vital. He sat up and saw his brother in a vacant, animal slumber, saw Jesse curled over the book like a monk. Bob wandered over and sidled into the pew.

Jesse licked an index finger and flipped a page. He said, "Go to the Good Book when you're sore distressed, and your soul will be comforted."

"Your mother sure seems to know her scripture."

"She's been an example to me all my life."

Bob rolled his head on his neck to relieve a crick and then canted a little to ascertain which section the man was on.

"The Book of Psalms," said Jesse. "Ever come across it?"

"Well, I've never read it one right after the other, but I've listened to that poem about the Lord being my shepherd."

Jesse recited, " 'Thou preparest a table before me in the presence of mine enemies.' "

Bob nodded. "You hear it at funerals."

Jesse let the book divide from his finger and sought Psalm 41, which he scanned, vigorously scratching his two-inch beard, gingerly petting it smooth. He ironed out the page with his fist and knee and smiled wryly at Bob and then began a private study of the words, as if he were without company.

Bob tried to imagine how Jesse's children saw him: he would be the giant figure who could fling them high as the ceiling. They knew his legs, the sting of his mustache against their cheeks, the gentle way that Jesse had of fingering their hair. They didn't know how he made his living or why they so often moved; they didn't even know their father's name; and it all seemed such an injustice to Bob that he asked, "Do you ever give your past life any thought?"

Jesse squinted at him. "I don't get your meaning."

Bob managed a grin and asked, "Do you ever give any thought to the men you've killed?"

Jesse moved the candle forward so that it was near his left hand and he angled a little in the pew. "Give me an example."

"I just thought you'd've imagined it maybe: how it must've been for that cashier in Northfield or that conductor you shot in Winston. You're doing your job, you've just ate maybe, you're subtracting numbers

or you're collecting tickets from passengers and then—bang!—everything's changed and a man you don't even know is yelling at you with
a gun in his hand and you make one mistake and—bang!—you're
killed.''

Jesse shut the book and rubbed a thumb across the two gold words
on the black leather cover. Rainfall was the only noise. He said, ''I've
been forgiven for all that.''

Bob said, ''You might've had a good reason for killing them. I
don't know. I'm just saying it must've been like a nightmare for them,
and maybe it is for you too, right now.''

Jesse said again, ''I've already been forgiven,'' and then leaned
to his left and blew out the candle.

BOB AWOKE with sunlight coming through the mosaic windows in
colors of red and blue. Charley was already slugging his feet inside
damp boots. Bob slunk up the aisle, looking down pews, until he found
Jesse rounded asleep inside his coat, his mouth open, his ankle twitch-
ing, a gun in his left hand. Bob then scuttled out of the church in his
socks and saw Charley meandering through the cemetery, reading the
inscriptions. He ambled over to him with his palms cupping his elbows.

Bob said, ''Craig gave me ten days.''

Charley considered an angled gravestone and the engraving GONE
ON TO GREATNESS. ''For what?''

Bob thought a moment, tugging up his right sock as he chose the
proper term. ''Arresting him,'' he said.

''You and me,'' Charley said.

''It's going to happen one way or another. If not us, then some
deputy sheriff in Saint Joe, or some Pinkerton man in Kearney, or
some simpleton with a pistol on loan like it was in the swamplands
when the Youngers were captured. It's going to happen, Charley; and
it might as well be us who get rich on it.''

Charley scratched his neck and looked across the road to a greening sward where cattle and sheep were mixed. Timberland was a blue
smear on the horizon. His sunken cheeks and cruel overbite made him
seem to be sucking a mint. He said, ''Nobody's going to get Jesse if
he's still live enough to go for his gun. He can kill ya with every
hand.''

''I'll go alone then,'' Bob said.

Charley glanced at his kid brother disparagingly. ''And besides
that, he's our friend.''

"He murdered Ed Miller. He's going to murder Liddil and Cummins if the chance ever comes. Seems to me Jesse's riding from man to man, saying goodbye to the gang. Your friendship could put you under the pansies."

Charley sighed and said, "I'll grind it fine in my mind, Bob. I can't go any further than that, right now."

"You'll come around," Bob said, and returned to the church, twisting the crick in his spine.

Jesse was by the altar and above the congregation in a pulpit of inlaid wood. He looked both pious and possessed. His face was stern as he flipped pages at the lectern, his fingers clenched the railing, and his blue eyes had silver fire in them as he put them on the Fords. He called, "From now on you two won't go *anywhere* without me! From now on you'll ask for *permission;* you'll ask to be *excused!*"

THEY MADE ST. JOSEPH by afternoon, with enough sun overhead to tarry at the railroad station and watch the men shunt cars, to number the cattle and sows in the stockyards, and to buy licorice and *Frank Leslie's Illustrated Weekly Newspaper* at an apothecary. Jesse asked what the clocktower said and Bob leaned from the store to read the time, almosting it, and they rode east through the mud and smoke of the city. Jesse carried himself like a chamberlain with two groundlings and intermittently winked or touched the brim of his fedora whenever a man called the name "Tom" in greeting.

Soon they were near the red-bricked World Hotel and Jesse told Bob to raise his eyes to the roller coaster of Confusion Hill more than a quarter-mile off. Bob looked over the roofs of bungalows and a steep ascent of timber to a high skull of land on which rested a white cottage with green shutters. He could see laundry swelling with wind on the clothesline, the measured white pickets of the yard fence, the swing in the sycamore tree.

Charley said, "Jesse finally come up with a place to match his prominence," a comment he'd plagiarized from Zee.

And Jesse said, "I could mow down a thousand scalawags with no more than a thousand cartridges. I'll never be surprised by anything again."

The horses strained up Lafayette Street and stopped as soon as they heard the children. Jesse crawled off his saddle and accepted his daughter in his arms as he knelt to kiss Tim, and then, with a general's arrogance, assigned Charley the stable chores, Bob the job of bringing their gatherings in, and moved off to the rear of the cottage, Mary clutching his right leg.

Bob skidded the packs and paraphernalia onto the stoop and eavesdropped on a conversation that was too remote to comprehend. Bob took off his bowler hat and bent close to the locked door, his pale forehead blotching against the screen. "Halloo!" he called and rattled the door on its hook. Zerelda James backed from the stove to see him and winced a little and said rather crossly, "You never mentioned Bob would be here." And yet she squeezed her hands dry in her apron and managed an indulgent smile as she walked across the room and unlocked the door.

"He didn't tell me you'd come along," she said.

"Maybe he was saving it as a pleasant surprise."

Little Mary was submerged in the woman's skirt and glowering at Bob. Zee combed the girl's hair and said to her, "You've got *two* cousins for company now," and then mothered the child back into the kitchen.

Bob threw clothes and whatnots inside and then removed his gunbelt and soldier's coat as he examined the room. The floornails had not been countersunk and were raised and silvered with shoe scuffs. A red rubber ball and two jacks were strewn on the tasseled green rug. *Five Little Peppers and How They Grew* was astraddle the rim of a straw portfolio that had been decorated with a gladiola seed package and nailed onto the wall. The sofa pillows had been shammed with lace and white doilies on the chair backs were tanned with the stains of hair oils and pomades. To the right of the door was an oak bed and a soogan quilt lighted by a tall window of flawed glass slatted by Venetian blinds. On the left was a corresponding window and a plaster wall that was papered with roses and an intricate scheme that had been scribbled upon with a child's crayon. Contrary to the fabrications of magazines and stage sets, there was no tapestry embroidered with the sentiment "God Bless Our Home"; instead there was an ornate walnut frame and a watercolor painting of a racehorse named Skyrocket. Jutting from a wicker sewing basket was a feather duster made from some blue and brown exotic bird. Against one wall was a rush-bottomed chair and wine table, cater-cornered was a rocker, against the dining and sitting room wall was a broad sofa and a black, ironworked, naked woman whose lewdly cleft legs were used as a bootjack. Staring at Bob was Jesse. The man walked into the kitchen and muttered to Zee with amusement, "That boy can make our sitting room look like a matinee."

BOB AND CHARLEY REMAINED at 1318 Lafayette Street until April 3rd, so more than a week was frittered away in inconsequential chores, afternoon naps on the sofa, and loudmouthed and lingering meals. The routine was to wake at seven, see to the care of the animals, then stroll down to the post office, where newspapers that Thomas Howard subscribed to arrived, each neatly rolled into a brown paper mailing sleeve. The three men would straddle wicker chairs and flatten pages on the dining room table until Zee carried in a farmer's breakfast to them and Tim was sent off to school. By nine they would have finished two kettles of coffee and the men would retire to the sitting room while Mrs. James cleaned the kitchen. They would mention the two- or three-day-old news items they'd read and comment on each crime or predicament in accordance with their own creeds and stances. Jesse would wind his pocket watch; Jesse would wind the clock. Jesse would clean a revolver and load it and then he would clean another. Weather might be introduced as a subject of conversation and for many minutes the weather would be rigorously considered. Questions might be lazily asked about spring planting and the crops. Bob cited locusts once and ascertained from the increased interest that he'd inadvertently entertained an exciting topic that was never before discussed.

Lunch was served at noon and then the three would nap or kill time on the kitchen porch, where they would watch Mary play with a girl named Metta Disbrow. They scrupulously pored over a collection of nineteen ambrotype photographs. Bob reread *Noted Guerrillas, or The Warfare of the Border,* by John Newman Edwards, the one contemporary book that Jesse owned. Jesse exercised in the sun with weighted yellow pins. He touched his toes one hundred times. He twisted horseshoes with his fists. He looked at his physique from various angles in the mirror of the shaded kitchen window. He made his daughter feel his muscles and laughed at her mystified reaction. He made Bob and Charley cup flexed biceps that were as round and solid as baseballs. He Indian-wrestled them one at a time and then struggled with them together, gradually becoming disgusted with their clumsiness and frailty.

At four they walked down for the evening newspapers and *The Police Gazette* and absorbed themselves in them until the main meal was served at six. Jesse never scolded the children, rarely even corrected them; the grammar, hygiene, manners, and temperament of his children, even if improper or inadequate, were either never noticed by

Jesse or else caused an anguished look from him and a call for his wife's ministrations. He spent the evenings in the crowded sitting room with one child next to him, another riding the jouncing pony of his knee, while Zee sewed and the Ford brothers simpered. Only when the children were asleep would the three men journey into the city, where they played pool in a South Jefferson Street saloon. By eleven or twelve they were asleep themselves, or at least they pretended to be.

After three days of this dreary routine, Bob was markedly nervous; by the fourth day, Bob was so skittish his legs jittered whenever he sat, he couldn't remain in a chair for more than two minutes, he chewed his fingernails and clawed at his baby-fine hair and generally carried on so much that Jesse said, "Appears to me you've got the peedoodles, Bob," and then compassionately prescribed Dr. George Richmond's Samaritan Nervine.

Bob once went to the kitchen and slurped water from the bucket dipper as Zee separated egg whites and yolks. She usually swiveled away from Bob whenever he was near or curtailed their conversations by inventing chore-girl activities. Now she simply lifted on her toes to find a bowl in the cabinet and ignored Bob's sulky consideration of her body. He saw the fine blond hairs raise from her neck as he stared and he sent his eyes to his feet. She moved to her mixing and Bob said, "If you want to clean your floor, you should first off scrub sand over it and follow that with a soda lye applied with a real stiff brush. You rinse it with warm water and when it's nearly dry, you know, sort of coolish to your feet, you wipe it down with hypochlorite of lime and let it cure overnight. I learnt that at the grocery store."

Zee sifted white flour into a bowl and said, "This isn't my kitchen. We're renting."

Bob let the water dipper sink in the bucket. He scratched his calf. Zee spooned bicarbonate of soda from a canister and set it down. Bob was about to reach for the canister in order to read it but Zee shot a glance at Bob's knuckles and he stalled. He sniffed a sliver of brown, gritty soap; Zee mashed cream of tartar into the bicarbonate of soda with a soup spoon. She asked, "Why are you so antsy?"

Bob improvised by saying, "It's just this cussed boredom. This sitting around inside the livelong day, getting into your hair, getting slow and sleepy, making jailhouse dogs of ourselves."

She looked at Bob with some animation and attention subtracted from her eyes, as if she were recalling something even as she spoke. "He's sometimes gone for months. We sometimes change houses five times in a year. It's gruesome being hunted, Bob. He can stay in his nightshirt all day if he wants; I'm just grateful that he's around.''

"You can see it's damaged his mind some," Bob said.

She ignored his comment by rubbing flour from her palms with her apron and returning to her recipe.

Bob watched her work a minute more and said, "You're making a cake.''

THEY WALKED TO A POOL HALL at nine on Saturday, and as the Fords shot eight-ball, Jesse maneuvered among the pool tables, letting players clap him on the back, making jokes, remembering names and relationships, visiting corner tables if anyone called him over, which was frequently and with gusto. A gunsmith chatted with Thomas Howard about a .22 caliber pistol the man carried inside his boot. Mr. Howard said, "You can't more than make a man itch with that article," and soon the two were in good-natured argument about marksmanship. They settled on a competition and walked outside to the alley with a starved-for-entertainment crowd.

Bob watched Jesse pry the lead ball from a cartridge and saw a notch in it with a skinning knife that he then fixed into the crook of a tree so that the cutting side was a thin, silver streak in the night. He worked a string into the cut lead ball and stomped his bootheel on it to close the nick, and that string he fastened to an overhead branch so that the ball swayed close enough to tick the skinning knife. He made a boy stand near the target with a coal-oil lamp. He took five strides from the oak tree and announced to the audience that the boy would set the cartridge ball in motion and the gunsmith and he were going to fire five times. The trick was to strike it just so and make the skinning knife shave both the swinging and the speeding bullets with one shot.

The crowd grumbled their grave doubts or murmured in awe or made side bets and the gunsmith raised a .22 caliber revolver with grim resignation. The boy flipped the ball into a metronomic swing and stood aside with the coal-oil lamp as the gunsmith shot at and missed the moving target five times, scattering oak bark and cursing the foolishness of the contest.

Jesse then removed his suit coat, rested his right hand on his hip, and with his left lifted the revolver he called Baby. The boy slapped the cartridge ball into a wide arc and retreated and Jesse squinted down the muzzle sights and fired. Wood chipped but the ball continued to swing. It ticked against the knife like a clock. Jesse jiggled his left arm by his side to relax it and then raised it again and missed a second time.

"Ain't nothing to be ashamed of," the gunsmith said. "It's next to impossible."

Jesse grinned at the gunsmith and said, "If I didn't know I could do it, I wouldn't have concocted it."

The ball still clocked but with shorter strokes and Jesse squinted a third time and then there was a gunshot noise of plank clapped against plank, a chime as two cartridge balls skinned off the knife, and the long song of the steel blade as it quivered and rang.

Silence followed the accomplishment and then some men applauded and yahooed and some others crouched at the oak tree and a gratified Thomas Howard was rushed to by people who wished to congratulate him and vigorously pump his hand and gladly introduce themselves.

The boy carved the cartridge balls out of the oak tree and walked around with them as if they were wedding rings on a silver tray. Bob lifted one and rubbed his thumb on the flat of it and the boy asked, "Is it still hot?"

Bob moved over to his brother. "He arranged that for our benefit."

Charley smiled. "You thought it was all made up, didn't you. You thought everything was yarns and newspaper stories."

Bob looked over at the shootist, who was then showing Baby to the gunsmith. "He's just a human being."

The Fords returned to the pool tables and Bob won the next rack. He supported his chin on the pool cue if standing; he snared his coat over his gun butt so that it showed when he leaned over the green felt and clacked the ivory balls. At midnight, Jesse winged his arms around Charley and Bob and weaved them out into the street, and on the climb up Confusion Hill gave them his recollection of the James-Younger gang's robbery of the Ocobock Brothers' Bank at Corydon, Iowa, in 1871: then nearly everyone was at the Methodist church as Henry Clay Dean pleaded the case for a contemplated railroad; the holdup attracted no attention and seven men were able to split six thousand dollars. Jesse now expected many people in Platte City, Missouri, to be at the courthouse on April 4th to see Colonel John Doniphan perorate in the defense of George Burgess, who was being charged with the manslaughter of Caples Burgess, his cousin. The Wells Banking Company—commonly called the Platte City Bank—would remain open for its commercial customers, but with only a teller or two in attendance.

They reached the cottage and Jesse reclined on the sitting room sofa, sending Charley out to collect firewood for the stove. Charley lolloped off and Jesse wedded his fingers on his stomach and closed his eyes. "How it will be is we'll leave here next Monday afternoon and ride down to Platte City."

Bob seated himself on the floor and crossed his ankles. "How far is that from Kansas City?"

Something in Bob's inquiry made Jesse resistant and he chose to answer around it. "Platte City's thirty miles south. You and me and Charley will sleep in the woods overnight and strike the Wells Bank sometime before the court recesses."

Bob asked when that would be exactly, but his voice was too insistent, his attitude too intense, and Jesse said, "You don't need to know that."

Bob scrawled on the floorboards with his finger and Jesse arose to a sit. He said, "You know, I feel comfortable with your brother. Hell, he's ugly as sin and he smells like a skunk and he's so ignorant he couldn't drive nails in the snow, but he's sort of easy to be around. I can't say the same for you, Bob."

"I'm sorry to hear you say that."

Jesse was silent a moment and then asked, "You know how it is when you're with your girlfriend and the moon is out and you know she wants to be kissed even though she never said so?"

Bob didn't know how that was but he said that he did.

"You're giving me signs that grieve my soul and make me wonder if your mind's been changed about me."

"Do you want me to swear my good faith like I did for your mother?"

Charley clattered wood into the stove's firebox and returned from the kitchen, slapping his hands. He saw Jesse glowering at Bob with great heat in his eyes, and said, "You two having a spat?"

"I was getting ready to be angry," Jesse said, and then smiled at Bob. He reached out and coddled Bob's neck and said in a gentling voice, "Sit over here closer, kid."

Bob vacillated a little and then scooched over, smirking at his brother with perplexity and shyness.

Jesse fervently massaged Bob's neck and shoulder muscles, communicating that all was forgiven, and he continued with his sketch of the robbery. "You'll stay with the animals, Charley, and The Kid and I will walk into the Platte City Bank just before noon. Bob will move the cashier over away from the shotgun that's under the counter and he'll tell the man to work the combination on the vault. They'll finagle about time locks and so on and I'll creep up behind that cashier and cock his chin back like so.'' And Jesse cracked his right wrist into Bob's chin, snapping the boy's skull back and pinning him against his knee as he slashed a skinning knife across his throat. The metal was cold and left the sting of ice on Bob's fair skin and for an instant he was certain he'd actually been cut and he slumped against the sofa, incapacitated, in panic. Jesse's mouth was so close his mustache snipped at Bob's ear when he said in a caress of a voice, ''I'll say, 'How come an off-scouring of creation like you is still sucking air when so many of mine are in coffins?' ''

Bob's eye lolled left to see the skinning knife vertical near his cheek. There was a crick in his neck and the man's wristbone was mean as a broomstick under his chin. Bob manufactured a smile and said, ''This isn't good riddance for me, is it?''

''I'll say, 'How'd you reach your twentieth birthday without leaking out all over your clothes?' And if I don't like his attitude, I'll slit that phildoodle so deep he'll flop on the floor like a fish.'' Jesse then retracted his arm and rudely shoved Bob forward and rested the skinning knife on the sofa cushion. Then his temper abruptly altered and he slapped both knees gleefully and grinned at Bob and exclaimed, ''I could hear your gears grinding *rrr, rrr, rrr,* and your little motor wondering, 'My gosh, what's next, what's happening to me?' You were precious to behold, Bob. You were white as spit in a cotton field.''

Bob examined his neck by finger touch. ''You want to know how that feels? Unpleasant. I honestly can't recommend it.''

''And Charley looked *stricken!*''

''I *was!*'' Charley said.

'' 'This is plum unexpected!' old Charley was thinking. 'This is ruint my day!' '' He looked from Bob to Charley and joked some moments longer, laughing coaxingly, immoderately, sarcastically, unconvincingly, and when at last the two laughed with him, Jesse adopted a scolding look and slammed into his room.

SO IT WENT. Bob was increasingly cynical, leery, uneasy; Jesse was increasingly cavalier, merry, moody, fey, unpredictable. If his gross anatomy suggested a strong smith in his twenties, his actual physical constitution was that of a man who was incrementally dying. He was sick with rheums and aches and lung congestions, he tilted against chairs and counters and walls, in cold weather he limped with a cane. He coughed incessantly when lying down, his clever mind was often in conflict, insomnia stained his eye sockets like soot, he seemed in a state of mourning. He counteracted the smell of neglected teeth with licorice and candies, he browned his graying hair with dye, he camouflaged his depressions and derangements with masquerades of extreme cordiality, courtesy, and good will toward others.

He played the practical joker and party boy. At suppers Jesse would make his children shiver by rasping his fork away from his mouth so that the tines sang off his teeth. Zee set down a soup tureen and he winked at Bob when he asked, "Is this fit to eat or will it just do?" He'd belch and murmur, "Squeeze me." He surreptitiously inched the butter or gravy dish under Charley's elbow so that the chump stained his sleeve; he hooked Charley's spurs together as he snored in the sitting room and then screamed the man off the sofa so that Charley farcically sprawled. He repeated jokes at the evening meals, making each more long-winded and extravagant than it was in his recollection, altering each so that it commented on the vices of railroad officers and attorneys—who were so crooked, he claimed, that they had to screw their socks on. But even as he jested or tickled his girl or boy in the ribs, Jesse would look over to Bob with melancholy eyes, as if the two of them were meshed in an intimate communication that had little to do with anyone else.

Bob was certain the man had unriddled him, had seen through his reasons for coming along, that Jesse could forecast each of Bob's possible moves and inclinations and was only acting the innocent in order to lull Bob into stupid tranquility and miscalculation.

Once Bob was occupying himself in the stables, scraping the clinging mud from the horses' fetlocks and pasterns with a wire currycomb. Then misgivings overtook him and he straightened to intercept Jesse peering in angrily at the window and in the next instant disappearing. And yet, when reencountered on the kitchen porch no more than five minutes later, Jesse dipped his newspaper to happily remark on the weather. On some nights Jesse segregated the two brothers and slept with Bob in the sitting room, a revolver, as always, clutched in his strong left hand. His brown hair smelled of rose oil and his long underwear smelled of borax; sleep subtracted years from his countenance. Bob listened to each insuck of air so he could tell when Jesse went off, and when the man's inhalations were so slow and shallow they never seemed to come out again, Bob cautiously rolled to a sit and placed his feet on the cold boards and the revolver was cocked with three clicks. "I need to go to the privy," Bob said.

"You think you do but you don't," said Jesse, and Bob obediently returned to bed.

On Monday, Zee worked outside in a wide brown dress with the cuffs rolled to her elbows, stirring a white froth of laundry in a cast-iron wash boiler that steamed into the blue sky. Charley dampened a red handkerchief and ran it along the metal clothesline in order to remove the rust. Bob cringed up to Zee and asked if she would wash his clothes and she consented with some annoyance. She swished his socks and shirts in a soapwater tub on the stove and scrubbed them against a Rockingham pottery washboard, but after they were rinsed and cranked through the wringer, Bob refused to clothespin them and returned with them to the sitting room, where he smoothed them out on the oak bed so that they would gradually dry.

Jesse walked in, slapping a rolled newspaper against his thigh, seeking company. He oversaw Bob's meticulous care in the arrangement of a shirt's sleeves and then espied an H.C. laundry mark on some white underwear. He asked, "Whose initials are those?"

"I beg your pardon?"

Jesse frowned and inquired, "What's H.C. stand for?"

Bob looked at the letters and then remembered that he'd confused Henry Craig's underwear with his own that night in the St. James Hotel. He couldn't fiction an answer.

"High church?" Jesse offered. "Home cooking?"

Bob fidgeted a little and smiled ingratiatingly. "I stayed in a workingman's hotel and saw them squished up in a closet. I couldn't find any cooties, so I kept them as a sort of memento."

Jesse either accepted that or considered it a subject not worth pursuing. He strolled out onto Lafayette Street. Bob sank down on the mattress and cooled his eyes with a wet sock; Jesse circled yard trees, scaring squirrels with sticks.

THE SITTING ROOM conversations were about Blue Cut that week: the Kansas City newspapers carried front-page articles about the movement of John Bugler, John Land, and Creed Chapman from the Second Street jail to Independence, Missouri, where there was a court trial over their complicity in the Chicago and Alton train robbery. The reporters called them stool pigeons. Creed Chapman had lost forty-two

pounds while incarcerated; John Land was rumored to be so apprehensive about reprisal by Jesse James that he refused to even mention the
man's name. "He evidently is in fear of bodily injury," one man
wrote, "and dreads the idea of ever again leaving jail."

On the afternoon of March 30th, a policeman meandered near the
cottage and then loitered on the sidewalk to inventory the geography of
St. Joseph. He wore a riverman's short-brimmed cap and a navy blue
coat with brass buttons and a brass star. A shoulder sling crossed the
man's chest to a black leather holster that housed a dragoon revolver.
He made a cigarette and, like a cat with its catch, seemed to look
everywhere except the cottage, and then he found cause to rest his
elbows on the white picket fence and lounge there, scrutinizing and
squinting.

Charley was sunk in a brown study: he creaked a rocking chair
forward and back and stared morosely at the marred wallpaper as he
smoked a cigarette. Jesse came out of the master bedroom with a
revolver tucked inside a folded newspaper, looking imperiled and
perturbed. He asked in a whisper, "Is anyone out there?"

Charley craned around to see out the screen door and saw the
policeman allow smoke to stream from his nose. "Yes!" Charley said,
and slid off the chair as Jesse crouched across the room. "How in
Heaven's name did you know?"

Jesse raised the revolver next to his left ear and split two bottom
window blinds with his fingers. He said, "I had a premonition.'s-5'

Charley squatted against the front wall, ground his cigarette out
on the floor, and suspected the governor had grown impatient and that
the cottage was at present encircled with perhaps fifty policemen and
two hundred state militia. Plaster would spew if they shot; glass would
sprinkle, pictures would tilt, even the sofa would move.

The window sash had been raised four inches in order to ventilate
the room. Jesse rested his .44's muzzle on the sill and steered it toward
the policeman's face.

Charley peeked out the screen door and saw the policeman screw
his boot down on his dropped cigarette and then cruise over to the
sidewalk gate. When the man's thumb tripped the metal latch, the
revolver cocked with its soft clicks and Charley prayed, *Go home*. The
policeman was only a suggestion away from stepping onto the rented
property when he lost either the gumption or the yearning and shut the
gate and strolled on.

Jesse uncocked the revolver and covered it with the newspaper.

He said, "An angel tugged on his coattails," and then with graceful nonchalance walked back into his room.

BOB WAS IN TOWN at the time. He'd told Jesse that the cash he'd earned at the Richmond grocery store was burning holes in his pockets and that he wanted to look for an Easter suit at the Famous Boston One-Price Clothing House. And 510 Main Street is indeed where he went, there buying a fifteen-dollar gentleman's suit of salt-and-pepper tweed. Bob told the salesman that his name was Johnson, and that he was a cousin to Thomas Howard.

The cattleman?

Bob lent his affirmation.

Good neighbors, the salesman said. Always polite and respectable, with a pleasant word for everybody.

Bob started toward Lafayette Street but then got a notion and instead skipped down alleys and cut through stores until he came to the American Telegraph office, and there Bob slanted into a standing desk for many minutes, scribbling twenty messages that he might send to Governor Crittenden or Police Commissioner Craig.

He could be a glib and even grandiloquent speaker, but writing was agony for him: the right words seemed to disappear whenever he grasped a pencil, plus he was hampered by the grim recognition that he really had nothing to say. He listed the chances for capture that Jesse had given him and came up with only two: Bob had gallivanted past the kitchen window and noticed Jesse asleep in a chair; and Jesse unbuckled his gunbelts to scrub at a washbasin and Tim had strapped them on. But Zee was ironing a blouse close by as Jesse slept, a shot would have stabbed her left breast; and Bob himself wore no gun on the second occasion and to go after Jesse with anything else was unimaginable to him.

For the man was canny, he was intuitive, he anticipated everything. He continually looked over his shoulders, he looked into the background with mirrors, he locked his sleeping room at night, he could pick out a whisper in the wind, he could register the slightest added value a man put into his words, he could probably read the faltering and perfidy in Bob's face. He once numbered the spades on a playing card that skittered across the street a city block away; he licked his daughter's cut finger and there wasn't even a scar the next day; he wrestled with his son and the two Fords at once one afternoon and rarely even tilted—it was like grappling with a tree. When Jesse predicted rain, it rained; when he encouraged plants, they grew; when he scorned animals, they retreated; whomever he wanted to stir, he astonished.

So some of Bob's telegrams were apologies, some were clarifications, still more were prognostications of when the criminal would be "removed," until finally Bob settled on a coded note to Sheriff Timberlake, providing him with clues about their living situation in St. Joseph and about the contemplated robbery in Platte City on the 4th. All he could think of as he jotted it down was Jesse's story of George Shepherd sending a telegram in Galena, Kansas, and then riding into a barrage of gunfire from the James gang.

It took five minutes for the telegraph operator to code and transmit the note and two hours for Timberlake to receive it because of the court session in Independence at which he was an expert witness. But thereafter the sheriff acted with great speed, arranging a company of fifty deputies who would ride their horses into two freight cars at sunrise on the 4th and surround the Platte City Bank while the James gang was inside. Timberlake even went so far in his preparations as to order a Hannibal and St. Joseph locomotive's engine ignited and kept fully steamed in the Kansas City roundhouse so that it could race to Platte City or St. Joseph without much delay. Having satisfied himself that the appropriate steps had been taken, the sheriff dined with Commissioner Craig on the night of the 30th and they toasted a victory that they seemed only days away from achieving.

GOVERNOR CRITTENDEN GAVE an interview that week in which he bragged about the many members of the James gang who were already in jail or in courts of law, going on to claim that certain arrangements had been made that could snag the James brothers themselves very soon. He could say no more than that, the governor smugly asserted, as if he had not already divulged enough to put the Fords in jeopardy.

On March 30th the Kansas City *Evening Star* carried a leading article that stated: "Commissioner Craig, Sheriff Timberlake, and Dick Little have been closeted in Craig's office all afternoon, the outlaw having been engaged in making an affidavit to all the operations of the old gang. The *Evening Star* is able to state as a positive fact that Little has been working with the officers for several months past."

And the *Evening Star* for Friday, March 31st, again concentrated its attention on Dick Liddil's confession in an article that was somewhat inaccurately titled "The James Gang." It accused the James gang of the robberies at Glendale, Winston, and Blue Cut, but then incriminated only Dick Liddil in the alleged murder of Wood Hite, even moving the gunfight to a location near Springfield, Missouri. "Jesse was greatly incensed at the murder of Wood," the writer stated, "and Little ran away from the gang to escape Jesse's wrath. Thereupon Jesse offered a reward of $1,000 for Dick Little, alive or dead, saying that he would prefer him dead. When Little learned of this offer, he surrendered himself to Commissioner Craig and Sheriff Timberlake, and betrayed, or pretended to betray to them, the whole gang."

And though the Kansas City *Times* published similar stories, Jesse's subscription to it meant it came by mail, so he couldn't read about Dick Liddil's collusion or make the correct inferences about the Fords until the morning of April 3rd. And yet he acted with the skepticism and suspicion of a man who already knew. He scarcely acknowledged Bob's remarks all day on the 31st nor spoke at supper except to complain about an overdone seven-bone steak that Zee promptly removed to the kitchen to steam. He then confided to Charley, "Her cooking always has been a scandal. Cut her meat and the table moves."

He passed the evening simply enough, sitting with Mary and Tim on the sofa and reading from *Five Little Peppers and How They Grew:* "The little kitchen had quieted down from the bustle and confusion of midday, and now with its afternoon manners on, presented a holiday aspect that, as the principal room in the brown house, it was eminently proper it should have."

Charley took apart his pistol, squinting away from cigarette smoke and chugging slight coughs as he twisted a screwdriver; Bob catnapped on the sitting room bed and didn't awaken until he heard Jesse swat Charley's foot with his hat and say, "Come on, Cousin; let's go for a ride."

Charley shot a scared look at Bob and then said, "Sorry, but I'm not much in the mood."

"Stomach ache?"

"Sort of."

"The night air will cure it," Jesse said and crushed Charley's wrist in his seizing hand as he yanked him to his feet.

Charley climbed sluggishly into a coat and boots and glanced again at his brother. "Don't you want to come along too?"

Jesse said, "Bob stays," and the two men walked out to saddle their horses.

They rode east near Pigeon Hill under a moonshade of interlaced shagbark trees. Jesse rambled to the right or left of Charley, riding the creeksides and cowpaths, rising into the woods, reconnecting with the road many yards behind Charley and then creeping up alongside.

He asked, "Do you ever count the stars?"

Charley looked overhead at the pinpricks of light. It reminded him of his father's badly shingled barn roof when the cat he was shooting at crouched on the rafters and everywhere else it was noontime but it was midnight whenever he sighted his gun.

Jesse said, "I can't ever get the same number; they keep changing on me."

"I don't even know what a star is exactly."

"Your body knows; it's your mind that forgot."

Charley slid an eye toward Jesse and said, "Riding was a good idea. I wonder if we could go back?"

"So early?"

"I don't know why but I've been poorly lately and the rocking makes my gut want to jump."

"You need to correct your way of living."

"Well; like I say, I've been poorly."

Jesse didn't say anything more. His horse nickered and clicked its bit and its rider dangled his legs off the stirrups and squirmed around with soreness. He turned up his collar and lowered his chin as if the wind was mean and then reined back slightly so that he slipped four feet to the rear and with grim foreboding and fright Charley tried to guess if Jesse's gun was already out. Greenery was high all around them as they climbed a grade and Charley began the only prayer he knew, getting to the words "my soul to keep" when a comet of golden fire careered down the road. It was the size of a cannon ball and instantly, spookily reeling at them, singeing the animals' legs, causing them to skirt aside and whinny. And then it was not there but gone. Smoke rose to the horses' noses and they jerked their heads at the smell.

Charley recollected the marvel to Bob and in the April 21st Liberty *Tribune* and was still not over his mystification, couldn't tell if it was lightning or a meteor or tumbleweed that a practical joker set a match to and rolled down the hill. But he said Jesse reacted with calm acceptance, with no more than a scolding look, and claimed that it was an omen, that fire had come to him many times in the past in various manifestations and each visitation was followed by an affliction.

Charley had grown accustomed to the man's grand manner of lying, so he did not challenge the statement but only glanced to see that he'd misjudged his plight, for Jesse's greatcoat still covered his guns.

Jesse swung his horse around to the west and on the ride to the cottage swore, "I've seen visions that would make Daniel swoon; I've been warned as often as Israel." Then he grinned at Charley as if it were a good wrench or rope pulley that they were talking about. "It's mighty handy," Jesse said.

SATURDAY INTRODUCED summer weather to the state: the skies were blue, the sun insistent, the temperature close to eighty at noon. The river flashed light from its rills and currents, and Zee could look up from her scullery work and see Kansas shimmer like a reflection in water. The Fords removed the storm windows and Jesse raised each sash so that sweet air could stir through the rooms, but they were too lazy or lumpish to attach screens, so flies crawled over the rising loaves and birds flew into the rooms.

Jesse went to the market with Tim and Mary and came back home at four with a crate of groceries and a black box clamped under his right arm. He kissed Zee and rubbed her fanny and asked her how she was feeling. She saw that he'd subjected his skull to a barber: a smear of white talcum powder was on his neck and his chestnut hair smelled of lilac water; but he looked much handsomer now than when she married him, a quality of aging that she'd often envied in men. Jesse sought Cousin Bob and she told him she thought Bob was resting in the children's room.

Sunshine was diagonal in the room and curtains flirted in the air. Bob wasn't sure what woke him. He pivoted in the child's bed and saw Jesse in a spindle chair, peering at him with great interest. Jesse said, "I never learned what your nationality was."

"How long've you been studying me?"

"You look French."

Bob rolled to a sitting position. "My grandfather married a French girl in New Orleans. He was with the Virginia volunteers in the War of Eighteen Twelve. I guess I take after my grandmom."

"You're gonna break a lot of hearts."

Bob arched an eyebrow. "How do you mean?"

Jesse revealed the black box from behind his back and reached it over to Bob. "It's a present."

Bob raised it and reckoned what it was. "Heavy," he said.

"You going to look inside?"

"Why are you being so nice to me?"

"You gave me that bawdy bootjack; this is my Christmas gift to you."

The wooden lid was nailed shut. Bob crammed a coin into the interstices and twisted it until the lid released. "It's April Fool's Day, you know."

"Isn't a joke," said Jesse.

Inside the box, nestled in red velvet, was a pearl-handled .44 caliber revolver, a New Model Smith and Wesson number 3, with a six-and-a-half-inch nickel barrel. Bob beamed at Jesse and said, "Such extravagance!" and then turned the revolver to admire it.

"Doesn't that nickel shine though?"

"It's more than I could hope for!" said Bob. He clicked the chamber around, cocked and released the hammer, cocked the hammer and aimed the revolver at a red ball on the floor, investigated the play in the trigger, squeezed the trigger until the steel hammer snapped forward, listened to the mechanisms as he recocked the revolver at his ear, straightened his right arm and shut his left eye, skated his thumb across the serial number (3766), measured the full length: twelve inches. "I want a gunsmith to engrave this; some sentence with our two names and the city and the year of presentation. It'll be a prize that can be passed on from one generation to the next."

"I figured that granddaddy Colt of yours might blow into frag-ments next time you squeeze the trigger." .

Bob grinned and said, "You might have something there." He substituted the New Model Smith and Wesson for the tarnished revolver in the scrolled black leather holster that he then buckled and let slant across his right rear pocket. He slapped it out like a gunfighter, snugged it, slapped it out again. The gun chuckled against the rigid leather but after repeated pulls and replacements it made no more noise than a man's swallow.

Zee called from the dining room, "Dave? You ready for supper?"

"Pretty soon, sweetheart."

Bob said, "I might be too excited to eat."

Jesse smiled broadly and rose from the spindle chair. "You know what John Newman Edwards once wrote about me? He said I didn't trust two men in ten thousand and was even cautious around them. The government's sort of run me ragged, you see. I'm going the long way around the barn to say I've been feeling cornered and just plain ornery of late and I'd be pleased if you'd accept the gun as my way of apologizing.''

"Heaven knows I'd be ornerier if I were in your position."

"No. I haven't been acting correctly. I can't hardly recognize myself sometimes when I'm greased. I go on journeys out of my body and look at my red hands and my mean face and I get real quizzical. Who is that man who's gone so wrong? Why all that killing and evil behavior? I've been becoming a problem to myself. I figure if I can get you right I'll be just that much closer to me."

Bob looked at the man in bewilderment and couldn't find the words for an answer, so he said, "I need to wash my hands if supper's on. The gun's made them feel sort of public."

"Go ahead," the man said, and graciously opened the door.

Bob exited from the children's room and smiled meekly at Zee as he entered the kitchen and leaned on the counter for a moment. He spilled pitcher water into a pan and as he sank his hands in it he listened to Jesse greet his children, listened to chairs sliding away from the dining room table and sliding underneath it again. Jesse began to say grace without him and Bob raised a brick of yellow soap to his nose, smelling its ingredients: rainwater, sal soda, unslaked lime; tallow, rosin, salt.

APRIL 2ND was Palm Sunday and Mr. and Mrs. Thomas Howard, their two children, and their cousin Charles Johnson strolled in sunshine to the Second Presbyterian Church in order to attend the ten o'clock service. Bob remained at the cottage, claiming he'd stomached all the religion he could when his father was a minister of a timber church that was called Jasper. So they went without Bob and he slyly migrated from room to room in his white-stockinged feet, a shining revolver slung near his thigh, a coffee cup near his mouth. He ate a slice of cold toast and walked into the master bedroom, where he rested the cup and saucer on the chiffonier and investigated each of the six wide drawers. Hanging from a mirror hook was an eighteen-karat-gold watch in a hunting case, made by Charles J. E. Jaeat and stolen from John A. Burbank in the Hot Springs stagecoach robbery of 1874. Bob listened to the ticks and chimings of the clock, gave it timidly to air, savagely grabbed it back. He walked into the closet and inventoried the clothes on the hangers and hooks; he slipped on one of Jesse's worsted wool coats and inspected its tailoring in a mirror. He ironed the bed's rumpled sheets with his hands, he sipped from the water glass on the vanity, he smelled the talcum and lilacs on a pillowcase that was etched here and there with snips of cut hair. He reclined on the mattress so that he could be in meeting with it and he situated each coal-oil lamp in the room by the smoke stains it made on the ceiling. He rolled to his left as Jesse must have rolled to marry with his wife in the evening. He resisted a temptation. His fingers skittered over his ribs to construe the scars where Jesse was twice shot. He manufactured a middle finger that was missing the top two knuckles. He imagined himself at thirty-four; he imagined himself in a coffin. Morning light was coming in at the window and pale curtains moved on the spring breeze like ghosts. Bob raised his revolver and straightened it on the door, the mirror, the window sash, a picture made from a fruit can label, a nightgown that hung from a nail. He went out to the sitting room. He considered possibilities and everything wonderful that could come true. He remembered the set-down coffee cup and saucer and removed them from the chiffonier, wiping a ring from the wood with his sleeve. And he was at the dining room table, oiling his gun, when the churchgoers returned to the cottage, each with a sword of green palm.

THEY WENT on a picnic at noon. Jesse and Charley and the boy skimmed stones off the river and skulked around the bleached bones of a sheep that rocked in a shallow pool. The sleeves of their white shirts were sloppily rolled up past their elbows, exposing the farmer brown of their hands and wrists and the gradations into white. A dog plunged into the river and struggled out and chomped at the water as if it were meat. Bob reposed on his elbow and exchanged pleasantries with Zee as she scraped corn relish out of a jar and onto some cold mashed potatoes. He chewed a blade of grass and coolly watched Jesse swing his screaming and then giggling daughter over the river. Bob asked, "How come you married him?"

Zee changed position to remove covered bowls from the market basket. Her gingham dress rose and subsided. Her pregnancy didn't yet show. She said, "Oh, he was so dashing and romantic and cast-out by the world, I couldn't help but love him." She smiled over the river, recollecting. She caught a strand of blond hair that flew near her eyes and refastened it with a small comb. "He was a figure out of a girl's storybook. Gentle, adoring, dangerous, strong." She looked at Bob. He was marking the checkered groundcloth with a spoon. "Surely you must've felt the same things. He has a magic about him. He steps straight into your heart."

Bob looked for an exit and asked, "Your middle name is Amanda, isn't it?"

She looked puzzled but replied that it was.

"I've got a sister whose name is Amanda."

Tim waded in six inches of water. A couple fifty feet east of them was singing gospel hymns. Somewhere a girl was being tickled. Zee uncorked a mustard jar. "Do you have a sweetheart, Bob?"

"I've kissed a girl or two, if that's what you're getting at."

"You don't have a sweetheart though."

"Nope." He tapped the spoon against his palm and then set it across a plate. He said, "That's the one thing that's been denied me. Otherwise my life's been a bounty."

"You're young yet."

Bob smiled uncertainly. "You hear people mention being in love. It's like a sickness I've never had."

Zee stared at Bob sympathetically and simply said, "I know."

JESSE LOUNGED as he ate and grinned at the sunlight and after their picnic lunch moseyed along the river with Zee, her right arm engaged in his left as he gave names to birds with his pointing finger. Charley put on the blue spectacles that were supposed to keep his identity unknown and galloped to the rope swings with Tim piggy-backed. Bob catnapped with Mary in shade and twenty minutes later opened his eyes to see Jesse squatted beside him. "You've got a habit of startling me."

Jesse moved a toothpick in his mouth and asked, "Can I talk with you a minute, Bob?"

Bob said, "I'm just lying here with nothing better to do."

Jesse looked straight ahead. "I've got a grapevine of spies; I guess you knew that."

Bob wasn't sure what to say. "I guess maybe I didn't."

"One of my spies told me you've spent a good portion of time in Kansas City lately. Could you tell me what your primary reasons would be?"

"I've been making purchases."

"You haven't come across Dick Liddil by any chance?"

"Nope."

"When would you say was the last time you saw him?"

Bob pretended to speculate. "December."

"That long ago!"

"If you've heard otherwise, they're mistaken."

"You don't have any idea where he might be?"

"Actually no. You hear plenty of stories but they contradict each other."

"He hasn't given himself up to get that reward?"

"Sorry I can't be more help to you but I've been sorely placed since Christmas—no one drops any good gossip in Richmond; it's mostly about who's been tippling or about some boys swiping pigs."

Jesse seemed to be in agreement. He gave his attention to Charley, who was walking in high grass in sunlight with Tim, his blue spectacles on his nose so that he could see over them and read aloud from a rain-damaged book he must have unearthed by the swings. " 'They were ready with their reins between their teeth,' " he read, " 'a loaded Colt's revolver in each hand.' "

Jesse got up from his squat, jiggling his legs out to get feeling back in them. He frowned and asked, "What sort of garbage is he reading to my boy?"

Charley continued, " 'A wild yell from Jesse, and the eight sprang upon the unprepared greasers, and before the first awful fire of Jesse and his clan, half the Mexicans were killed.' "

Jesse strode over and Charley smiled hugely at him. "I'm getting to the good part. 'The miserable Bustenado missed his mark but Jesse, quick as thought, sent a bullet between the Mexican's shoulders, and he fell upon his horse's neck, as dead as a bag of sand.' " Charley grinned again and showed a book cover that read *The James Boys Among the Mexicans*. "Someone forgot it over yonder."

Jesse slapped the man's cheek with his left hand and the blue spectacles flew. Charley staggered a little and became pale except for the hot pink of the skin where he was struck. Jesse yelled, "Don't you ever read them lies to my boy again! You understand me? My children are growing up clean!"

"I'm *sorry!*"

Bob could see water in Jesse's blue eyes. He said to the Fords, "I'm *real* angry," and then gently lifted his sleeping daughter to his shoulder and crooned words of affection as he walked away with Tim.

LATE SUNDAY NIGHT Charley scrunched close to the wall in the sitting room bed. His mouth was so muted by the pillow that Bob could just barely perceive that his older brother was crying. Bob asked what was the matter and Charley said one word: "Scared."

Bob snuggled close to his brother and curled his left arm around him. "He isn't going to kill us."

Charley sighed and shook a minute and scoured his nose with the pillowcase. Once he'd collected himself he said, "Yes he is. We're going to leave here for Platte City tomorrow and he's going to shoot us like he shot that conductor at Winston. Maybe he'll wait till we're asleep in the woods and then slit our throats like he said about that cashier."

Bob looked over his shoulder to check the room and then murmured into Charley's ear, "I'll stay awake so he can't."

Charley rolled to his back and gazed at the ceiling and then glanced at his kid brother. "This was the ninth day, right? And Craig gave you ten? So maybe we'll get surrounded up here and maybe we'll go to the bank and when we run out it'll be a crossfire and maybe fifty guns'll be shooting every whichway at Jesse and who gives a golly goddamn about the nobody Fords or if you and me get killed in the bargain?"

"You're imagining things."

Charley covered his eyes with his arm, respirated great, calming breaths of air, and coughed rackingly. Quiet came to the room again and then he said, "Isn't going to be no Platte City. That's Jesse fooling with us."

Bob considered the notion for a minute and then slipped out of bed and into his clothes. Charley looked at him and asked what he had in mind but Bob merely said in a low voice, "Go to sleep," and walked through the sitting room, dining room, kitchen, and stepped off the wooden porch into the night. The earth was cold as marble to his feet and the grass stabbed like a broom. He wore gray wool trousers over his longjohns but the chill convinced him to shawl his shoulders with a tattersall quilt that was being aired on the clothesline. He could see a mare asleep on three legs next to the stable—the fourth leg was canted rather coyly, as if a curtsy were coming. The wind in the sycamore branches made a sound like "wish." He could make out Severance, Kansas. He could smell fruit trees in the way that one can smell a neighbor's cooling pie. He settled himself on a plain bench under the clotheslines that sagged from the cottage eave. A mangled spoon was in the dirt; a straw doll was in a tin bucket.

He heard the screen door creak and clap shut, heard his brother limp over and stand to the rear of him. He seemed to ponder their predicament, the past, the galaxy. He lowered onto the long bench like a man who weighed six hundred pounds, and Bob saw that it was Jesse.

"So you and me are the nighthawks."

Bob made no reply.

"Mrs. Saltzman cut out a garden plot here. The Turners say it was a marvel: rabbit wire, noontime shade, clematis on the bean poles. I've been lazy about my seedlings."

"I don't like to garden; I just like to eat."

Jesse clutched his trousers and craned his legs into alignment. He said, "Maybe I'll nail together a Martin box." He peered at his right knee and his left and rapidly pounded them with his fists. "I've got pains in every *inch* of my body. My ears ring; my eyes are itchy. I'm going to lose my gift of second sight."

"Do you see future things like they were long gone, or do you just get inklings about what's to come?"

Jesse showed no inclination to answer. He paused for some time and then asked, "Did you know Frank and I looked for my father's grave over in Marysville, California?"

"You've mentioned that, but not at any length."

"I could picture the grave and the wooden cross but I couldn't get the geography right. They said it was cholera that killed him. They might as well've said the bubonic plague. You can always tell when it's Satan's work."

"How?"

"Trickery. Empty promises." Jesse scratched at his skull hair with all his fingers and then scratched at his jawbeard. He rubbed his eyes with his wrists. "You missed the Palm Sunday service."

"I used to go every week but that was because my daddy put a gun to my head."

Jesse shut his eyes and recited, " 'For it was not an enemy that reproached me; then I could have borne it: neither was it he that hated me that did magnify himself against me; then I would have hid myself from him. But it was thou, a man mine equal, my guide, and mine acquaintance. We took sweet counsel together, and walked unto the house of God in company.' "

Jesse said, "A good preacher will match that up with Matthew twenty-six." He coughed meanly and spat to the right. He squeezed his mouth with his palm. "Sometimes I get so forlorn and melancholy. Do you ever get that way?"

Bob shrugged.

"Do you know what it is you're most afraid of?"

"Yes."

"What?"

"I'm afraid of being forgotten," Bob said, and having admitted that, wondered if it was true. He said, "I'm afraid I'll end up living a life like everyone else's and me being Bob Ford won't matter one way or the other."

"It isn't always up to you, Bob. It may not be in the cards for ya." Jesse looked over to Kansas and leaned on his knees for a minute. "Do you ever get surprised when you see yourself in a mirror? Do you ever find yourself saying, 'Why do they call him by my name?' "

It seemed to Bob that Jesse expected no response.

"You're wrapped in a ragged coat for your three score and ten and nobody gets to see who's inside it."

"It's getting chilly," Bob said.

Jesse's thoughts seemed to fly and he concentrated on something that Bob couldn't see. "His voice is like a waterfall."

"Whose voice?"

"If I could stand in it for a second or two, all my sins would be washed away."

"I honestly can't follow this conversation."

Jesse approximated a smile. "Do you know who I'm jealous of? You. If I could change lives with you right now, I would."

Bob said, "I guess this must be a case of the grass always being greener on the other side of the fence."

"You can go away right now if you want. You can say, 'Jesse, I'm sorry to disappoint you, but the Good Lord didn't put me here to rob the Platte City Bank.' You can go inside and get your gatherings and begin a lifetime of grocery work. I'm roped in already; I don't have my pick of things; but you can act one way or another. You've still got the vote. That's a gift I'd give plenty for."

Bob thought negligently, as a young man might—totally within his body and his own history, without etiquette or any influence other than his hunger and green yearning. He gripped the tattersall quilt at his neck, smelling borax in it. He said, "I don't know. I'm not acting according to any plan. I'm just getting myself out of spots and pressing for my best advantage."

"You can't always make things happen, Bob."

"Well, like I say, I'm just taking what comes my way."

Jesse rose up and crimped his fingers over the metal clothesline, sagging a little on it, looking at the ground. "You Fords show your teeth like apes."

Bob couldn't imagine where their dialogue was going but the man's gloom seemed vaguely dangerous, so he decided to go back inside. He threw the tattersall quilt over a raspberry bush and shoved his hands in his pockets. "I'm going to call it a night."

Jesse was slumped forward dismally, swinging his weight on the clothesline, making the metal hooks complain. He asked, "Why don't you stay with me a little longer?"

"I'm sort of sleepy, Jess."

"Go ahead then," he said.

Bob was perplexed by the man's despondency. He walked to the screen door and then said, "I appreciate your frankness with me. This has been illuminating. I'm going to ponder all you said."

Jesse moved off into the darkness. "Don't make anything out of it," he said. "I was only passing the time."

MUCH LATER Bob would remember that he woke at sunrise on April 3rd looking at the racehorse named Skyrocket. Charley was climbing into a rough wool shirt that he wore whenever he worked with the animals. Bob dangled his fingers to the floor and walked them over his gun. Zee was already at the stove and Bob could see steam escape from a covered saucepan in shy phrases of smoke. Tim was in the children's room annoying his little sister.

Bob would recall that Jesse then came out of the master bedroom and scolded the children for pestering each other when it wasn't more than seven. He wore the crisp celluloid collar and the dazzlingly white linen shirt that he stole from the Kansas hotel highboy, and he adjusted the silk cravat in a looking-glass that revealed a section of shut door, a chair woven with rushes, a marred wall with the heights of Tim and Mary designated in crayon. Bob slithered from under the covers in order to conceal an erection and struggled his legs into nut brown trousers, then struggled his stockinged feet into boots that were so worn in the heels that his ankles caved out. Charley clomped to the stables via the front door and the screen door clapped off a sinking mist of street dust. Jesse buttoned a black cashmere Prince Albert coat over a vest and over his two crossed holsters and guns. He informed

Bob without nastiness that he could stay inside and sleep some more, and he walked out into sunlight just as Zee angrily banged shut the oven door, muttering, "Oh, shoot!"

Bob tucked in a yellow shirt and called, "Is that you making all that smoke?"

He saw Zee flip some burnt cottage biscuits from a blackened baking pan and say to no one, "This ornery stove!" He fingercombed his ginger brown hair in the looking-glass and slipped through gray oven smoke to go out to the privy.

He stepped over puddles that an overnight rain had put in the yard and he closed the privy door behind him. The temperature forecast was eighty degrees and already the April morning seemed as warm and moist as cooking vapors. Mary crouched outside with a coffee grinder that she'd ruined with sand; Tim propelled himself on a rope swing that rasped against a sycamore bough. Bob walked over to the backyard cistern, buttoning his fly, and the cistern pump brayed mulishly when he worked the iron handle. Charley came up from the stables and scraped off manure on a rusted rake that was forgotten in the grass, and though Bob said good morning to him, his only gesture of recognition was to slouch down the slope of the yard a ways and squat for some time inside cigarette smoke.

Jesse caught the swing set and gentled Tim down to a stop and then the two strolled down Confusion Hill for the subscription newspapers. Cold water that was slightly orange splashed into Bob's lifted white enamel bowl and spotted his trouser cuffs and boots. He brought the water to his face gratefully, as a man might a sweetheart's fingers, and he imagined without willing it the gruesome fish he'd caught in September. When he looked up Zee was peering at him through the porch screen.

"How much do you want to eat?" she asked.

"Just a smidgen," Bob said, and got up on his legs. "I'm feeling sort of peculiar." He pushed Mary in the swing for a while, responding to a two-year-old's questions, and then grew weary of that, flung her higher than before, and straggled into the front yard, where he leaned over the white picket fence to look down Lafayette Street. Sunlight flashed off the city's windows. The railroad yards to the west were ceilinged with smoke. The river moved with the slow advancement of blood. He lingered there for five minutes or so, his thumbs cocked by his pockets. He could have been a man at the races, a gambler with money on Skyrocket. Craig and Timberlake would be sitting at breakfast perhaps, making preparations for Tuesday, eating sweet croissants.

Craig would enrich his coffee with cream. A crew would be in the freight cars strewing straw for the deputies' animals.

Bob watched the great man and his child climb the steep ascent of the sidewalk with shoes on their feet and grand aspirations and a common language between them, but Bob figured that only meant they were slightly more intricate animals. It meant they were given more mechanisms than guns. Bob saw Jesse move a cigar in his mouth and squint his eyes from the smoke. He said, "How come you're looking so interested?"

Bob asked, "Do you think it's intelligent to go outside like that, so all creation can see your guns?"

Jesse ignored him and threw the cigar so that it sparked and rolled, screwing smoke. And then he rushed his daughter, monstering, catching Mary as she ran squealingly to the screen door and swinging the girl around so wildly her right stockinged foot lost its shoe.

Zee called everyone in to a breakfast that was cooling and Mary hugged her father's neck as he gracefully walked to the dining room. Tim carelessly threw down the rolled newspapers in the sitting room and climbed up next to his sister's highchair. Bob slit open a brown paper sleeve and spilled out the Kansas City *Times,* seeing instantly a story about the arrest and confession of Dick Liddil. Charley slouched into the dining room late, looking meek and afflicted, lying about some complaint with the horses to which Jesse paid scant attention. Bob slipped the newspaper under a shawl and strapped on the gun he had been given, tying the leather holster to his thigh with a string. Zee called Bob again, slightly irritably, saying everything was getting cold, and Bob seated himself across from Jesse, accidentally scarring the chair with his gun.

Zee jellied a biscuit for Mary and mentioned she'd invited a girl from across the street to go shopping with her for Easter clothes that afternoon. She asked Jesse to give her some money and he removed two five-dollar bills from a small roll secured with a rubber band. She asked if Jesse wanted some sandwiches for his journey. She asked if he'd come back for the Holy Thursday services.

Jesse frowned at his six-year-old son, who was staring blankly at the sunshine, woolgathering, his oatmeal spoon in his mouth. "What do you think goes on in that noggin of his?"

"Nothing," said Charley Ford.

Jesse laughed. "I was referring to *his* mind, not yours."

Bob snickered cravenly and Jesse looked askance at him. He then stood from his chair and fetched the newspapers that Tim had abandoned on the sofa, almost missing the Kansas City *Times* that was incompletely concealed by a shawl. He sat again with solemnity and stirred a spoon in his cup, swirling ghosts from the coffee.

Bob noticed every motion, every physical event: the crease in the man's brow, the fret in his reading eyes, the stain on a finger from the cigars he smoked. Bob slid the second newspaper around and scanned the items on its front page: legislation and politics, advertisements for curatives and clothes, the outrages visited on a young woman in Memphis, the shedding of innocent blood. A man in Grandview was ruled insane; a farm was lost to incendiaries; it was the twenty-second anniversary of the start of the Pony Express.

Jesse unfastened his Prince Albert coat and snared it over his guns. Tim excused himself from the table with a rasher of bacon in his mouth and Mary climbed down from her highchair after him. Jesse flattened the Kansas City *Times* over the newspaper he'd finished and lowered his crossed arms to scour the articles. "Hello now!" he said. "The surrender of Dick Liddil."

Charley said, perhaps too urgently, "You don't say so!"

Jesse lifted a coffee cup close to his mouth and stared at Bob through the vapors. "Young man, I asked you yesterday and you said you didn't know anything about Dick."

"And I don't."

Jesse moved his finger down the page, guiding his eyes as he read. "It's very strange," he said and made no other comment as he continued to the conclusion. Zee was scraping the children's breakfast plates in the kitchen and immersing them in soaped dishwater. They thudded together with the wooden sound of a muscular heart pumping blood. Jesse sipped some coffee without looking up from the newspaper. He said, "It says here Dick surrendered three weeks ago." He glanced at Bob with misgivings. "You must've been right there in the neighborhood."

"Apparently they kept it secret."

Jesse slumped back in the chair with his fingers knitted over his stomach and glared at Bob and then Charley. "It looks sort of fishy to me."

Bob said, "If I get to Kansas City soon, I'm going to ask somebody about it." And then he left the dining room with his right hand on his gun. He raised the Venetian blinds and the screenless sitting room windows and reacquainted himself with the rocking chair, his body fidgeting. Tim hunkered down on the stoop outside, coercing the crank on the coffee grinder. His little sister squatted beside him, pushing her pale dress down between her thighs, stabbing at the earth with a crooked spoon, and repeating, for some reason, "Don't."

Jesse retrieved some remedy from the medicine cabinet in the pantry and murmured privately with his wife. Charley walked into the sitting room and remarked on the sultry weather, said the afternoon would be hot as a pistol. He sat on the mattress and looped his holster off the bedpost, looking significantly at Bob as he put it on.

Jesse paused at the sitting room entrance as if to reconsider a scheme and then proceeded across the tasseled green rug with a long linen duster over one forearm, the other cradling packed saddlebags and a folded newspaper that carried a gun. Bob jumped up from the rocker and it reared and rowed, clubbing the floor, until he could still the chair with his hand. Jesse asked, "You two ready?"

And Charley said, "I will be by noon."

Bob strode over to the hanging straw portfolio, and as he snatched out a children's book he could feel Jesse glare at his gun. Bob shouldered into the floral wallpaper and vagrantly read to himself the first sentence of chapter one: "The little kitchen had quieted down from the bustle and confusion of midday." Jesse rammed a raised window sash higher, making the snug fittings moan.

Clouds were shipping in and accumulating and most of the eastern sky was the color of nails. "It's an awfully hot day," Jesse James said, and Charley thought so much of his earlier statement that he said once again it was going to be hot as a pistol. Jesse took off his Prince Albert coat and Bob concentrated on the man, stowing *Five Little Peppers and How They Grew* among some magazines. Jesse folded the fine black coat on the oak bed and then removed a six-button black vest that was extravagantly brocaded with red stitching. Charley shambled over to the screen door to scan Lafayette Street.

Sunlight streaked off Jesse's two revolvers. He leaned on the windowsill and gazed at the skittish weather. A suspender was twisted once across the back of an ironed shirt that coins of sweat made the color of smoke. He proclaimed in a sentence that seemed composed just for Bob, "I guess I'll take off my pistols for fear the neighbors will spy them if I walk out into the yard."

Charley instantly turned from the screen door with vexation in his face and saw his kid brother's right thumb twitch as Bob lowered his hand to his gun.

Jesse unbuckled the two crossed holsters with their two unmatched revolvers and carefully placed them on the mattress, as if creating some exhibit, and it seemed to Bob that the man was pretending: each motion seemed stressed, adorned, theatrical, an unpolished actor's version of calm and nonchalance. Jesse lent his attention to the race-horse named Skyrocket and said, "That picture's awful dusty," and withdrew from a wicker sewing basket a furniture duster that was made from the blue-eyed feathers of peacocks. He could easily reach the picture by standing, but he skidded the rush-bottomed chair across the rug and climbed onto it as if the floor were inclined and uncertain.

Bob slunk from the wall in order to stand between Jesse and the two revolvers. He shook loose his fingers like a gunfighter and instructed his brother with scared eyes as Jesse stood above them and feathered the walnut frame. Charley winked and the two Fords slipped out their guns. Bob was the speedier and had his .44 extended straight out from his right eye as Charley was still raising his and Jesse appeared to hear the three clicks as the Smith and Wesson was cocked because he slightly swiveled his head with authentic surprise, straying his left hand toward a gun that he'd forgotten was gone.

Then Robert Ford's .44 ignited and a red stamp seemed to paste against the outlaw's chestnut brown hair one inch to the rear of his right ear, and his left eyebrow socked into the glassed watercolor of Skyrocket. Gunpowder and gun noise filled the room and Jesse groaned as a man does in his sleep and then sagged from his knees and tilted over and smacked the floor like a great animal, shaking the house with his fall.

He looked at the ceiling, his fingers curled and uncurled, his mouth worked at making words, and the two Ford brothers saw he was dying. Charley leaped out the window and into the yard and as Zee rushed into a room that was blue with smoke, Bob slowly retreated and straddled the sill.

She screamed, "What have you done?" and the boy looked as if he wanted to apologize but couldn't. Zee knelt and cried, "Jesse, Jesse, Jesse," and cradled his skull in her apron and smothered his right ear in petticoats that soaked red with his blood. Tim was at the screen door, seeing everything, and Bob was still crouched at the sitting room window, gawking at the man. She asked with anguish, "Bob, have you done this?"

And he answered, "I swear to God that I didn't."

The man sighed and grew heavy on her legs. His eyes seemed yellow, his muscles slack; the blood was wide as a table. He made a syllable like "God" and then everything inside him stopped.

Charley skulked inside the cottage to collect the Fords' two hats and riding coats and to look again at the man they'd shot. He told Zee James, "The pistol went off accidentally."

Then Charley was outside again and the two Fords ran down Confusion Hill, their coats flying, cutting through yards and down alleys until they achieved the American Telegraph office, whence was sent to Sheriff Timberlake, Henry H. Craig, and Governor Thomas Crittenden an abbreviated message that read: "I HAVE KILLED JESSE JAMES. BOB FORD."

Part Three

———

AMERICANA

———

6

———

APRIL 1882 –
APRIL 1884

*Outside my window about a quarter mile to the west stands a little yellow
house and a crowd of people are pulling it all down. It is the house of
the great train robber and murderer, Jesse James, who was shot by his
pal last week, and the people are relic hunters. They sold his dust-bin
and foot scraper yesterday by public auction, his doorknocker is to be
offered for sale this afternoon, the reserve price being about the income
of an English bishop. . . . The Americans are certainly great hero worshippers,
and always take their heroes from the criminal classes.*

OSCAR WILDE
in a letter mailed from St. Joseph and dated April 19th, 1882

T HEN THE FORD BROTHERS ran over to City Marshal Enos Craig's
office in order to surrender, but a man there told them Craig was
at coffee and that a deputy marshal had just left for Confusion Hill,
that a woman had called on the telephone to report a gunfight on
Lafayette Street. The man was going to begin interrogating them about
their intentions with Craig but the two were already running east, and
they caught up with Deputy Marshal James Finley as he commenced
his search for the slain man's two cousins.

Charley was coughing from his exertions, so it was Bob who
gathered his wind and made introductions, saying next, "I'm the man
who killed the person in that house. He's the notorious outlaw Jesse
James, or I am mistaken."

The confession was so cold and conceited, with nothing in it
extenuated or softened by excuse, that Finley suspected it as a stupid
prank or as a calculated interruption of his pursuit. And yet Bob
persisted with his claims, specifying the articles in the cottage that
would signify the owner's name or initials, depicting physical scars

and appearances that Bob incorrectly thought most people would recognize as characteristics of Jesse James.

Just then Marshal Enos Craig was climbing Lafayette Street with Dr. James W. Heddens, the Buchanan County coroner, and with John H. Leonard, a police reporter for the St. Joseph *Gazette,* so Bob Ford forsook the deputy marshal, running down to meet Craig. Bob asked him if they could talk privately and the city marshal lingered on the sidewalk as the coroner and reporter walked on to the cottage.

Rubberneckers, neighbors, and children were collected in twos and threes in the yard or were peering through the sitting room windows when Heddens and Leonard arrived. The two men went inside the cottage and saw the body on a green carpet, the left eyelid closed, the right blue eye asleep, the mouth slightly ajar. A coat and vest and two revolvers were on an oak bed; the room smelled of gunpowder. Dr. Heddens knelt to listen to the man's chest and lifted his wrist to check for a pulse. He examined some mean lacerations on the man's left brow and then removed the soaked swaddling and examined a nickel-sized hole in the skull. He asked, "Do you know who it is, John?"

The reporter was making notes about the contents of the sitting room. He said, "Haven't the slightest idea," and then saw a pretty girl of sixteen come out of a sideroom.

The girl said, "His wife's in here."

Zee was sitting on the wide bed and crying in her hands. Her calico dress was streaked with blood and was redly saturated in the middle and hem. A fat woman sat with a sweatered arm over the widow's shoulders, and a girl of twelve was crouched with the children. Zee looked to John Leonard and realized he was recording whatever he saw. She pleaded, "Oh, please don't put this in the paper," and Leonard said, "I'm afraid that's my job."

The coroner came to the door and asked, "What's your name, madame?"

"Mrs. Howard," she said.

"Is the body that of your husband?"

She nodded.

The *Gazette* reporter turned to the sitting room to see Enos Craig and the two Fords come inside. The coroner asked Zee, "Do you know who killed him?" and Leonard could hear the widow answer, "Our two cousins, the Johnsons."

City Marshal Craig stared at the strong, spiffily outfitted body on the floor and sidled over to Leonard. "Do you know who they say that man is?"

"Someone named Howard."

Craig shook his head. "The boys claim it's Jesse James."

"Go on!"

The city marshal spied the widow in the sideroom and slipped off his broad white hat as he approached her. Enos Craig was a skinny and very stern man of fifty-three, with a crossed left eye and a vast gray mustache that he continually petted with a red handkerchief. He was not at all related to Henry Craig but *was* the younger brother of Brigadier General James Craig, a United States congressman, and he could exert in special circumstances the mellifluence that his brother made customary. He glared at the fat woman and the girl until they left the room, and then sat on the mattress with Zee. He remarked in an amenable, soothing voice, "Mrs. Howard? It is said that your name is not Howard but James and that you are the wife of the notorious Jesse James."

Zee frowned at him. "I certainly can't help what they say."

"The boys who have killed your husband are here. It's they who tell me your husband is Jesse James."

She looked at him with consternation. "You don't mean they've come *back?*"

Craig let the widow slump against his shoulder and weep rackingly as he stroked her fine blond hair. He crooned some comforting words and then said, "You know, it would be a lot more restful for your soul if you'd speak the truth. The public would think mighty highly of you; your children wouldn't ever again want for anything."

She rubbed her eyes with her sleeve, like a child. "I want to go see him."

"How's that?"

"I want to see my husband."

"Just lean your weight on me," Craig said, and the two walked into the sitting room.

Bob shrank back when he saw Zee and Charley moved to the screen door. She screamed, "You cowards! You snakes!" She surged at them but was restrained by the city marshal and, struggling, she cried, "How could you kill your friend?"

Charley slouched outside and Bob followed him, slapping the screen door shut. John Leonard scurried after them and went over to the sickly brother with the smudge of a mustache who was then squatting against the white picket fence, making a cigarette. Leonard asked, "You mean that really is Jesse James?"

"Isn't that what we've been saying since we come?"

The crowd ogled them and a small boy ran down the street, shouting what he'd overheard about Jesse James to whomever he encountered. Bob strolled over, slapping his palm with a stick. He said, "Have someone twist off that gold ring on his finger. You'll find a script with the name Jesse James inside."

Leonard jotted that down and then asked Charley, "Why'd you kill him?"

Bob intervened, "Say: we wanted to rid the country of a vicious and bloodthirsty outlaw."

Charley smiled in agreement and craned his neck to see the flight of the reporter's scribbled shorthand. He said to Leonard, "You should mention the reward too."

"You shot him for money?"

"Only ten thousand dollars!"

Leonard looked at Bob and saw that the young man was scowling. He said, "I'll mention that you are young but gritty."

Charley grinned. "We are *all* grit." He licked a cigarette paper and said, "You never expected to see Jesse's carcass in Saint Joe, did you? We always thought we'd create a sensation by putting him out of the way."

Zee gave in to Craig's gentle interrogation and admitted the truth. She wished she were in Death's cold embrace; she wondered what would become of the children; she talked about Jesse's love and kindliness and promised to speak further if the city marshal would guarantee no entrepreneur could get at the body and drag it all over the country.

Shortly after ten o'clock the body was carried to the Seidenfaden Undertaking Morgue in a black, glass-sided carriage that was followed by a procession of mourners, including Mrs. James. Snoops and onlookers swarmed around the cottage, viewing what they could through the windows, appraising the horses in the stables, swapping stories about the James gang, stealing whatever would slide up their sleeves, so that the cottage was soon closed, the sashes nailed shut, and a policeman stationed on the sidewalk to scare off looters.

Removed as evidence by Enos Craig were a gold ring with the name of the gunman inside, a one-dollar gold coin made into a scarf pin and cut with the initials J.W.J., a set of pink coral cufflinks, a Winchester rifle that Jesse called Old Faithful, a shotgun that was nicknamed Big Thunder, four revolvers (Pet, Baby, Daisy, and Beauty), an eighteen-karat-gold stem-winder watch stolen from John A. Burbank in the Hot Springs stage robbery in Arkansas, and a Waltham watch in a gold hunting case stolen from Judge R. H. Rountree when the Mammoth Cave sightseers' stagecoach was robbed in 1880. Mrs. James was not relieved of a resized diamond ring that was owned by Rountree's daughter, Lizzie.

An onlooker came over to the boy Tim and smiled as if they knew each other. "So you're Jesse Edwards James."

The boy frowned at the man.

"Do you know who Jesse James is?"

The boy shook his head.

"Do you know what your father's name was?"

Young Jesse was mystified. "Daddy."

The man laughed as hugely as he would have if Jesse James had joked with him and tried to get the gathering reporters to jot down the story along with his name, spelled out.

Jesse Edwards James and Mary were sent to stay with a woman named Mrs. Lurnal, and the manager of the World Hotel gave Mrs. James accommodations there. She displaced her grief by fretting a great deal about finances, so an auction of unnecessary household items was suggested. Zee's uncle, Thomas Mimms, sent telegrams to Mrs. Samuels and the family; the girl she was to shop with for Easter clothes packed a suitcase. Alex Green informed Zee that she was an accessory-after-the-fact in the multiple crimes that her husband committed but consented to represent the widow for a retainer of five hundred dollars; then R. J. Haire ruined Green's scheme by volunteering his services as an attorney in loving remembrance of a much-maligned and magnificent man.

POLICE COMMISSIONER Henry Craig received Bob Ford's telegram at his law office in the Kansas City *Times* building, but made no effort to inform the newspaper staff of the assassination; he merely sent a return message to Bob that read: "Will come on the first train. Hurrah for you," and then notified William H. Wallace, the Jackson County prosecuting attorney, of the extraordinary news. And since the wait for a regular run would have been many hours, Craig rushed north in the readied Hannibal and St. Joseph locomotive and coaches, stopping once, in Liberty, to collect Sheriff Timberlake and a stunned and saddened Dick Liddil.

Thomas Crittenden's secretary saw Bob Ford's communiqué only after perusing the morning's correspondence, but he immediately telegraphed the St. Joseph authorities for particulars and made arrangements for the governor to go there as soon as Crittenden returned from a meeting in St. Louis. The governor groaned when he was greeted with the news, and according to Finis C. Farr, the secretary, Crittenden said over and over again on their walk to the executive mansion that he regretted the Fords did not apprehend Jesse James alive.

At noon in St. Joseph, O. M. Spencer, the prosecuting attorney for Buchanan County, scheduled a coroner's inquest for three o'clock that afternoon and visited the Fords in Enos Craig's office in order to inform them that he didn't actually believe their stories about acting in concert with the government and that he intended to prefer charges of murder against them. He said, "I don't care if Mr. James was the most desperate culprit in the entire world; that fact wouldn't justify you in killing the man except in self-defense or after demanding his surrender, and the law is very explicit on that point."

Bob looked at the floor but Charley smirked at O. M. Spencer and asked Enos Craig when lunch would be served.

At Seidenfaden's funeral parlor on Fourth and Messanie streets, the cadaver was made void and then swollen by a cavity injection that was the substitute, then, for embalmment. A starched white shirt was exchanged for the stained one, but the cravat and remaining clothes were the same that Jesse James wore when he walked to the cigar store that morning.

On his second day of work with the Alex Lozo studio, a man named James W. Graham got the chance to become renowned at twenty-six by gaining the city marshal's permission to be the only photographer of Jesse Woodson James. He set a single-plate, eight-by-ten-inch studio camera on a box and, with William Seidenfaden and two men, carried the cadaver from the laboratory into the cooling room where those who'd expired were exhibited in a case of ice.

Correspondents from Kansas City, Independence, Richmond, and Kearney were already in the city and clustered behind the crimson cord and stanchions in the cooling room, writing their impressions and comparing the physical features on the remains with the two available photographs of Jesse at seventeen and twenty-seven.

Graham and the undertaker's assistants strapped the body to a wide board with a rope that crossed under his right shoulder and again over his groin, then they tilted the man until he was nearly vertical and let the camera lens accept the scene for a minute. The man's eyes were shut, the skin around them was slightly green, and the sockets themselves seemed so cavernous that photographic copies were later repainted with two blue eyes looking serenely at some vista in the middle distance.

Likewise missing in the keepsake photographs was the mean contusion over his left eyebrow that would convince some reporters that it was the gunshot's exit wound and others that it showed the incidence of Bob Ford's smashing the stricken man with a timber. The body's cheeks and chest and belly were somewhat inflated with preservatives, necessitating the removal of the man's thirty-two-inch brown leather belt, and making his weight seem closer to one hundred eighty-five pounds than the one hundred sixty it was. His height was misjudged by four inches, being recorded as six feet or more by those who wrote about him.

Graham carried the photographic dry plate back to the Lozo studio for development and many in addition to the newspaper reporters followed him, awaiting prints that sold for two dollars apiece and were the models for the lithographed covers on a number of magazines.

The body of Jesse James was lowered onto a slab that was surrounded with crushed ice and Mrs. Zee James was escorted into the cooling room by Enos Craig. She was so overcome with anguish and sorrow that she swooned in the city marshal's arms and then catatonically sat in a chair, disinclined either to cry or talk, unmindful of other visitors, merely staring at the slain thirty-four-year-old man until two in the afternoon.

Bob and Charley were in the midst of perfunctory interviews with reporters by then. Many noted that the Fords appeared to be proud of their accomplishment and contemptuous of the men who'd sought the James gang of late. Their comments were sneering, snide, argumentative, cocky, misleading. Charley preempted most of the conversations, exaggerating his role and responsibilities in order to insure the governor's indulgence. Bob lied about being an employee of the Kansas City Detective Agency, about being twenty-one, about Jesse's wearing four revolvers instead of two .45s, about never having joined the James gang, about shooting Jesse through the left temple, when the man turned around, rather than to the rear of his right ear. When they were asked whether they feared retribution from Frank James, Bob answered in a sentence that seemed rehearsed: "If Frank James seeks revenge, he must be quick of trigger with these two young men; and if we three meet anywhere, it will be Bob Ford who will kill Frank James if there's anything in coolness and alertness."

A policeman returned from the cottage with clean clothes for Charley, a gray tweed suit for Bob, and after they'd washed and changed, the Fords were issued shotguns for a short walk under rain-lashed umbrellas to the Buchanan County Courthouse.

The circuit courtroom was on the second floor and was already more jam-packed than an immigrant ship, with pallid women in the pews and children squeezed between the balusters of the bar and boys piggy-backed on their fathers' shoulders. Sitting in the aisles and pushing down the alleys and shoving into every cranny were correspondents from all the closer towns, shopkeepers with aprons on under their sweaters, intimidatingly mustached businessmen in nearly synonymous suits and slickers, farmers with droopy hats and fierce-looking beards, everyone staring as six policemen and the Ford brothers strode to the reserved seats on the defendant's side, their bootheels clobbering the oakwood flooring, their suit coats stuffed behind their pistol grips.

Mrs. Zee James was sitting with Marshal Enos Craig on the plaintiff's side, wearing a black silk dress and dark brown veil; in the second row was Henry Craig with a yellow legal pad on his knee, his round spectacles far down his nose. He gave Bob just a glimmer of a smile and then found justification to make some sort of notation. Bob crouched forward and saw that Zee was crying, he saw the prosecuting attorney instructing Coroner Heddens at the clerk's table, he looked around the room. People began making comments on his attractiveness, expressing surprise at his slightness and age, gossiping about his peccancy, sending him looks of scorn; but Bob governed his own emotions, reading his fingers as Coroner Heddens and a jury of six men came in from the judge's antechambers and a bailiff announced the inquisition was in session.

Charles Wilson Ford was the first witness called to the stand. He testified that he was twenty-four years old and in residence on the Ray County farm of Mrs. Martha Ford Bolton when he first made the acquaintance of Jesse James in 1879. He said, "He was a sporting man and so was I. He gambled and drank a little, and so did I." Charley claimed he'd never stolen anything with the James gang, but most of his further statements were true. His lisp was not much noticed. Rain fell straight as fishing line outside and gradually cooled the courtroom. Heddens asked if Bob came to St. Joseph to assist in robbing a bank and Charley apprised the coroner of their plans for a Platte City attempt. "Jesse said they were going to have a murder trial there this week, and while everybody would be at the courthouse, he would slip in and rob the bank, and if not he would come back to Forrest City and get that."

The coroner stood near the plaintiff's table with his hands in his pockets. He was unpracticed at cross-examination and all too aware of the many attorneys observing his performance. He lamely asked, "What was your idea in that?"

Charley continued as if the man's inquiry were logical and incisive. "It was simply to get Bob here where one of us could kill Jesse if once he took his pistols off. To try and do this with his pistols on would be useless, as I knew that Jesse had often said he would not surrender to a hundred men, and if three men should step out in front of him and shoot him, he could kill them before he fell."

O. M. Spencer was aghast when Dr. Heddens then released Charley without a more exacting interrogation but chose to let the matter rest until he could manage the questioning at the Ford brothers' trial. Charley swaggered back to the wooden chair and slouched down in it so that all the eyes would be off him. Bob said, "You did fine," and Coroner Heddens called Robert Newton Ford to the stand.

People strained their necks and rose from their seats and jumped to see the shootist. He strode with confidence to the bailiff, calmly swore not to perjure, and then complacently revealed himself to the courtroom audience, smiling with arrogance and gladness. He was twenty years old but looked sixteen. His gray suit was new, he seemed exceptionally well groomed, his short brown hair was soft as a child's. He was very slim but sinewy, with stark bones that seemed as slender and hard as the spindle struts on a chair. His facial features were refined, his complexion was flawless and without color (sunburn was then tantamount to dirt), and except for something cruel about his mouth Bob Ford might have been thought rather pretty.

The coroner commenced his easy catechism and Bob answered with a voice that was authoritarian and certain, even haranguing in its tone. He presented a comparatively accurate narrative of the preceding four months, misspeaking some dates and making the ten-thousand-dollar reward seem his only motive for the murder.

Heddens asked, "What have you been doing since you came here?"

"My brother and I go downtown sometimes at night and get the papers."

"What did you tell Jesse you were with him for?"

"I told him I was going in with him."

"Had you any plans to rob any bank?"

"He had spoken of several but made no particular selection."

The coroner was a little confused about the variation from Charley's statement about the Platte City Bank but went on. "Well, now will you give us the particulars of the killing and what time it occurred?"

"After breakfast, between eight and nine o'clock this morning, he, my brother, and myself were in the room. He pulled off his pistols and got up on a chair to dust off some picture frames and I drew my pistol and shot him.''

"How close were you to him?''

"About six feet away.''

"How close to him was the hand that held the pistol?''

Bob sent the coroner a reproachful look for the pointlessness of the question and said, "About four feet I should think.''

"Did he say anything?''

"He started to turn his head but didn't say a word.''

"Was Jesse James unarmed when you killed him?''

"Yes, sir.''

The coroner gave Bob permission to step down and the court was adjourned until 10 a.m. on Tuesday. O. M. Spencer moaned.

Henry Craig said, "You'll get your chance, Spencer,'' and the two attorneys strolled to a restaurant in order to argue their strategies.

In the meantime, the Fords tardily returned to jail in a cold rain. A cluster of black umbrellas were raised over them by policemen and a crowd followed them with admiration, congratulations, catcalls, jeers, and surly looks. Sheriff James R. Timberlake rose from a chair when the two scurried inside. Door locks were thrown and the window shades were drawn as Timberlake walked the Fords back to their cell. He told them to make no agreements without consulting Henry Craig or William H. Wallace, to make no arrangement about an attorney since a good one was already considering the case, and to get their accounts of the assassination straightened out—according to the reporters he'd chatted with, there were too many inconsistencies; in some versions Charley was not even in the room when the shot was fired.

Bob Ford explained, "I was just having a little fun.''

"Fun,'' said the sheriff.

Dick Liddil was resting on a cot next to theirs. He stood when the Fords came in and exchanged greetings with Charley, but it was clear that Dick was aggrieved and he could only stare with anguish at Bob. Timberlake suggested that it might be safer for Dick if he remained in jail overnight and Dick said, "It's all right, Jim. I've gotten used to it.''

Sheriff Timberlake was intercepted outside by a correspondent with the St. Louis *Democrat* and used the occasion of an interview to correct some misconceptions, saying Jesse knew that Bob Ford was there on a mission and was only waiting for the right time to kill the boy. "For ten days I suffered mortal agony, expecting any hour to hear that Bob was dead, and when at last I did hear of the killing, and how it was done, I knew in a minute that Jesse had only taken off his revolvers in the presence of Bob to make him believe that he stood solid. He never dreamed that the drop would be taken upon him then. That very night, on the ride toward Platte City, which had been seemingly agreed upon, Jesse would have shot Bob Ford through the head sure.''

Railway companies had by then rather gleefully scheduled special coaches that would carry the inquisitive to the city at greatly reduced rates; thus a thousand strangers were making spellbound pilgrimages to the cottage or were venerating the iced remains in Seidenfaden's cooling room. Reporters roamed the city, gathering anecdotes and apocrypha, garnering interviews with the principals, relentlessly repeating themselves, inaccurately recording information, even inventing some stories in order to please a publisher.

The man who offered thirty thousand dollars for the body of Charles Guiteau sent a telegram to City Marshal Enos Craig offering fifty thousand for the body of Jesse Woodson James so that he could go around the country with it, or at least sell it to P. T. Barnum for his "Greatest Show on Earth." Notwithstanding his guarantee to Mrs. James, Craig appears to have given the proposal some strong consideration, and appears also to have craved the criminal's guns, for on Wednesday Governor Crittenden angrily interceded in the matter with a wire to O. M. Spencer that said: "Just informed your officers will not turn over the body of Jesse James to his wife nor deliver his arms to me. I hope you will have done both. Humanity suggests the one, and a preservation of such relics for the state the other. His jewelry should be held for the present." The governor also sent the state militia to St. Joseph on the 3rd in order to preserve the peace and to protect his increasingly threatened clients.

However, the militia had not yet arrived when six horsemen in raincoats and slouch hats rode inside the fence at 1318 Lafayette Street. They had short rifles or shotguns in saddle scabbards, revolvers made their coats wide at the waist, and they were laughing at some sally or jest when a policeman in navy blue walked out of the cottage to meet them. They were unnerved when they saw him, some were affrighted, but one man merely scowled and asked the policeman what happened to the owner. When they received word that the man they sought was shot, one of the six groaned, "Oh, God, no!" and because they steered away and left the city at once, it was thereafter conjectured that they were recruits to the James gang that not even the Fords knew about; which of course lent credence to Bob's claim that Jesse meant to kill them. Little was made of the six men's unanticipated appearance and precipitate departure—there was simply too much frenzy and ferment in the city for the episode to make an impression on the authorities.

Mr. Seidenfaden concluded his day by noting in a black ledger: "Apr. 3. Mr. Jesse James killed. Number 11 S. casket with shroud, $250. Shroud $10. Paid." That was an extravagance: the casket was an imitation rosewood that was made with galvanized iron; the lifts and lugs were silver; the mattress and pillow were cream-colored satin. Two hundred sixty dollars was more than ten times the price of a standard funeral, but the costs were entirely covered by "gentlemen who wished to remain anonymous." It was only much later that the gentlemen were revealed to have been James R. Timberlake and Henry H. Craig.

Jacob Spencer, the man who owned the St. Joseph *News,* went into his library late that afternoon and began seven nights' work on what would become *The Life and Career of Frank and Jesse James,* a two-hundred-page book that sold out as soon as it reached the stores on April 12th. (Spencer claimed later that five hundred thousand copies would have been needed in order to meet the demand.)

A man crept into the cottage that night and cut out a swatch of the blood-stained carpet; the next afternoon he was in Chicago selling square inches of the material for five dollars.

The governor wanted to be certain that the man on ice was Jesse James, so a party of acquaintances and Clay County neighbors (including two cousins) were sent to St. Joseph via a Missouri Pacific train and at midnight viewed the remains. Mattie Collins was the most greatly affected by the sight: she called Bob Ford a cur and a scoundrel, rashly cursed William Wallace and Henry Craig in their presence, maintained that it was that slut Martha Bolton who'd orchestrated everything, and carried on like an overexercised actress until Wallace commanded, "My dear lady: cease!"

One by one the identifiers were asked by Craig if they recognized the man, and all corroborated that it was indeed the man they'd schooled or soldiered or been on the scout with. Dick Liddil said, "That's Jess all right. I'd know his hide in a tanyard." Four of them then signed a statement certifying "that we were well-acquainted with Jesse James during his lifetime, that we have just viewed his remains now in the custody of the coroner at this place and have no hesitation in saying that they are unquestionably his."

Soon after they left, at about 1 a.m., Coroner Heddens and three other doctors, among them George C. Catlett, the superintendent of the insane asylum, stole into the cooling room in order to perform an autopsy. They noted the cadaver was "a man of fine physique and was evidently possessed of unlimited powers of endurance." They sawed open the skull and followed the .44 caliber bullet's route from its entrance at "the lower part of the occipital bone on the right of the median line" to "the junction of the suture which divides the occipital, parietal, and temporal bones of the left side." According to Catlett, "The brain was a most remarkable one, and showed the great will power, earnestness, and determination of the man. It also showed thought and courage and in most men would have accomplished wonderful things."

They saw two round scars within three inches of the man's right nipple and after surgery realized, with some astonishment, that the man had managed a vigorous life without the service of his right lung. They also recorded a bullet wound in a leg, the scar of a lanced abscess in the right groin, a fractured interior anklebone of the left foot, a missing inch of the left middle finger, a brown birthmark above the right elbow. The doctors then restitched the sectioned skin and cleaned and dressed the cadaver with such care that their post-mortem was secret for more than a week.

The remaining night was calm.

ON TUESDAY MORNING, Police Commissioner Henry Craig, Sheriff James R. Timberlake, James Andrew "Dick" Liddil, and Deputy Marshal James Finley were tactfully examined by a tired Coroner Heddens. Little that was unanticipated was said. Timberlake stated he'd known Jesse James since 1864 and recognized the cadaver as being that of the criminal. (His words at Seidenfaden's were "Jesse, I've looked for you for a long time.") Timberlake volunteered the theory that Jesse would have killed the Fords if Bob hadn't shot him first, that Jesse only removed his revolvers in the Ford brothers' presence in order to pacify them. He reminded the court that Jesse James had announced his intention of killing Governor Crittenden, Dick Liddil, and one or two others in the gang "as they were surrendering too fast, and he would be in danger if they were permitted to live."

Henry Craig admitted that Bob "was not regularly employed by us, but acted in good faith, and according to our instructions, and assisted in every way he could to aid us," an acknowledgment that caused a stir of rebuke in the courtroom but meant so much to the careers of the Fords that Bob smiled with gratitude and relief when he heard it said.

In the course of the Tuesday proceedings, Mrs. Zerelda Samuels arrived at the railroad station and was greeted by a great throng awaiting her on the platform. She moved in their midst like an Amazon queen—six feet tall, two hundred twenty-eight pounds in weight, the largest form in the crowd, but with a sovereignty that made her seem even grander. She accepted solace and sympathy from a great many there, gathered sprays and nosegays of wildflowers, and then rode in a carriage with grave indignation to Seidenfaden's parlor.

She tottered as she walked to the stone slab on which her third-born son slept. She was too mentally and spiritually limited to contemplate the sorrow that the man she mourned over had caused the wives and mothers of his many victims; she only contemplated her own grief and wept as she stroked his white sleeve. A man asked if the remains were really Jesse James and she said, "Yes, it's my son; would to God it were not." She then caressed his cold cheek and cried with great lamentation, "O, Jesse! Jesse! Why have they taken you from me? O, the miserable traitors!"

Mr. Bowling Browder, a Kentucky hotel owner who'd married the sister of Zerelda Mimms, then steered Mrs. Samuels out to the carriage that carried her to the courthouse. Some correspondents accompanied them. She said, "You know, he must've had a foreshadowing that this was about to happen. One of the last things he said to me was 'Mother, if I never see you on earth again, we're sure to meet in Heaven.' " She was practiced enough with reporters to pause while they wrote down that statement, and then she continued with vituperations against the government and angry professions of her son's charity and goodness.

They reached the circuit courtroom just as Deputy Marshal Finley was concluding his brief testimony and as Coroner Heddens was preparing to call for a recess. The Ford brothers were removed from the courtroom through the judge's antechambers in order to avoid the press, so they missed the attention-getting entrance of the magisterial Mrs. Samuels in a long black gown and veiled sunhat. She was seated with Mrs. James and the two children but then saw Dick Liddil slumped on a side bench. She rose at once and, with the vast courtroom audience attending her, shook her mangled right arm damningly at Dick and railed, "O, you coward! You did all this; you brought all this about! Look at me, you traitor! Look upon me, the broken-down mother, and on this poor wife and these children! How much better it would be if *you* were in the cooler where my boy is now than here looking at me! Coward that you are, God will swear vengeance upon you!''

The courtroom assembly strained to see Dick's reaction, some further off even climbing onto the seats; Dick looked around with annoyance and bewilderment and then meekly said, "*I* wasn't the one who killed him. I thought you already knew who did it.''

Henry Craig peered across the room at Dick and shushed him with a parental finger to his lips. Coroner Heddens wisely interrupted the scene by calling first the mother and then the pregnant wife of the deceased to the stand, asking them merely to give their names and current residences and to verify the identity of the remains. Then, lacking any reason to continue the inquest, he requested that the coroner's jury of six men, "all good and lawful householders in the township of Washington,'' be impaneled until they could render a judgment as to how and in what manner and by whom the said Jesse W. James came to his death. Their verdict was returned before noon and the Fords were summarily indicted for first-degree murder.

The St. Joseph *Gazette* was sold out by then and its seven-column account of the assassination was being reprinted verbatim in many newspapers throughout the country. Scare headlines were not yet in use, so that JESSE, BY JEHOVAH was wedged into a single column and was followed by five three-line decks that read: "Jesse James, the Notorious Outlaw, Instantly Killed by Robert Ford—His Adventurous Career Brought to an Abrupt Close on the Eve of Another Crime— Ford Gets into His Confidence and Shoots Him from Behind While His Back Is Turned—Jesse a Resident of St. Joseph Since the Eighth of November Last—An Interview with Mrs. James and the Testimony Developed Before a Jury.''

The account began: "Between eight and nine o'clock yesterday morning Jesse James, the Missouri outlaw, before whom the deeds of Fra Diavolo, Dick Turpin and Schinderhannes dwindled into insignificance, was instantly killed by a boy twenty years old, named Robert Ford, at his temporary residence on the corner of Thirteenth and Lafayette, this city.

"In the light of all moral reasoning the shooting was unjustifiable; but the law is vindicated, and the $10,000 reward offered by the state for the body of the brigand will doubtless go to the man who had the courage to draw a revolver on the notorious outlaw even when his back was turned, as in this case.''

And there followed a narrative of the assassination as set forth by the Fords. John Leonard wrote that the news of the shooting "spread

like wildfire'' but that few people gave it credence. Inevitably, the
excitement in St. Joseph and Kansas City was compared to that created
nine months earlier when President James A. Garfield was shot by
Charles J. Guiteau.

On the afternoon of the 4th, Zee consented to an interview, in
which she said she was thirty-five rather than thirty-seven and went on
to prevaricate about her late spouse. She said Jesse was not a good
scholar and that his spelling was rudimentary, but that he read incessantly and could compose letters like he was pouring water, and never
striking a word. She said he was quiet and mild and affectionate, never
smoked tobacco nor consumed alcoholic beverages, was always playing with the children. She talked about his practicality and acumen at
finance and then made the familiar claim that the circumstances of
geography and history compelled him to commit the very few crimes
for which the James gang was actually accountable. She stated, without
close questioning or contradiction, that the couple had worked in
contentment on three farms at various times but authorities had always
conspired to drive them off and confiscate their property. The correspondent mentioned that it was estimated the James gang had collected
over a quarter of a million dollars in fifteen years, and Zee replied by
saying she hadn't an inkling where the money could've gone, she only
knew they'd always been poor.

Cole Younger was interviewed in the Stillwater penitentiary but
magnanimously tempered his antipathy for Jesse by limiting his
comments to tales of the Civil War and a physical description of the
outlaw. And a girl who'd once thrown snowballs with the man she
knew as Thomas Howard said she'd ''never met a more perfect gentleman. Whenever I came to his house he bowed very politely, and in a
dignified manner offered me a chair and conversed in the most accomplished manner. Much has been alleged against him but I don't believe
half of it.''

Many newspaper editorial pages on Tuesday carried columns
applauding the assassination because it was cheap, expeditious, and
successful, but the newspapers' correspondents were at odds with that
judgment, seeming only to record conversations with people who were
sympathetic to the victim or skeptical that he'd really perpetrated all
that the government said he did. In consequence, antagonism to the
Fords was increasing. It was rumored that some Crackernecks intended
to steal and enshrine the remains, that Bob would be lynched on the
day that the body was interred, that Frank James was in the city with
vengeance on his mind—this ''mysterious stranger'' was eventually

revealed to be a German barkeeper who was known as Dutch Charlie. By afternoon the Fords had received at least two menacing letters, one of them crudely printed under the official seal of the Tennessee House of Representatives. It read: "To the Ford Brothers you have Killed Jessie James but you did not get his Pal so Jessie James shal be Avenged i will kill you both if i have to follow you to the end of the earth you cant escape my Vengeance."

A reporter asked the Fords if they were at all cowed by the threat and Charley was again the one who answered, "No, sir, we fear no one. You tell this fellow from Tennessee to give us his name and we'll meet him on even ground."

Bob added, "Give me my guns and let me know who he is and I will meet him anywhere he will name in the United States."

The writer was clearly impressed by the boys' courage and resolution and said in summary, "If the worst comes, they will sell their lives as dearly as possible."

Governor Crittenden came up from Jefferson City on the 4th and graciously shook hands at the polling places, urging people to vote the Democratic ticket. The Republicans swept the city elections except for a Democrat who was preferred as city marshal over Enos Craig.

Crittenden granted a good number of interviews, denying in each that he'd meant that Jesse James be killed. He was sure though that his actions would meet with the sanction of law-abiding citizens of Missouri and throughout the United States. "If not killed when he was," the governor said, "he would have attacked the bank at Platte City, and in perpetrating the robbery would have killed in all probability some one or more of the officials in the ill-fated bank; then he would have gone to Kansas, returned and attacked the bank at Forrest City and killed one or more of its officials. Should not these things be considered? Must we overlook not only his past but anticipated robberies and murders in the future and grieve over his deprivation? I say no, a thousand times no. I have no excuses to make, no apologies to render to any living man for the part I played in this bloody drama; nor has Craig nor has Timberlake. The life of one honest law-abiding man however humble is worth more to society than a legion of Jesse Jameses. One is a blessing, the other a living, breathing, putrid curse."

Crittenden's secretary, Finis Farr, then substantiated the governor's claim that no murder was intended by indicating the July proclamation that promised a reward only for the arrest and conviction of the man. Off the record, however, the secretary confided that studies showed real estate values in Missouri would increase by thirty-three percent once the desperado was gone, and noted that one man who was selling his farm had already raised the price by five hundred dollars.

Meanwhile the crowds at Seidenfaden's grew and now were gaining admission to the cooling room only after contributing fifty cents. Another photograph was taken of the renowned American bandit constricted in a small walnut coffin, with his head canted to the left and with three sullen, scraggly men around him, and it was that shot that was most available in sundries stores and apothecaries, to be viewed in a stereoscope along with the Sphinx, the Taj Mahal, the Catacombs of Rome.

JAMES WILLIAM BUEL ARRIVED on Wednesday to cull information about the shooting for a reissue of his two books about the James brothers, *The Border Outlaws* and *The Border Bandits;* and Frank Triplett was in the city to sign a contract with Mrs. James and Mrs. Samuels and a St. Louis publisher, giving them fifty dollars as an advance against royalties. (*The Life, Times, and Treacherous Death of Jesse James* was written at the rate of sixty pages a day, and while not actually dictated by the two women, as was alleged, it was as congenial to the Jameses and as contemptuous and critical of Governor Crittenden and the Fords as any chronicle could be; yet it claimed that Frank and Jesse were criminals, and for that reason Zee repudiated the book in May, and Governor Crittenden unintentionally cooperated with the widow by suppressing it.)

Ex-Governor Brockmeyer visited both the cooling room and the jail cells and then communicated to a correspondent his glancing impressions of the slain man and his remover, saying Mr. James could have been distinguished in whichever course he undertook, that he was obviously a man born to control subordinates, and his general appearance showed a sagacity and power that but few men can ever possess. Of the Ford boy, there was a youth who could look green and uncouth except when cornered. That he was courageous, self-reliant, and prepared for any emergency, those who looked into the depths of his cool blue eyes could not doubt for an instant. He could cope with anything, although his manner was quiet, self-centered, and of a retiring character; and it was possibly the corresponding singularities in the fugitive's make-up that conceivably caused him to take young Ford into his confidence.

Mrs. Moses Miller, the mother of Clell and Ed Miller, also looked in on the cooling room, moving inchingly on two canes and shivering with palsy as she stood over the remains. Many reporters insisted on her opinion of the man more or less responsible for the deaths of her two sons, but she refused to speak a syllable and simply pressed a laced linen hankie to her eyes.

Meanwhile, an eight-year-old boy named Tom Jacobs was gallivanting through greening woods in countryside east of Richmond, calling for his mongrel dog. He followed its barking around scrub oak, box elder, and crab apple trees and saw it gambling miseries with a skunk, wagering to the right and left as the skunk showed its sharp white teeth and maneuvered in the scraggle and muck of a rain-changed creek. The boy saw that the skunk had been eating. He recognized a muddy wool blanket, menacing teeth, and a withered left hand with three missing fingers, and then ran with fright to his father.

Perry Jacobs was so convinced by the child's horror that he rode straight to Richmond and collected Constable John C. Morris and Coroner Richard Bohanon, and they followed Tom Jacobs onto the Harbison acreage that was rented by the widow Bolton, finding the rotting cadaver of Robert Woodson Hite in a shawl of clay and apple tree leaves that slid from his chest in the rain. His eyes were plucked out, his mouth seemed to scream, and a bullet hole in the man's right temple had been exaggerated by birds. The men wincingly carried Hite's weight to a wagon and wound him in a rubber sheet, and then arrested Martha Bolton and Elias Capline Ford on the suspicion of murder.

Elias acknowledged that the cadaver was Wood Hite, but Martha claimed she'd only known the man as Grandfather Grimes; otherwise their statements about the December gunfight matched in attesting that it was Dick Liddil who'd committed the killing. They were released on their own recognizance since two brothers already in jail seemed a satisfactory guarantee that they wouldn't "high-tail" it (the constable's words). Wood Hite was deposited on the plaintiff's table in a Richmond courtroom, pending a coroner's inquest, and then Constable Morris, with unseemly haste, sent a message to Governor Crittenden that read: "I have the body of Wood Hite and am ready with evidence for identification. What shall I do with it? I claim the reward."

The governor was so incensed by the constable's greed that he considered charges against him, but guiltily decided that Morris's reaction was partly of the governor's own making, so that he merely sent the reply: "On account of the weather, rebury it. No reward offered for *his* dead body."

The Ford brothers were remarkably unbothered by the revelation in Richmond. Perhaps their distractions and perturbations were already too plentiful for them to register the significance of the discovery, or perhaps they'd made a blithe assumption that the governor would pardon all previous crimes. At any rate they continued to comport themselves as if they'd done nothing terribly wrong, and Charley even acted hurt when he was informed that they would not be allowed to attend Jesse's last rites on Thursday.

THE RAINS CONTINUED into the afternoon of April 5th, and surreys and rigs were mired in the slime of the streets, and yet more than four hundred mourners slogged after an express company wagon that carried a boxed iron casket to the Hannibal and St. Joseph Railroad depot. A covered hackney summoned Mrs. James and the two children at six, then Mrs. Samuels, a cousin named Luther James, and Sheriff Timberlake. Thomas Mimms, Henry Craig, and deputies, correspondents, and the city marshal came after them in carriages that were somberly festooned with black crepe ribbons and bows. Crowds lined the sidewalks and watched the cavalcade from beneath wet umbrellas and men stood lugubriously in the rain with their hats off, their hair washed slick against their skulls. A crackpot no one knew raised a purse pistol and shot at Mrs. Samuels, and Luther James and Henry Craig leaped out, tackling the manifestly intoxicated man in an alley. Craig punched him once in the stomach and once in the cheek and the man staggered away until he sprawled sloppily into a gutter. Craig regained the carriage and shook out his fingers and smiled when he was clapped on the back. "I needed the exercise," he said. No charges were made against the crank.

Sheriff Timberlake and the deputies slid the boxed casket into a railway express car, then shut and locked the sliding door behind them, mindful of the irony in the situation. The remaining parties climbed onto a coach that included regular passengers who stared so rudely and pryingly at the veiled and weeping women that City Marshal Craig issued some minatory instructions and then sat with Mrs. Samuels's left hand engaged in his right. They were old acquaintances from the Civil War when Enos Craig was the Buchanan County sheriff and oversaw Zerelda Samuels and her daughters in the county jail. They chatted about their gardens.

A special Hannibal train was scheduled to meet them at Cameron Junction but the crowds made them tarry so long in St. Joseph that they missed their connection and were forced to stay over in the town until a Rock Island train could be sent. Sheriff Timberlake and Marshal Craig vied over who would nightwatch the remains, for each mistrusted the other as a man capable of selling the corpse. An argument followed and Enos Craig reached for his gun, but realized the childishness of the fight when a station agent yelled from across the room, "Gentlemen, gentlemen! Don't pull your pops in here!" Craig returned his revolver to its holster and then sourly walked the railroad tracks, snuffing Maccaboy tobacco.

Dick Liddil, Marshal Bill Wymer, Mrs. Katie Timberlake, and two other ladies had arrived in Kearney around noon on Wednesday and word went out that the funeral cortege would be coming soon, so that the railroad line between Cameron and the Samuels farm was fenced by the afflicted and curious even when the Rock Island freight train and single coach actually coasted by after midnight. Mary and Jesse Edwards James slept on the seats inside and Mrs. Samuels continued her inexhaustible commentaries on the caitiffs who'd slaughtered her son. Sheriff Timberlake lashed the container to the coach's rear platform and sat on the box during the journey, sucking on a cold Calabash pipe, letting the wind comb his hair.

Once Kearney was attained, the casket was removed from the box and rested in the candle-lit lobby of the McCarthy House so that residents could look through the coffin glass at a man that many there had known only as a storybook legend. His skin was yellowing a little and the contusion over his left eye was orange but otherwise the man seemed more attractive than the Jesse they'd seen as a child. Mrs. Samuels came in from the sitting room at 3 a.m. accompanied by her mincing husband, and she again gave in to wild lamentations, screaming, "How can I stand it? How can I stand it? How can I stand it?" Zee James stood quietly at the foot of the casket, gently caressing the metallic rosewood with her light, gloved fingers. A silver name plate was affixed to the casket and German Gothic lettering had been used to inscribe the words "Jesse James." Dr. Samuels recounted an uninteresting story about seeing his wife for the first time in that very hotel, and the New York *Herald* correspondent muttered a wisecrack to one of his colleagues. It was almost five in the morning when the writers at last went to sleep.

Sheriff Timberlake had arranged for the president of William Jewell College to officiate at the services on Holy Thursday, but after agreeing to that the Right Reverend W. R. Rothwell was reminded that a sophomore, George Wymore, had been slain by the James-Younger gang in the robbery of the Clay County Savings Bank, and Rothwell claimed an incipient malady, recommending in his stead Reverend J. M. P. Martin, pastor of the Mount Olivet Baptist Church.

Kearney was a main street town with only six hundred residents then, and yet five hundred people moved through the McCarthy House between sunrise and noon. Freight and passenger trains made unscheduled stops at the Kearney depot so that travelers and railroad crews could see the desperado, and sharecroppers were walking into town from shacks that were sometimes as far as sixteen miles away. Then it was two in the afternoon and the casket was screwed shut and carried out to the flatbed of a spring wagon. A procession of twenty teams and carriages followed the remains to a one-storey red-brick church that was already so filled that two hundred spectators were laughing and smoking on the lawn. The sky was cerulean blue, the temperature was sixty degrees, and a slight wind mowed over the grass.

Sheriff Timberlake was the supernumerary among the pallbearers and was mistaken for Frank James by many in attendance. The five others were Deputy Sheriff J. T. Reed, a boyhood friend of the outlaw's, and J. D. Ford, the mayor of Liberty; then Charles Scott, James Henderson, and James Vaughn (who much later became mentally ill and claimed he was Jesse's brother). The casket was situated on a short table in front of the plain altar and relatives and close acquaintances were seated beside it as the congregation sang "What a Friend We Have in Jesus."

Reverend R. H. Jones read from the Book of Job: "Man that is born of woman is of few days, and full of trouble. He cometh forth like a flower, and is cut down: he fleeth also as a shadow and continueth not."

Mrs. Samuels moaned, "O merciful Jesus!" at strategic intervals then and throughout the reading from Psalm 39: "Lord, make me to know mine end, and the measure of my days, what it is; that I may know how frail I am. Behold thou hast made my days as an handbreadth; and mine age is as nothing before thee: verily every man at his best state is altogether vanity." Jones then offered a prayer for the bereft mother, wife, and children, asking the Lord to make their anguish a blessing to them by bringing them to wonderful knowledge of Himself.

The Mount Olivet congregation rose for the hymn, "Oh, Where Shall Rest Be Found?" and Reverend Jones retreated next to Timberlake as a stooped and sullen Reverend J. M. P. Martin sorely climbed to a raised wood pulpit that was slashed across with sunlight. He looked grimly at the casket through his spectacles and glanced apologetically at the family and assembly before dividing his Bible with his finger. He said, "We all understand that we cannot change the state of the dead. Again, it would be useless for me to bring any new information before the congregation respecting the life and character of the deceased."

Some reporters were annoyed by the prim and politic tack the minister had taken, recognizing that there'd be no story in it, and they audibly sighed and sank deeper in the pews as Martin peered into his Good Book. "The text which I have chosen today is the twenty-fourth chapter of Matthew, forty-fourth verse: 'Therefore be ye also ready: for in such an hour as ye think not, the Son of man cometh.' "

It was a sleepy, unimaginative, uninspired sermon that concentrated on the certainty of the grave, the need for repentance, the salvation of the righteous. Zee James no more than sniffed as Martin spoke, but Mrs. Samuels sobbed and swayed and rolled her eyes to the roofbeams, swoonily repining, then made the smaller Dr. Samuels crutch her flamboyant, chest-striking exit from the church at the conclusion of the service.

Only those closest to the James-Samuels clan were invited to the hundred-fifty-acre farm three miles northeast of Kearney, for Mrs. Samuels was afraid that the commotion would be a vexation to her boy Johnny. In spite of the minister's instructions to the contrary, however, more than eighty followed the casket on the Greenville road and another vast number from the countryside was encountered in the yard.

Confederate Army soldiers had cut a grave into seven feet of loam and roots beneath the giant coffee bean tree in which Yankee soldiers had hanged Dr. Reuben Samuels by the neck. It was close enough to the kitchen window that the apprehensive mother could easily look out for body snatchers. The cadaver was shown one last time to Johnny and then was carried out into the shade where it was rested on chairs so that the company could see Jesse Woodson James in the sleep of peace.

Mother and wife were then overmastered by grief and hysteria and they cast themselves upon the casket, screaming for God to avenge the man slain by a coward for money. The two women were gently encouraged from the ground but Zerelda Samuels wrenched away from constraining hands and, having become convinced of some skullduggery, insisted that the casket be reopened in order to make certain that her son's arms and legs had not been sawed off and replaced with limbs made of wax. Sheriff Timberlake went dutifully for a screwdriver but was called back after Reverend Martin soothed the woman with practiced words about a calculus in Heaven that adjusts for our privations and compensates for our losses. And as those gathered sang "We Will Wait Till Jesus Comes," the casket was jarringly lowered on ropes and gradually covered with earth.

MEANWHILE LIFE WAS BEGINNING to be glorious for Charley and Bob. The manager of the Théâtre Comique in Kansas City proffered one hundred dollars per night to them for presenting their interpretations of the assassination. Sojourners in the city, who might only have visited the Pony Express station previously, now patiently lingered outside the jail for Sheriff Thomas to show them to "the man who shot Jesse James." They peered at Bob as if he were an anomaly from P. T. Barnum's Grand Hippodrome, and they were inordinately pleased if the young man raised his eyes from his reading or spoke unimportantly to them.

It was even considered good advertising to capitalize on Bob's patronage, as in this newspaper item from that week: "It may not be developed in the evidence, but it is no less a fact that Ford, the slayer of Jesse James, while under the assumed name of Johnson, only a few days ago purchased a genteel suit at the Famous Boston One-Price Clothing House, 510 Main Street. This is not mentioned to indicate that this has anything to do with the capture, but merely to suggest that when anyone wishes to personate a gentleman or wear good clothes of any kind, they are sure to buy them at the Boston."

The Fords stayed in their jail cell until Easter, accepting no gawkers at all on the day that Jesse was interred in the grave. They spent their time chatting with Sheriff Thomas and Corydon Craig, the city marshal's son, or they played cards or tiddlywinks and read the many newspaper recapitulations of past meetings with them. Charley's lung congestion and stomach complaints seemed to have been aggravated by the week's excitement, for he coughed persistently in the night, recurrently vomited his suppers into a bedpan, and pitifully informed the reporters that he hadn't enjoyed a single day of good health in all the preceding five years.

Whereas Bob was learning to thrive on the attention, even to be thrilled by it. He began smoking cigarettes in order to appear more experienced and dangerous and cosmopolitan. He weighed the advantages of growing a mustache. He smelled gunpowder on his fingers. He could still feel the jolt of the gun going off, could still hear the groan as Jesse sagged from the chair, but that was all, he'd seen no phantoms, listened to no incorporeal voices, was not subjected to nightmares. He would ask on second thought, as a passing fancy, if anyone had yet sighted Frank James, but revenge was not a worry really, it was as if no person could physically harm him once Jesse was underground.

In order to satisfy the many requests for his picture, Bob agreed to sit for a studio photograph in the second week of April. He wore green wool trousers and a gray tweed coat that was buttoned just once at the short lapels and then curtained away from a green vest. He resisted sitting on a chair and suggested instead a gracefully scrolled and sculpted staircase, seating himself on the fifth step, his right hand dangling slackly off his right knee as his left grasped a gleaming Peacemaker, a photographer's prop, that was artificially rested on his left thigh and calling attention to itself. He looked like a grocery clerk accidentally caught with a long gun in his hand. A correspondent asked why, if Bob was right-handed, he'd gripped the gun with his left, and Bob answered, as if nothing further needed saying, "Jesse was left-handed."

And it was also in early April that the Fords rode to Kansas City with two deputies as chaperones, and they stood in the wing of the Théâtre Comique, next to the fly lines and counterweight pulleys, rephrasing the tragedy in their minds and watching a Russian in opera clothes fling daggers at playing cards poised by a pretty woman. Charley was agitated and sick and smoked cigarettes so continuously that he used one to light another; but Bob was beguiled and delighted—the atmosphere was exciting, sympathetic, eccentric, provocative; it seemed precisely the sort of place that would bring him happiness. He chatted with the stage manager, regarded a man juggling white supper plates inside his dressing room, got a crick in his neck from looking into the loft at the curtains and teasers and scenery suspended from the overhead gridiron. An elderly woman highlighted his eyelashes with the licked point of a charcoal pencil and then smeared red coloring onto his lips with her little finger. Charley endured the same cosmetics and said, "I don't know what we're doing here." Bob combed his ginger brown hair in a mirror and said, "Educating."

The deputies let the Fords strap on their holsters and emptied pistols and then took seats in the orchestra pit with shotguns cradled across their chests. And a comedian with a spiraled mustache and waxed goatee rounded out his waggish stories about a baffled and bamboozled visitor from Boston by grandly indicating, "It is now a singular privilege to welcome to this performance hall the two courageous young men who brought to justice that wild beast to society, the notorious Jesse James.'' He checked the wing and saw Charley woozily clutching the curtain but saw too that Bob was readied and impatient to go on. He swept off his top hat and swung it stage right, saying, ''I therefore urge you to give your undivided attention to the report of their daring exploit, and I present to you in their premier public appearance, Charles and Robert Ford!''

Bob strode onto the gray stage apron and Charley sluggishly followed as a man at the piano accompanied them with processional music that wasn't meant as sarcasm. The balcony and mezzanine were vacant and the main floor was only spottily filled with an audience that was principally couples in evening clothes and smoking men in the lobby. Some peered at their playbills to read if the act was explained (it was not even mentioned), but most gaped at the Ford brothers, getting their measure, gossiping, audibly recalling what they'd read.

Charley's eyes slid shyly to Bob and then to the deputies in the orchestra pit who progressively slumped down in chagrin at the Fords' prolonged aphasia. Stagefright stripped Charley's language away and he wondered rather hopelessly if it would be enough to just stand there and be seen. Then he was caught by surprise upon hearing words easily come from Bob, astonished at seeing his younger brother enjoying the presentation, pronouncing a speech for which there was no script, gesturing gently in the air, portraying himself with apologies and subtle immodesty, and then inviting questions.

A man stood and asked, ''Why did you decide on April third instead of any other time?''

Bob said, ''Ever since Charley and I were with Jesse, we'd been watching for an opportunity to shoot him, but Jesse was always heavily armed, guns everywhere on his person, and it was getting to be impossible to even look to our weapons without him noticing. Then the chance we had long wished for came that Monday morning.''

Another man stood and Bob shaded his eyes from the stage lights to see him. The man asked, ''What were Jesse's last words?''

Bob glanced at Charley and signified it was Charley's turn at answering, but Charley stammered inconsequentially and glowered at the footlights as he pursued words and impressions that kept disappearing. Bob spared him further hardship by surging on with the story he'd already related to many correspondents, except that this time he spoke Jesse's comments with compelling accentuation, physically representing the great man's stroll into the sitting room, his painstaking removal of coat and vest, the imprudent removal of his pistols on the mattress, the featherdusting of the picture of Skyrocket. ''Getting back to the subject," Bob said, "I guess his last words were 'That picture's awful dusty.' "

Some of the audience laughed.

A woman asked where Mrs. James was at the time; another asked the children's ages; a gunsmith wanted to know the makes of all the guns in the cottage and Bob's opinion of their accuracy and ease of operation, only to argue with him about his prejudices; the master of ceremonies came on stage and suggested that it would be fitting to conclude with Bob's interpretation of the fatal shot.

Bob transfigured his expression into something hard and sepulchral and slapped the deputy's gun from his hip, slowly crossing the audience from left to right with it, closing his left eye as he sighted the muzzle on the most appalled and upset faces. Then the gun's hammer snapped forward and pinged into a cleared chamber. Someone in the audience gasped and others edgily laughed, for Bob was grim-visaged and villainous, with scorn in the sour set of his mouth and mean spite in his eyes. He relaxed his right arm and the crowd's anxiety left; he shoved the gun into its holster and lingered next to the footlights, looking stonily at as many in the audience as he could, and the comedian said, "How about a big round of applause for these two courageous young men?" And Bob and Charley walked off the stage to the gratifying sound of clapping hands.

Charley said, "You surprise me, Bob."

Bob collapsed onto a chair and grinned with ecstasy. "I was really good, wasn't I?"

Some professionals who saw Bob play the slayer thought the boy showed an aptitude for acting and encouraged him to study stagecraft. So he begged release from jail to attend matinee performances at Tootle's Opera House, pantomiming the leading man's style, incorporating his gesticulations even if not appropriate. It was generally acknowledged that he ought to have been preoccupied with the impending court trial in Buchanan County and the coroner's inquest into the death of Wood Hite, but Bob was instead becoming starstruck by Miss Fanny Davenport in her role as Lady Teazle in a comedy of manners called *The School for Scandal*.

ON FRIDAY, APRIL 14TH, Henry Craig arrived from Kansas City with Colonel John Doniphan, a powerful attorney and orator who'd recently completed the Burgess trial in Platte City (getting the gunfighter off on a five-year sentence). Doniphan was an austere, misanthropic man with no generosity or high regard for the Ford brothers, whom he'd agreed to defend. He sat with Charley on a cot in the jail cell and listened intently as Craig conducted Bob through a recapitulation of his conversation with the governor during their meeting in the St. James Hotel, and then through the peregrinations that resulted in the killing of Jesse James and a charge of first-degree murder. Craig completed his orientation and sat back; Doniphan crossed his long legs and asked, "How do you two feel about your situation?"

Bob looked at Charley and then replied, "I sleep fine."

Doniphan then indicated what their problems were: that they had no written agreement with the governor, that Crittenden himself was susceptible to charges of conspiracy to commit murder, that public sentiment could coerce the governor into changing his mind about his pledge to the Fords. Suppose Crittenden denied ever making a promise of pardon, as he repeatedly had to the press? Were they not public nuisances on whom no pity should be squandered? Will the claims of two gunslingers and petty thieves carry much weight in a jury trial? What could the disposition of even their supporters be once the corrupted body of Mr. Hite had been discovered on their property?

Charley glared at Doniphan through the cataloging, and when the attorney was finished, asked, "Do you want me to answer those questions?"

Doniphan said nothing.

Charley said, "I'll wager the governor does what's right."

Colonel Doniphan put his pencil away. "You'd better hope he does not."

On Monday, April 17th, O. M. Spencer took his case to trial. The second-floor courtroom was as crowded then as it was on April 3rd, but there was little grandeur in the Fords' progress through the gathered spectators now. Charley was angry and banged out of his way anyone who pressed close to him; Bob was grinning but fidgety and though he worked at aplomb and courage, it was read as arrogance.

For reasons of politics and prestige, Colonel Doniphan was unwilling to be the sole counsel to the Ford brothers, so he invited William Warner and W. A. Reed to collaborate with him, and they congregated with four deputies around the Fords in order to prevent any violence against the two who were sitting at the defendants' table.

Judge William H. Sherman took his seat at the bench after one o'clock and once the court clerk crossed to the recorder's table, O. M. Spencer stood and requested that Robert Newton Ford be the first arraigned. Bob rose and swayed a little as the prosecuting attorney read a grand jury's accusation that on the third day of April, Ford had willfully, feloniously, and with malice aforethought, killed Jesse W. James and was now being summarily charged with murder in the first degree. Spencer turned to the prisoner and with great formality asked, "What plea do you make?"

Bob responded, "Guilty!" as if pestered by ceremonies, and then presumptuously sat down.

Spencer raised a second grand jury indictment and with some irritation and frustration read the name of Charles Wilson Ford, pronouncing a premeditated murder charge and receiving the same reply.

The courtroom was then filled with controversy and whisperings and Bob reveled in it. He swiveled in his chair and crouched around the deputies to wink at his brother Elias and at Henry Craig, wave to some reporters he'd met, and pugnaciously smile at those who clearly wished him ill. Doniphan nudged him around.

Judge Sherman ruminated for many minutes and inscribed some thoughts in his elegant longhand before sitting toward the bench and saying, "Under the circumstances, there is only one thing I can do and that is to pronounce sentence here and now. You have pleaded guilty to murder in the first degree, and it only remains for me to carry out the provisions of the law. It remains for others to say whether the sentence is carried out." Sherman glanced at his writing and commanded, "Robert Ford, stand up."

Bob smirked but arose.

"Have you anything to say as to why sentence should not be pronounced upon you?"

"Nothing," said Bob.

The judge looked at him sternly but without passion or righteousness. He said, "Robert Ford, you have pleaded guilty before the court to the crime of murder in the first degree, and it becomes my duty to pass the sentence of death upon you. It is therefore the sentence of this court that you be taken to the Buchanan County Jail and there safely kept until the nineteenth day of May 1882, and at that time to be taken to some convenient place and hanged by the neck until you are dead."

Bob then lazily slumped down in his seat and Charley was ordered to stand and receive the same sentence. Charley listened with aggravation and outrage that he might be executed without having fired a shot, but Bob simply laughed at the judge in a haughty and mocking way that he thought would be interpreted by correspondents as audacity and pluck. It was not.

Then Sheriff Thomas and the deputies and attorneys walked the

Fords back to jail and checked all newspaper reporters for firearms before they were admitted. Bob was asked how he felt and he answered, "Bully." Charley was asked if he'd actually hang and he answered, "Why, I should smile. The governor will attend to that part of the business; that's in the contract."

City Marshal Craig couldn't abide the Fords any longer, so he collected the revolvers and rifles and articles that had been stored as evidence and carried them to 1318 Lafayette Street. Zee James received him graciously and served him sponge cake and coffee.

Meanwhile the Fords were packing their clothes in luggage that Elias had brought and were predicting that the pardon would come by evening. Bob wrapped his .44 caliber Smith and Wesson in yesterday's newspaper but then weighed the gun with repugnance and gave it to young Cory Craig in gratitude for the many errands that boy had gone on. His only instructions were that Cory should get a gunsmith to engrave on the nickel sideplate: Bob Ford Killed Jesse James With This Revolver At St. Joseph, Mo. 1882.

Charley sat up from a nap and patted his pockets for cigarette papers. He'd apparently overheard the impromptu presentation, for he commented to Bob, "Your shoes must be starting to pinch."

"I don't need any mementoes," said Bob. "I've already got everything fast in my head."

At 3:45 p.m., Colonel John Doniphan climbed onto a box in the city marshal's office and soberly read aloud to the assembled press a telegram in which the governor granted an unconditional pardon to Charles and Robert Ford.

Henry Craig ran to the jail cell and greeted the Fords with the news but few others joined him in congratulating the two.

ON APRIL 19TH, 1882, two days after his unconditional pardon and release from jail, Bob Ford was arrested in Richmond, Missouri, on the charge that he'd murdered Robert Woodson Hite, and Bob was obliged to beg two thousand dollars in bail from J. T. Ford, the father he'd always made efforts at forgetting. "Isn't this typical?" Mr. Ford said with spleen and all too apparent pleasure. "You come to me crying and pleading and whimpering like a little girl, please give me the money, daddy, and I'm the one to clean things up."

Bob glared as the elderly man jerked his shoestrings tight with a grunt. He said, "Maybe you're the one I should have killed."

Mr. Ford glanced with anger and fright at his youngest child and saw that the boy was grinning. He considered the garden outside his window as he often would when he composed his sermons and then pulled himself up from the overstuffed armchair and prepared to make a trip to town, only adding nastily, "How perfectly our good Lord put it in the parable of the prodigal son." By the time the cashier's check was made out, many customers at the Hughes and Wasson Bank had come by to say Bob shouldn't take to heart the words of John Newman Edwards.

Edwards was then living in Sedalia, about sixty miles west of Jefferson City, and was managing editor of the *Daily Democrat,* which was singular among Missouri newspapers in its attenuated suspicions that Jesse James couldn't have been killed in such a manner. Soon the corroborating evidence was overwhelming, however, and Edwards considered making a pilgrimage to Kearney to attend the funeral, but instead purchased six bottles of whiskey and "went to the Indian Territories." And it was not until one week after the interment that the Sedalia *Daily Democrat* published his scathing philippic on the subject of the murder.

It began: "Not one among all the hired cowards, hard on the hunt for blood money, dared face this wonderful outlaw, one even against twenty, until he had disarmed himself and turned his back to his assassins, the first and only time in a career which has passed from the realms of an almost fabulous romance into that of history."

He continued with a mixture of apology, reprimand, and angry screed, saying Jesse's transgressions were outgrowths of the Civil War. "Proscribed, hunted, shot, driven away from among his people, a price put on his head, what else could he do, with such a nature, except what he did do? . . . He refused to be banished from his birthright, and when he was hunted he turned savagely about and hunted his hunters. Would to God he were alive today to make a righteous butchery of a few more of them."

Edwards called the murder "cowardly and unnecessary" and castigated the commonwealth of Missouri for having "leagued with a lot of self-confessed robbers, highwaymen, and prostitutes" in having a citizen assassinated without confirming "that he had ever committed a single crime worthy of death." The government and the conspirators had succeeded, Edwards acknowledged, "but such a cry of horror and indignation at the infernal deed is even now thundering over the land that if a single one of the miserable assassins had either manhood, conscience or courage, he would go as another Judas and hang himself. But so sure as God reigns, there never was a dollar of blood money yet obtained which did not bring with it perdition. Sooner or later there comes a day of vengeance. Some among the murderers were mere beasts of prey. These, of course, can only suffer through cold blood, hunger, or thirst; but whatever they dread most, that will happen.''

Bob Ford read that commentary, of course—he'd acquired from Jesse the daily routine of reading every newspaper available. He read without much resentment its implicit denunciation of Crittenden, Craig, Wallace, and Timberlake (''sanctimonious devils, who plead the honor of the State, the value of law and order, the splendid courage required to shoot an unarmed man in the back of the head'') and its imputation of his sister Martha (''into all the warp and woof of the devil's work there were threads woven by the fingers of a harlot'') but nothing upset and preoccupied him like the phrase *whatever they dread most, that will happen*. It seemed more than a simple curse; there was the ring of something presaging and prophetic about it, it was the sort of thing Jesse would say.

On May 13th a justice of the peace in Ray County accepted the two thousand dollars in bail along with Bob's promise that he would be present for the court trial. Bob reportedly told him, ''I keep my appointments, Your Honor.'' Then Bob and Charley went to Kansas City with Sheriff Timberlake in order to supply further information about the James gang to the government. The journey was announced in the press against all instructions and a pro-James newspaper invited the public to greet the Fords ''in some appropriate way'' at the railroad depot. However, the sheriff let Charley and Bob jump from the caboose upon arrival, and they nipped around the train to a waiting carriage as Timberlake escorted two cuffed and camouflaged policemen through the gathering. One policeman was struck in the cheek with a rock and needed eight stitches to close the cut, the second policeman got into a fistfight and only Timberlake's strong intervention kept him from getting disfigured.

Then Finis C. Farr joined the Fords in Henry Craig's law office in order to present them with their rewards, but first he spoke at dulling length, explaining and adapting with the intricacy, circumspection, and loftiness that was regarded as a signal of good breeding. He made a preamble about the governor's July 1881 proclamation, saying the extra five thousand dollars that was promised for the arrest and conviction of one of the James boys couldn't be justified in the circumstances of manslaughter and, second, funding depended upon the railroad companies and their complete cooperation in providing the money. Some of these companies had proven themselves to be irresponsible, Farr said, still others were parsimonious. And there was a third component to consider, that it was not only the Fords who'd made the capture possible, there were good men who'd struggled for many years at great risk, and these civil servants too, the governor felt, should take some part in the profits. (Henry Craig diplomatically slipped from the room.)

Charley was exasperated. He slumped deeply in a chair and stared gloomily at the ceiling, sighing as the governor's secretary moved from point to point. Finally he asked, "Are we going to get a plug *nickel?*"

Bob sneered at Finis Farr. "It's just that there's these raspberry cough drops that Charley's got his heart set on."

They each were given a large brown envelope with two hundred fifty dollars inside. Farr anticipated them by saying, "You two can complain if you want but that's the only cash available; anything else would come straight from the governor's pocket."

Charley said, "Well, let's not be too hasty in turning that down neither. I mean, it spends just the same, don't it?"

Farr reacted testily. "Many prisoners would be happy to *pay* five thousand dollars to get a governor's pardon. Don't bite the hand that feeds you."

Charley put the envelope inside his shirt and responded, "Appears to me we already did."

So THEY WERE READY for a change of atmosphere and providence when George H. Bunnell arrived in Richmond squiring a poshly costumed actress who'd apparently patterned herself after the great Lillie Langtry and spoke with an emphatic and highly suspect English accent. Bunnell was a New York showman with a museum of curiosities and living wonders in Brooklyn and a repertory company that played one-night stands in cities and resorts throughout the East. He made a party of a cheap cafe supper that evening and as Bob and Charley gaped with aspiration at the actress, he persuaded them to sign a contract with his "players guild," guaranteeing them costly publicity and promotion, repeated engagements before large audiences, payment of fifty dollars for each of six evening and two matinee performances per week, plus an aggrandizing script "crafted by one of America's most accomplished playwrights" and the professional improvements of a Broadway director. He'd misinterpreted the newspaper stories about the Fords: he presumed they were explosive and stormy men of great prominence who'd already rejected multiple opportunities while the actual case, of course, was that nothing had yet happened to make them feel either prosperous or respected and by May even the town of Richmond was inhospitable to the Fords. People crossed the street to avoid passing them, shop clerks refused to acknowledge them, every mailing included letters of asperity, reproof, and warnings that they too would be shot when next their backs were turned. By the time George H. Bunnell came around they were living in protective custody inside the Ray County courthouse and splitting a nightwatch at the single high window, often scaring children away by clapping saucepans together.

William H. Wallace procured the necessary permissions for the Ford brothers to quit Missouri and they proceeded, incognito, to New York City in June, gaping at the strange new geography outside the passenger coaches, their noses against the windowglass like snails whenever the train precariously crossed a gorge or hairpinned up a steep mountain. George Bunnell generally stayed close to Bob during the journey, as if the young man were an invaluable object to which he'd just gained possession. They would sit in the dining car with a silver service between them and with men of color refilling their coffee cups at brief intervals, and Bunnell would ask Bob yet again to give an account of how he killed Jesse James, designing a stage presentation from those story ingredients that Bob rarely forgot.

The Ford brothers' try-outs quickly verified Bunnell's prior conviction that Bob possessed some acting talent and Charley not a jot, and the unaccredited playwright made allowances for that incongruity by casting the script as Bob Ford's proud and complacent reminiscence, calling it *How I Killed Jesse James*. Bob was taught not to saw the air with his hand nor to split the ears of the groundlings but to give temperance to his passion, to keep within the modesty of nature, and to imitate humanity; Charley was only expected not to slouch or mutter and to transport his sicknesses to the alley before letting them go.

They practiced the skit for two weeks and then previewed it with music hall and carnival acts at seaside resorts such as Atlantic City, Jersey City, and Ocean Beach before they opened in a splendid theater at Ninth and Broadway in Manhattan. Bob was as groomed as a European prince; his ginger brown hair was recut and marceled with irons, he'd glued on a dignitary's clipped mustache, his gentleman's suits were tailored in England throughout the range of grays and greens, he gained nearly four inches in height from exaggerated Wellington bootheels and lifts. Charley was simply given a Prince Albert suit and striped cravat and a glued chestnut brown beard and mustache that matched Jesse's, along with rigorous promptings throughout the performance due to his inadequate memory.

Saucy girls danced in the French style, cowboys sang anthems and gunslinger ballads around a gaudy cardboard fire, an Appaloosa mare displayed feats of arithmetic by stamping on the floor, a railway coach was robbed by a snarling gang to gasconades of opera music, and then the Fords walked onto a set that resembled the sitting room of the cottage atop Confusion Hill. Stage right contained an oak bed and an easy chair with a crimson shawl on it; to the center was a round dining room table and chairs and canvas wall with two artworked windows and a wide door; stage left showed a wicker chair and two picture frames, one of which enclosed a spurious reward poster that announced Jesse was wanted dead or alive and included an etched portrait of the outlaw, and next to that a shabby, made-to-order painting showed Julius Caesar being stabbed by conspirators in the Senate.

How I Killed Jesse James began with Charley clomping across the stage in the apparel of Jesse James and pumping Bob's hand imperatively as his mouth seemed to make imploring words. Bob looked out to the audience and said: "When Jesse James came to me at the grocery store, he told me that my brother Charley was with him and that they had planned to rob a bank in Platte City. It would take three men to do the job and he needed my help."

Charley sat down at the dining room table like a gruff town burgess and rattled out a newspaper; Bob sat informally on a wicker chair beneath the pictures and polished a silver pistol. Charley scowled across the stage at Bob and Bob again confided to the audience: "After we got to his house in the suburbs of St. Joseph he seemed suspicious of me for some reason and never allowed me out of his sight for even a moment. He had me sleep in the same room with him and he even followed me when I would go out to the stable."

Bob laid down the pistol and collected some newspapers placed under the chair rungs, then moseyed over to the dining room table. "Each morning before breakfast he would take me downtown with him to get the morning papers which he read every day. He would buy the Saint Joseph and Saint Louis papers and I wanted to get the Kansas City papers to keep track of things, and after we had read them we would exchange."

Bob straddled a chair across from his brother and the two traded what they'd been reading. Bob perused a page and flipped to another and, without raising his eyes, said: "I had been told that I must keep the papers from Jesse if I could, as the reporters were on to the fact that something was in the wind and it might leak out and be published that Dick Liddil had surrendered, which fact, up to that time, had been kept secret.''

Charley slammed his fists on the dining room table, astounding some in the audience, and jolted up as Bob registered amazement. Charley then careered around, wildly jawing, wagging a finger at his brother, overplaying wrath, as Bob shrugged and professed his guilt-lessness according to the accepted conventions of stage acting. By way of explaining the foregoing, Bob stated: ''Soon after my arrival in Saint Joseph, Jesse questioned me closely about Dick Liddil and I told him I had not heard anything about him for a long time.''

Charley resettled on the dining room chair and suspiciously eyed Bob as the young man walked to the footlights and invited everyone he could see to participate in his intrigue. ''The days kept slipping by and it was getting hotter for me every hour. I knew anything might happen at any time to tip my hand to Jess, and I scanned the papers each morning eagerly.'' He moved a little to the right in accordance with the director's suggestion that Bob indicate a transition from summary to scene. ''On the morning of April third, Jess and I went downtown as usual before breakfast for the papers. We were to go that night to Platte City to rob the bank, and I was afraid that I might need to go through with the prospect and that innocent people might be killed.''

Bob had by then circumnavigated to the oak bed; Charley squared on the audience and crossed his legs and looked at everything with belligerence. Bob raised the newspaper from the mattress and slowly rotated downstage. ''We came back to the house at about eight o'clock and sat down in the front room. Jesse was sitting with his back to me, reading the Saint Louis *Republican*. I looked over the Kansas City *Journal* first, and seeing nothing of interest, I threw it on the bed and picked up the Kansas City *Times*.'' Bob then glanced at the newspaper front page and his eyes signified aghast surprise. ''The first thing I saw in big headlines, almost a foot long on the first page, was the story about Dick Liddil's surrender. My only thought was to hide the paper from Jesse.'' Bob perceptibly noticed the crimson shawl on the easy chair and pushed the newspaper under it with some expense of motion.

A pretty girl made to appear twice her age glided across to the dining room table with a porcelain coffee service on a tray. ''Please sit down, Bob,'' the actress said. ''Breakfast is ready.''

Charley hackled a tooth as Bob sat and, seeming to prefer alternative company, Charley moved over to the easy chair where he conspicuously accomplished each action as Bob explained it: ''Jess couldn't have seen me conceal the *Times* but he sure enough picked up the shawl and threw it on the bed, and snapping open the newspaper, returned to his seat. I felt that the jig was up and I moved my belt around so that it was close to my right hand. I proposed to die game if Jesse began to shoot.''

The girl playing Zee poured cold coffee into painted cups and settled into her skirts at the table, sweetly facing the audience. Charley spread the newspaper over his plate and propped his chin on interlaced fingers as he joylessly read. Bob illustrated each of his director's interpretations of panic, consternation, fright, and hopelessness. ''My heart went up in my throat,'' he said, without straying his eyes from the reading man. ''I couldn't have eaten a bite to save my life. All at once Jesse said—''

Charley surged in on signal: ''Hello, here! The surrender of Dick Liddil!''

''And he looked across at me with the pitiless glare in his eyes that I had seen there so often before.''

''Young man,'' Charley said, resticking a sinking wing of mustache, ''I thought you told me you didn't know that Dick had surrendered.''

''You mean he *did?*'' Bob asked. ''I didn't know!''

''Well, it's very strange. He surrendered three weeks ago and you was right there in the neighborhood. It looks fishy.''

The actress carried the coffee service off-stage, Bob removed to the easy chair as Charley continued to scowl at him and stood from the dining room table, his Prince Albert coat slung to the rear of his large revolvers.

Bob abstractly buffed his boots with a red bandana and slyly looked to the audience as Jesse loitered in the room. ''I expected the shooting to begin right there, and if it had Jesse would have got me, for I was nervous. But then he was smiling and said pleasantly—''

''Well, Bob, it's all right, anyway.''

Bob submerged a little in the chair in an attitude of judgment. ''Instantly his purpose flashed upon my mind. I knew I had not fooled him. He was too sharp for that. He knew at that moment as well as I did that I was there to betray him. But he was not going to kill me in the presence of his wife and children, and so he was smiling and pleasant to throw me off-guard, intending when we were on the road that night to finish me.''

Charley strode to the oak bed with a general's carriage and after some overacted deliberations in which his eyes squinched and his mouth screwed to the left and right, Charley painstakingly uncinched the cartridge belt and in a challenging way flung the two revolvers on the mattress. Charley had been coached to remember the balcony seats and his voice was consequently a little too like a yell: "In case you're wondering why I took my guns off, it's because I might want to walk into the yard!"

Bob revealed: "It was the first time in my life I had seen him without that belt on, and I knew in an instant that he threw it off to further quiet any suspicions I might have that he had tumbled onto my scheme."

Charley's brown eyes cast about the stage with what seemed mania and Bob helpfully clarified: "He seemed to want to busy himself with something to make an impression on my mind that he had forgotten the incident of a moment before at the breakfast table."

Charley fetched a feather duster from a wicker stand and then flagged it toward the implausible painting of a dying Caesar and, with some tardiness in matching gesture to utterance, said: "That picture's awful dusty."

Bob surreptitiously got up from the easy chair and sneaked down-stage as he softly divulged: "There wasn't a speck of dust that I could see on that picture." He swiveled to watch Charley flick the feather duster over the frame as one might watch a man at a petty crime and Bob let the audience espy his five-fingered right hand as he gradually rested it on his gun. His back was turned three-quarters to them, so he amplified his speech as he confessed: "Up to that moment the thought of killing him had never entered my mind, but as he stood there, unarmed, with his back to me, it came to me suddenly, 'Now or never is your chance. If you don't get him now he'll get you tonight.' " Bob moved within six feet of a man who was then muffling a cough and straggling the duster onto the canvas wall, making the gray illusion undulate like a slowly luffing sail. Some people in the audience stirred with anticipation.

Bob said: "Without further thought or a moment's delay, I pulled my revolver and leveled it." Bob did so. "He heard the hammer click as I cocked it with my thumb in throwing it down on line with his head. He recognized the sound and started to turn to the right as I pulled the trigger."

Bob let the hammer snap and a light charge of gunpowder ignited and the great noise on the stage made some of the audience gasp and later complain of the percussion still in their ears. Charley reeled on the chair, clapped his palms to his chest, shut his eyes, and then crashed unauthentically to the floor, stopping his collapse with his left foot, then his left elbow, but smacking flatly on his back and issuing one word: "Done!"

Bob stepped back and with a perfect imitation of marvel, puzzlement, and regret, confronted the witnesses to the assassination. "The ball struck him just behind the ear and he fell like a log, dead. I didn't go near his body. I knew when I saw that forty-four caliber bullet strike that it was all up with Jesse."

The girl playing Mrs. James ran onto the stage from the right, paused to see a man who was suppressing his breathing on the stage apron, and then permitted herself that which the script described as "a blood-curdling scream." Then nothing happened; they froze. The houselights dimmed almost to darkness for many seconds and brightened once again on a stage that contained only Robert Ford. He slung his gun and glared at the susceptible and with gravity proclaimed to the crowd: "That is how I killed Jesse James."

The curtain rang down to magnanimous applause, rose to show Bob and the actress and Charley accepting their compliments, then sprang noisily down again as boys in knickers scurried onto the stage in order to change the scene.

HOW I KILLED JESSE JAMES was mentioned in only one newspaper and then as a skit of mild curiosity value in an evening of middling entertainments—by Thursday so many seats in the Manhattan theater were empty that George Bunnell couldn't meet his expenses and he moved the show, on the 25th, to his Brooklyn museum on Court and Remsen streets, where the competition for theatergoers was not nearly so dismaying and public captivation with the Ford brothers was emphatic.

The crowds there were without Southern loyalties or strong emotions about the Yankee railroads and banks, and if they thought about the West it was with contempt, as a region of Baptists, Indians, immigrants, cutthroats, and highwaymen that only the savage and stupid could take much delight in; or they thought of it with a dreamy worship inspired by nickel books, thought of it as a place of dangers, deprivations, escapades, knightly contests, and courtly love. And in that prejudiced and uncomprehending atmosphere, the Fords attained the peculiar type of respect and approval they'd sought when they started out rustling horses as teenagers.

It was an age in which common wages were twelve cents an hour, so at fifty dollars a performance they could easily think themselves rich; they were from a territory that was so critically short of women that marriages were still arranged by correspondence, and yet the Fords were everywhere accompanied by pretty, teenaged dancing girls and singers who did not vigorously protect their chastity or reputation, and who thought that Charley and especially Bob were menacing, moody, ungovernable, and wickedly appealing. They were recognized on the seashore, in grand hotel lobbies, in Brooklyn, and were warily accommodated, wisely adjudged, gossiped about as if they were Vanderbilts; they could walk into shops and see the aproned sales clerks cringe, they could jeer at waiters and maids and hackney drivers who would make the ridicule seem jolly, they ate in elegant restaurants with giggling girls who were painted and powdered in the superior fashion of the arrogant rich but who made no efforts at genteel politeness or responsibility. A significant amount of their days was without requirements or planned activities, and yet the temptations were now greater and interestingly multiplied: Turkish tobaccos, Scotch whiskies, English gins, nights spent gambling on cards or fighting dogs, Sundays spent with expert prostitutes. On the afternoon that Bob read about the flamboyant surrender of Frank James to Governor Crittenden, he was sitting in an apothecary awaiting a prescription for a stomach complaint, and when he received the telegram that ordered him back to Missouri, he'd already missed a Thursday matinee on account of intoxication. So that when Bob and Charley arrived for the court trial in Plattsburg—a change of venue caused by extreme anti-Ford sentiments—they were written about rather chidingly, as corrupted representations of the evils of city living. They were dissipated, intemperate, petulant, and over-indulged. Charley's consumption and indigestion had only become more lacerating; his eye sockets were as deep and dark as fistholes in snow, his gums were strangely purple, he wore extravagant gold rings on every finger and a clove of garlic around his neck according to the guidance of a gypsy named Madame Africa. Bob was skinny, sallow, peevish, his complexion spoiled with so many pimples that some correspondents thought it was measles.

He was beleaguered in Plattsburg, cornered in strange rooms, gracelessly stalked and surrounded on sidewalks, greedily nagged for opinions and hypotheses about Frank and Jesse, the James gang, Governor Crittenden, Wood Hite. Everything was exaggerated and magnified— if he was not religious then he was slavishly in league with Satan; if he slept little it was of course a consequence of nightmares; and it was generally agreed upon by all that Bob was plagued by apparitions, by incorporeal voices, by grim imaginings of his own grave and the stinging judgment of history—even the indignant silence that he gradually adopted was guessed to be charged with meaning.

By October of 1883, Bob Ford could be identified correctly by more citizens than could the accidental president of the United States (Chester Alan Arthur); he was reported to be as renowned at twenty as Jesse was after fourteen years of grand larceny, and though it was by then a presumption on his part, it was unanticipated by others that a poised but unscrupulous young man could be thought dapper and tempting to women: the courtroom was as packed during his second-degree murder trial in Plattsburg as was the Mount Olivet Baptist Church when the corpse of Jesse Woodson James was prayed over and dispatched to his Maker, and as the correspondents noted the crowds inside and on the courthouse steps, they were surprised by the presence of otherwise sophisticated ladies, reading in this a proof of the young man's beguiling powers.

Bob was represented by Colonel C. F. Garner and the case against him was put by the prosecuting attorney for Ray County. An agreement was reached with the James-Samuels clan that if they neglected to respond to subpoenas requiring them to testify, Bob would repay the indulgence when and if Frank James came to trial, so the cross-examinations at Plattsburg were far less spectacular than many who visited the town might have hoped. Colonel Garner opened the case for the defense by introducing an affidavit sworn to by James Andrew Liddil (who was then in an Alabama jail and in no jeopardy) stating, according to Garner, that Dick and Wood "suddenly became involved in a personal difficulty but that few words passed between them until both drew revolvers and commenced firing at each other . . . the firing being rapid and continuous, occupying a few seconds of time; that Liddil received a flesh wound in the leg, and Wood Hite was fatally shot, dying instantly; that Hite brought on the fight, was the aggressor, made the attack, and was firing at Liddil when he was shot and killed by a bullet from a pistol fired by Liddil, and that Robert Ford, my client, knew nothing of the difficulty until the firing commenced."

The expected group of deponents were called to the stand: Constable Morris, who recovered Wood's body, Dr. Mosby, who examined it, Henry H. Craig, residents of Richmond who could remember nothing derogatory ever having been said about Robert Ford's character, and especially Mrs. Martha Ford Bolton, whose aplomb and placid deposition of even recklessly obvious lies very nearly stupefied the appalled prosecution.

It was a raucous and unruly trial interrupted by snipes from the spectators, by laughter at provocative or funny comments from the witnesses, and by applause at particularly rousing passages in the attorneys' summary arguments. Bob ignored the exchanges to a great extent, seeming to be engrossed only in the cartoons he scribbled on a yellow pad or in smuggling silly notes to girls who flagrantly admired him. He even appropriated a piece of Henry Craig's office stationery and scrawled out a misspelled and mispunctuated letter.

President Dear sir as have forgoton your name & addess as President of the Wabash St. Louis + Pacific R.R. will you please grant Myself and Family a monthly pass over your Road from KC to Richmond the distance of 45 miles
I Remain yours truly

Bob. Ford
Slayer of Jesse James

ON OCTOBER 26TH, after forty hours of deliberation, the jury arrived at a verdict and deputies spent the morning combing the county in order to bring back the defendant. Sheriff Algiers found him on the railroad tracks, walking a rail like a tightrope, his arms kiting out and his body hooking left or right for his precarious balance. Bob glanced at the road and grasped why the sheriff was there. He jumped to the cinders and as he swaggered to the sheriff's buggy said, "The judge can hang me if he wants. I'm not scared of dying." And when Bob walked into the courtroom it was with carelessness and insouciance; sitting next to Colonel Garner he seemed a worker called in from the cornfields for coffee and apple pie.

The jury foreman gave a folded note to the court clerk and Judge Dunn acknowledged that the court clerk could read it. " 'We, the jury,' " the clerk announced, " 'find the defendant, Robert Ford, not guilty of charges as indicated in the indictment.' "

Colonel Garner gleefully shook Bob's hand and then the hands of the Ford family, and the large crowd exited as if from a play that was not entirely satisfying. Bob crossed over to the jury box, grinning a little crazily and saying, "You did the courageous thing." One man wiped his palm on his pants leg after Bob Ford clasped it.

Practically as soon as the Plattsburg trial was over, the Ford brothers traveled east again in order to bring back to the stage *How I Killed Jesse James*. The repertory company went south to Philadelphia, Baltimore, Washington City, and the Ford origins in Virginia, then was rerouted north again with a Christmas in New England.

Charley was increasingly superstitious, increasingly subject to the advice of gypsies and tarot card readers and poor women who lived in the slums and who promised to cure his miseries with green teas, pipe smoke, poultices, hypnosis, even jolts of electricity cranked into his jittering wrists with a magnet generator. And yet his coughing continued, his fatigue grew greater, his stomach fought all his body's cravings, he was convinced that tapeworms were eating his organs and once hung upside down over a goblet of syrup and milk, his mouth gapingly open, tears sliding into his dangling hair as he prayed the parasites would grope out of his esophagus into more acceptable food.

Charley was initially delighted with the East and with the progress he'd made from his poor beginnings. He would slog through an ankle-deep ocean at Atlantic City with his suit coat gathered over his right arm, his shoes clamped together in that hand as the other shaded his eyes from sunlight so that he could see more unmistakably the pretty women in their thigh-length bathing dresses and knee-length bloomers, their sturdy white calves exposed. They would step into the sheeting water higher up on the sand and a larger wave would curdle foam over their feet and they'd squeal, and Charley would grin magnificently, looking around for Bob so he could share his enjoyment. A young girl might venture out and dip into the ocean, bravely swimming toward Europe as Charley's aghast eyes followed her every stroke. And when she came out, the frills of her bathing dress would be sagging low and the black cloth would be clinging to her body, making everything significant and generating such excitement in Charley that he'd run to get Bob and show him the sight.

"She was a beauty, was she?" Bob said once.

"She didn't have one more bump than necessary. And you could tell she liked you noticing too." Charley sniggered a little and added, "I would've stayed put till the tide came in but I was afraid I was starting to bulge."

By the time they were living in Brooklyn, though, Charley was getting no great pleasure in hungering for women and was going out of his way to avoid meeting them. If Bob brought along one of his dancing girls on their evenings out in Manhattan, Charley managed to speak only when protocol demanded it or when he had something ugly to say, smiled without good humor when Bob nudgingly joked, and glimpsed the girl leeringly on the sly. He whispered to one girl, "I know exactly who you're working for. You won't get your hooks in me."

Charley was becoming an onlooker, a playgoer, judging but not joining, given to long days alone in his room, where he read strange pamphlets and testimonies and circled his bed with garlic and black candles. He called Bob's girlfriends Jezebels and temptresses, begetters of greed and jealousy, and warned Bob that his "wrong-living life will carry you into the perpetual burning." He compared all females unfavorably to Mrs. Zee James, whom he spoke of as certain priests might the Madonna, and composed long, soul-describing letters to her, begging her forgiveness, none of which he mailed. He said once, "I'm going to look for somebody like Zee. All my spots will disappear." And on another occasion Charley disapproved of something by pointing out that a soothsayer named Perfecta had put him onto just such a scheme.

Bob said, "You're spending too much time with gypsies."

"You mark my words, Bob. They'll pluck out your eyes. They've got your name written in goat's blood."

Hence Bob grew more estranged from his brother. He was appalled by Charley's peculiarities, his progressively worsening illnesses, his mixture of puritanism, piety, black magic, and gullibility. He squandered no money but possessed no savings and it seemed probable to Bob that Charley was giving his earnings away, having been counseled by some crystal-ball gazer—who was no doubt the beneficiary—that this was the only means of assuaging his guilt. And guilt was pumping like poisoned blood through the chambers of Charley's heart; he'd confessed that many times he'd lain on a mattress, calling for sleep, but was instead visited by gruesome imaginings of a coffin and of the subjugation of earth on his chest, and more than once he'd bolted upright at night to see a grisly form fly out through the window. Perhaps in consequence, there was something changed in Charley's stage portrayal of Jesse: his limp now seemed practiced, his high voice was spookily similar to the man's, his newly suggested dialogue was analogous to a script that Jesse might have originated, he said he was "getting to know him" with the unopposable conviction of a man who'd just been in colloquy with a spirit made flesh. It was a gradual transmogrification, but it was no less frightening to Bob. Too many gunshots on the stage and too many resignations to Bob's betrayal were separating the Ford brothers as Charley accepted the obligation of personifying Jesse James. He was given to private yearnings, wistfulness about the past, all of the commonplaces of death like weeping and glamorized memory, and he began to look at his younger brother with spite and antagonism, as if he suspected that in some future performance he might present himself to a live cartridge in Robert Ford's gun.

So Bob avoided Charley insofar as that was possible, and sought only to repair his evil reputation. Ironically, it was in New York that Bob first heard the song written by a Missouri sharecropper whose name was Billy Gashade. Bob was sitting in a Bowery saloon, a green bottle of whiskey on the crate to his right, a shot glass in his fingers, when a man with a banjo announced he was going to sing "The Ballad of Jesse James."

He began: "Jesse James was a lad who killed many a man. He robbed the Glendale train. He stole from the rich and he gave to the poor, he'd a hand and a heart and a brain." The man strolled the room, coming so near Bob that Bob pulled back his crossed legs as the man sang the chorus in a higher pitch. "Oh, Jesse had a wife to mourn for his life, three children, they were brave; but that dirty little coward that shot Mister Howard has laid Jesse James in his grave."

A stevedore put a nickel in the singer's palm; he tipped his head in appreciation and continued: "It was Robert Ford, that dirty little coward. I wonder how he does feel? For he ate of Jesse's bread and he slept in Jesse's bed, then he laid Jesse James in his grave."

The man with the banjo, whose name seemed to be Elijah, sang the chorus again and Bob worked at registering no change in attitude or expression. He was so drunk by then that his head jerked when he shifted it and one arm hung slack by his side, but his mind was stubbornly unasleep and could make out that there was an incorrect stanza about robbing a Chicago bank and another about the shot coming on a Saturday night and one about Jesse being born in the county of Shea. The singer concluded: "This song it was made by Billy Gashade as soon as the news did arrive. He said there wasn't a man with the law in his hand could take Jesse James when alive."

Bob capped the green bottle with his shot glass and stood, gripping the bottle neck. His chair tipped over and he staggered a little with intoxication, gaining balance as he moved by sliding a hand against the saloon wall. "*Two* chilrun," he said. "Munnay mornin, na Saurday nigh. Cowny of Clay. You said Shea." He gave the bottle and shot glass to the saloonkeep and tilted slightly to the right as he took a boxer's stance versus the singer. "You gonna fight me, see who the coward is?"

Elijah glared at him with repugnance but said without anguish, "I ain't gonna fight you, boy. You get on outta here."

"*Huh?*"

A man at the rail yelled, "Sleep it off!" and slapped Bob forcefully on the back, sending him walking a step or two before he regained himself. "Any you wanna fight me? Huh? Who's gonna be?" He fell off his legs somehow and sat down on peanut shells, looking flabbergasted. He crawled up to his feet and swayed without words for a moment, his fists raised only gingerly at his sides, and his eyes glinting with tears.

The saloonkeeper said, "Get on home now, son. Go on! Get yourself outta my place!"

Bob guided himself through the door and got lost in the night and awoke at sunrise on Houston Street, a dog licking his mouth.

SOON EVERY SALOON'S piano man could sing the song and stock companies were incorporating it into their romances, and because the simple chorus came up no less than eight times in the course of the ballad, even the stupid or dipsomaniacal could recall that it was Robert Ford, that dirty little coward, who laid poor Jesse James in his grave.

Charley seemed to agree with the allegations of cowardice but Bob always challenged them, punching more than two street buskers, insisting on gunfights or meetings in alleys, stopping the stageshow at any gibe and asking the man if he wanted to investigate Robert Ford's courage in some mutually agreed upon way.

On New Year's Eve in the Horticultural Building in Boston, a rough who'd argued with Charley that afternoon (calling him a barbarian), came to the Fords' evening show and guyed them throughout the act, yelling so many insults that Bob eventually sprang from the stage, jolting the wind from the man, swinging punches at his skull, maybe socking him a dozen times before others yanked him off. And then Bob smashed into them as well, his fists striking blood from the lips and noses of gentlemen who tried to discourage his rage, as Charley pitched into a second group, misapplying his pistols until a policeman finally appeared, fetching a lump from Charley's head with a single swipe of his billyclub.

Only sixteen from an original audience of over three hundred had stayed in the Horticultural Building; the rest had stampeded outside, some even crashing through windowglass as if the place were on fire. Five men were lying on the floor, cupping their mouths or noses, their starched shirt fronts crinkled and spotted red. The policeman said as he shackled Bob, "You may be the Ford brothers or the James brothers, but you cahn't drink blood in Boston."

Articles about the fight appeared in many newspapers over the next week, inspiring the St. Joseph *Gazette* to comment: "Since one of them acquired notoriety by shooting another assassin in the back, the pestiferous pair has traveled the country under the apparent assumption that they were protégés of the state of Missouri. These fellows ought to be locked up in the interest of public morals or put under bonds to keep the peace by holding their tongues."

George Bunnell coincidentally came to a like opinion that the slayers of Jesse James had lost their stage appeal and he called in their repertory company, claiming the competition for shows like theirs was already too plentiful. J. J. McCloskey's *Jesse James, the Bandit King* was still in New York; Charles W. Chase brought his *Mammoth James Boys' Combination* to the West, playing Mosby's Grand Opera House in Richmond in May 1883; another company stayed for a two-night engagement at Tootle's Opera House in St. Joseph; and a show called *The Missouri Outlaws* was being reviewed by P. T. Barnum. And yet the Fords continued on the road with their own company, The Great Western Novelty Troupe, presenting seven thespians and a composition called *Jesse James* throughout Ohio, Pennsylvania, Massachusetts, upstate New York, and New Jersey.

The playwright was a glamorous actor from Buffalo who gave himself the title role and rearranged American history to gain an enlarged arena for his gifts. The makeshift story commenced with an archetypal robbery with many killings, jumped rapidly to the cottage in St. Joseph where the swag was apportioned to the gang, the greatest amount going to Jesse. Angered by that, Bob shot the outlaw after supper on a Saturday night, but only now, on this stage in Cincinnati, Ohio, or Newark, New Jersey, did gallant and gritty Robert Ford see that he'd slain an impostor, for striding from the wings was the genuine Jesse James, and following a vainglorious dialogue, the two desperadoes met in a gunfight and Bob again vanquished the lion. Bob was then congratulated on his courage and accuracy with a gun and the tragedy was strangely forgotten as Bob began a shooting exhibition, firing many blank cartridges at apples that were jerked from Charley's mouth with strings.

Charley called the road shows "a regular picnic" and claimed weekly receipts of nine hundred dollars, but they actually made only a fraction of that, and as they journeyed west they played to apathetic or antagonistic crowds. On September 26th, 1883, *Jesse James* played Louisville, Kentucky, and the management of The Great Western Novelty Troupe was agreeably surprised upon learning the Buckingham Theatre was completely sold out and that sitting rights to the aisles and galleries cost as much as regular box seats might. Only when the curtain was raised did Bob recognize that the great crowd was there to hiss and jeer at his every sentence and fling garbage onto the stage, and when he uneasily raised his gun at Jesse the audience rioted, according to Bob's recollection, surging to the footlights, calling him a cur and a murderer, children scrabbling onto the stage to destroy the set and sneer at Bob in the sing-song of playgrounds.

And when Bob returned to his hotel that night he was given an unsigned letter that conveyed an account of Judas that was never accepted into the gospels. It said the disciple lived on after his attempt to hang himself, providing an example of impiety in this world. He grew huge and grotesque, his face became like a goatskin swollen with wine, his eyes could not be perceived even by an examining physician, to such a depth had they retreated from the sunlight, and his penis grew large, gruesome, a cause for loathing, yellow pus and worms coming out of it along with such a stink that he could stay in no village for long before he was chased away. After much pain and many punishments, Judas died in the place he belonged and, according to the account, the region still permitted no approach, so great was the stench that progressed from the apostate's body to the ground.

EXCEPT FOR A MONTH as sideshow attractions with P. T. Barnum's Greatest Show on Earth, the Ford brothers stopped performing in 1883 and their company dispersed into other productions as Bob and Charley sought more private lives, though that was problematical, even impossible, for many of those who'd once been in the presence of Jesse James.

Bob was going on twenty-two when he went back to Kansas City to gamble for a living. He was dapper, glamorous, physically strong, comparatively rich, and psychologically injured. By his own approximation, Bob had by then assassinated Jesse over eight hundred times, and each repetition was much like the principal occasion: he suspected no one in history had ever so often or so publicly recapitulated an act of betrayal, and he imagined that no degree of grief or penitence could change the country's ill-regard for him.

He thought he might have committed suicide in the cottage on April 3rd, gripped the smoking gun barrel in his teeth and triggered his skull into fragments, painting his red regrets on spattered wallpaper he gruesomely staggered against, but even that might have been judged just one more act of cowardice. He thought he might have begged no clemency from the governor and been hanged on May 19th, but even with his own strangling descent to the grave, Bob guessed he would not be any more forgiven than Judas was long ago. So Bob played the renegade and rogue, stooping to no repentance, struggling with no phantoms, expecting no compassion, accepting no responsibilities, no pressures, no contempt. He was smug and disagreeable, arrogant and dangerous, as aggressive as a gun.

He thought, at his angriest, about visiting Mrs. William Westfall in Plattsburg, the McMillans in Wilton, Iowa, the Wymore family in Clay County, Mrs. Berry Griffin in Richmond, Mrs. John Sheets in Gallatin, perhaps even Mrs. Joseph Heywood in Northfield, Minnesota. He would go to their homes and give his name as Robert Ford, "the man who killed Jesse James." He imagined they would be grateful to him. They would graciously invite him in and urge him to accept extravagant gifts in exchange for his having made their grief a little lighter. But in actuality Bob made only one irregular journey and that one was to Kearney, Missouri, under the cover of night when even dogs were asleep. He crept up to a nine-foot-high marble grave monument beneath a huge coffee bean tree and glided his fingers over an inscription reading:

In Loving Remembrance

JESSE W. JAMES

Died April 3, 1882
Aged 34 Years, 6 Months, 28 Days
Murdered By a Traitor and Coward
Whose Name Is Not Worthy To
Appear Here.

BOB JOURNEYED into Kansas and the Indian Territories in 1885, gambling with cowboys in saloons, sleeping on ground that still remembered the sun, riding west without maps. A rattlesnake once snapped at his spur and then slithered gracefully away. Bob crept after it with a machete, chopping off the snake's head and giving the body to a gunnysack until he could cook the meat that night. Hours later when Bob stripped off the gunnysack, the snake slashed out and socked Bob's neck, striking hard as a strong man's fist, only then spilling onto the sand, its spirit spent and at peace.

7

MAY 1884–JUNE 1892

*Some may think different but all the men I know who've killed anybody
would give all they're worth to get away from their reputation.*
BOB FORD
in the Creede Candle, *1892*

CHARLEY FORD was all that his countrymen wanted an assassin of
Jesse James to be: agitated, frightened, groveling, his melancholy
unmanageable, his sicknesses so actual and so imagined that days
would pass when he could do no more than nap under smothering coats
and catch spiders with his glances. He had married in May 1883, a
Miss O'Hara from St. Louis, but by April 1884, her peevishness and
disappointment with her pale, phthisic, and ghost-ridden groom had
separated the two and Charley was staying with his parents in order to
cure his consumption with some good country air. Though he was only
twenty-six years old, he was given to the fatigue and fragility of the
aged; he weighed just ninety-eight pounds, he complained of the cold,
the outcries of children, the plots against him by Martha and Bob, the
purloining that kept him impoverished. He would shrink into a rocking
chair on the roadside porch in May, his skeleton covered with woolens
and shawls, his skull made idiotically jolly with a purple and gold
stocking cap. He had by then developed secondary infections to his
alimentary tract and in order to calm the searing pain in his lungs and
organs, Charley ate ten or twelve grains of morphine per day, with the
result that a stupid and sprightly playfulness could give way to deep
sleep and then sleepless depression in which he wept and whispered
plainsongs of remorse to Jesse.

But on May 6th, 1884, Charley was merry enough to go hunting
with Tom Jacobs, the boy who'd chanced upon the body of Robert
Woodson Hite two years earlier. Quail were startled from the weeds of
the Jacobs farm, their wings chattering in flight like the sound of riffled
pages, but Charley would only gape at the sky as the birds disappeared,

as if sight were as tardy as description and their presence had not yet pierced his eyes. He lingered over ordinary things—a gnarled finger of Dutch elm root emerging from the earth, the spade marks of a plowhorse's shoes in a muddy cornfield, a clearing peppered with the pawprints of rabbits, a crow that sliced down near his ear. Tom lost the sickly man in the woods and after a prolonged absence saw Charley again with his shotgun hinged open over his arm, slouching back toward home, his clubfoot jerking his walk. Tom cried out if anything was wrong, but Charley gave no answer.

He angled the shotgun against a staircase and gave his mother a smile as he climbed to the upstairs room where he slept. He hung his heavy chinchilla coat on a closet nail and snagged his slouch hat over it. Though there were scraps of paper and pencils in the room, he composed no apology or goodbye. He removed a .45 caliber Colt revolver from a frayed holster looped over the bedpost and reclined on a duck feather mattress, crossing his calf-high boots at the ankles, fingercombing his dark brown hair. He twinged as he pressed the gunsight against his chest, then quelled his heart with a single shot, the gun sliding to the floor as the singe mark on his shirt lightly smoked.

The suicide was reported in a great many newspapers and the private ceremony that the Fords preferred was changed by circumstance to a large public gathering. No government official paid his respects, but Henry Craig and Sheriff Timberlake attended, as did Dick Liddil, whose release from jail had just been arranged.

Bob was plagued by questions from people seeking the reasons why Charley killed himself, some appraising the victim's kid brother as he spoke, trying to anticipate if Bob would make his escape from shame and reproach by employing the same procedure. Bob responded to the pressures imprudently, by pushing away from the reception crowd and going into the woods with his gun and shooting the shagbark off a tree.

And yet he stayed on the Ray County farm for another year, playing cards with his sister and Dick, making Ida his audience for acts of prestidigitation, puttering around the house, mowing hay, corn-husking with his brother Wilbur, slaughtering pigs and chickens. But by the summer of 1885, the scrutiny of passersby and the contempt of the Richmond community were all too persistent, and Bob journeyed west in order to make a new reputation.

Elias Ford sold the grocery store and purchased a farm near Blue Springs that he worked on with Wilbur in the plain and simple way of ordinary people. Martha gave up the Harbison place soon after Bob departed and moved over to Excelsior Springs to be with her twin sister, Amanda. Dick Liddil was still Martha's paramour but the spell was beginning to wear off for her. His appearance was no longer exemplary, his skewed right eye was going blind and was sometimes red as a radish, and he whispered, when alone with her, that Jesse had put a hex on them, that everything they attempted from then on was predestined to fail. So Martha separated from him in the late eighties and accepted a marriage proposal from a man whose occupation and personality were unimpressive but sustaining. Except for Bob, the Fords were alike in that: they completed their lifetimes peacefully and disappeared from history.

JOHN SAMUELS, who'd lingered on the brink of death for more than four months in 1882, got better as soon as his stepbrother Jesse was sent to the grave, and he gave the world an undistinguished life until his dying at seventy-one, in 1932.

Dr. Reuben Samuels grew progressively more affected by the mental injuries he'd suffered when strangled in the coffee bean tree during the Civil War. By 1900 the man was so violent that he was finally confined in a straitjacket and conveyed to the state asylum, where he spent the last eight years of his life in a condition of childishness and rage.

His wife, Zerelda, remained on the Kearney farm, which she subdivided among her surviving children until it was little more than a two-storey house, slave quarters, ramshackle barn, and garden. Her greatest source of income began to be the twenty-five-cent tours of the grounds and rooms, in which she perorated against the government and the courts, and gave gasconades about her slaughtered sons, Archie and Jesse, gladly showing her amputated right wrist or the combination steel knife and fork she'd made so that she could eat left-handed.

She was an inveigler. She would cozen many of her guests, invite them into her confidence, make them feel especially privileged, at last agreeing to sell them a stone from the grave or, at much greater cost, a worn shoe from one of the James boys' steeds (these she bought from a village blacksmith in wheelbarrow loads; the stones were shoveled from Clear Creek and spread on the grave once a week). If they asked to take a photograph of Zerelda in her black rocking chair in the yard, she would appeal to them to mail back a copy as a sweet remembrance, and these snapshots she'd sell to new visitors as soon as she received them. She petitioned for and accepted a free pass from the Burlington Railroad in atonement for its crimes against her family, and then spent each trip lumbering down the aisles, steadying herself on the seats as she chronicled her life for the passengers and castigated the Burlington company.

She remained a strong and overwhelming woman even as she crossed into the twentieth century. She outlived three husbands and four of the eight children she bore and she showed no signs of sickness when she retired to a Pullman sleeper in 1911 and there died of a stroke at the age of eighty-seven.

On the Monday after Easter in 1882, Zerelda Mimms James auctioned off most of the contents of the cottage on Lafayette Street. A common coal scuttle that was once warmed by the great man's hand garnered twice its cost, the coffee mill that Mary played with on April 3rd brought the widow two dollars, Mary's highchair, seventy-five cents, the chair Jesse stood on and the feather duster he fiddled with went for five dollars each. Two horses and saddles in the stables were confiscated as stolen goods, slivers of the floorboards were ripped up as mementoes, painted wood siding was being stripped off the cottage when the police came to restore order.

And yet Zee was penniless and she would remain that way in spite of many generous efforts to bring her to solvency. Someone enterprising signed Zee onto a speaking circuit but she was unwilling to exaggerate and actually too shy for public address, so an orator was paid to retell the legend with extravagant histrionics as the crying widow looked on. The preview rehearsals were atrocious, however; Zee kept shaking her head at the man's preposterous hyperbole and she couldn't be heard when she responded to questions from the audience. The program was judiciously canceled and she accepted work as a cook for a while, but she suffered a miscarriage in July, recuperated slowly, and soon depended upon a subscription of several hundred dollars that was raised for her by Major John Newman Edwards.

Zee moved back to Kansas City in 1882 and worked there as a cleaning woman and seamstress in a manner that many construed as penitent. She joined Mrs. Samuels in suing J. H. Chambers, publishers, for royalties from *The Life, Times, and Treacherous Death of Jesse James,* a book they'd earlier denied collaborating on. A jury awarded them $942 and the article about that was the last news about Zee; she thenceforth retired from the public eye, shunning reporters, seeking retreat, staying with one of her five sisters and brothers for months at a time and then regretfully moving on.

She felt crippled, forsaken, marooned. She saw no other men, she mixed with other women solely at church socials, her only company was her children, most of her clothing was black. She thought of Jesse as her vitality, her vigor, her crucial ingredient; once he was gone she was a prey to fatigue and sickness and instability until she gratefully accepted death in 1900 at the age of fifty-five.

Her daughter, Mary, grew into an intelligent and pretty but rather inconspicuous woman who married Henry Barr, an affluent farmer much older than she was, and gave birth to three boys on property across the road from her father's birthplace. Her hair changed from ash blond to chestnut brown as she aged and it delighted her that she resembled Jesse at least in coloring, but she called no particular attention to her heritage and many who knew her when she passed away in 1935 were surprised by her maiden name.

Her brother took great advantage of the name Jesse Edwards James. He was a sprinter in high school and, in the summer, an office boy in the real estate investment company run by Governor Crittenden's son. He played semi-professional baseball, ran a cigar stand in the courthouse, received a college scholarship from Thomas Crittenden, and became an attorney-at-law in Kansas City and Los Angeles. He was once accused of robbing the Missouri Pacific Railroad at Leeds in 1898, and Finis C. Farr, the governor's private secretary in 1882, acted as counsel for the defense without fee. Mrs. Zerelda Samuels gave her grandson an alibi by claiming he'd been sitting on the porch with her when the robbery occurred, just as Jesse James, Sr., seemed always to be when earlier crimes were committed. The jury acquitted the man but the judge was rumored to have said, "Jesse, I find you not guilty, but don't do it again."

When Jesse was twenty-four he wrote the memoir *Jesse James, My Father;* in 1921 he financed and acted in the movie *Under the Black Flag,* and some years later was a highly paid technical advisor to Paramount Pictures when they produced their counterfeit *Jesse James,* starring Tyrone Power. Jesse Edwards James died in California in 1951. Of his four daughters, one was an escrow officer for the Bank of America, another worked in the Federal Reserve, and a third sold Liberty Bonds.

IN MAY 1882, the Missouri state legislature was asked to vote on a resolution "to commend the vigilance and success of the civil officers of Clay and Jackson counties and the citizens of western Missouri for their efforts in bringing the [James gang] to justice." Spittoons were thrown at the sponsor of the resolution and he was upbraided with such outrage and ridicule that the session was soon adjourned.

It is not very startling then to see that Timberlake, Craig, Wallace, and Crittenden were politically ruined by their involvement in the conspiracy to assassinate Jesse James. James R. Timberlake could read the signs clearly enough that he sought the county collector's job rather than reelection as sheriff, and yet he was roundly defeated and moved to New Mexico to work as a cattleman. Governor Crittenden called him back as deputy United States marshal but he retired from office soon after his wife died and returned to his Liberty livery stables. He started taking morphine to cure insomnia, and he succumbed to an accidental overdose of the narcotic in 1891.

Henry H. Craig ran for Kansas City marshal in 1882, but received only a small percentage of the vote. He never again gained even a party's nomination but he did acquire some prominence in the private practice of law and it was partially because of the sponsorship of Henry Craig that the junior Jesse James could study for the legal profession.

William H. Wallace stayed on as prosecuting attorney for another year but couldn't resist attempts at a higher office. He lost races for Congress in 1884, the United States Senate in 1901, Congress again in 1906, and governor in 1908 before he gave up and applied himself to the cause of prohibition.

Thomas T. Crittenden once realistically assumed that he would be reelected governor, then join his uncle in the United States Senate or join his childhood friend John Harlan on the United States Supreme Court, so he was shocked and stung when the Democratic Party withheld even its nomination for governor from him, preferring the former Confederate general John S. Marmaduke. Senator George Vest came to his aid by suggesting Crittenden as a foreign ambassador but President Grover Cleveland rejected the motion on the grounds that Europeans would recognize the ex-governor as the man who "had bargained with the Fords for the killing of Jesse James." Cleveland instead made him consul general to Mexico City, and, after a change of presidential administration, a friend whom Governor Crittenden appointed as a judge repaid the favor by making Crittenden referee of the Kansas City Bankruptcy Court, which he manfully accepted as a great honor and responsibility. He suffered a stroke at a Kansas City baseball game and died in the stands in 1909.

In the late eighties Dick Liddil joined Bob Ford in Las Vegas, New Mexico, and acted as his partner in a Bridge Street saloon, but he

really wasn't much help. He was hopeless with arithmetic, lackadaisical with cleaning up, and in his despair would strip off his apron and
stroll out of the place, preferring the companionship of horses that ate
apples off his palm in the livery stable next door. J. W. Lynch made
the attractive proposal that Dick sample a thoroughbred named St. John
and a string of other racehorses on the Eastern and Southern circuits
and the partners split up. Dick would never again see Bob or Martha,
nor would he admit any past association with the James gang. He
competed at Saratoga, Pimlico, and Churchill Downs and produced so
well that he came to own a good many racehorses himself, and he was
grooming one in Cincinnati, Ohio, when he grew oddly weary and
went to sleep on the straw floor of a stall, and there James Andrew
Liddil died of natural causes, at age forty-one, in 1893.

Of the Younger brothers, only two survived the nineteenth century.
John had been killed by Pinkerton detectives in 1874. Bob yielded to
consumption in the Stillwater prison infirmary in 1889, his last words
to Cole being "Don't weep for me." A significant segment of Jim's
ruined jaw was surgically removed after the gang was arrested near
Madelia and his only nourishment for twenty-five years was whatever
could be sipped from a spoon. Cole lost most of his hair and added
forty pounds in prison. Mostly as a relief from routine, he and Jim
volunteered as subjects for phrenological studies that concluded Cole
was a loyal and steadfast but unforgiving man who could have made
an excellent general; and that Jim had considerable artistic and literary
talent but no faculty for getting money.

The two were released from Stillwater in 1901 and took jobs
selling cemetery monuments for the P. N. Peterson Granite Company.
Jim sought to wed a writer named Alice Miller but was forbidden a
marriage license because the Minnesota attorney general ruled that a
man still under a life sentence must be considered legally dead. Soon
thereafter his fiancée changed her mind about Jim and in 1902 he
committed suicide in the Reardon Hotel in St. Paul, leaving an anguished
letter in which he said he was "a square fellow, a socialist, and decidedly in favor of Woman Rights."

The governor attested to his sorrow and remorse for the tragedy
by granting a full pardon to Thomas Coleman Younger, and with mingled
gloom and gladness Cole returned to Lee's Summit, Missouri.

ALEXANDER FRANKLIN JAMES was in Baltimore with his wife and
child when he read the news about the assassination of Jesse James.

He had spurned his younger brother for being peculiar and tempera-
mental, but once he perceived that he'd never see Jesse again, Frank
was wrought up, perplexed, despondent. The East seemed a foreign
country to him, and whichever city he visited seemed an uninhabited
island without Jesse alive. He was suddenly lonely, nostalgic, morose;
he might have yearned for suicide were it not for Annie and Rob.

He was inaccurately sighted in St. Joseph, Kansas City, and Kearney in April and May 1882, but in fact stayed on the coast through
spring and summer, writing letters of overture and negotiation to the
journalist John Newman Edwards, who routed them in turn to Governor Thomas Crittenden.

Frank assumed the alias of B. F. Winfrey and moved west in
autumn, meeting with the governor on October 5th, 1882, at five in
the afternoon. Crittenden had jubilantly invited state officials and
approving reporters to his Jefferson City office in order to share in the
opening of a "Christmas box," a surprise which they presumed referred
more to Major John Newman Edwards than to the grave, august stranger
who was with him. But then Edwards gestured to the stranger and
grandly introduced Mr. Frank James and the man strode forward,
removing a revolver and Union Army cartridge belt, and presented
them to the governor, saying, "I want to hand over to you that which
no living man except myself has been permitted to touch since 1861,
and to say that I am your prisoner."

One day later, Frank James gave an interview to the St. Louis
Republican in which he said: "If I were governor charged with uphold-
ing the laws of a great state cursed by such a band of outlaws who
terrorized the state, I would take desperate measures to meet such
desperate men. They would have to go as in this case they have gone.
Such is the fate of all such bands. But what must be the suffering of
such a pitiful creature as Bob Ford? For a few paltry dollars he has,
while on the verge of manhood, brought upon himself a blighting curse
that will never leave him in all the years to come."

The government accorded privileges to Frank James; he was given
parties, genteel receptions, magnificent presents and accommodations,
an opulent coach on the train that carried him to Jackson County; to
some it seemed the state of Missouri surrendered to Frank James rather
than the other way around. People learned of his journey north and
swarmed to the railroad stations along the way, at which Frank needed
only to show himself and shyly wave to receive a wild ovation.

Prosecuting attorney Wallace couldn't construct a convincing case
against Frank in Independence, so the outlaw was sent to Gallatin to

stand trial for the murder of John Sheets in 1869, and for the murders of Conductor William Westfall and Frank McMillan in the Winston train robbery of 1881. Edwards was able to recruit seven aspiring politicians as counsels for the defense, including a former lieutenant governor and a former congressman who was a commissioner of the Supreme Court of Missouri. Since the courtroom was too small to accommodate the crowds, the trial was moved to the Gallatin Opera House, where the sheriff sold tickets of admission.

The prosecution's case depended upon the confessions of Clarence Hite, Whiskeyhead Ryan, and Dick Liddil; but Hite died of consumption before he could take the stand, Ryan was already in jail on a robbery sentence and had nothing to gain by angering Frank James or his confederates, and although Dick was precise and persuasive in both his testimony and demeanor, the accusations of a convict, horse thief, profligate, and roustabout were not given much credence.

Frank James, however, evinced dignity, intelligence, rectitude, and sobriety. He represented every quality that gentlemen then were eager to possess. He could speak passable German and French; he could recite one thousand lines of Shakespeare; he was not suspiciously attractive; he had fought for the right side in the Civil War.

A jury that was already partial to James when first impaneled moved to acquit the defendant and the courtroom erupted into prolonged applause.

Frank wasn't free for more than a year when he was arraigned in Alabama for the robbery of a paymaster at Muscle Shoals, and again the verdict was not guilty, but right after the announcement a sheriff arrested the man for the robbery of the Missouri Pacific Railroad at Otterville in 1876. The charge was dismissed in February 1885 because the principal witness died two days before the case went to trial.

So it was that in spite of more than circumstantial evidence linking Frank James to a great many crimes, the man never served a day in the penitentiary.

What he did was act as a race starter at county fairs, increasing attendance with each appearance; he worked in a shoe store in Nevada, Missouri, and in the Mittenthal Clothing Company in Dallas, Texas, until monotony or annoyance with the overawed customers goaded Frank into leaving. He curried and cared for the racehorses of a rich man in New Jersey until his generous paychecks seemed too much like philanthropy. Then for seventy dollars a month, he accepted tickets at the Standard Theatre in St. Louis, refusing all invitations to see the saucy burlesque show inside.

He was mentioned as the new sergeant-at-arms for the Missouri legislature in 1901, a post that he anticipated would be a reprieve and an open display of his reformation, but the Democrats who recommended Frank foresaw his presence in the assembly as a political handicap, and the offer was retracted. So it was with regret and resentment that Frank capitulated to some of the many propositions from stock companies and performed, with chagrin and great nervousness, secondary roles in the plays *Across the Desert* and *The Fatal Scar.*

He was a survivor and it made him feel slightly guilty. It seemed to Frank that grace had come upon him without merit, that he'd been pardoned without justification or purpose. He once visited the scene of the 1864 Centralia massacre with a *Missouri Herald* reporter and strolled the Pleasant Grove cemetery looking for names he recognized. He gardened around an ill-kept grave and said, "The marvel to me is that I am not sleeping in a place like this. What have I been spared for when so many of my comrades were taken?" He straightened and roughed the earth from his hands, quoting from the Gospel according to Matthew: " 'Then shall two be in the field; the one shall be taken, and the other left.' "

When Cole Younger came back to Missouri in 1903, the two sick, aging men became reacquainted. Cole was pious, penitent, overweight, aching from the twenty-six gunshots he'd subjected his body to. Frank was sour and skinny and gray-haired, a chain-smoker and teetotaler with a minor heart condition. A Chicago circus management company signed the two to appear together in a Wild West show called *Hell on the Border,* in which Cole mixed with the audience and signed autographs and waved a white hat when his celebrated name was announced. Frank sat grumpily in a stagecoach that was robbed by city boys playing the James-Younger gang and then rode on an ornate spangled saddle and Arabian horse in the grand finale alongside Sioux Indians and ex–cavalry men and bronc riders and girls who did rope tricks.

Frank considered it crooked, silly, and unmanly and he moved on within months, settling once again on the Kearney farm. His son, Rob, was by then an auditor for the Wabash Railway in St. Louis; his wife, Anne, provided Mrs. Samuels with company and went into angry seclusion whenever gawkers stopped by. Frank raised cattle, rode in a buggy pulled by a plow horse named Dan, shot at paper targets in the woods, and taciturnly walked from room to room with tourists who now paid fifty cents to see Reverend James's diploma from Georgetown College, a sampler stitched by Zerelda Cole at St. Catherine's Academy, the Holy Bible that Jesse read, one of the guns he shot. If asked about Jesse, Frank would recite from *Julius Caesar:* "The evil that men do lives after them; the good is oft interrèd with their bones."

Alexander Franklin James died of a heart attack on February 18th, 1915, at the age of seventy-two. As he grew older he'd become plagued by visions of scientists making judgments about the configurations and weight of his brain, so Annie granted his wish that his body be cremated and the ashes stored until they could be interred with her own, which they were, in 1944, when she died at age ninety-one.

Thomas Coleman Younger died, unmarried, at age seventy-two, and was survived by one daughter, Pearl, a prostitute whose mother was Myra Belle Starr. After leaving the Wild West show, Cole returned to his birthplace in Lee's Summit, Missouri, and continued making public appearances, speaking at churches, tent meetings, and ice cream socials on the evils of whiskey, *What Life Has Taught Me,* or simply *Crime Does Not Pay.*

ROBERT NEWTON FORD meandered southwest to the Las Vegas hot springs in the late eighties, having recollected that Jesse once thought about going straight in that region. He was a professional gambler then and owned a plug horse, the clothes he'd rolled into a green tarpaulin, and the shaggy chinchilla coat that had belonged to Charley, with eight hundred dollars in poker winnings sewn into the coat's sagging skirts. He registered in the Old Adobe Hotel, then made a sightseer of himself for a week, playing cards for pennies, gathering information about the town and Billy the Kid and Pat Garrett, going to the hot springs to cogitate and get clean.

On a sashay along Bridge Street one evening, he saw a stooped man gum to a saloon window a sign saying the place was being sold and the owner going back East. Bob spent the night on a stool there, counting the sales that were rung up, figuring out what he'd change, and the next morning negotiated an outright purchase of the inventory and a year's lease of the property, putting down a fifty-dollar deposit. He then sent a telegram to Dick Liddil in Richmond, and a month later, when Dick jumped off the train, Bob was happily at the depot, looking groomed and genial in a crisp white shirt and buttoned gray vest, a long white apron concealing his legs and angling off his gun. He grinned at Dick and said, "Say hello to prosperity," and hung an arm over Dick's shoulders as Jesse might have as he guided him on a ramble through the Mexican vegetable and poultry market and then across Old Town's plaza with its gazebo and gardens to a street of orange-colored clay.

Bob Ford's saloon was advantageously located in Las Vegas, on the major east-west thoroughfare over the Gallinas River, and it might have gathered commercial men of San Miguel County as well as those going west forty miles to Santa Fe, but gossip about the proprietors was circulated, *The Daily Optic* even reminded its readers of their inglorious careers, and though a few shepherds and miners straggled in to gawk at the renegades of the James gang, a large contingent, under the outraged influence of Scott Moore (Jesse's boyhood friend), boycotted the place in fury over the assassination.

Bob paid boys to pass out fliers to people crossing the bridge and even went into the street himself in order to prevail upon pedestrians to appease themselves inside. He ordered an upright piano shipped over from Albuquerque, gave away boiled eggs and sweet pickles and crackling pig skins painted with red chili sauce; he persuaded the governor's son, Miguel Antonio Otero—who was just about his age and grew up in Missouri—to give a Saturday night party there; he even sought singers and dancing girls through advertisements in Colorado newspapers; and yet the saloon was bypassed, signs were ripped down, gentlemen crossed to the southside sidewalk in order to get to the plaza.

Bob was spending capital accumulated over five years on weekly expenses and saw poverty approaching with each payment to a supplier, so when Dick presented Bob with Lynch's proposal that Dick run St. John and some other racehorses on the Eastern and Southern circuits, Bob gave up and without pain cooperated in pushing the animals into a Santa Fe freight car and in packing the inventory into a Studebaker wagon. Dick went East and got lucky again; Bob went north to Walsenburg, Colorado, and began another sorry saloon, bringing in a meager number of customers with sideshow bragging about himself: the man who killed Jesse James. He moved on again, going forty-five miles further north to Pueblo, where he earned some recognition as a wily professional gambler and then managed to get together the capital for a "pretty waiter saloon" in a section of town called the Mesa. He invested all his savings in gambling equipment that was shipped south from Denver and spent many hours in the countryside or at the railroad depot meeting sixteen- to twenty-one-year-old girls who looked poor or put upon or in flight from mail-order marriages and jobs in the cantaloupe fields. He promised them an eight-by-four room, three meals a day, and clean white dresses that were cut so short they showed their white bloomers and thigh-length black stockings. He guaranteed them protection and pleasant society, quietly giving them the option of prostitution without really requiring it—they were only expected to speak gladly with the patrons and persuade them to purchase liquor and beer at outrageously increased prices.

The gambling and the pretty waiter girls in Bob's third saloon made all the difference. Bob flourished in Pueblo as he hadn't since his years as an actor with George Bunnell. And his life in Pueblo *was* by then in great part a performance; his personality was compressed to that peculiar emptiness of a man whose public appearance is only a collection of gestures and posturings, of practiced words and affectation. He was a peacock, a swain, a swaggerer: one account of Bob accused him of "running off at the mouth" and of playing gunfighter around the Mesa, another reported his belligerence and umbrage, and yet another account mentioned his jumpiness and unhappiness and a panicky desperation that could make him seem possessed. His mean and cowardly reputation preceded him, of course, but there were plenty of other stories that could explain, at least, his uneasiness and suspicion. It was at this time, for example, that a man who owned a barbershop ingratiated himself and cringed around Bob for a month or so before letting on to a companion that he planned to avenge Mr. Jesse James by killing Robert Ford. The companion whispered the news to Bob, who approached the barber in his shop, jostled him out into the yard, and supplied him with a pistol. "Go ahead," Bob yelled. "Draw your gun and let her fly!" Instead the man got down on his knees and begged to stay alive. Bob chopped his pistol into the barber's nose, crushing cartilage and bone, and as the man gushed blood over his mouth, chin, and belly, Bob dragged him over to his saloon, where the barber was compelled to beg again for pardon in the presence of Bob's pitiless cronies.

On another occasion Bob happened into the Bucket of Blood saloon in Pueblo and sipped whiskey at the bar in order to oversee the gambling operations and compare their gross income with his own. A boy with a guitar was singing anything suggested and it wasn't long before a man in the audience sought to anger Bob Ford by calling for Billy Gashade's song. The boy began "The Ballad of Jesse James" and according to an eyewitness named Norval Jennings every gaze attached to the dirty little coward in their midst. As the song went on it seemed Bob would not react to its jeering, but he gradually grew indignant enough to swing around on his high stool and sweep the right side of his coat over his gun, scowling at the singer as the boy ignorantly continued. According to Jennings, Bob then jerked up his Colt and shot at the guitar with miraculous accuracy, cutting through the catgut strings and stinging the boy's playing fingers as the tightened strings sprang free. The boy yowled and gathered his right hand to his chest and Bob swaggered out through gunsmoke, inviting disgust with a grin.

He was regarded as arrogant, dangerous, pigheaded, savage, with no redeeming qualities beyond a capacity for liquor and a scary gift in handling guns. Yarns were relayed around town in which Robert Ford was gallant or magnanimous—yarns about his giving Christmas suppers to the indigent, about his slipping fifty dollars into the pocket of a Mexican with a poor family, about his chasing off a gang of toughs on a sidewalk merely by menacing them with his cane—but anything congratulatory was judged to be bogus by those who thought they knew him and the accounts were forgotten in favor of disparaging tales that seemed more fitting.

He brought much of their antagonism on himself: he *was* argumentative, garrulous, haughty, intoxicated more than often, petty about anything that involved money, perturbed only by injuries to his property and reputation, and pestered by an everlasting fear of assassination. In his private life, however, he was agreeable, forgiving, even loving, a gentleman of means and intelligence who was plagued by a guilt that he could not acknowledge.

He had given work to a nightwalker named Dorothy Evans and gradually became beguiled by her. She was a plump, pretty, cattleman's daughter, pale as a cameo, with the sort of overripe body that always seems four months pregnant. Her long brown hair was braided into figure eights and pinned up over her ears in the English countrygirl style. Grim experience was in her eyes, many years of pouting shaped her lips, but everything else about her expression seemed to evince an appealing cupidity, as if she could accept anything as long as it was pleasing. She was canny, practical, sympathetic, purposeful, with a ready tally of the profit and loss she made on each hour she passed with her employer; and Bob was willing to pay for her attention, her pity, her open displays of high feeling and respect.

Dorothy had initially appeared at his saloon in response to a newspaper advertisement that read:

GOOD STEPPERS, make yourselves some money.
FUN GALORE! FINE CLOTHING!
The wages of sin are not death, but wealth,
fame, and the chance of a proper marriage.

It was July and Bob was pulling ice in a child's red wagon because he couldn't afford the five-penny delivery charge when he came upon a young woman in a long green gown of dainty frills and ruffles. She wore gem-buttoned gray gloves and a Georgia sunhat and she angled a parasol over her right shoulder, rolling it slightly in a way that suggested pleasure at the sight of a man pulling a child's red wagon. She said, "I was expecting somebody old and ugly."

Bob said, "Pueblo has a supply of them: just who in particular?"

"You *are* Bob Ford?"

"And proud of it too." He figured she was a big-city journalist like Nellie Bly and there to get yet another story about Robert Ford's disgrace and ignominy.

But she said, "I sing and play the piano. I've come to see you about that position for a good stepper."

"Oh golly." He'd been getting his fingers into yellow gloves in order to carry the ice inside but now he yanked them off and with chagrin jerked a swinging door open for her and invited her out of the sunlight and high temperature.

She said her name was Miss Evans and that she was brought up in an orphanage run by the Sisters of Mercy. Her only skirt was a flour sack until the age of fourteen when she'd married a mining engineer in Denver. Pneumonia had taken him from her, however, and desperation had pushed her into the life of a courtesan.

"You mean you're a prostitute," Bob said. Her gloves were together on the oak saloon table. His finger jiggled one of the gems and he recognized that it was only colored glass. He said, "You don't have to sugar things with me."

Miss Evans said, "I'm not ashamed of it; I just like the word."

"I've got some call for it, if you're willing."

"Could be," she said, and then forgot her pert good taste. She pulled a gold case from her purse and Bob lighted her cigarette. A man who worked for Bob barged inside the saloon, swinging ice between his legs with iron tongs. He saw the cigarette in her fingers and stopped long enough to pepper the floorboards with waterspots and make a happy face at Bob, then lunged back into the storeroom.

Bob asked, "You know who I am?"

She nodded a little too eagerly, like a girl slightly in love with her teacher. "Bob Ford."

He recrossed his legs and gazed at the flooring. "The man who shot Jesse James."

"I've seen your picture."

He glanced at her with suspicion. "So you were lying."

"Excuse me?"

"You said you were expecting somebody old and ugly, when you knew just what I looked like."

She wasn't sheepish, she didn't look into her lap or pout or pretend to be embarrassed. She said, "I was making conversation," and was especially pretty with him.

"How much of that is true, about the orphanage and the Sisters of Mercy and the mining engineer?"

She blew cigarette smoke and said, "Hardly any."

He glared at her with a cocked eyebrow that betrayed how engaging he thought she was. "Do you have a given name or do you just generally make something up?"

"Dorothy," she said.

"You *can* sing though, can't you?"

She got up and glided over to the upright piano, putting her cigarette in a tin cup there. She sang "Only a Bird in a Gilded Cage" and "Home, Sweet Home" and Bob gave her a job at higher pay than the other girls'.

She garnered attention in Pueblo with gaudy clothes and brazen, unblushing displays of her body; she sang serenades on street corners as riders lingered their horses, teamsters looked on from their wagon seats, and young clerks forgot their shops to gaze with delight and longing; her picture was on a poster that read: "Prizes like this may be captured nightly at Bob Ford's Saloon." She brought in enough new customers to greatly augment Bob's earnings, but she could have justified her wages with only her generous attentions to Bob. She was deeply interested in Bob's overpublicized life with Jesse and listened almost rapaciously, sitting absolutely still as he spoke, showing no expression beyond that of rapt absorption, her mind seeming to accept his words as a mouth does water.

It was only with Dorothy Evans that Bob spoke revealingly or plainly, and it was with her that he spoke of things he didn't know he knew. He told her about playing poker with Thomas Howard in the dining room of the cottage. Jesse would flap his bottom lip with his

thumb and smack his fist on the table with every card he played. He'd
folded on one or two winning hands and never caught on to Charley's
bluffs. He rubbed his teeth with a finger, Bob said, he nibbled his
mustache, he purified his blood at night with sulphate of magnesia in
a glass of apple cider. Bob told Dorothy that he had no real memory of
the shooting and its aftermath: he could remember lifting the gun that
Jesse had given him and then it was Good Friday and he was reading
about the funeral proceedings as if they'd happened a long time ago.
He explained that he'd kept the yellowed newspaper clippings from
April 1882 and repeatedly pored over them, each time feeling aped,
impersonated, cruelly maligned by the Robert Ford that the correspondents chose to put into print. He'd acted lightning-struck and stupefied,
mechanical and childish. He was ashamed of his persiflage, his boasting, his pretensions of courage and ruthlessness; he was sorry about
his cold-bloodedness, his dispassion, his inability to express what he
now believed was the case: that he truly regretted killing Jesse, that he
missed the man as much as anybody and wished his murder hadn't
been necessary.

"Was it?" Dorothy asked.

Bob looked at her without comment.

"How I mean it is: why was it you killed him?" There was a
gentle tinkling to her voice that Bob had grown accustomed to in
actresses.

Bob said, "He was going to kill me."

"So you were scared and that's the only reason?"

He sipped from a German stein of beer. "And the reward money,"
he said.

"Do you want me to change the subject?"

Bob reset the stein and glanced at her in a calculating way. He
asked, "Do you know what I expected? Applause. I thought Jesse
James was a Satan and a tyrant who was causing all this misery, and
that I'd be the greatest man in America if I shot him. I thought they
would congratulate me and I'd get my name in books. I was only
twenty years old then. I couldn't see how it would look to people. I've
been surprised by what's happened."

IT WAS AROUND THIS TIME that a cowpuncher and prospector named
Nicholas Creede began producing great amounts of silver ore from the
Holy Moses and Amethyst mines in the San Juan Mountains of south-
west Colorado. A tent town in the gulch of Willow Creek was given

the man's name and a spur of the Denver and Rio Grande narrow-gauge railroad was rapidly developed to join the camp to Wagon Wheel Gap in the east, and only deep snows in the high canyon passes prevented many thousands of miners from swarming over the mountains. They waited impatiently for the spring thaw in Pueblo, bringing good profits to the saloons and hotels and boardinghouses where they slept three or four to a room. Bob Ford was not exempt and put in with him in the Phoenix Hotel was a man named Edward O. Kelly, making a very unhappy pairing.

Kelly was from Harrisonville, Missouri, just twenty miles south of Cole Younger's farm in Lee's Summit, and he gave even friends the improper opinion that his sister was married to one of the Younger boys. He was a child of a physician who'd given him a good education and he was employed as a policeman in Pueblo, but by 1890 the man had the mean, scrawny, unintelligent look of the regularly intoxicated. He forgot to shave or change his clothes, his shirts and coat were much too big for him, his green eyes showed no glint of humor, he had only repugnance for women, and he thought Bob Ford was a disgrace to the good name of Missouri.

They generally said nothing when in the room together, they glanced everywhere but at each other, they even hung up a flagged string in order to split the room area and separate possessions. And then one day Bob was rummaging through his belongings in search of a four-hundred-dollar diamond ring that he was going to present to Dorothy as a sign of their common-law marriage. Bob saw Kelly sniggering and saying words to himself and he jumped to the wrong conclusion, charging Kelly with stealing the ring.

Kelly glared at Bob for a second or two and then groped for his six-gun, raising the .45 at Bob when a janitor ran in from the hotel corridor and beleaguered him, grappling his strong arms over Kelly's and jolting the slight man against the room's wall. Kelly looked between his feet and jerked the gun's trigger, obliterating the man's big toe and then going down with him as the janitor fell in agony. Kelly wriggled away to a corner and glared at the janitor as the man rolled with his pain. Bob was sitting in a chair like a passenger, looking aghast at the damage he'd caused, and Kelly said to him, "You've always got an angel, don't ya. Some fool's always rushing in to save your sorry hide."

The police came and Kelly gave up his gun to a pal, and in the course of the explanations that followed, Bob Ford slipped out of the room as if he could disappear.

He stayed away from Kelly after that and moved into the store-room of his saloon, sleeping on a cot with Dorothy there, letting vagrants and spongers and hungry young men sleep on the gambling tables and bar for fifty cents a night.

Everyone, it seemed then, was going to Creede; grubstaked strangers from as far away as Indiana were loitering around the railroad yards in order to gather the latest exaggerations from the King Solomon Mining District, or they grouped around the big fires in the cold, goading the sting from their fingers. Bob joined the rings of men around the fires or in the congested hotel lobbies, chatting with gandydancers who'd put in the railroad spur and with the rugged mountain men who'd strung the telegraph lines. According to them there was no government in Creede, no taxes, no lodgings, not many stores, no fancy women in sight; the only saloons were cold canvas tents rigged over log walls and the whiskey was cut with plugs of tobacco.

So Bob bought green sawmill lumber and got the many stragglers around Pueblo to raise and carpenter a grand dance hall on ground that was swept free of snow. He bought extravagant furniture and draperies and oil paintings of naked goddesses and with a practiced eye appraised how everything looked in the place. When the building was complete, he ordered a crew to cautiously take it apart and pile it on a railroad flat car, and by the time Wagon Wheel Gap was opened in April and the Denver and Rio Grande was operating in the high country again, Bob was moving on with his common-law wife and his pretty waiter girls to the city where he could begin a new life.

He became a man of property and exemplary reputation. He squandered a magnificent sum of money and made his Exchange Club a palace. The rough boards on the outside of the gambling hall and bagnio disguised eight gaming tables of green felt and sculpted mahogany, an intricately scrolled and filigreed Eastlake bar of forty-foot length, a long brass rail four inches off the floor, brass spittoons at each junction, brass fittings on each cabinet and door, and glassware exactly like that used in the Teller House in Central City. Overhead lighting came from crystal chandeliers, muslin cloth of dark green concealed the pinewood walls, and everywhere were copied paintings of Aphrodite and the apple, Leda and the swan, the rape of the Sabine women, Venus at her toilette, Venus and Cupid, even La Primavera.

Downstairs were eight pretty waiter girls, many croupiers in crisp white shirts and yellow ties, and two or three mixologists with gartered sleeves and great waxed mustaches. Upstairs Dorothy oversaw the expensive activities of prostitutes with made-up names like Topsy, Lulu

Slain, the Mormon Queen, and Slanting Annie. Everything was meant to be as high-class and congenial as an Eastern gentlemen's club, without gunplay or fights or conniving; corporation presidents and their mine managers visited after supper, a glee club of Yale graduates sang around the piano, prospectors galumphed around the place bragging about their claims, assayers, grocers, and storekeepers made their evening elapse over newspapers there, and earnings changed hands at an average of nine hundred dollars per hour, sixteen hours per day, six days a week—meaning, of course, that Bob Ford's gambling hall could garner more in one year than the James gang could in thirteen.

Creede itself was nothing like the Exchange Club. It grew in a gully between two great mountains, so that the sun only gave it eight hours' light in a day and the snow run-off guttered along the single main street from April to July, obliging pack animals and pedestrians to slog through stocking-high muck and manure. The altitude was eight thousand eight hundred forty feet, so it was infrequently anything but cold (twenty degrees below zero in March was not uncommon) and the only water for months at a time came from pails of snow cooked over a fire—many negligent or already overworked men were consequently filthy, infested with body lice, and so foul-smelling that the Cyprians kept perfumed hankies to their noses as they gave up their pleasures.

A great variety of humanity was coming to Creede: cowhands, cardsharps, shopkeepers, tramps, mining engineers, crew managers, speculators in precious metals, foreigners from every country in Europe, Mexicans, Ute Indians, common laborers, cattle rustlers, circuit riders, petty thieves, physicians who had no license to practice, one or two lawyers who'd been disbarred, and a good many men whose lives were money. They were coming at the rate of three hundred per day, with the railway passengers sitting two to a chair or squeezing so tightly together in the aisles that a man could lift both feet and not fall. The Denver and Rio Grande recovered the cost of its railroad construction to Creede in just four months and lodgings were so scarce in the camp that each night they rented out ten Pullman cars on a sidetrack. Shanties might give refuge to eight or nine men, as many as sixty cots were jammed into one hotel dining room, the poor taught themselves to sleep upright supported by ropes that were strung across storage rooms, some people limped around Creede on crutches, having lost their feet to the cold.

And though it was against all odds and expectations, the man who governed all of them, the grand authority in Creede, was the slayer of Jesse James, Robert Newton Ford. Bob made the judgments and regulations, oversaw the punishment of criminals, the paltry disputes of commercial men, the controversies between saloonkeepers and their patrons; he arranged many civil matters, approved sketches of construction, appointed the sheriffs and tax collectors, paid the yearly salary of the justice of the peace. If he was not appreciated or very often praised, he was nonetheless complied with as a man of power and strong opinion who could not be crossed without peril. He gave permissions, exceptions, dispensations; he gained prerogative, reputation, prestige, satisfaction.

His was a night life. He slept late and read the Colorado newspapers in an elegant silk kimono as Dorothy brought in doughnuts and coffee and straightened the dark green room. His eyes moved speedily over the pages, skipping the lists of mine applications, stopping only on stories of gruesome accident and crime. He wore his ginger brown hair longer now than when he was twenty, in a gentleman's cut that gently waved and was scented with European fragrances. His distinguished mustache gave him years and panache but his boyishness wasn't gone yet, and when he stripped in front of his common-law wife, his slight but scrappy body seemed that of a juvenile. His clothing was English and high-fashion, his starched white shirts always seemed just bought, actor's lifts made him seem long-legged and six feet tall, he cocked his bowler hat to the right and was genial on the street.

He walked gracefully even in snow and affected a certain jauntiness by flicking his hat brim with a finger in greeting and by swinging an Italian cane, tilting against it as he gossiped and joked. He was gregarious to everyone and genuine to his companions. He smoked good twenty-five-cent cigars. He greeted all regulars to the Exchange Club and gave away to every gambler shot glasses of an overnight whiskey he concocted on a stove, though he himself would lounge at a corner table with J. and F. Martell cognac or a green bottle of Jackson's sour mash. He might stay eight or nine hours there, inviting acquaintances over to join him, giving orders to the dancing girls and prostitutes in gestures and sign language.

If he did not forget to eat he partook of a huge meal at seven, getting it over with at one sitting and never seeming to gain weight. Then he'd spin roulette or play poker in his gambling room, often giving up on straights or perfect combinations of cards rather than bring on a challenge that he'd been cheating. He could in fact perform magic tricks, practice sleight-of-hand, cut to the royalty at will, guess accurately what a player was holding, move the aces anywhere he wished as he swiftly shuffled the Bicycle deck. His fingers were nimble, his mind was quick, his blue eyes caught every nuance; he recognized patterns and strategies and was rarely swindled or captivated except when it suited his purpose.

He laughed often in an overeager, miscarrying voice and could talk engagingly at great length, but his subject was all too frequently himself; a glance from him could cut the tongue from a man, and he aggravated at the slightest suggestion of insult when among spectators, going for his gun with no more misgivings than if he were reaching for change. He was physically strong and wild with his fists, a grappler and aggressor who could go straight at anyone without regard for their size. And yet he was cautious, fidgety, high-strung, vigilant. He kept his back to the angled meetings of walls or kept his eyes on the long saloon mirror that was just lately imported from France. If doors were left open, he shut them; he never lingered near windowglass, never gave his back to strangers, never climbed ladders or chairs; a gun was string-tied to his thigh all day and slipped under his pillow at night.

He noticed the comings and goings of the nightwalkers he managed and was gentle with them, called them daughters, savagely cudgeled any man who was rough with them in their sleeping rooms or paid them less than they'd agreed upon. He would periodically prowl the upstairs corridor, putting his ear to the sleeping room doors, and if she wasn't then employed, Bob would ask Dorothy to prettify herself and join the company at his corner table. Already there would be his rough good friends in Creede: Joe Palmer, who would be run out of town in April, "Broken Nose" Creek, a cousin of the Younger brothers, and Jack Pugh, a horse thief who'd come to Creede to run a livery stable. They would speak together of appalling crimes that they never actually committed; Bob would exaggerate his participation and accomplishments in the James gang's last years, going on and on with his misrepresentations as Dorothy pampered him with courtesies and pleasantly simpered at his guests. If there was a dispute about the long career of the James gang, Bob was the authority, for he recognized every legend, consumed every history and dime novel, he was basically as engrossed in the man as a good biographer could be and even called the Jameses his cousins, a heritage that nobody argued with.

He openly collected the prostitution receipts from Dorothy at midnight, giving the money to a cash register that was scrolled and plated with nickel. He kissed his common-law wife goodnight and sent the dancing girls out or upstairs, and then gradually shooed his patrons from the saloon so that he could make an accounting of his profits from faro, birdcage, roulette, and stud poker. The croupiers helped him sweep the floor and wipe the counters and tabletops with soaped towels, then Bob adjusted the pipes and pans and stovetop temperature for his overnight whiskey, paid the two mixologists for their evening's work, and locked and barred every door.

Then he might pour a big glass of Chapin and Gore and clean his pistol by candlelight. He could hear the girls pillowfight upstairs, could hear one of them slip down to be with a paramour, could hear a boy creep into the privy in order to pass the night in its dry protection. Bob would point the Colt at objects in the saloon and make the hammer snap the quiet in the great room. And he'd say a word or two to Jesse as he went upstairs to sleep.

THE COMING OF SOAPY SMITH to Creede began the change in Bob. He was a mountebank, swindler, and confidence man who was born Jefferson Randolph Smith in Georgia in 1860, grew up throughout the South, and graduated from moving cattle in Texas to carnival work in Colorado. He was a glib and magnetic talker with a glad-to-meet-you jubilance and a way of getting delighted attention whenever he joined a crowd. He would gull men who thought they were cunning and wily into collaborating with him on an illegal project and then make them the target of the intrigue before they could get out of it, finagling so many in that manner that the city of Denver was no longer safe and he thought it wise to go west.

And so he came to Creede in February 1892 on a Denver and Rio Grande passenger train that rammed a giant plow along the rails in great surfs and tempests of snow. He went there with a gang of sixteen bodyguards, gamblers, and underlings and gradually made his way through the town, introducing himself to every shopkeeper and cardsharp, a joke for each man he stopped on the street, a gift of beer for everybody in whichever saloon he barged into, always acting the scamp and rogue and good sport, a man who was rich and leisured, who had the common touch.

He progressed in such a way along Amethyst Street that he got to the Exchange Club over a week after he arrived, and Soapy placed himself at the gaming tables so that he could peer across the room at the lord of the place, Bob Ford.

He saw a jittery, laughing man of thirty sitting magisterially in a corner, eating cake with his fingers, inviting company over, pouring cognac for all comers. His rough friends sat around the circular table in Mackinaw and astrakhan coats, snow becoming water on their big crossed arms and sliding into beads on their mustaches, their ungloved and grimy hands blackly smudging the glassware. Though Bob Ford's birthday was weeks past, his age was apparently a topic, for Soapy once overheard him say, "I always thought I'd go off like a skyrocket, but now it looks like I'll just be petering out"; and then Bob pursued other issues, monopolizing the conversation, paying little attention to what was said by others or even to his own replies, only talking ceaselessly like a man trying to clean every scrap of language out of his puzzled mind. And always he was looking to his right or left, looking into the many assorted mirrors, looking at every gun, until he appeared to spy an enemy in the gambling crowd and got up to intercept one of his pretty waiter girls and say, "Don't give him anything."

The man he said that about was Edward O. Kelly. He'd journeyed downward into dipsomania and depression since his gunfight with Bob in the Phoenix Hotel and he'd come to Creede without hope or plan. The police department in Pueblo had pressured Kelly until he paid a Fourth Street physician for surgery on the janitor's foot, sharpening the man's stupid prejudice to such an extent that he shot and killed a man of color named Ed Riley for a simple act of clumsiness. The common bigotry of the age salvaged Kelly and he wasn't charged with a crime, much less found guilty, but he was expunged from the police department, finding work only as a streetcar driver and begging for coins on the sidewalk until he'd gathered enough for passage to Creede.

And then he gained entrance to the Exchange Club, ogled its extravagance, gripped and regripped his cold fingers at a fire, and when a girl came by, Kelly had the gall to order a complimentary shot glass of whiskey in a gruff voice that Bob recognized.

In accordance with the saloon owner's instructions that Kelly ought not to be given anything, the girl returned to the bar with the shot glass on a tray and Bob imperturbably paused by one of the gaming tables to study the dexterity of a poker dealer he'd recently hired. Bob stacked coins and looked to an overhead mirror and saw Kelly shrug off his long wool coat as he argued with himself. The man seemed wild, insane, and fifty years old, though he would have been thirty-five, and Bob caught a glimpse of Wood Hite in Kelly as the man adjusted his long pistol. He was wearing a blue policeman's jacket with the insignia buttons cut off and a cartridge belt and gun were strapped over it so that they middled him. Kelly gave some learning to his right hand and unsnugged his gun in its cracked leather holster as he jostled through the gambling hall crowd to close on the man he thought of as his antagonist.

Kelly pulled up his pistol and a girl shouted, "He's gonna kill you!" but Bob only smiled and pretended he was Jesse as he approached Kelly sociably, his arms sweeping out as if he accepted all humanity and especially his present company. "Hey!" Bob said. "Hey, you ought to let bygones be bygones!" And then he grinned so congenially that he surprised Kelly and slowed him just enough to unexpectedly slap the man's cheek with his right hand and clasp the pistol with his left, jolting Kelly low and awry as Bob jerked the gun from his grip. He then snapped his right knee into Kelly's mouth and the ex-policeman collapsed with a split upper lip and Bob cruelly rapped the man's skull with his own long pistol, the knock like a knuckle on wood. "Get out!" Bob yelled. "Get out and don't you ever set foot in my place again."

"I guess I will if I want to, " Kelly said.

Bob stamped the floor and Kelly shied, cringing under his lifted arm. Bob laughed at the sight and gave up, walking back to his corner table with gamblers clapping him on the back and giving him their approval. And Bob was sitting with his Creede gang and getting only some of their jokes as he watched Kelly barge over to his long coat and then out into night and a snowstorm. Bob said, "It just goes on and on and on."

Dorothy said, "I can't hear you," but Bob said nothing more.

Soapy Smith got into his black mink coat and straggled out after Kelly, catching up to him under an arc lamp and speaking compassionately. Blood was dripping off the man's chin and he spit out chips of teeth like gravel. Kelly said, "Second time I've tried to get that son of a bitch," and Soapy winged an arm around the man's neck, saying, "Why don't we see if we can't get you stitched up."

BY THE FOLLOWING AFTERNOON the justice of the peace had arranged for Soapy Smith to go upstairs to Bob Ford's apartment and give his regards to the man who so coolly managed the agitator. Bob greeted the confidence man rather graciously, giving him a green leather chair and cognac in a brandy snifter and along with that some good advice about possible commercial enterprises in Creede if Smith was going straight.

Soapy was delighted. "So you know who I am!"

Bob shrugged. "You hear stories; not that I put much stock in what those goddamned newspapers say."

"You couldn't, could you."

"Meaning what?"

Soapy ignored that, and when the subject changed he ignored Bob's business suggestions, neglected to acknowledge his questions, but only gave his attention to the objects in the room, moving about the apartment with a cigar in his mouth, weighing things and gliding his fingers over them, interrogating Bob about their cost and the city of acquisition. He was a dapper, appealing man with clipped brown hair and a two-inch brown beard, who appeared for their meeting in a black suit and a black cravat that was kept in place by a two-carat diamond stickpin. He was genial in dialogue and forbidding when his thoughts strayed off and as Bob gazed at the man's arrogant progress around the room he couldn't dodge the feeling that he was looking at a reincarnation of Jesse James, Jesse James, Jesse James.

Bob asked, "Just what was it you had in mind with this meeting? Outside of making an inventory of all my worldly goods?"

Soapy resettled in the green leather chair and swished cognac from cheek to cheek as he scoured Bob with his eyes. He asked, "Do you know what you shoulda done about Jesse?"

"No; why don't you tell me."

Soapy grinned. "I will then." He crossed his legs and looked into the glass. "One night you oughta gone out and sorta lagged behind old Jess on your horse. You get your gun out and yell his name and once he spins around, bang! You coulda said you two had an argument and shot it out and you come out the victor. I guess you never thought of it though."

"I wasn't big enough."

"You sure done the wrong thing, killing the man with his wife and kids close by, and his guns off and, well, you know what you did. You oughta said you were sorry."

"I figure if I'm sorry or not, that's my own business."

"Don't matter! You ought to apologize and give 'em what they want! Say you were on this train there was no getting off and you did the only thing you could do. A man looks at Bob Ford now and you know what he sees? He sees pride and greed and no regrets."

Bob scratched an itch at his neck. His grin was a dagger. "I'm going to make them forget all about ten years ago. I'm not going to be begging for forgiveness. I'm going to get people to respect me because of my accomplishments, just like Jesse did."

Soapy tilted his head to gaze out at sunlight and snow. He scratched at his beard and asked, "Do you know Joe Simmons?"

"I've said pleased-to-meetcha."

"Joe and me we've been talking about you and Creede and how things are and we thought maybe we'd begin a saloon and gambling hall like yours over to Jimtown. I figured maybe I'd get rich by pushing de booze over de boards."

"Do you think there's much call for another saloon? They say there's one for every five men as it is."

Soapy grinned at Bob with more antagonism than joy. "I'm going to get in while the getting's good and then make the others get out."

Bob struck a sulphur match off his shoe and stood it under a Corona cigar. "Just out of curiosity: how are you going to do that?"

"My gang, Bob! I'm going to be the government! I'm going to run things around here! Y'all come over to the right way of thinking or, bingo, out you go!"

Bob sucked on the cigar, squinting his left eye from the smoke. He changed his angle in the chair. "I forgot how to get scared ten years ago."

"I figured that too."

"I'll give Creede to you though."

"You're saying that because you know I can take it."

"Just stay away from the Exchange. You and your bodyguards and thugs. You don't have guns enough."

Soapy poured his cognac into a green fern and then pulled himself to standing with the green arms of the chair. He adjusted his big black sombrero on the crown of his head and ground out his cigar on the rug. "You and me, we're exactly alike. If the time comes for killing Robert Ford, I guess you know what I'll do."

"Like I said: I've already been as scared as I'll ever be."

And then Soapy went out and Bob went to the ceiling-high windows that looked over the street. He saw Soapy laughing with his bodyguards as he slogged through the snow; he saw shopkeepers greeting the man and giving way on the sidewalks. Bob slumped against the green wall and said without feeling, "Bang."

THE GOVERNMENT OF CREEDE WAS, in fact, reorganized. Soapy's gang strong-armed the commercial men, jerked pedestrians into alleys and put guns to their ears as one of Soapy's lieutenants told how things had changed; they got to new arrivals to Creede as soon as they stepped off the train and injured more than one man by twisting a wrist until it snapped. Soapy appointed himself as president of a Gambler's Trust and imposed membership in it on every saloonkeeper except Robert

Ford. He manipulated people and preferences to such a degree that within weeks his good friends were made mayor, city councilmen, coroner, and justice of the peace, his brother-in-law, John Light, was made city marshal, and as a special insult to Bob, ex-policeman Edward O. Kelly was made deputy sheriff of Bachelor, a mining camp on the mountain of that name, just three miles away. Meanwhile, Soapy Smith opened the Orleans Club in the east canyon section called Jimtown, financing purchase of the gambling hall with the monthly percentages paid him for municipal operating expenses. And he did what he could to get Bob to resign his ownership of the Exchange Club: rocks with auguring messages tied to them crashed through the batwing doors at closings, glowering men in grizzly bear coats slouched outside the club with shotguns all day and followed Bob anywhere he went, and on April 3rd, 1892, the geography on which the club had been constructed was designated by the city government as the site of a forthcoming school and the gambling hall was ordered closed.

Bob ignored the ruling and gave not an inch to Smith's commands and injunctions, and yet his bearing changed as his influence lessened, he was accused of cowardice and accommodation, of living up to his pusillanimous reputation, and he kept to his apartment all day or in a private room at night, getting drunk on his overnight whiskey as he pensively flipped over playing cards, looking at his destiny in every king and jack.

He complained to Dorothy that despising Robert Ford had become a peculiar kind of sport. He sometimes wondered in a self-pitying way whom people would peer upon, snipe at, sneer about, threaten, if Bob Ford weren't around. Even as he circulated in his own saloon he knew that smiles disappeared when he passed by, that it was his overweening pride that the patrons whispered about, that it was quiet jeering that snagged their mouths like a fishhook, that there was always someone to spy on him and repeat his every word to Smith, to tally his sins and trespasses. And even Dorothy seemed unsympathetic, she seemed to perceive Bob as an impostor, as a boy of impulses but no principles, incapable and apprehensive and forever repeating the same mistakes.

Bob paged through his scrapbook from 1882 and grinned as he reread newspaper stories about the Ford brothers going East to perform on stage; then he glimpsed a correspondent's report of the execution of Charles J. Guiteau, the man who shot President Garfield. He was a changed man, "meek as a child," and on the night before his hanging Guiteau recited his own poem, "Simplicity, or Religious Baby Talk."

A scaffold was constructed in the jailyard and the public paid as much as three hundred dollars for the right to see the man strangle. A black sack was slipped over Guiteau's head and a noose was snugged around his neck and he sang, "I am going to the Lordy; I am so glad," until he dropped through the trapdoor and the rope jerked him rigid and he dangled in the air. The jailyard audience applauded.

On Holy Saturday night in April Bob Ford wagered a good deal of his savings on a prize fight between a professional named Johnson whom Soapy Smith had brought in and a Colorado boy whose magnificent strength could not compensate for his ignorance of boxing or of the newly inaugurated Marquis of Queensberry rules. He was one-eyed and practically unconscious by the seventh round, when he sloppily collapsed to the canvas and could not respond to the referee's count. The professional was declared the victor and Soapy was clapping the man on the back in his corner when Bob irately jumped into the ring and swung a stocking that was weighted with coins at the fighter's jawbone, instead breaking a bodyguard's right arm before Bob could be dragged off.

Bob stayed awake that night and all Easter, grieving over his losses with Joe Palmer and four quarts of whiskey, at last going out to kill the prize fighter at eight o'clock Sunday night. But they could do no more than digress along the way: Bob made a shopkeeper jig by cocking his pistol and pounding in bullets around the man's high-button shoes, spattering mud on his pants cuffs; he shot through a preacher's dining room window and made a milk glass crash apart; the city's pride were the arc lamps that illuminated Amethyst Street and prompted the saying "It's day all day in the daytime and there is no night in Creede," so Bob Ford rode underneath them on his horse and straightened his gun overhead, destroying all but sixteen. He encouraged his horse into the genteel lobby of the Central Theatre and there grandstanded with a long justification of his life, his reasons for thinking the prize fight was rigged, his high regard for his good friend's boxing skills, his willingness to meet in a gunfight with anyone who thought he could match the man who shot Jesse James. By midnight all Bob's cartridges were gone and he rode back to the Exchange Club yelling an old Kentucky brag: "Size me up and get goosebumps, boys. I'm the widowmaker and the slayer of jungles, the mean-eyed harbinger of desolation! I've ripped a catamount asunder and sprinkled his fragments in my stew; one screech from me makes vultures fly, one glance puts blisters on grizzly bears, devastation rides on my every breath! Where is that stately stag to stamp his hoof or rap his antlers to these proclamations! Where is the mangey lion what will lick the salt off my name!''

A COMMITTEE OF ONE HUNDRED was organized in Creede overnight and after long argument and a vote of fifty-three to forty-seven, they decided against lynching Bob Ford and Joe Palmer, choosing instead to urge them out of town. They pulled Bob from his sleep at six in the morning and reported the committee's verdict and Bob pushed by them to drop the poisons of his stomach out an upstairs window. He then slipped to the floor, wiping his mouth on his sleeve as he looked up at a man in an astrakhan coat. "I'll come back, you know. I always do. Getting rid of Bob Ford isn't easy."

"You're a mighty big talker, ain't ya."

"I've got all your names on my list."

The committee transported Bob to the railroad depot in a hackney and put him on a train to Colorado Springs, where Dorothy later shipped his possessions. Bob took a cheap hotel room there and permitted an interview in which he said, "I'm going back to Creede in a day or two with a gun in each hand," but he sojourned in Colorado Springs for almost a fortnight.

He would go out in the morning sunlight and range over grasslands as Jesse might have, feeling the earth gain height until the green mountains abruptly jutted from it and changed their color to blue and gray in the distance. Or he would sit like a chair all day in the hotel lobby, gazing at the Regulator clock, reimagining the sitting room and the racehorse named Skyrocket and the gun that Jesse had given him, and everything would mingle with the stageshow and it would be Jesse who cocked his head to the right as Bob clicked back the hammer but it would be Charley with fright in his eyes, Zee who sagged from the chair to the floor, and then Bob himself who looked at the ceiling, blood pooling wide as a woman's lap under his injury.

He was moving out of history with each year beyond 1882, and yet mentions of Robert Ford appeared periodically in the Colorado and Missouri newspapers, some displeased reports implying it was a pity the coward was still around even as one or two accounts every month contained the news that the slayer of Jesse James had his throat cut in an alley in Oklahoma or expired from consumption or pneumonia and was put in a paupers' cemetery. No account that he'd read had the grace to remark on when or where he was born, who his kin were and how he was raised; they never remarked on the Moore School, Blue Cut, the grocery store, his agreement with the government; it seemed enough to say that Bob Ford was the man who shot Jesse James, as if his existence could be encompassed in that one act of perfidy. He recognized that he would never be forgiven, that he would not be granted eulogies nor great attention at his death, correspondents would not journey to Creede, his skull would not be surgically opened nor phrenologically measured, photographs of his body on ice would not be sold in sundries stores, people would not crowd the sidewalks in rain to see Bob Ford's funeral cortege, biographies would not be written about him, children would not be named after him, no one would ever pay twenty-five cents to stand in the rooms he grew up in. He yearned for much less in Colorado than he had as a boy in Missouri, but he did yearn for this: that Robert Newton Ford might go down in history as more than a gunshot on April 3rd, 1882.

In such a mood, Bob mailed letters of penitence and supplication to commercial men in Creede, apologizing for his temporary insanity and asking permission to come back as a man of peace. And on April 27th he was sitting in the green chair of a Denver and Rio Grande passenger car as it coasted into Creede, but he was depressed to see upon looking out that the railroad depot was populated with competitors and opponents, even some of Soapy's men twisting stockings with pennies packed in the toes. So he gripped his possessions and rushed back to the caboose, jumping down to the rock bed when the train jolted to a stop, and slipping through shops and down alleys to the office of the *Morning Chronicle,* where he composed, with the help of an editor, an article that was published the following day:

> Bob Ford is again in Creede. Why the possibility of his return should have carried terror to the hearts of certain citizens is hardly possible to understand. Since he has been in Creede there has been no quieter man except on the unfortunate Sunday night two weeks ago. For his action upon that occasion he is extremely sorry, but after all, he only displayed then the Western idea of staying by one's friends. This idea is one which Eastern people, as a general rule, cannot comprehend. It is true, nevertheless, that when a true Westerner starts out to stand by a man he does it thoroughly, even though it is simply a matter of getting drunk and shooting up the town. This is the cardinal idea which distinguishes the West from the East. Bob Ford has many interests in Creede,

and if he chooses to stay here and watch his investments, he
has as much right to do it as anyone else. A fighting chance
is all anyone wants and Ford should at least be granted that.

Bob then appeared before the justice of the peace, pleaded guilty
to a misdemeanor, and gladly paid a fifty-dollar fine, but the Committee of One Hundred (many of them Easterners) was persuaded by
Soapy Smith that Bob was a pestilence to the community and ought to
be expelled from Creede under penalty of death. The committee sent
as its representative City Marshal Theodore Craig and Bob replied only
that it was a peculiar coincidence in his life that he was always being
ordered around by a man with a star and the name of Craig. He said
he'd had just about enough of that and wasn't moving on again, and
when the Committee of One Hundred came after Bob in the Exchange
Club, they found gathered around him the many he'd given work to,
the pretty waiter girls and gamblers and scary men like Jack Pugh and
Broken Nose Creek, all of them aiming guns. "I'm staying," Bob
said. "You pass that along to Soapy."
    Craig said, "You give us no choice but to fight you."
    And Bob said, "You can't kill me; I'm already dead."
    The committee gave in and Bob subsequently challenged the city
government by keeping the gambling hall open and by going about
Creede in his swank English suits and gentleman's look, with only a
derringer for a gun and that in his hip pocket. He knew the regular ill-
regard of strangers and could feel great hate for him come into the
gaming room each night. His history was pried into, his private life
was made public, men stopped on the sidewalks to gape at him, reporters impeded his progress with impertinent and predictable questions.
(On being introduced to one correspondent Bob said, "You're going to
talk me to death, I guess, and then go home and roast me like all the
other goddamned papers do.") He was compared to every reptile and
animal, most of them predatory, and was persecuted by the catcalls of
children and the loopy pronouncements of miners who were deep inside
whiskey bottles. Spoiled vegetables were dumped on his doorstep,
intoxicated Southern men sometimes pitched inside his saloon with
pistols gripped in their hands, people ducked into shops to avoid him,
he received so many menacing letters in the mail that he could read
them without any reaction except curiosity and then smirk as he crumpled them up, a slaughtered cat was nailed to his closet door along
with a note that read simply, "Get out of town." The bogus signature

belonged to an Ed O'Kelly and the words were written in chicken blood.

And yet he did not change his name, camouflage his identity, dodge the press, go off to a foreign country, or seek refuge in the wilderness. Instead he played the scapegrace and rogue, pretended that he was appreciated by many, professed that he knew just when and how he would die and did not feel imperiled.

ON THE NIGHT of June 5th, some persons unknown (perhaps inspired by Soapy Smith) spilled coal-oil around the Exchange Club and put a match to it. The fire grew like ivy over the wooden walls and gained entrance to the gambling room, peeling the wallcoverings up from the floor, exploding the glassware, and mangling iron until it got out again and joined itself to the wood around the club. It soon became a conflagration, eating not only Bob Ford's place but every canvas, clapboard, and pinewood building in the gulch, ravaging much of Creede and creating such great heat that men gave up pitching their pails of Willow Creek water on the fire itself, instead cooling their panicky animals by splashing their steaming hides.

Bob managed to preserve only a few cases of liquor and his upright piano, and yet he persisted with the doggedness and incorrigibility that were typical of him throughout his life. He prospected the unincinerated sections of Willow Creek gully and purchased in Jimtown a big canvas tent shored up by scantlings, with a long wooden floor and a ceiling eighteen feet high, a onetime inn between a mining office called Leadville Headquarters and an eating cabin called The Cafe. Bob then salvaged a good length of his Eastlake bar and a mule team dragged it up Rio Grande Avenue and into the tent, the greater area of it being given to dancing, the one activity not available in the Orleans Club or the Gunnison Club and Exchange.

Bob called his fifth saloon the Omaha Club and the grand opening was on Tuesday, June 7th. He engaged two musicians to play violin along with the piano man and charged his eager and agog patrons one dollar to dance a five-minute mazourka, schottische, or waltz with pretty girls they'd only gaped at with longing in the past. An intermission followed each song, during which the girls were encouraged to get their partners up to the bar or go back with them to private tents, splitting the receipts of each enterprise with Bob. So many yearning men crowded into the Omaha Club by eight o'clock that a good deal of the dancing took place on the streets, and it looked so much as if Bob and his girls would be getting rich that Nellie Russell sought Mr. Ford out, saying she'd accept any job with him, even one as a prostitute.

They strolled together up Rio Grande Avenue and Bob made the usual interrogations, learning that Miss Russell grew up in St. Joseph, Missouri, and would have been a girl of ten when Bob was living there in the cottage. She said at night children would crouch by the sitting room windows of 1318 Lafayette in order to frighten themselves by seeing the ghost of Jesse James. She'd never seen it but a boyfriend said the apparition once spooked him, appearing near a looking-glass, like vapor from a teapot except for his scowling and piercing blue eyes. She said the place had been such an upsetting experience for the people who'd rented it over the past ten years that the cost had dropped from the fourteen dollars per month that Thomas Howard had paid to the bargain price of eight, and still no one would stay there. It was being sold for taxes when she left to come West.

Bob used that advantage to change the subject and ask why she'd come to Creede.

Nellie shrugged. "You go down any street in America and you'll see signs about folks getting rich in Creede. And I guess I liked the sound of it; I mean the word Creede. Don't you?"

Bob guffawed at her ignorance and said, "It isn't even the man's actual name! His real name was William Harvey! Only reason N.C. came West was his girlfriend jilted him and married his older brother. Shouldn't make it religious or anything."

"Still. You get a good feeling from it."

"You don't always," he said.

The canyon's cliffs and buttes castled over them, deep black against a deep blue sky. The conflagration had gutted a good many lodgings in Creede and the uprooted had been transplanted into Jimtown, where they slept on the ground like island people, like serfs. Bob could see the lights of cooking fires and cigarettes in the foothills, and as they strolled along with their practical conversation, he could hear the happy uproar of the Omaha Club as the musicians played "Pop Goes the Weasel," but under that he could pick out the hopeful talk of shop-keepers, prospectors, workers, and clerks who'd lost what few things they had.

She angled her head to regard him. "I could've recognized you anywhere. You're just like your photograph."

He glanced at her with slight annoyance. "I'm not just like the boy in that photograph though. I've aged."

"I thought you were so daring and romantic. I thought you were the most glamorous man alive."

"I get along fine with girls of ten, it's when they grow to be eleven or twelve that I'm a goner."

She giggled and then her thoughts must have anguished her for she grew taciturn, her gray eyes looked at something remote in the night, she gripped a shawl around her with a pale fist at her breasts. Two minutes passed and then she became embarrassed by her own silence. "I guess an angel must be flying over us."

Bob made no comment.

She said, "The mountains are so steep everywhere! It's like you're inside an envelope!"

Bob spied her profile and her especially pretty smile. He said, "You were going to ask me about what Jesse was like."

"How'd you know?"

"They always do." Bob gentled Miss Russell's elbow to guide her around for the descending walk to the Omaha Club, and then he glided his right hand to her lower back, feeling the girl's letting through her cool gown. He said, "He was bigger than you can imagine, and he couldn't get enough to eat. He was hungry all the time. He ate all the food in the dining room and then he ate all the plates and the glasses and the light off the candles; he ate all the air in your lungs and the thoughts right out of your mind. You'd go to him, wanting to be with him, wanting to be like him, and you'd always come away missing something." Bob looked at the girl with anger and of course she was looking peculiarly at him. He said, "So now you know why I shot him."

Miss Russell sighted the ground as they walked, and when she spoke again there was grief in her voice. "My father would read to us about it from the newspapers he bought. He said we were living through a great moment in history. He thought you'd done the world a big favor."

Bob said, "On your right is the Leadville Headquarters. Over there is the smithy's shop. You can't see them from here but I've got four green tents behind the club and men go in and out all night."

She said, "You're making me sad."

He could see by the lights in her eyes that the girl was crying. "You ought to go back."

She shook her head in the negative but wouldn't say anything.

He said, "Don't work for me."

"No?"

"You've got your dignity yet; I wouldn't give it away for money."

Dancing had given way to an intermission and groomed men in ugly brown clothes were lingering around the club and standing on Rio Grande, smoking cigarettes, spitting juice, glowering at Bob and the girl.

She said, "Maybe I'll go then," and Bob suggested she might find other work in Jimtown. And though she said she might try some stores in the morning and even seemed grateful to Bob, Miss Nellie Russell of St. Joseph, Missouri, instead purchased whiskey and some grains of morphine and that night committed suicide.

IT WAS MIDNIGHT when Deputy Sheriff Ed Kelly righted himself from his cot and gave an ear to the nickering of a horse. He sought out his gun and scurried across the earthen floor of his cabin, getting to the rough board door just as it was rapped. He opened it with his gun cocked and peered out at a man he didn't recognize, with a brown jawbeard and mustache and orange beaver coat. The man grinned at Kelly's longjohns and said in a high Southern voice, "You and wash soap ought to meet once or twice."

"Do I know you?"

"You got your eyes open?"

"You woke me."

The man sagged against the cabin logs and looked down Bachelor mountain into the gulch and the fog of light that was all they could see of Jimtown. "You hear that music?"

Kelly stepped out with his pistol by his hip. He could just make out a piano.

The man lighted a cigar and said, "It's the Omaha Club. Bob Ford's having his grand opening tonight."

Kelly spit to his right. "I'll give him a grand opening one of these days."

The man ticked his head. "I come to tell ya regarding that. He's got on one of his periodicals and he's puffed himself up to say he's going to kill Ed Kelly on sight."

"Why, that son of a bitch!"

"And Bob's one of the most plausible talkers I ever seen."

"I expect he'll ask me to turn my back first."

The man sucked on his cigar and looked at it as he blew smoke. "You oughta do something."

Kelly agreed. "I'll go down there now and give him a straightening."

"I'd give it till around afternoon if I was you." He then put the cigar in his mouth and soon thereafter disappeared.

ON THE MORNING of June 8th, 1892, the body of Miss Nellie Russell was brought in by railroad crewmen and on the instigation of Dorothy Evans a subscription paper was made up to cover her funeral expenses. The Omaha Club prostitutes accepted the responsibility of collecting the philanthropies, and Dorothy went upstairs to raise Bob from sleep.

She said, "You know that girl you were talking to about a job? She went and killed herself."

Bob sighed, "Oh God!" and gazed at nothing for some time.

Dorothy could find nothing to say that would subtract from his grief, so she only read a distillery's mail-order form out loud to Bob as he dressed in his gentleman's clothes. He flexed a stiff celluloid collar around his neck and closed it with a gold collar button that Soapy Smith would eventually carry as a good luck charm; then he adjusted a yellow cravat around the collar and affixed the cravat with a milk white opal pin. He asked Dorothy, "How do I look?" and she answered, "Very distinguished," without lifting her eyes.

He ate a segment of her sugar doughnut and checked his mustache in a looking-glass and he slumped against a closet door as he thought about Miss Russell. Sunlight was coming in around the green window shades and a light breeze made them angle inside the room and subside again, lightly tapping the sill. Bob said he thought he would go for the mail; Dorothy thought she would stay inside with her sewing and magazines. She said, "You were right not to give her a job," and Bob went out without saying goodbye.

Dorothy Evans would be married in 1900 to a Mr. James Feeney of Durango, Colorado. She would adopt two daughters, one of them nearly deaf, and, according to gossip, she would mistreat them. Her legal marriage would be no more joyous than her common-law marriage was and Mr. Feeney would leave her to make book at the races in Trinidad and Pueblo. She told a neighbor in June 1902, "My husband is gone, my health is miserable, I've mortgaged all the furniture, we scarcely have anything of our own," and on Friday the 13th she sent a daughter to a drugstore with a note asking for fifty cents' worth of chloroform. On Sunday morning she got into her green silk wedding dress, telling her daughters she was going to take a nap. She then poured the chloroform into a cloth and pressed it to her nose until she slept so deeply that she perished.

Bob skimmed the mail and then collected his subscription newspapers and rode a mare down to the Rio Grande River to read them. He hung his suit coat on a limb and sat on the brown paper sleeve that the Denver newspaper was mailed in. Shade dappled him; the grass whispered. Sunlight glinted on a river that would still be cold with snow. Boys with fishing poles were near the water, plunking out hooks that were yellow with corn. The Republican National Convention was meeting in Minneapolis. President Benjamin Harrison was expected to be renominated. The Dalton gang robbed the Sante Fe Railroad at Red Rock in the Indian Territories and a manhunt was under way. Bob smiled and said, "Good luck." He got an apple from his coat pocket and ate it as he flipped pages. He saw a stick-float spin in the water and then dip and he sat up to watch a boy pull the fish to land. It curled out of the water once and then splashed wildly and abruptly disappeared. The boy complained and Bob put on his coat, giving the apple core to his mare before he rode back to Jimtown.

Deputy Sheriff Edward O. Kelly came down from Bachelor at 1 p.m. on the 8th. He had no grand scheme, no strategy, no agreement with higher authorities, nothing beyond a vague longing for glory and a generalized wish for revenge against Robert Ford. He ate a sandwich and soup at Newman Vidal's restaurant and was joined by a French Canadian named Joe Duval. Duval would later maintain that Kelly informed him then about a message he'd been given, Kelly saying, "I'm not gonna give the dirty cur a chance to shoot me like he did his cousin, Jesse James." The two acted accordingly. They walked to a machinist's shop and there sawed a lead pipe into eighth-inch sections that French Joe chiseled in half. Duval was carrying with him a ten-gauge shotgun with twin barrels. Kelly removed the shells, cut off the paper tops, and emptied the shot pellets onto the ground, repacking the shells with extra gunpowder before reinserting them into the gun. He made a paper funnel and poured the pipe shrapnel through it into the right shotgun barrel and then the left. Duval shut his long coat around the shotgun and walked away with the walnut stock against the leggings of his right boot.

Edward O. Kelly would be ordered to serve a life sentence in the Colorado penitentiary for second-degree murder and French Joe Duval, his accomplice, would be given a term of two years. Over seven thousand signatures would eventually be gathered on a petition asking for Kelly's release, and in 1902 Governor James B. Orman would pardon the man. Kelly began writing gruesome letters to Bob Ford's widow in Durango but otherwise did nothing except get arrested on charges of vagrancy and ramble from one insignificant town to the next. He begged Jesse James, Jr., for room and board and the young attorney obliged Kelly for more than a month, but then the man strayed off again, going at last to Oklahoma City. And there, in January 1904, Kelly tangled with a policeman arresting him for burglary, chewing on the policeman's ears as they fought until the man got out his pistol and shot Kelly through the head. His body was put in a potter's field without rites or ceremony.

Robert Newton Ford worked in the Omaha Club on the afternoon of June 8th, stocking the bar with his overnight whiskey and getting jiggers of it for some of the Cornish miners sitting there. He removed his suit coat and hung it on a nail and then unfastened his cartridge belt, winding it around his gun and snugging it against the cash register. A man named Walter Thomson from Kansas City commented on Bob's opal stickpin, saying opals brought bad luck.

Bob said, "My luck isn't very good as it is. I guess an opal couldn't change it much."

The man said he knew what Bob meant.

The sun was high and the day growing hot. Some men had given a burro a pan of beer rather than water and they were laughing as the pack animal staggered down San Luis Avenue. Deputy Sheriff Plunket saw Ed Kelly crouched in an alley's shade, looking at the Omaha Club, but considered it only another example of the man's peculiarity.

A pretty entertainer named Ella Mae Waterson crossed into the Omaha Club with the completed subscription papers for Miss Nellie Russell and Bob perused the list of contributors, giving his opinion of each. She said Soapy Smith signed up just before going off to Denver that morning. Bob ascertained that Smith had pledged five dollars, so just below that line Bob printed his own name along with a pledge of twice that. And, paraphrasing from an epistle of Peter, he appended the inscription "Charity covereth a multitude of sins."

It was twenty minutes to four when French Joe Duval, with whiskey in him, lunged around the corner of The Cafe and up toward the Omaha Club, struggling a shotgun out from under his long coat. A boy named Albert Lord scooted from the smithy's shop to the club in order to change a twenty-dollar bill for his father and Edward O. Kelly was right behind him, slowing only long enough to grab the shotgun from French Joe and then pressing the cold metal to the boy's neck like a kiss as he whispered, "Step aside, Albert."

The deputy sheriff of Bachelor crossed from sunlight into the yellow light of the tent and caught the man who shot Jesse James laughing with Ella Mae Waterson, giving his back to the street. Kelly sighted down the shotgun and said, "Hello, Bob!" And as Bob was turning as a gentleman might to a greeting he recognized, the shotgun ignited once and again from five feet away, clumped sprays of shrapnel ripping into the man's neck and jawbone, ripping though his carotid artery and jugular vein, stripping skin away, and nailing the gold collar button into scantling wood. His body jolted backward, jolted the floorboards, and Ella Mae Waterson screamed, but Robert Ford only looked at the ceiling, the light going out of his eyes before he could say the right words.

ACKNOWLEDGMENTS

My sources for this novel have principally been the Missouri newspapers of the period and the following: *The Man Who Shot Jesse James* by Carl W. Breihan, *The Crittenden Memoirs* by H. H. Crittenden, *Jesse James Was My Neighbor* by Homer Croy, *The New Eldorado* by Phyllis Flanders Dorset, and *Jesse James Was His Name* by William A. Settle. I would like to express my gratitude to those authors for their information and guidance, and to the National Endowment for the Arts and the University of Michigan Society of Fellows for grants that helped me complete this novel.

R.H.

A NOTE ON THE TYPE

The text of this book was set in a film version of Times Roman, designed by Stanley Morison for *The Times* (London) and first introduced by that newspaper in 1932.

Among typographers and designers of the twentieth century, Stanley Morison has been a strong forming influence, as a typographical adviser to the English Monotype Corporation, as a director of two distinguished English publishing houses, and as a writer of sensibility, erudition, and keen practical sense.

Composed by Centennial Graphics, Inc., Ephrata, Pennsylvania. Printed and bound by R. R. Donnelley & Sons Co., Harrisonburg, Virginia. Typography and binding design by Virginia Tan.